PAI

Happy birthday
2018

Craig

Craig Newnes is an author, editor, musician, dad, grandfather and gardener. He has six children and spends his time between the UK and France. Until retiring after a near-fatal road accident, he was a Consultant Critical Psychologist and ex-Director of Psychological Therapies for Shropshire's Mental Health (NHS) Trust. He has published numerous book chapters and academic articles and is editor of *The Journal of Critical Psychology, Counselling and Psychotherapy*. His books include *Clinical Psychology: A critical examination* from PCCS Books and the edited volumes: *Making and Breaking Children's Lives; Spirituality and Psychotherapy; This is Madness: A critical look at psychiatry and the future of mental health services; This is Madness Too: A further critical look at mental health services*. He is author of the novel, *Tearagh't*. A book on the *Malaysian Emergency*, and a *Critical A-Z of ECT* are due in 2018. Tracks from his band Sandghosts are available from Amazon.

Like all of us he lives in a constant whirl of today and yesterday and sometimes he stops for a moment to write it down.

Paris

A novel

Craig Newnes

THE REAL PRESS
www.therealpress.co.uk

Published in 2018 by the Real Press.
www.therealpress.co.uk
© Craig Newnes

ISBN (print) 9781912119547
ISBN (ebooks) 9781912119530

To Isabel

Acknowledgements

I spent years in villages France and England, months in the British Museum and Paris doing my utmost to understand the experience of ordinary folk living six hundred years ago. In the end, not much changes and we all do our best. As ever, my thanks to my family. Without Balzac, Zola, Picasso and Simone de Beauvoir the world would be a duller place. Without the support of David Boyle, the author would be searching for ways to get all these words into print.

I

To spoil the page. Carefully places nib onto paper. Scrawls:

Can I write this all down? I am no Rousseau, no Balzac, no real use as a man now. I shall try.

Imagine Paris as a village. Streets are now so wide whole villages could have lain across them. Two might be encompassed by the Quai de Tuilleries alone, the Seine a vast waterway, each tributary offering water to a close-knit community devoted to serving the land. It wasn't quite like that.

The Île de la Cité was dominated by Notre-Dame, a labour of faith and crushing manual labour that had taken five hundred years to build. Unlike Chartres, which took a mere fifty six; at least Chartres is finished. You don't have to go far from Notre-Dame to find peasant life. Tiny villages, hamlets...

In one such, we find la famille Picard, so central to local life and custom they seem cast in the imagination of a Zola. This family is not so easily relegated to the fantasies of a novelist. The Picards are real. As real as the stones forming the walls surrounding their allotments or the text you have before you.

Perhaps, if we look hard enough, we shall see Pierre Picard. He is Pee-pee to his few friends and "the dunce" to all and sundry. Like some yokel from a Hardy novel he struggles along one of the muddied tracks on what will become the L'avenue Jean Jaurès.

He carries faggots.

With spite some mutter it is all the dunce can do. But the girls know he can do more, much more; in the fields, behind the barn, once in a byre as an elderly cow lowed in the background, her eyes as wide as those of the girl giving herself up to desire: "Tiens moi. Tiens moi!"

He stoops beneath his burden, trudges a little further, halts to wipe the sweat from his brow and stiffens as he hears his name called.

"Pierre. Pee-pee. Ça va? Will there be a fire tonight?"

"Ça va. Bien sûr. Non, demain. So they say."

It is Guy:

"Are we celebrating?"

"A répas for Jerome's return."

Guy walks on. Pierre, now lost in thought, is pre-occupied with the homecoming of Jerome Mazerme. From war. From a war they said might last a hundred years.

Pierre knows nothing of time measured thus. "Many summers since the drought of my youth," is a common phrase for Pee-pee. It captures him perfectly; the worldly ignorance, the wisdom of the season, the unashamedly preposterous notion that he has earned the right to refer to his "youth" as some by-gone era. Pee-pee is but twenty years of age. As he walks on away from Guy, he thinks of Jerome. Not quite four years older, fair-haired, a strong, tanned face and a smile to make the few village girls blush.

The Mazermes had been horrified at their son's

determination to go to war.

"What good will come of it?" his mother had said, adding, "Sure, you'll find yourself killed before the month is out."

"Quiet, woman!" came the reply, "You will bring the boy bad luck with such words."

So it was that Jerome the proud, Jerome the smiler, Jerome the dancer (a man who would "twirl any young thing off her feet," as his mother would have it) left the commune and struck out for adventure and more.

His father had been wrong. Jerome was not killed. As he had trudged from hopeless battle to fearful aftermath alongside men exhausted beyond comprehension the spirit was sapped from him. Not for Jerome the quick death of an enemy's blade or arrow. No, the slow death of knowing that tomorrow shall be as grim and harrowing as today.

Should you be of unquiet disposition, you should read no further. This is a heart-rending story. In part of Paris, of persons you think you must know – Picasso, Monet, Genet, Marie Antoinette. And persons you have already glimpsed; Jerome, certainly. Pee-pee. And one for whom words are hardly adequate. Can you sense her approach? She that loves the honour of knowing a good man; his courage, his integrity, his dancing.

But she who loves more the promise of love; the pleasure, the caresses, the abandon. An abandon that shakes her to her core – leaves her sated, glowing, demanding, lost to all but the moment when she gives herself utterly, life beyond the physical forgotten, her duty cast aside as a mere quirk of fate, her name echoing as her lover whispers, "J'aime ta chatte." This woman will kill.

II

Of course obituaries of Malcolm Maclaren made much of his Sex Pistols years. His so-called exploitation of Messrs Rotten, Vicious and the rest, running amok with *Sex* alongside Vivien Westwood on the King's Road, all of Chelsea – so it seemed – falling at the feet of a couple who dared to drape their manikins in bin-liners or ripped jeans fastened with safety-pins. Why not cling-film; surely, more iconic? After all, when asked what had been the major, indeed world changing, outcome of the lunar landings Truman Capote – he of *In Cold Blood* – had opined, "Cling-film."

Maclaren's musical progeny had included the pubescent Annabella of Bow-Wow-Wow, his own output apparently, to most obituarists, best exemplified by *Duck Rock*. But one album has slipped through the net, only *Le Monde* mentioning it in passing; *Paris* is Maclaren's legacy. Hard to find now, it is a full-blown love letter to the city. A salacious beginning with his highness declaiming words that even the libertarian Zappa may have deemed *de trop*, is followed by glorious, glorious music encompassing gentle jazz, an African chorus (*Anthem*), extraordinary drumming and – wait for this – both Françoise Hardy and Catherine Deneuve on vocals.

You half expect Jane Birkin to show up; *Je t'aime* is there but in MM's inimitable style so no Gainsbourg. No

Edith Piaf either but Miles gets a mention.

The Deneuve track includes a moment of genius. She is encouraged to sing: "Sing away Catherine." In halting English – perhaps the sexiest voice ever committed to vinyl – she declines, her questioning, "Sing away?" echoing for a few bars. And then she does, indeed, sing and this questing, pale Englishman has conjured up a never to be bettered intensity from this beautiful French siren.

But, hey, that's *Paris*. And how could you better Paris; in song, celebration, in love or in soul? It is the city of love, no? Various Presidents have had a similar claim to fame to dear Malcolm in the love stakes – nearly all the wives and lovers were taller than their spouses.

III

Jerome stares at the grate, now cold with the ashes of last night's fire. There are tears in his eyes, his blond hair awry. The curls are ruffled by his habit of running his hands through them. He knows tonight there will be another blaze, this time a bonfire set in the field beyond the stable. A fire of welcome, of homecoming and thanks. For the moment he is quiet, lost in thought and memory. Four years! Not a long time in a war said to last a hundred but almost a sixth of his life to date and a third of his adulthood if you count twelve as the age he was first considered a man.

Those years before he left had been hard. A time of work and little rest; helping with the harvest, husbanding his father's trees, cutting enough hardwood for the lintels and beams, sawing the softer boughs for repair-work and chopping the rougher, gnarled boles for kindling and winter firewood. Working alongside Pierre in the cobbled yard had been serious toil from which he had drawn great pleasure. He would groom his father's cart-horse. "That old nag not fit to make a frog fart at dawn" as Pierre would say.

Jerome grins at the memory and runs his hands through his hair. Coaxing the dam's neck he would gently buckle her knee and raise one or other front leg for the smithy. Pierre and Jerome harness her with leather buffed and gleaming bridle before leading her through the yard and on into the field for ploughing.

The fields stretch as far as the eye can see. Bisected by the river, they run across the hillside where copses stand out against the sky-line. This is woodland where as a child he had played hide-and-seek, archery or "let's see who can climb the highest" (it was always Pee-pee). Sometimes they sing ditties made up in the instant by Jerome and forgotten just as quickly. Depending on the crop, the landscape could be almost any colour but, whatever grain or grasses were planted, in April the fields were a blaze of red and blue. Poppy and cornflower.

It was in just such a field after a day spent gathering firewood and kindling that Jerome had sat open-mouthed as Pierre, then barely sixteen to his own twenty years, had spelled out the art of love-making. And in that hour's education Jerome had understood that he could never love a woman as she might want to be loved until he had proved himself in war, in battle, anywhere but in the seasonal labour of woods and fields.

It had been hot, unseasonably hot. The friends had attacked the smaller branches with fervour before axing and sawing the trunks into submission. Hornbeam mostly and pine sticky with sap that bled from where their axes first split the bark; a smell of resin that haunts him still. By evening both are tired beyond fatigue and collapse against the grassy river bank, the Seine idling past with all the time in the world.

The steam from their bodies mingles with the haze rising from the field of wheat and barley. Poppies flare red wherever Jerome's gaze wanders. Soon the crop will rise higher than its crown of poppy red and cornflower blue.

"I'm fucked," says Pierre. "Trompé. You look done for, aussi."

"My body feels like the cart-horse has been sitting on me for a week. My shoulders and arms are so sore. Fatigué. Fatigué."

"Too tired for you-know-what with you-know-who?"

Jerome remembers sitting bolt up-right at the question.

"You-know-who?"

"Don't play the innocent with me. Our queen of the village, Marie."

"What about her?"

Jerome has shifted his position and is rubbing his legs back to life.

"Well, you're obviously stuck on her. Have you made your move yet? She's of age, you know."

Jerome stiffens. He feels horribly aware of the shameful confession he is about to make to his younger friend.

"I'm not much good at, at … action."

"How do you mean?"

"You know. Action. Stronger stuff. I … just think all the time. All the time. In the stable, at home. Sometimes just staring into the ash in the grate I get lost."

He pauses, slightly out of breath, searching for an example, Pierre now looking at him as he might a wounded bird.

"That pair of trees over there."

"The hornbeams?"

"Yeah."

"What about them?"

"You look at them and you see trees?"

"Ummm... D'accord. What do you see? Fish?"

"Work, chat with you, seasons, other trees I remember from last year, the silhouettes of a pair of lovers turning away from us. On and on."

Pierre raises an eyebrow.

"Just those two there? Or is it any trees?"

"It's worse than that. It's anything, anybody, any plan I make. It's why I can't make love to Marie."

"You see her as a tree?"

"No, you donkey! When I think of talking to her about being (he reddens) ... together I imagine her older, us together as an aging couple, children, arguments. Daft. Useless. The moment is gone."

"Well just make something up. Lie to her."

"Lie?"

"Tell her you love her and want her forever."

"But that wouldn't be a lie. I do."

"Which?"

"Both. I think I love her and I'm fairly sure I'll want her forever."

"But you only think it. You don't know it. So say it and it's a kind of lie."

"How's that going to help?"

"Girls, sorry women, expect to be lied to. So say anything you like as long as it sounds good. She won't believe you but she'll know what you're thinking. Anyway, it's all a lie. Love, forever. All of it."

Jerome hasn't considered the world this way before. Nor has he witnessed his friend being so loquacious albeit – to his mind at least – ruthless.

"But, but it's not meant to be a lie."

"What?"

"Love. It's ... eternal, blind, glorious. It even goes on when everything else is burning down."

"Burning down! You've got it bad. You should have been a troubadour."

"I speak words to her sometimes. Well not to her, but it's like she's standing in front of me listening. If I could write, I'd write a lay for her. She's, she's, just glorious. She's about the only thing that keeps me here."

"She's not that glorious."

Jerome opens his mouth to reply but stops. There is a certainty to Pierre's manner he hasn't noticed before.

"How, how do you know?"

"I've had her."

The response is short, jarring and all too obviously honest. His world spins,

"You're lying."

"No. I wouldn't lie to you. It was towards the end of last Autumn, just after her birthday. The first time."

Jerome can hardly breathe.

"And when was the last?"

"Last week."

Jerome feels sick. He can't think. He is flooded with images of Marie and Pierre. Pee-pee of all people! In the woods, in the byre, soaked in the sweat of passion, entwined in each others' arms as dawn approaches...

"Like I said. She's not glorious. Randy, yes. Glorious, no."

"I thought you were my friend! Mon ami!"

"I am, chump, but you and Marie hadn't done anything but walk. Or talk, or hold hands. And she wanted more."

"From you?"

"No, from you fat-head, but you were lost in day-dreams and your imaginings of love. She wants passion not words. Or maybe both. But words aren't my best face. Voilà! Pass me that axe."

That was the moment Jerome Mazerme resolved to go to war. For honour, for his man-hood, for Marie Leclaire.

IV

In June 1995, France had been gripped by reports of a missing child. Headlines and stories even appeared briefly in England's *Daily Mail.* A short piece in *Der Spiegel* made much of the possibility that the child, a girl, had been seized by slavers. Then, as these things happen, she slipped under the radar. Her desperate parents had appeared on television, on the radio and on the front pages of *Figaro* and *L'Independant. Le Monde* covered what story there was for less than a week and not once on the front page.

As ever, political machinations, the economy, even Algeria took precedence along with a puff piece for *Le Monde* itself prompting the reader to turn to its debunking of fears about the increasing size of the EEC. *Le Regard de Plantu* was in place (bottom left corner) but the cartoonist thankfully did not set his sights on the abduction. Nor did *Le Monde*'s readers get to see the photograph of a smiling ten-year-old clutching a teddy bear. Typically, captions in the dailies were variants on, 'Search for little Louise goes on.'

Even the townspeople of Evreux where her (already grieving?) parents lived soon dropped the saga. What was there to say? "Have you heard? Is she still missing? Her poor mum and dad!" The local journalist moved on after penning, 'M and Mme Burle to appear on national radio in new appeal.' He had been asked to seek out local views on the ever-expanding EEC. Slowly all but the Burles' neighbours and family forget. For them it is as if Louise is still among them; laughing as she opens birthday presents, smiling at the school gates.

Louise's parents don't forget either, of course. Every day they stare into the abyss and wonder, wonder...

V

Gaston isn't fat. Jerome cannot call him fat. Gaston is –
what is the word – énorme. Kind, gentle, a great gap-
toothed grin on his face on even the most gruelling days
and a jerkin of a soft, kid-like leather "like a rich
woman's chemise" (as Jacques had said) but legs so
vast it might be possible to go to sleep on his right thigh
alone. The rest of Gaston is perfectly in proportion to
his tree-trunk appendages. Neck wider than his head,
great shoulders carrying arms like hams and a belly ...
Jerome sits and looks at Gaston's belly and pictures his
mother's sow at litter.

"A drink?"

"Merci."

Jerome takes the proffered cup from a hand the size
of his own head. There are boudin-sized fingers, nails
bitten to the quick, but the smile, the smile... Always
there even... It is raining. They have been travelling for
four days, the company picking up fellow would-be
combatants at each hamlet. Most, Jerome sees, are
peasants, land-workers, many young, very young and a
few more seasoned men who arrive with arms,
crossbows, strong boots. These men have fought before;
for a pittance, a harsh diet, the familiar company of
fighting men. Gaston is one such.

At the first rest-halt Jerome had seen two lads of
perhaps fifteen run out from a field to the head of the
group and shout excitedly at a man with the appearance

of authority. There had been no hesitation. They were recruited. One absconded during their second night but the other, Jacques, now sits beside Gaston chewing on some mutton. Jerome has already understood that the diet will be whatever is to be begged from villagers. Gaston warns him they have been lucky.

"Went four days with now't but water at the start of the month," he says, dolefully. "Four days! I felt quite faint."

"You could go four months and you'd be fine. All that blubber on you."

At this Gaston shoots out an arm to grasp Jacques. Laughing, the boy squirms from his grip and leaps to his feet.

"Catch me big boy!"

And he dances away, still laughing, a slew of mutton fat at his chin.

They are in Giverny, a village of no more than thirty stone houses and a beautiful church. They sit now in the church-yard, Jerome propped against a lichen-covered head-stone. He can make out carved shapes in the stone and wonders again at the men who must make their living from chiselling what he knows to be words into the rock. 'Can the stonemasons read? Or do they follow a script already inscribed by the bereaved?' And what is this script? Latin. The language of those with power and an education that won't have included learning how to set a fire, cook in the open air or sleep on the hard ground.

"You are always thinking, my friend. What are your thoughts now? You stare at the rock as if you can see the future."

The future? No-one can see the future. Jerome knows that, without reading; he cannot even see the past beyond his father's tales, stories from *his* father and his before him.

"I was thinking about the people buried here. How we all return to the soil. To be eaten by worms and rot to nothingness."

"Cheerful! Perhaps these people had good lives. Well, at least decent food. Still died though, didn't they?"

"And their souls?"

"Flown. As ours' must. Do you always think about such things? Eating, sleeping, working? When making love?"

Jerome blushes and turns away. He suspects he would. If only...

"Love-making not your strong suit then? Desolée, mon ami. I don't mean to embarrass you, though I would recommend it!"

"You? You.."

"Bien sûr. I may be big but I am in proportion! Ha!"

Gaston puts a great hand between his legs and grasps at his groin pulling upwards as he does so and smiling broadly. Jerome laughs and runs his hands through his hair, now matted from the constant drizzle. It's really the only part of the last days he hasn't enjoyed. The company, well Gaston's, has been good, the food, always mutton, more regular than he might have hoped. And there have been sunflowers, in field after field, to brighten his heart if not the sky; so far a continuous grey. He has even managed a swim; cold but refreshing as Gaston threw pebbles from the bank. He is not a good swimmer but his friend doesn't even attempt to enter the water fearing what may "lurk beneath." This is new for Jerome and not an idea he allows to disturb his splashing. But he finds it is a common terror, any number of men warning him about eels, "vast" pike, even snakes. He doesn't know if his natural confidence is earned or ignorance. He has never *seen* a river snake. Either way, he swims, relishing the feel of the water and the moments after as Gaston rubs him down.

"You are in proportion as well, mon ami."

The remark keeps coming back to Jerome. Is he big, small? Does it matter? Would it matter to Marie? And he closes his eyes, her image floating around him like a protective angel.

"You've gone again."

"Desolée. I was thinking of a woman at home."

"Ah, a lover!"

"Non, mais je l'espère. Quand...si...je reviens."

"Return ! You are confident at more than swimming. You will need luck, my friend. And a little guidance, je crois."

Jacques reappears. He looks sidelong at Gaston who gestures for him to sit. Tentatively the lad settles beside the older man and, resting his head on the enormous thigh, is soon asleep.

"Do you know any songs?"

"I don't think so. Pierre and I sometimes made up silly things when we were working."

"Silly?"

"You know, spur of the moment things ... we forgot them straightaway."

"Try this. Frère Jacques, Frère Jacques. Dormez vous, dormez vous..."

"What's that? "

"I don't know. Some of the others used to sing it to try and get us up in the mornings. Sleepy-head here reminded me. It's a song about Jews."

"Jews? What are they? Do you know any Jews?"

"No idea? I don't think so, but it's a nice song. Let me teach you."

And Jerome sits while his new friend, a boy asleep in his lap, teaches him a song, a song of the nursery and better times.

VI

It is impossibly smoky. Dimly, through smarting eyes, you make out the bar. It is but three metres away, a hubbub of French voices fill what was once air and is now pure, exhaled tobacco smoke. Behind you less voices but more noise; a drone, like something you might hear from an approaching ferry in the fog. This drone has a logic to it, repeating ululations with only the slightest fluctuations reminding you that that the sounds do not emanate from some infernal machine. They are man-made. Man and saxophone made. You are listening to Roland Kirk. Not far from the Place Pigalle you imagine yourself to have truly arrived. A jazz bar, a Parisian jazz bar at that.

You have bribed your Parisian lover. She is French and you only half French, raised in England after your father's 'escapades' (courtesy of the Royal Air Force) by an English mother who herself claimed to be part French. She refused to speak the language. And your lover has brought you to Paris for the weekend. Gauloises and Crème-de-Menthe dutifully choked over and absinthe illegal, the real Paris must be in a smoke-filled jazz bar.

The Paris of Miles, Coltrane, Mingus, Monk and Dexter Gordon. Who happens to be at the club tonight? None other than the blind, black, sun-glassed purveyor of impossible multi-instrumentalism, Rahsaan Roland

Kirk. The drone drones. On and on over an occasional flurry of higher notes piercing the smog. You shift and stare through the gloom.

"C'mon, we've got to see him. Let's get closer."

Easier said than done. Prising yourself up-right you stand and several "Excusez-mois" later you haven't moved at all.

"Just push. That's what we French do."

What is it about the English part of you that prevents this simple physical contact? She grasps your arm and you both lurch forward.

"Merde!"

"Monsieur, mademoiselle!"

"Faites attention!"

"Jesus, watch out!"

But you have lurched into a less crushing part of the club. There are tables here and groups of three or four listeners all sit with faces turned towards the drone. Then you see him as another series of arpeggios splits the numbing base notes of the tenor and a new trilling of piccolo-esque demi-quavers cascades above both. There he stands, not massive as you have every right to expect but absorbed so absorbed, beyond the crowd and behind his Raybans.

He is, for what it's worth, spot-lit, a yellowish haze surrounding him as fingers and hands blur. Now he is on tenor, now soprano and – how can this be? – a third, the piccolo. You stare. This blind, black, beautiful man is playing all three at once! All the sounds you hear come from Kirk. They are not discordant, raucous or stark. It is quite, quite sublime. In that smoke-filled club off the Place Pigalle you know heaven for the first time.

You turn to her. Through the smog she suddenly appears so beautiful.

"Je t'aime. I love you. Will you have my baby?"

"Ah, oui. Bien sûr."

VII

"You need to get your end away my man."

"My end?"

"Mon dieu! That beauty between your legs. Your cock!"

"Why do you say that?"

"You're always moping. Anyway, it's been a week since we picked you up. I couldn't have gone a week at your age."

"And now?"

"Well, I'm no more than... Hmmm, twenty something I think and I get it regular enough."

"How?"

"You must live in a world of your own. Think about it. Men, boy! I have men. And there's no shortage here is there?"

Jerome is startled upright. They have been resting in the midday heat not far from the beginnings of a forest. Like low-lying cloud the haze rises above the trees. There is fresh water and enough cold mutton to allow them to enjoy the "calm before the storm", as Gaston has called the day.

"I. I ... didn't know. I assumed..."

"What? That I had a nice woman and six brats at home? No, my boy. Je préfère les hommes, toujours."

"Pourquoi?"

"Why? Well that's a good question coming from a virgin. Pourquoi? Pourquoi non? Men are easier."

"Easier?"

"Well, there's more of them for a start. Especially here. But they don't have their heads full of chores, children, getting pregnant."

"Isn't the whole point to get pregnant?"

Gaston stares at Jerome and offers his most sympathetic smile.

"No, my young friend, the point is to enjoy yourself. And men know what they're doing! And what another man wants."

Jerome shifts uncomfortably. He runs his hands through his hair.

"I think I'd rather start with a woman."

"Then, we'll find you one. There was one we passed this morning. Did you see her by the ditch? Kept looking our way. Come on!"

It is evening. True to his word, Gaston has found Jerome a woman. She had been quietly squatting by a ditch when they came upon her. Pushing her skirts down and with a look of perhaps welcome on her face she had seemed pleased when Gaston whispered something in her ear, an ear Jerome couldn't help but notice seemed to have been chewed. It is ruby red. Bulbous. The woman grins at Jerome and beckons, her hand plump and filthy. Her grin is marred only by the lack of teeth, the few that remain blackened. He wonders what she has been chewing on.

"Do you want a little, young man?"

"Er, I, I, think so."

"Don't be shy boy. I'll be careful."

With that she reaches out and takes Jerome's hand pointing to some bushes at the lane's edge. Jerome looks pleadingly at Gaston.

"Go on, lad. I'll keep a watch out. Give her one for me!"

The bush is laurel, its foliage offering some sort of privacy as he finds himself steered into its midst. He stands before her, his head ducking low to avoid the branches.

"Do you want me on my back or front, lovey?"

"I, I..."

"You ain't as forward as your fat friend are you? C'mon loverboy, let's see what you've got."

As if watching through fog, Jerome sees the plump hands hauling at his belt. He feels his breeches pulled down past his knees. Instinctively, he pulls away.

"Oh dear. What have we here? He's a soft fellow isn't he? Fat though. I like 'em fat. We'll soon get you up to size!"

Still in a dream, Jerome feels the woman's soft mouth, softer than he expected, close around him. He wonders if it's the lack of teeth... Despite himself, he is getting hard, her tongue tickling him, arousing him. He is swelling...

"Oh God, I'm sorry. I didn't mean..."

"Gwmm, you taste good. Mild. No harm done. Just another lick. Look, you're getting big again already. Lovely. Slower this time lover. I'll just hitch these blessed skirts up. Now easy does it."

He feels relief, embarrassment, his stomach muscles

still flexing as she turns, kneels and pushes out to him. Her bush is black-haired, the fur tracing a line through her behind. This time it is Jerome who moves, pressing into her as he has witnessed the dogs at home. Her skin feels soft – not so different from her mouth. She is younger than she looks. He is hard now, more in control, pushing in and out, sliding, deeper, deeper...

"Oo, that's lovely that is. Push him in big boy. Ahhh..."

"Ur, aagh, aagh."

He grasps her hips. With one more thrust the sensation of release is such that he almost faints. Collapsing beside her he just spies a pellucid oozing before she pulls her skirts back in place.

"That was nice, that was. Now let's have a nice cuddle."

"What's your name?"

"My name! Oh, so now you're all done, you want my name? Put those big strong arms around me and I'll tell you."

He notices the powerful smell of rosemary as she nestles her head into his chest. It seems to be coming from her hair: 'Is this contentment? Is this how it always is afterwards?'

"People like me don't have a name, lovely boy. But you can call me Coquette."

"Coquette? Really?"

"Why not? What does it matter? Nice cock, I must say. You got any food?"

Before he can answer a familiar hand is reaching through the leaves, grasping him by the jerkin.

"Come on sunshine. Hide that manhood of yours. We've got to make tracks."

"I thought you or the boy might have a little food. What I swallowed won't last me long."

Jerome blushes and adjusts his tunic. He runs his hands through his hair and is about to speak when Gaston presses his finger to his lips.

"Don't worry my friend. She won't need food where she is going."

"Here, what are you doing? Leave me be you lump!"

But Gaston doesn't leave her or let go his grasp, now rough and powerful. Dragging the woman out from under the laurel as if she is no more than a sack of leaves, he pushes her head back. Her neck is suddenly exposed and with a sharp twist he turns her head. From somewhere a vicious looking blade appears in his right hand. Her vein stands proud, but only for a second, and then Gaston cuts fast and deep, the blood flowing over his own hand and onto the ground. The woman struggles, breathing hard, trying to twist away. But the blood flows stronger. There is a gurgling sound and a smell, a smell...

"Dirty whore's shit her-self! What a stink!"

The woman lies still. But a few feet away, Jerome is standing transfixed.

"What have you done? Why? What harm could she...? I don't understand."

He crumples and sobs a little.

"You'll get over it. Last thing we'd want is her ratting on us. Or worse..."

"Worse?"

"Getting with child. No good at all, my lad. No good at all. Let's go."

And he had thought this man kind....

"Well done, Jerome! You are a man now. Tu es un homme fait! Killing's next."

VIII

By the 1950s, Paris saw itself as the literary capital of the world; Proust, Gide, Malraux, Genet, Sartre, de Beauvoir. All had written in and of the city and prospered though Genet was not to be fêted until the explosion of liberal attitudes of that era nostalgically known as the 'sixties.

Suddenly a man who had lived in sometimes abject poverty was rich. The English translation of *The Thief's Journal* sold three million copies effortlessly even though its author had been regarded as a pornographer in the war years, his work selling under the table to the middle class literati. Sartre adored Genet, the latter finding his admirer ultimately a bourgeois with his love of *France Musique*, the piano duets with mère Sartre and his need for de Beauvoir to read, edit, copy and inspire his work.

In his early twenties Sartre claimed to be reading upwards of three hundred books a year – not slim summaries of the "Philosophy for Idiots" variety (momentarily putting Russell to one side there were few of those to be had) but the real thing; Plato, Aristotle, Husserl. Into his thirties he was writing for six hours a day in two three-hour shifts sandwiching his relentless note-taking in cafés and debates with friends and Gauloise after Gauloise. What did he take notes about? He assiduously recorded everything *he* said. He knew that only his interpretation and responses would have meaning. By his sixties, already the author of hundreds of articles, several biographies, the monumental *Being and Nothingness*, plays – both acclaimed and unpublished – film scripts, *Nausea, The Roads to Freedom* and *The Words,* he was world renowned *and* had declined The Nobel Prize for literature. And still he envied Genet.

For her part, de Beauvoir matched him in literary output and prowess. She read, corrected or produced commentaries on everything her beloved Jean-Paul ever published.

But in the early 'fifties one author took the public's gaze and garlands. A Hammett with added garlic he was translated, filmed, interviewed and lauded by intellectual and manual worker, spiv and stage-hand. The *Maigret* novels swept all before them, Simenon somehow conjuring up a world of suspense, inquiry, leisure, murder and the vicarious satisfaction of a distantly heard classical recital playing on Maigret's gramophone.

For readers he was a policeman who worked into the small hours, sometimes pursuing villains down fin-de-siècle staircases, sometimes sitting quietly, pipe clenched between his teeth. And yet still managing a midday meal almost beyond parody for an English readership in the grip of the last years of rationing. Two (or more) pastis at 11.30 a.m., an hour later snails or perhaps pâté accompanied by a Beaujolais (Simenon was meticulous about the year and provenance of the delights on offer in his hero's wine cellar), poached sole with a Montrachet, a hearty coq-au-vin (time for the Burgundian red), then a pause.

Mme Maigret might say,

"Did the fellow fall from the balcony? How do you think he could have smuggled the sapphire out of Paris? I do think those curtains need a thorough shaking. They do so show the dust!"

Meanwhile, our Inspector will nod, lost in thought, reach absent-mindedly for his pipe and then remember le fromage has yet to arrive. And arrive it will; a brie (à pointe) a beaufort, some rocquefort (served with a pre-war Chateau D'Yquem). The only doubt will be a question mark about pudding. Maigret has put on a little weight and is considering that archetypal fad of his era – a diet. Only just freed from the austerity of the war years and people are trying to be thinner, not through hard work – they have had enough of that – but by eating less. Profiteroles duly turn up, followed by coffee and, at last, thirty minutes with his pipe. A little cognac. Why not? It's now gone four in the afternoon.

There we might still find him at five, fingers interlocking under his chin. His right index finger occasionally toys with the pipe stem. He is now deep in post-prandial thought.

Four pages of this kind of thing for a rationed, book-buying British public were just too much. So they put him on television.

IX

The fog doesn't bother him at first. Jerome has known worse. He can make out three men walking line abreast to his right and another five or so to the left. 'Is this the nature of war?' he wonders, 'Tramping through a wood with who-knows-what in front of us. Making enough noise to make sure that anyone who's not stone deaf can hear us for two leagues!'

The men trudge on, the occasional curse, a whispered, "Silence!" or two. Bracken crunches beneath their tread. They are not yet weary. But there is no spring in their steps. Only fear. If it were not for the arms they carry it might almost be possible to take them for a hunting party. But a hunting party stretching for as far as the eye might see if only the fog allowed. There is now a full company; over a hundred footmen with fifty horsemen and the cross-bow carriers bringing up the rear. The crossbow-men themselves are in a group of another hundred or so far to the left of the main body. "Keeping out of harm's way," one of the group leaders had said.

Jerome wonders at the respect given to these men. Has he not brought down quail and pheasant himself in the fields? The fields! How he misses the fields. But this was with a bow of ash, not a cross-bow so heavy that a serf has the task of carrying it. How he yearns for a day with Pee-pee in the fields. Never again would he think of those days as dull, however necessary for survival.

They had been slow, peaceful, warm; even in the evenings. And safe. He tries to push the horror of Gaston's violence from his mind but his thoughts keep returning to the woman's look of terror, her blood ... It was only hours ago, yet seems like a year. His mind wanders a little more. 'Marie? What of Marie?'

She sits in front of Pierre, her legs astride his. Her index finger strokes his chest.

"You make me shake all over."

Her legs part a little more.

"It's easy loving you. You want it so much."

"Like a man?"

"Some men. Well, me anyway."

And with that he presses her back to the straw and, kneeling now, he lowers his head between her legs deliberately brushing her thighs with his hair as his tongue flicks teasingly, achingly against her soft skin.

At first he thinks the quiet voices to his right are those of his companions. But there is something, something different. The accents! These men speak French, certainly. But their muted conversation is slower, more guttural. Normands! How can that be? Surely they are a long way, a very long way from the north? He thinks hard. How long have they been marching, how many nights camping under the stars made invisible by cloud or by the roof of a byre? Perhaps it is longer than he thought, but surely not long enough to ... To what?

Make a friend? Lose his virginity? Witness a killing? In any case, he has no idea where 'the North' is meant to be and how long getting there should take. They have been criss-crossing the river whenever the waters allow. They may have gone barely any distance in their efforts to avoid the enemy. He stiffens.

"This is no enemy. We were told they are men of the woods and fields who could hear a fox a league distant!"

It is a stranger Jerome hears.

"Shhh..They don't know we're here."

"If they're as tired as me they won't care."

What can this mean? Jerome hurries to settle himself under a tranche of leaves, silently cursing the rustling around him. He hears a twig snap. Someone is moving. Closer ...

"Be quiet, you oaf. They will hear us. Attend! Que-ce que c'est!"

A boot is digging into Jerome's side. He flinches. Through the leaves he can see a shape above him. A shape that moves down. Two eyes meet his. He just has time to think, 'such tired eyes' when he feels a sharp pain in his side. As the pain bites he hears, as if down a long tunnel,

"Ambush! Mon Dieu! Ambush! Ambush!"

"The bastards are upon us!"

"Ambush!"

He can dimly see Gaston not far away. This huge man, the first to have offered him friendship; Jerome still sees the great, strong, brown hand offering wine from a mottled leather flask. Hears again the kindly voice, "Take some, your need is greater than mine," the grinning face, brown eyes darker than night...his blade at the woman's throat...Then he drifts, drifts...

-

"Do you want more, cherie?"
    "You're insatiable!"
    "Well?"
Marie shifts her weight under Pierre. She can feel him inside, growing again.
    "Encore. Tiens moi encore. Pierre ..."
    She feels his weight as she pushes her hips to meet him. 'Nothing beats the weight of a man.' Her last thought as she closes her eyes.

Something is lying on top of Jerome. Something heavy. A weight that doesn't stir. He smells the harsh, rank aroma of bloodied leather. This something is dead. All around is silence; no more hushed voices approaching, no more ghosts with northern accents. His side is numb, heavy. As carefully as he can he squirms from under the body and claws his way through the leaves: 'some protection they were!' He tries to stand and a sharp pain bends him double. Pressing his hand to the place he feels warmth seeping through numbed fingers. More gradually now he stands. The fog has lifted. Before him is a scene of carnage to rival any abattoir.

"What do you think he is doing now?"
    "Jerome?"

"Oui, Jerome."

"Do you think of him when we're at it?"

"Non! Well, sometimes."

"Thanks! He'll be safe. Probably holed up in a warm barn feasting on a partridge or two. You know Jerome. He'll stay well away from danger."

Not far away lies an arm – hacked off, the blood not yet dry. A man – friend or foe? – lies with two crossbow bolts protruding from his neck. Another is kneeling. Where his head should be there is a mass of gore and bloodied hair. Jerome retches, the only sound in the wood. The sound of fear, of horror. He stumbles forward, wincing at the pain in his side. Wherever he turns there are bodies. Most look as though they have been butchered and hacked to death. He can see many more companions than dead northerners. But where are the living? Where? He slumps down, suddenly cold.

Ahead he hears voices, harsh voices.

"They'll be around here somewhere, they couldn't have gone far."

He has never heard English spoken before. It is not so different from Normande with the same guttural quality, much the same haughty slowness to the speech. It is coarse and he can only imagine the kind of men who speak thus. He can see none of his companions, scattered, scythed down where they stood. He seems to remember Jacques not more than a strong whisper away, first surrounded then hacked to death, his screams louder than the triumphant cries of his butchers. He vaguely recalls men striding away from him into the wood, blades red with his friend's blood. And how many others? He crouches and tries to cover himself again with leaves. He notices the powerful scent of rosemary above him. 'Romarin.' His mind drifts to Coquette... and Marie...

"Here's one!"

As he is hauled to his feet he has one – not very helpful – thought, 'Next time I won't trust leaves for cover!'

"Put him with the others."

"Les autres?" He understands. Voilà! There are others. He catches sight of them. Mostly crossbow-men, all captive but alive. And Gaston is with them. Alive! Jerome is manhandled by a ruffian pulling and pushing him ahead. He does his best to avoid the dead bodies sprawled and spread-eagled at his feet but he knows it is no sin to touch them. Their souls are flown. The dead are dead. It is dying that terrifies him. Some are contorted in death agony, others simply appear to sleep. At peace. Ahead he can see perhaps thirty of his own standing while their captors laugh around them.

"Ça va?"

"Ça va. Et toi, ça va?"

"C'est dur. So many dead."

Jerome turns and surveys the scene, his throat suddenly dry. He tries to understand. What had happened? He had only seen perhaps half a dozen enemy when they first found him under the accursed leaves. An advance party only. For the ambush. He can imagine the scene – remembers again Jacques - 'Frère

Jacques.'

His exhausted companions had been caught by surprise. Mostly peasants, not soldiers, they couldn't have out-fought real infantry. The crossbow-men would have been too far distant, their bolts impeded by the trees. He can see more of his own on the ground with no sign of weaponry All butchered where they had stood or lain. Others had fought well, but were now as dead as their companions. He chokes back a sob.

"What now?"

"We don't know. We've been stood here for hours."

As the bowman speaks, one of the enemy approaches.

"Do you remember Crécy?"

"Que-ce que c'est, Crécy?"

"A great victory. But our bowmen paid a terrible price after. The time has come for revenge."

Four men rush forward and grasp a crossbow-man. Forcing him to his knees, one of them, a grim looking brute, grasps a wrist and pulls. Hard. Panic is in the captive's eyes. A knife appears in the enemy's free hand. Pressing the bowman's hand to the earth his tormentor forces the blade into soft flesh just above the knuckle of the middle finger. With a cruel twist and downward thrust the blade slices, tears, splinters skin, muscle and bone. The man roars:

"Bastard!"

"Not finished yet, Willam Tell!"

Taking the bloodied maw in his left hand the infantryman again wields the blade with his right. Now he is quicker. Two fingers lay on the crimson ground.

Jerome stares at them, the nails curiously beautiful.

"Next!"

Another crossbow-man is dragged forward and pushed to his knees. Jerome turns away. He doesn't know if his captors understand he has never loosed a bolt in his life. He feels a rush of shame. 'Besides, if they know, they will kill me anyway. What use is an extra prisoner, another mouth to feed?' Or perhaps this mutilation is just a prelude to another mass killing. A scream rends the air and he sees Maurice Laguoile – he of the knives – collapse grasping his mangled flesh.

"Next!"

"C'est moi."

Jerome steps forward.

X

Matisse, Monet, Mondrian. Is there significance in each name beginning with the alphabet's thirteenth letter? Like maître and master. They all knew Montparnasse, Madame Toussaud's, Montmartre. Would they have liked Malcolm MacLaren? How could they not? *Both* names begin with the thirteenth.

At the Louvre Claude Monet witnessed students copying from the old masters. He preferred instead to go and sit by a window to paint what he saw, something of a contrast to Matisse who took eight years to copy *one* work to the satisfaction of his teacher, Bouguereau.

In June 1861, Monet joined the First Regiment of African Light Cavalry in Algeria – supposedly for seven years. But, two years later, after he had contracted typhoid fever, his aunt intervened to get him out. Her condition was his agreement to complete an arts course becoming, in 1862, a student of Charles Gleyre in Paris. There he met Sisley, Bazille and Renoir. In Paris Monet also met Manet. Impressionism was about to begin.

Monet painted *Camille* or *The Woman in the Green Dress* (*La femme à la robe verte*), in 1866. The model is Camille Doncieux. Three years later, still his model, Camille falls pregnant and gives birth to their first child, Jean.

They marry in June 1870, moving the following year to Argenteuil. Despite becoming seriously ill, Camille gives birth to their second son, Michel, eight years on. That same year, the couple move to the village of Vétheuil to stay with Ernest Hoschedé and his wife, Alice. Bankrupt, Ernest soon leaves for Belgium. On 5 September 1879, Camille died of tuberculosis (some say cancer) at the age of thirty-two. Monet painted her on her death bed. Alice took his sons and her own six children to live in Paris. Then she and the children rejoined Claude in Vétheuil, later moving to Poissy. Looking out of a train window, not far from Vernon, he discovered Giverny.

Following her estranged husband's death, Alice Hoschedé married Claude Monet in 1892 and so he arrived in Giverny with eight children. He was 42.

The family rented a house and two acres from a local landowner. There was a barn that doubled as a painting studio, orchards and a small garden, the house close enough to the local schools for the children. The surrounding landscape offered vista and views to inspire and seduce. How he loves the gardens; his Japanese bridge crosses the Ru, a branch of the Epte, tributary of the Seine. And how he works; he paints it all.

Seven years later he was famous and prosperous enough to buy the house, the surrounding buildings and the land for his gardens. During the century's last decade he added a greenhouse and a second studio, a building bathed in light from its skylights.

At Giverny, in the 40 years to his death in 1926, Monet pioneered modern art. Some might claim he was imitating the serial painting methods of the Japanese woodcut artists Hiroshige and Hokusai in depicting the town and his garden from different viewpoints and in different formats. The "Early morning on the Seine" series shows varying weather and follows the changing light. In the later, vast, paintings of water lilies, water, light and reflection mix natural and reflected realities to the point where the viewer can't tell the difference. The "Poplars" series seems inspired by Japanese woodcuts with a dash of Van Gogh. Meanwhile haystacks from the "Grain stacks" series brought him into the world of abstraction soon to be dominated by Kandinsky.

His second wife, Alice, died in 1911 and then his oldest son Jean, who had married Alice's daughter Blanche, died in 1914. After Alice's death, Blanche looked after and cared for him

Claude Monet died of lung cancer on 5 December 1926. He had already had two operations for cataracts. Some claim they influenced the redness to be seen in his later works. He was 86 and is buried in the church cemetery at Giverny. Monet had insisted that the occasion be simple. The grave is tended still, covered in flowers and marked by a stone cross and a simple plaque. Only about fifty people attended the funeral.

In contrast to the master of Giverny, Matisse had known poverty, material poverty. Exploring colour and, like Picasso, finding inspiration in found objects (Picasso's famous goat started life as an old basket that somehow evoked a rib-cage), or rugs, or pots, or the simplicity of a window open to the blue of the Mediterranean, Matisse lacked for nothing in creative wealth. But food, new linen, clothing not spattered by oils from his palette ... these were something else altogether. He would buy drawings from Van Gogh to enable Vincent to eat. Or a very occasional Cézanne purchase. It made little difference to the master. His sponsor and supporter – Zola no less – having died (in bleak and, it is said, deeply suspicious circumstances at the hands, perhaps, of the French secret police), Cezanne remained impoverished. By 1906 he is writing to his son, another Paul, "I have nothing to do but paint." The paintings of his final years remain the most treasured of his life.

For Matisse, art was irresistible. On the day Mme Matisse finally bought new bed linen what had he done? Unable to resist a rug filled with red, gold and crimson shades that enchanted him, he took it home and draped it across a wall for her admiration. And her response? No mention of the linen and knowing they couldn't afford both the rug and new sheets she returned the linen and made do yet again.

And the rug? Painting it, re-painting it, positioning it such that the eye is positively burned by the colour rather than the more obvious subjects – an open window, a woman's figure, table-wear – he gave the world *Harmonie en Rouge*. Incredibly, it had started life in blue. Bought by the Steins, some of Matisse's only moneyed friends, for some 30 Francs, it now hangs in the Hermitage and last exchanged hands for millions. How Matisse might have sighed; rich folk buying his work, sometimes to hang or lend to galleries, at other times to hide in attics hoping the investment well made. Could these collectors paint? Some, perhaps? Could they understand? Can anyone? What to make of a portrait where the sitter's face has green streaks across the forehead and along the nose, the lips slashes of pink, yellow and green? Not because that was how she appeared, but because, in Henri Matisse's words, "She would one day."

The sitter for *La Femme au chapeau* was the ever-tolerant Mme Matisse, the buyer, Sarah Stein, sister of Gertrude, who in the autumn of 1906 at one of her soirées introduced one master (Matisse) to another (Picasso). At the time Picasso lived and worked in Montmartre. His new friend and rival had first moved to Paris in the 1880s. Twenty years on Matisse had scandalized the art world, invented Fauvism, survived on hand-outs from sympathetic friends and collectors in Collioure, prompted outrage and derision at the Salon and still he borrowed money to buy fresh canvasses and oils. Then came Céret and the two of them could be found with Jean Gris, Braque and Soutine founding a gallery. Cubism arrived. Soon, Picasso was the darling of Paris.

XI

They don't first meet at a party. He doesn't do parties. She does - wonderfully – but he doesn't know that yet. It is Montmartre. Sitting with his ubiquitous coffee he glances up to see a vision walking – no, striding – his way. She smiles; beams. And he turns. There is no-one behind him. She is smiling at him.

"Do you play games?"

"Pardon?"

"J'aime jouer. You look like a man who plays games."

"Sudoku good enough?"

"Hmmm, not the most sociable of choices. Drives me nuts watching people give up their lives to numbers. And you could just cut it short and phone a help-line at some outrageous price. You can't do that with someone else opposite you. No, I prefer proper games. Je suis en joug aux jeux. A joke, non? A play on words on play. Words beat numbers every time."

She sits beside him and looks for the waiter, gazing intently at the café door as though he no longer exists.

"Can we start again?"

She turns her beautiful eyes to him,

"Chlöe. Enchanté"

"P…"

"Pardon! Garçon, garçon…! Tu voudrais un autre café?"

"Très gentille. What kind of games do you have in mind?"

"What? Oh, the games ... Let's start with a word game."

"Ok."

He suspects he already loves this woman. He has sat at the same table how many times? Sometimes deep in *Le Monde*, Sudokuing away, sometimes day-dreaming. Occasionally he notices a pretty woman go by or an older woman struggling with a shopping basket. Once he had smiled and a woman had smiled briefly back, only to sweep on past into the arms of Laurent, the café owner. But now, now. A complete stranger sweeps him off his feet – or chair – with no hesitation, utter confidence and breath-taking panâche.

"You have quite some panâche. Are you Parisienne?"

"You're funny. Parisians are an aloof lot. I don't know if they talk to their neighbours, let alone strangers in cafés."

"But you do."

"I liked your face. I like your face."

"Merci. What kind of game?"

"A kind kind."

"Je ne comprends pas."

"Whatever we play, we must be kind. No insults, no nastiness. I'll give you a word and you must entertain me for five minutes around the word. Then it's my turn to be entertained. Fish."

"Fish? Is that my word?"

"The clock's ticking, lovely."

Caught by the "lovely" he tells her what little he can muster up around fish. From somewhere he dredges up a memory of Maigret preferring Montrachet with his sole, how as a child he had only tried fishing once – a disaster as he couldn't get the hook out and he had watched with tear-filled eyes as the poor thing had flopped about desperately on the river bank; of a film he had seen with John Cleese and, and...

"Jamie Lee Curtis. J'aime Jamie. Ha! More word play. *A Fish Called Wanda.* Didn't you think the man with the awful stutter hilarious? The Jamie character loved words too. Well, Italian words. Anyway that wasn't bad. My turn."

"Fate."

"Good word. I think we're fated to go to bed together very soon."

They don't wait for Laurent to bring the coffee.

It is later. And raining. They watch the artists in the Place du Tertre frantically clearing easels and palettes. He feels a glow of content. And horny. So horny. She admitted to having seen him at his table and had booked a room at the nearby hotel before she'd even approached him.

From what little he now remembers of the room he has the impression it was five-sided, a tiny en-suite shower with a window overlooking a courtyard and a balcony off the bedroom with a view - if you stood on tip-toes - to the Sacré Coeur. They had stayed just long enough to know they would happily spend a long time learning more about each other.

Now he wants her again but has agreed to sit watching the performance for a while longer. A few of the artists are calmer, going about their business sketching rapid caricatures of children, their sketchbooks protected by make-shift canopies. An elderly gent sits stock-still as a grey haired, older man sketches away, his hand a blur, the charcoal occasionally pressed side-ways to the pad to produce shading or back-ground. Until the wind swirls through the square instantly transforming umbrellas into pirouetting parachutes and charcoal lines to grey smears. Two of the children run shrieking in the rain to a table behind Chlöe.

"That's impressive."

She is pointing. Following the direction of her outstretched finger he sees the elderly gent still sitting impassively on a wooden stool, the artist, oblivious to the wind and rain, sketching away.

"Which? The artist or his model?"

"Both, but the old man more so. He must be getting cold."

She is right. The damp air has lowered the May afternoon's temperature. It feels like Autumn. They sit under the protective eaves of the brasserie, a corner café. "With gingham table-cloths. Like The *Wizard of Oz!*", as Chlöe had exclaimed. She is making time stand still. He can't begin to guess how long they have been there but surely it has only been a few hours since they first met? He gazes at her and gets lost in her eyes as they gaze back. She is attentive, always alert. She points to incidents or people with exclamations of happiness or surprise. When she laughs, she chuckles, then chortles, sometimes a real belly-laugh complete with snorts. Their first coffee has turned to two. Now a third. The incidents multiply; a painter drops an oil-laden palette. The artist curses. Chlöe thinks two approaching women are dressed in *Givenchy*.

"Look, the Hepburn twins! And look at their poodles. The collars!"

He suspects he wouldn't know a fake diamond at this distance but the collars are studded with sparkling gem-stones.

"Do you think they're real?"

"Add the *Givenchy* to the way those two walk like they own the place and what do you get? Money! Serious money. Those collars could feed us for a year, lovely."

That "lovely" again. And an "us"! He's never been called lovely. Perhaps it is just her way. But she sounds like she means it. He has already noticed the way she sounds like she means everything.

"Some serious jazzers have played down the hill, you know."

"Serious? Like who?"

"Coltrane, Miles, even Roland Kirk."

"Who's Roland Kirk?"

"Blind guy. Dead now, I guess."

"I thought it was bluesmen who were all blind. Blind Lemon Jefferson, Blind Blake. Ray Charles."

"Ray Charles wasn't really blues."

"Ok, but he was blind. What was so special about your Roland Kirk?"

"He used to play three instruments at the same time."

"Guitar, piano ... xylophone?"

"No, there are limits. He played reeds. Clarinet and sax. My dad saw him near here."

"Why didn't he take you?"

"I wasn't born. But he always said I was conceived that night."

"Wow! And now you're just round the corner!"

He sits quietly. Remembering. Even if he'd been around there would have been an argument, his mum voicing reasons why his father shouldn't take him.

"You'll get drunk Phillipe. And all that smoke. I couldn't think of anything worse."

"Well I'm not asking you to go am I? You would have done once."

And they'd be off. Old grudges, other women, nights out with the boys. All would be dredged up. Then money and the amount his dad spent on Gauloises.

"My dad had some of his records."

"Good?"

"Amazing. You'd have thought there were three or four musicians playing lead but it was all him!"

"Maybe there were."

"What?"

"Three or four. You can't tell on a record can you?"

He pauses, mid reply. How can she be so critical? But she may be right. No, she isn't right.

"My dad saw him, though. It was my mum who'd brought him to Paris to give him a blast of the real scene. He did the lot. He even saw the infamous Charlie Mingus concert at the Salle Wagram, 'sixty-four I think."

"Infamous?"

"The one with Eric Dolphy."

"Where *do* they get their names? What happened?"

"His trumpet player was so ill he had to be carried off-stage."

"Drugs?"

"Stomach ulcer. Probably the same problem as my dad's but they said it was an ulcer."

"And your dad…?"

"His Paris trips started him on the Gauloises. And the Crème de Menthe."

"Yuk!"

"He'd have tried absinthe if it hadn't been illegal."

"They have an absinthe fair now, you know. As many different strengths as you can imagine. Awful."

"Not your poison then?"

"Non!"

"What is?"

"It might be you, baby."

Somehow, he finds himself living with Chlöe within what? Days? Hardly that. She checks them out of the hotel and four Mêtro stops later they are inspecting her apartment. Another six stops and they give his the once over (as she puts it). He suggests staying there the first night. Within a week she has moved in – as if nothing could be more natural. The Place du Tertre becomes a regular haunt.

He looks at her as she plays with her coffee cup. Eyes shining, she looks right back. The wind has died down, the rain all but stopped. A few artists have returned to their easels but most have retreated to the brasseries as evening closes over Montmartre. She had suggested an absinthe "to honour" his father. Then another and another. They both regret it, Chloe's eyes smarting as she chokes down the virulent liquor.

They talk about his parents, jazz, the beauty of Sacré Coeur and the mystery of Père Lachaise; Wilde, Morrison, Balzac. All still there. Morrison's admirers still gather to smoke weed. By the fourth absinthe, honour seems to have been replaced by a barely focussed slurring and a coffee duly arrives. She tells him the gruesome story of S. Major Bertrand. As she plays listlessly with the cup, he suggests she should lecture on the macabre exploits of Parisians

"It's too strong, trop fort!"

"The coffee?"

"The absinthe. I don't feel so great."

"Let's go back."

"You only want me for sex. I thought...Fuck you!"

With that Chlöe stands unsteadily and, blundering into a table, staggers away to sit, a little forlorn, on a nearby step. What is this? Passion? Booze? Some deep-seated madness? He is confused. An immediate sense of loss. Somehow empty, he too stands and walks towards her. What can he say?

"Don't go. I didn't...Merde!"

He stands waiting for her to say more. But, "Don't go," is enough. He waits patiently, still confused but already relieved. Love, with a new sympathy for this extraordinary creature, floods back.

"What?"

"Please don't go. I'm ..."

"You think I'm pissed? "There you go aga ..."

"No, lovely. I'm not accusing. It's just that..."

"Leave me alone! No! Putain, putain. I feel sick."

"Wait for it to pass. We'll go back when you're ready."

XII

Zola's wife so adored her husband that she insisted on climbing back into the marital bed with his corpse as soon as she recovered from the asphyxiating fumes that had already suffocated her beloved Émile.

In Paris Balzac found a kind of happiness at last with the Polish countess who rejoiced in his writing. Une comedie humaine? Only as grotesque pantomime. His body so bloated with oedema it is said that at the moment of death Honoré de Balzac (the 'de' was his own invention) burst, showering the aghast attendants with ... let's not be too specific.

Louis? Marie Antoinette? More lovers who paid the price. Unusually for a king, Louis XVI had no extramarital affairs. At least, there is no record; he seems to have genuinely loved his queen. In contrast, Marie Antoinette, to her horror, was accused of sleeping with her son, the Dauphin Louis Phillipe. Marie disappeared into the popular imagination as a figure of fun, a wealthy parasite mocking the poor by building a perfect hamlet in the grounds of Versailles and becoming the model for inspired self-starvers keen to imitate her fourteen inch waist.

But Marie was a true queen dedicated to her children and the union between Austria and France, if not to the French. She regarded them as backward. When Louis, almost paralyzed by a combination of the political events around him and the emetics prescribed for symptoms of tuberculosis, took to his bed for a week, it was his wife who seemed to grow in strength. A strength grounded in a passionate faith in kingship which she hoped would save the citizens of France despite themselves.

When Axel Fersen, her lover of eight years, heard of Marie-Antoinette's death he vowed to keep the sixteenth of October as a day of mourning for the rest of his days. He kept his promise for seventeen years. At the funeral procession of Christian, heir to the Danish throne - a man the crowd believed Fersen to have poisoned - the long dead queen's ex-lover was quite literally torn to pieces.

And Sartre? Tended by Simone de Beauvoir (her 'de' no affectation) to the end as she washed and bathed a body no longer in control, he was eased toward nothingness. They lie together now in Montparnasse.

So much tragedy, so much beauty. Braque, Rousseau, Pissarro, Meissonnier (he of *La Campagne de France*), Delaunay, Ingres, Géricault and Eugène Delacroix all died there. The list could go on. By the mid 19th century Paris was the artistic capital of Europe, rivalled only by Madrid. Artists gravitated to the capital and died there as moths drawn to a flame. Even a partial index of those born and buried within the city boundary startles; Boucler, Robert, Moreau, Corot, Manet, Degas, Seurat, Rouault, all Parisian by birth, death and nature.

And this only the art of the brush, the oil. For now we exclude those with their studios in the city, their lives elsewhere. We don't mention the composers, writers, sculptors and poets who either brought their vision to Paris or found it there. For now, no Morrison, Wilde or Balzac.

Well, perhaps a little more Balzac. It is said that at his funeral the streets were lined with those who had seen themselves in *La Comedie Humaine*. Victor Hugo walks beside the cart carrying the swollen, diseased body of the master judiciously out of the public's gaze in its casket. But the cart hits a cobble and lurches sending the coffin inches from Hugo's head. His comment?

"I was killed by Balzac in life only to be almost killed a second time in death."

XIII

He once looked out of train windows – the fields, the trees, the sunflowers, the sky a pale blue at the apex of the hills and azure high above him. The journey from Vernon was perfect. From the calm of Monet's garden at nearby Giverny to the bustle at l'Orangerie where the variations on the window of Rouen cathedral drew gasps all around - or respectful silence; and left him breathless. How many had there been? Seven? Eight? Some grey shot with pink, at least one – so he remembered – almost night-blue with the leaded window framed in near-black.

And then life had changed. He still walks through l'Orangerie, still sits at his café on the Left Bank across Le Pont Neuf. But now he has two train rides to work. He no longer arrives at St Lazare. He takes a crowded carriage from just beyond the banlieu – a place where to look out of the window is to see your own good fortune through the glass panes. And le Mêtro. How he hates le Mêtro. Always crowded, unbearably hot summer and winter. The first because of the sheer number of tourists, the second because in winter Paris is impossibly cold so everyone crushes into the heated train carriages wearing scarves, thick coats and hats better suited to the windswept winters of St. Pierre. You can almost see the sweat turning to steam and adding to the humid fug in the carriages.

But the banlieus! At least he can lose himself in imagining the squats, tower-blocks, broken windows and shattered, blackened balconies as it all must have been: fields, woodland perhaps, streams and the Seine a vast life-giving force. He can almost, almost see peasants going about their business. No fear of arrest, no fear of random arson or gang-fights. How far back must his imagination run? Five hundred years? Not enough – Paris would already have been growing. Six hundred then.

Lost in this reverie, he barely notices the woman elbowing him on his left, *Le Figaro* grasped in her hand as she pores over today's Sudoku.

"Pardon."

"De rien."

He looks up. Red hair. Has he seen her before? If so, she has blurred and blended with the many commuter faces he sees every day.

It hadn't been this way in Giverny. Tourists, yes. Sure - the place had become a shrine. But in the winter life was calm. Calm and for almost three years the closest he had come to contentment. Three years with Chlöe; a (small) garden, walks in the snow, in the rain, love in the firelight. Every moment seemed to last forever, every bird sang for him and him alone, even the stars – cold, distant, silver nails, immortal beyond imagining – gave their blessing.

He could remember – if not feel because to recall intense love you must be in love, even with someone else – the almost unbearable excitement of looking forward to seeing her. Planning, yearning, for a future of waking beside her, loving her.

He had discovered passion in the oddest things; how would that chaise look in a room where Chlöe had already arranged flowers? How might it be to walk in, drenched from the rain, knowing she would be there to dry his hair with a rough towel, maybe the one they used to dry the dogs after a muddy day in the field around their cottage? Cottage? Dogs? From somewhere he had conjured up a future idyll to match his mood of utter content. And all of this before they lived together, before the bickering American couple, the cottage, the – one – dog and before the *Confessions.*

They had come, tourists themselves, to Giverny towards the end of the millennium. Overwhelmed by love, beauty, Monet's Japanese bridge they had lingered. Idling an afternoon away in Vernon they had looked into an immobilière's window. The houses were outrageously priced, not a cottage to be seen. His dream had cracked a little. And then, then... The arguing couple. Americans he thought – unkindly. But who else could be so noisy? They were to his mind as brashly dressed as they were loud. And they had seemed furious.

"So much for your goddamn French paradise! Why don't you go and live with your Parisienne whore?"

"Lucille ain't a Parisienne whore. And why the fuck should I go? I found your perfect house. I paid the rent.

I even bought the damn dog!"

"Christ! The dog was tax-deductable. Honey, you're embarrassing these people."

He hadn't had time to feel embarrassed. They had both stood transfixed as the prelude to their future life together played out. The Americans were spitting bile now.

"This is the realtor's. We can settle this right now. We'll both leave!"

"Hey, what about my deposit? That's six months' rent. You know the French. They'll find an excuse to pocket it all if we don't give notice to quit. And there'll be dozens of forms to fill in."

"It's your choice Jack. We do it right now or I stay while we work the notice. You can go and live with little Mademoiselle Hot-pants, or whatever her name is and I get your goddamn arse out of my life."

"Pardon. Monsieur."

Where had he found the courage? What moment of mad hope was this? Perhaps, he had only wanted the row to stop. He had hated his parents' rows. And what did he expect to say, his English no better than his Chinese. He didn't speak Chinese.

"Vous avez une maison, à louer?"

"What's it to you, Bud?"

"Jack, you're a dog. The guy looks OK. Be nice."

And the American had gathered himself. Visibly controlling his temper, he addressed Chlöe,

"Sure, we've a house. Geevernee. Do you speak English? Parlez-vous Anglais?"

"Oui, un peu. A little."

She was at her most demure. If he could have had her there and then... But the American was speaking,

"Guess I don't know what you comprehendayed, but we need to move out. Fast. It ain't much of a place. Bathroom, kitchen you can't swing a cat in. Two chambres. Living room's OK. Good log fire, beams, all that."

"Un jardin? Does your 'ouse 'ave a garden?"

"Sure. No Japanese bridge. You can even sit outside when the neighbours' kids ain't screaming at each other."

The woman speaks, quieter now,

"Guess we need some time out,"

The man had glared.

"Are you looking for a place?"

"Oui, mais c'est impossible. The 'ouses are so expensive! Even the rents sont des chiffres astronomiques!"

The woman looks at the man, now a little subdued.

"Well, honey it's your call. We have a break for six months. You do your thing, I go back to the States. Who knows? Jesus, we could *give* the place to these guys. And the dog!"

"Jeez, you never liked the dog did ya?"

The woman turns again to Chlöe,

"It's a deal. You have the place rent free. Don't worry, he can afford it. The company'll pay. Then you give it back and pay us what you can."

"Where is it?"

"Not far from le centre. Nice little place."

"And the dog, le chien?"

"Yours. If you want him."

Still in a daze an hour later they had seen the cottage, its overgrown garden, the tiny kitchen, the ash-filled grate. Over a bottle of Perrier and a half bottle of Calvados they had signed a makeshift contract including the clause, "We agree to say nothing to anybody about this deal."

He had stumbled from the cottage brushing aside the rose hanging over the porch as if in a dream. A dream that lasted the first six months, then another and another until they both forgot about the Americans who had almost certainly forgotten about them. His future became his present; the garden, the love-making, the crazy hunting through brocante sales seeking out bargains.

Even the dog. A great floppy beast somewhere between a Pyrénéean Mountain Dog and a Setter.

Two years of commuting through glorious countryside, his head stuck in *Le Monde* or gazing out of the window. At Les Halles he would think about what to pick up for dinner and imagine her smile as she opened the door on his return, know that dinner would have to wait a little longer as they made love or talked. He had never known such - what was that dreadful 'sixties word? – connection like this. She would say something, he would reply and in mid response he would want to say something again, not always on the same subject but because he just wanted the conversation to go on. Hours would pass this way. Talk full of love, energy, new ideas. And sex, of course. She had once carried on their kitchen conversation at the brasserie and, oblivious to the incredulous couple sitting behind them, had almost shouted how much she loved his cock.

So much passion, so much contentment. And then came *the Confessions*.

XIV

De Sade's *Justine* was published in 1791 and sold well until 1801, when the Marquis was arrested for writing his now ten-year-old immoral novel. The publicity did no harm to its continuing sales. Incarcerated in Charenton, the national asylum for the insane, the libertine so enraged the medical hierarchy they implored the authorities to remove him to prison. It was a time when doctors were declaring their expertise in not only treating an ever increasing range of sexual perversions – from erotomania to onanism via satyriasis – but, crucially, in distinguishing the private sexuality of the many from the insane public sexuality of the few.

Fetishists, inverts, onanists and erotomaniacs were debated over by the judiciary and the emerging medical speciality of alienism, later to be re-named psychiatry. Was the disturbing conduct simply a vice or did the supposedly degenerate deserve sympathy due to their morbid pathology, in all likelihood of family origin? Zola, with his naturalism, championed the cause of heredity; the entire cycle of the Rougon-Macquart novels traces its psychopathy back to Tant Dide in *La Bête Humaine*. It is her sadistic treatment of her great-grandson that leads him to seek sexual fulfilment in slashing women's throats. Public scandals involving hideous sexual practices fuelled the imaginations of novelists. Their writing soon added vicarious evidence to court-room dramas played out by a burgeoning number of experts. Some even had the temerity to describe Zola himself as a monomaniac fetishist due to the lucidity with which he could describe smells; this more than a century before Suskind's *Perfume*. Whatever would they have made of that?

But even Zola couldn't compete with the sensation caused by François Bertrand, the 'Vampire of Montparnasse.' In March, 1849, Bertrand – a sergeant-major in his mid-twenties - presented himself at the Val-de-Grâce hospital with horribly injured legs. He had been caught in an explosive trap set by the authorities at le Cimetière Montparnasse to catch the infamous vampire. Cross-examined by a military tribunal he had no hesitation in confessing in July of the same year to having exhumed and mutilated corpses over several years.

He seemed to take almost Rousseauan delight in his public and eventually published – though only in medical journals – confessions. He admitted to, as a boy, finding sexual gratification with first objects, then dead animals and live dogs and finally, as a man, corpses. He claimed that, as a teenager, he had masturbated so continuously it was a wonder he found time to eat. His fantasies increasingly included the torture of women and then eviscerating the dead bodies. None of the medical experts disagreed with a diagnosis of monomania. Debates, instead, centred on the exact nature of Bertrand's disorder.

There seemed strong evidence that S-Major Bertrand had chewed on the labia of some of the cadavers he exhumed. The term 'necrophilia' was yet to be coined so deeming him a cannibalistic necrophile was not possible (as if naming conduct would somehow explain it). Instead, the arguments focussed on the ontology of his erotomania; were his actions the result of good, old-fashioned immorality or a deranged mind – and only medical experts could read the mind.

Ultimately, the courts rejected the defence of monomania – an inherited disorder Bertrand could not resist – and found him guilty of the desecration of mortal remains. After a year in prison he was freed. A successful plea of insanity would have meant incarceration in the Bicêtre or, like de Sade before him, Charenton. For life.

XV

"Merde!"

"Un problème?"

"Not if you don't mind treading in dog shit! Why don't they ever clear up after their dogs – or at least walk in the field like we do with Pantam?"

Pantam raises his head at his name; then carries on sniffing. He raises a leg. They have only walked thirty metres from the cottage. Chlöe is furiously scraping her boot against a kerb-stone. This is all part of the domesticity for him, a walk with the dog, the occasional "Bonjour" to a half-familiar face, strolling hand in hand in the fields by the river and then back to "their" brasserie.

"It's the same wherever you go. Except, maybe, Paris. But that doesn't count. Paris isn't France anymore."

"Not France? What is it then, Spain?"

"You know what I mean. There's a *McDonalds* outside the Gard du Nord now. It's the first thing you see. Not exactly French is it?"

"The Louvre? La Tour Eiffel, the Left Bank, Notr…"

"They don't count. You'll be saying L'Arc de Triomphe next."

"I was thinking of Montmartre."

She pauses, unsure whether the argument is worth the energy.

"Anyway, you'd think that anywhere as touristy as this could manage to clear up the dog shit. Voilà!"

Satisfied the boot is clean she links her arm through his.

"Let's not argue. You do know what I mean."

"I like our arguments. It means we get to make up after."

"Well I don't. Puts me in a mood. And today's no day for a mood. It's our anniversary!"

"It is?"

"Don't pretend you didn't know. You're hotter on these things than me."

It has been a year. He still can't believe his luck. A whole year! He had woken next to her this morning and felt a rush of happiness. Twelve months made a relationship real didn't they? Solid.

"Let's take Pantam to the brasserie. He likes it there."

"He likes the attention."

"He likes the croissants Raymonde gives him on the sly."

"I thought he looked upset last week."

"Pantam?"

"No, baby. Raymonde."

"Let's go. Pantam will cheer him up."

They turn as one and soon secure their favourite table in the sun. Pantam, panting now, looks expectantly at the doorway. Right on cue Raymonde walks through and heads their way. Leaning forward he ruffles the dog's head and turns to Chlöe,

"Café? Et croissants?"

"Bien sûr, Raymonde. Ça va?"

"Oui, ça va."

But Raymonde's look belies his words and he walks quickly away.

"He is miserable. You were right. What do you think it is?"

"Well it's not money. This place is heaving nine months of the year and he seems OK with Etta."

"We haven't seen her for a while. I hope she's not ill."

"Who's going to make you the éclairs you love so much?"

"I didn't … Anyway, she gets the éclairs from the boulanger."

At this moment Raymonde reappears. He has three croissants on two plates in his left hand. Three coffees perch precariously in his right.

"Voilà! Un croissant pour Pantam! Et, trois cafés pour nous."

"You're joining us? Excellent!"

Raymonde gently places Pantam's elevenses in front of him on the flagstone and sits, cautiously it seems, alongside Chlöe.

"We were just saying, we haven't seen Madame for a while. Raymonde! Have I said something wrong? Your hand is shaking, you'll spill your coffee."

"Pardon. Non, cherie, you have said nothing wrong. Can I trust you?"

"Bien sûr. Has something happened?"

"Etta has left me! Voilà"

"What? When?"

"A week ago for....for another, another. A woman."

Chlöe is transfixed. Raymonde looks crumpled now, his head sags forward as he slumps in his seat, a picture of defeat.

"What can we say? Poor Raymonde."

"What can anyone say? She just came out with it: "I've found someone else." Just like that. She didn't tell me the worst part until the morning she left. It's a woman! And I didn't suspect anything. I thought we were ... fine. Well, not the sex but you know what they say, "It's downhill after the first child" and we have four! But a woman ... Excusez moi. Clients."

And Raymonde stands and walks slowly to a woman and child who are staring at the day's menu pinned, as always, to the door frame. They exchange a few words before Raymonde points to the adjacent table. As the couple approach, Chlöe leans forward.

"Well! Poor Raymonde. Do you think it makes it worse?"

"What?"

"If a woman goes off with another woman."

"I don't see why it should. After all, men go off with other women."

"You can be so obtuse. Look at that couple over there."

"By the gateway?"

"Oui."

"What about them?"

"Do you think ugly people get it when they can?"

"What?"

"I just think Sartre's right. Hell is other people and all that. We can't guess what anyone else is up to. Like Etta. I reckon some people just have less options than others. Etta was a bit of a stunner but it's not like Monsieur or Madame Ugly can walk into a bar and all heads turn, is it? I just wondered if ugly people grab it at any opportunity."

"It?"

"Love, sex, coitus, intercourse, FUCKING!"

The recently arrived woman at the next table looks up, her face like thunder. With cupped hands she makes a show of covering the child's ears and, stumbling slightly, quickly stands. She glares at Chlöe as they leave.

"If this goes on Raymonde will ban us. Customers evaporate around us."

"We're only talking."

"Yes, darling. But I think you were yelling again."

"You love it when I yell."

"I ... I know, but that's at home and in the middle of ... Don't say it!"

Too late. She is off again,

"Coming" Orgasm! Lifting my bottom to get you deeper!"

She looks around. With no-one too obviously alarmed, Chlöe drops her voice.

"Anyway. Ugly people, what do you think?"

"What sparked this off?"

"That couple by the steps. I saw them before Raymonde dropped his bombshell. They don't have much going for them. Her face is all pock-marked and he's fat. I just felt, I dunno, sorry for them. His hair looks like it could do with a wash."

"Maybe she likes it that way."

"Maybe, beggars can't be choosers."

"That's an awful thing to say. Love is blind though, isn't it? You know; blind, eternal, beyond reason."

"Like us?"

"We're not beyond reason. You're the most beautiful thing that ever happened to me."

"Ah, baby."

"Sounds like a song title... Maybe even people with pock-marked faces have hearts of gold. She obviously isn't ugly to him."

"Maybe, but a heart of gold with dirty fingernails doesn't turn me on."

"What if I had dirty fingernails?"

Chlöe is about to answer but checks herself. Her brow furrowing (how he loves that look of concentration), she plays with her coffee cup.

"Let's try it."

"What? Dirty fingernails?"

"You're always in the garden this time of year but you shower as soon as you come in. And I bet you clean your nails."

"Only if there's dirt stuck in there."

"But it's not really is it?"

"What?"

"Dirt. It's soil. And soil's not dirty. It's not like it's three day old motor-bike grease or bits of food."

As ever, with Chlöe, images flood him; making love. No, having her, seriously having her. In the garden, on the compost heap (where did *that* come from?). Upstairs, on the stairs, under the stairs. Now it's his turn to pause. He isn't sure they even have an under-stairs.

"You've gone all quiet. What are you thinking about?"

"Cellars."

XVI

"Where are the young? There only the old here and they look as if dying. A walking death."

"Gone to fight?"

"But the children. There are no.... Oh!"

They have walked into the village hoping not for a welcome but at least the chance of food. Hunger tracks them now like a wolf. A wolf that doesn't hesitate nor cease its determined loping. This wolf is grey, death in its yellow eyes. The last two villages have been deserted, no sign of man nor beast. Their steps have become slower as the hunger gnaws at them. Jerome has seen at least two men wander away, first stumbling from the track and then haltingly walking into a field, terrain as inhospitable as the villages. No-one tried to stop them. There would be two less mouths to feed.

Unbelievably, their captors had let them go, a sorry bloodied group. Jerome had made out voices in the darkness that had overtaken him.

"He's alive!"

And as if from some subterranean mist-filled cavern his vision had cleared. He could just make out concerned faces peering at him. A hand was placed gently on his shoulder. That hand!

"Ça va?"

He couldn't tear his eyes from the butchery at his shoulder. From the middle two finger sockets thin blood trickled. Suddenly seized by excruciating pain from his own right hand, he carefully raised it to eye level. Tears welled as he examined the abomination. Two fingers cut from his right hand, his best hand, the hand he used for grooming, for buffing the leather...

"Ma main!"

"Trompé! Mais, tu as ta vie."

What good would life be now? He buried his head in his throbbing hand and then, smarting with pain, in Gaston's jerkin, for it is Gaston comforting him.

"They're going to let us go. Bastards. Won't feed us. Don't want to kill us. Bastards!"

Jerome has eased himself to his feet, wincing with pain at the momentary pressure as he tries to push himself upright. His companions are mostly silent, a few muttering and gazing in the direction of their captors who seem disinterested now, the damage done. They begin to limp toward the setting sun, their arms hanging limply at their sides. A few have makeshift slings exposing their hands to the cooling, healing air. Only Gaston seems uninjured but he, too, is silent.

A few had died within days, the gangrene spreading fast from their mutilations. The crossbow-men had been deemed harmless – unable to hold their weapons, let alone fire them. Jerome's act of bravery had been irrelevant. The enemy were tired of slaughter and not wanting to spare what little food they had for themselves had simply cast adrift Jerome and his companions. Not knowing what else to do, though longing to retreat, the company had continued its progress to the west.

This village had seemed more promising; smoke rising from one chimney, a dog gnawing at a bone in the doorway of a straw-roofed house. But the thatch has not been repaired, a gaping hole at the ridge. The dog looks up briefly, its fur matted, one eye almost closed, the other seeping a vile yellow puss. It returns to chewing. Jerome has seen first one, then a second bent-backed woman, their eyes cast down as they shuffle toward Gaston. The yeoman stops and stares long and hard at the first crone who seems to shrivel under his gaze. Moments later a third appears only to turn away seemingly crest-fallen.

"They're as hungry as us," mutters Gaston, "If that's possible."

It was then that Jerome made his remark about the lack of children. Only seconds later, he sees the first; if child she be. Curled up on the rough ground ahead of them is a bundle of grey rags. A foot protrudes and wispy hair can just be made out where he thinks the head must be. But this child doesn't move and there is something about that foot – so thin, so, so...

"Maggots! There are maggots eating that girl!"

The ankle is alive, or at least the teeming maggots make it seem so.

"Do not stay here. We have no food. Only plague."

The third crone is speaking, her face covered. She coughs and her rough shawl drops a fraction, just enough...

"O Lord, her face!"

The woman's face is a dull ochre. The remains of

recently suppurating boils mar one side. Her left eye is barely open, her right, like the dog's, seeping yellow. She only has the appearance of a crone. Jerome sees that she can be no older than Marie.

"It is nothing."

"Nothing!"

"The flesh is dying. She has the plague. La mort noire. We cannot stay here."

"But there is no plague now. C'est ne pas possible. It is finished."

"Not everywhere my young friend. As you see."

"But can we do anything?"

"For them?"

"Oui, d'accord. For them."

"Only this."

Gaston draws his blade. The woman doesn't flinch though she makes a gentle choking sound. Jerome steps in front of her and presses Gaston's hand away.

"I didn't mean..."

"It would be a mercy."

"I know, but a sin all the same. We should leave. The others are ahead. We should move fast."

"Ha! Fast! You walk on my young friend. I shall catch you up."

Jerome takes one last look at the bundle of rags at his feet and the woman, now bowing her head before Gaston. He thinks of his own village. Happier days. A time of peace; disease and death, of course. But not disease that strikes all before it, the few that survive too weak to bury the dead. As he turns west again the sun is sinking to the horizon. The sky is a red and orange shot with gold. Automatically he thinks, 'A fine day tomorrow,' and laughs low to himself. Fine days seem a thing of the past now.

XVII

In part it is the vans he loves; an illusion of village life in a place long since grown to a bustling town. Giverny is by no stretch of the imagination still a village. But the vans still come; two, often three, boulangers a day, fish twice a week, two travelling epiceries. He has lost track of the cheese sellers – Camembert, of course, several times weekly, a goat cheese lady on Saturdays, a ewe cheese lady on Tuesdays. The meat man comes Fridays, the horsemeat van every Monday and twice a week in the winter.

All this despite a fine butcher in the town, a boulangerie, even a busy and prosperous fish shop. And all that excludes the supermarkets not so far away; *Geant, Intermarche*, a gigantic *Carrefour*. They would usually buy wine from the *Carrefour*, ridiculously cheap with a section divided into Bordeaux, the Loire, Champagne, Burgundy, Provence, the Corbieres, the list went on. They had discovered local wines too, harsher than those from the earthy south west or the fine appellations of the Medoc but still astonishingly good, many at two or less (less!) euros per litre.

In a burst of adventurism that previous weekend they had travelled deep into Normandy and, following a sign saying *Calvados*, had driven up an increasingly narrow farm track – to a farm no less; their car a black *Renault Clio* Chlöe had persuaded Raymonde to lend them. Thinking the farm deserted Chlöe had walked around to a dung-strewn yard and on into an empty kitchen where she gazed at a faded Calvados menu propped against an empty bottle on the make-shift bar. The newest was priced at 12 euros, older for more and then, at the bottom of the list a 1948 *Calvados Ancien* for... She cried out. Thinking her in trouble he dashes across the cobbles and into the kitchen.

"Ca va?"

"Look at this!"

Relieved that her cry had been only one of surprise he looks, then stares.

"Mon dieu! Fifty euros! For 1948. Bargain or what?"

"Where are we meant to leave the money?"

Neither had heard the woman approach. Her question was all the more startling,

"Voulez vous déguster quelques choses?"

From somewhere at the back of the room a door had opened and the propriétaire now stands before them. She could have been a peasant from a Cezanne; long skirt, a round belly with a blouse stretched taut, the ubiquitous kerchief around her head. Even, he notices (instantly ashamed at his judgementalism), a small moustache on her upper lip.

"Le dix neuf quarante huit. C'est possible deguster?"

"Non. Mais, le nouveau est bon. Voilà !"

So they had tried the most recent and, slightly drunkenly, had bought the 1948 from the beaming woman.

But it is the vans he loves here – the gathering of local folk, all too few dressed as he thinks villagers should be. How many true locals would wear *Armani* or, in two cases, skin hugging *Donna Karan*? But still they chat, the nouveau riche, those from millionaires' row as Chlöe would have it, Raymonde from the brasserie, Jean et Madeleine, his neighbours. He thinks it's like a place where time continues to stand still, not so different from the place he drifts to when looking at Chlöe.

The highlight – highlight! – of the weekend is the melon man. How could he have known as a teenager that one day he would stand in a square (Monet's square no less!) awaiting the arrival of a grey-bearded man in his – what? – sixties driving a clapped out Citröen filled with melons, tomatoes and (if you knew how to ask) home-brewed Calvados kept tucked under the driving seat?

No-one is too proud to wait for the melon man. He is meant to arrive at ten. He is often two hours late. What did he do in those two hours? His breath has established a, perhaps unkind, local suspicion that he imbibes a little morning Calvados himself. He wonders if the melon man has other – female – fish to fry. Perhaps he is gay, indulging himself in the young men to be seen cruising the cafés in the evening. Or perhaps he is just late. After all, the best of folk are late; busy lives, children, markets to go to, trains to catch, all the things out of their control. Whatever. The melon man's tardiness allows people to chat as they wait.

Robert, the gnarled octogenarian, Mme Bordette, the *Yves-St-Laurent*-attired woman of indeterminate age (Chlöe had once remarked that the good madame's breasts were equally indeterminate; sometimes held high like a pert twenty-something's, at others like newly baked dough slapped onto her chest), the twins, Sebastian and Sebastianne ("The parents! How could they?" from Chlöe), and a veritable queue of people he only ever sees on melon man day. But the melon man duly arrives to shuffle from the driving seat, heaving his frame upright.

He is red-faced, his grey eyes sunken into puffy flesh. Stroking his beard, as grey as his eyes, he starts to call, "Melons, tomates, les pamplemousses. Oui, pamplemousses!" All this after he has heralded his arrival for a good ten minutes by pressing hard on the horn, a 'blaaahhh', that can be heard for miles. Perhaps he thinks some people don't know it's melon-man day. Unlikely; Robert had told him that the melon-man had been coming to Giverny for thirty plus years.

"They all do it."

"What?"

"Press their horns like they're announcing Armageddon."

"Maybe they're saying 'Come now or arm a geddin out of here. Hee hee."

"Hmmm…C'mon we've all day. Let's take Pantam to the café. We'll tell Raymonde about the Calvados. Let's go."

"Again! People will say we've got nothing to do but

sit and chat at Raymonde's."

"I don't think they notice, baby. And anyway, most of them are passing trade. It's not like it matters what they think. Let's go. Please."

Thirty minutes later they are sitting at the familiar table and while the dog waits patiently for his first croissant, he makes a note to see if he can one day resist her, "Please." It is not yet midday, the day already sultry, a haze over the reeds on the river bank. He stretches back, runs his fingers through his hair and then arches back, arms reaching toward the flagstones behind him.

"You'll break your neck!"

"You sound like my dad sometimes."

But he pulls himself back to the upright.

"Café. Merci Raymonde. Très gentil."

"Mon plaisir. Et pour le chien?"

Pantam has wrested himself into a sitting position, tail thumping. His eyes don't leave the proffered croissant for an instant. A moment later it is gone, the dog gasping slightly as he swallows. Then he resumes a more expectant posture.

"Un. C'est suffisant. Oh, look at that couple!"

He turns.

"Look at that?"

"What?"

"What? The luggage. Look at their suitcases! You could pack a sofa in his. And an armchair in hers."

Two new customers have been struggling to a table. They have already dragged two cases on wheels up the stone steps onto the café terrace and the man is returning to the open door of a parked taxi for a third. He is saying something to the driver and turns to the woman. He does his best to shout without making a public announcement. He fails:

"Attend, Marie-Claire. Attends. Tu as la monnaie?"

The woman takes a deep breath and, sighing, walks back to him while digging in a pocket for change. She leaves her case next to his on the flagstones.

"Do you think they're tourists?"

"Smugglers more like. That third one's even bigger. They must have the kitchen sink in there!"

Finishing with the taxi driver, the couple haul the third suitcase up the steps. The man is panting heavily now. He is tall and thin and wearing an old, battered looking brown raincoat. His brow is covered in droplets of sweat, some already running into his eyes. He attempts to mop his forehead with his free hand. He stumbles and Chlôe's eyes are drawn to his shoes.

"Wow! How about that for a contrast. Raincoat from a charity shop and three hundred euro shoes. Immaculate!"

"The things you notice! Don't stare, baby! And how would you know how much they cost?"

But he looks at the man's feet. Sure enough the shoes are gleaming patented leather with thin soles, wholly impracticable for the haulage work being attempted.

"*Givenchy*, I wouldn't be surprised."

"How on earth do you know that?"

"The little buckles. *Chanel* are more like a 'C'"

"I didn't even know *Chanel* and *Givenchy did* men's shoes!"

"Your teenage years were wasted. No fashion mags, no Paris fashion shows on the TV?"

"My old man wasn't much of a one for TV, except when Paris St Germain were playing and it was live."

"Well, trust me. Those are *Givenchy*. You see so much of it round here it's a wonder they haven't rechristened the place. It would only mean changing a couple of letters. Now look at them! Why doesn't he just leave it outside?"

The couple are dragging the leviathan into place besides the other two bags. It dwarfs them.

"Well if they're tourists, they're obviously planning to stay the whole summer. They *must* have brought the kitchen sink in that monster."

The couple are now unzipping the larger case, he from the left, her from the right. Just as Raymonde arrives at the table, the man pulls the flap open with a final flourish and slumps into his chair. Raymonde is on the point of his usual welcome – "Bonjour. Ca va? Voulez vous quelques choses?" – when he stops. He is staring into the suitcase.

"Deux cafés, s'il vous plait."

"Oui, d'accord. Et encore?"

"Seulement des cafés."

Raymonde is grinning broadly as he walks back towards them. He directs his gaze at Chlöe. Making an effort not to speak too loudly he almost whispers,

"Villeroy et Boche."

"Pardon?"

"Villeroy et Boche! The sink in that bag is Villeroy et Boche!"

Chlöe starts to laugh. First a snickering, then more of a cackle, then a throaty chuckle, not so different from a drain emptying and finally a series of snorts as the tears roll down her face. Barely able to speak, she says,

"I'll give you ten euros if they have a bidet and basin in the other two!"

The couple sit sipping their coffee, seemingly oblivious to Chlöe's convulsions and the man at her side running his hands through his hair in an orgy of frantic energy. He is trying to keep his head from falling off as he laughs loud and long.

XVIII

The queen was spared the sight of her husband's death. The guillotine had only been declared the universal form of execution the previous March. Considered humane and swift, the Assembly saw it as a symbol of equality. Louis was taken from the tower of the Paris Temple where his beloved Marie Antoinette was imprisoned in a separate apartment – more a cell – on the morning of Monday, January the twenty-first to be marched across the cobbles in an almost silent city and beheaded. His wife joined the silence.

But she had not been spared one hideous scene. The previous September hundreds had been massacred by the mob sweeping through prisons and hospitals for the insane. In Bicêtre and Salspêtrière children younger than nine had proven especially difficult to kill due to their fierce tenacity for life. The mob surged to the Temple and, her head hacked off, the eviscerated body of Marie Antoinette's favourite – many say lover – the Princesse de Lamballe was paraded just below the queen's apartment window.

IXX

"There are nuns in there."

"And?"

"Nuns. Women!"

"You wouldn't!"

"Well I wouldn't Jerome. But I think the lads might be interested."

L'abbeye stands silent; mostly a ruin now. The gardens, tower, cloisters and main hall are all that remain of a monastery. It had started life as a home, work place and spiritual centre for men who preferred prayer and toil to – to what? Toil and more toil. Peasants mostly, they had gathered around a local priest's wooden hut. After seventy years and the supposed piety of a succession of Frankish kings who were buying their way into heaven it had encompassed some eight hectares laid to vine and vegetables and paddocks for sheep. One was reserved for the Abbot's horse – an ass (not the horse, the Abbot). By the thirteenth century it housed nuns and, seamlessly – so it seemed – had become a convent.

Chlöe stands at the broken wall surveying what remains of the gardens – still tended, though now by men, mostly commuters she knows, from large, certainly too large for retired couples, houses around Vernon. It is one of their favourite walks. Along the old railway track, Giverny left quickly behind, and almost into Vernon. She stands now, gazing at the tower – wondering.......

"How many sins is it possible to cultivate on the march?"
"Sins! Sins? This is war, my friend. Is war not the greatest sin? What do a few more matter?"
"But nuns......"
"I give up. Hey, look! They're even coming out to greet us!"

Through the iron gate Jerome sees a small bevy of black-clad figures, heads covered, gathering at the vast arched doorway to the convent. They are talking. One points at Gaston and Jerome and takes a hesitant step forward.

Chlöe imagines the peace of prayer and work. Shudders at the thought of getting up at three in the morning to start the day. Then smiles; she and her man sometimes start the day at three in the morning. Then again at five....

"Do you want food?"
    "That would be kind mademoiselle."
    "How many are you?"
    Gaston turns. Five more men are approaching. They

gaze at the closed gate where Jerome and he are talking to the Prioress. She is young, older than Jerome, but to his eyes young for one in authority. Gaston turns back to her.

"Six or seven your, er, what do I call you?"

"Thérèse. My name. We don't stand on ceremony here. Sister!"

She beckons to the woman closest to her who walks forward and quickly unlatches the gate. It swings open.

"You're lost in thought, baby."

"Sorry mister. Pantam! Where *have* you been?"

The dog wags his tail, walks to his mistress and with a burst of energy, vigorously shakes himself. A none-too-fine spray of water covers her smiling face.

"The river!"

"You're hopeless. You know he shakes himself when....Pantam?"

Chlöe is smiling less now as spray covers her from head to foot.

"Sorry, babe. It's only wa.... . Pantam!"

The five others have caught up and follow Jerome and Gaston into the grounds. Jerome glances left and right. The vegetable patches are extraordinarily neat and weed-free, each allocated to a different vegetable. Some he recognises. Some ...

"Hey, Gaston! What are they?

"Blessed if I know. Something to eat I suppose.

Leaves are a strange shape."

The prioress beckons to the men who walk proud, hesitantly at first and then with lengthening strides. One of the nuns walks away, two others whisper and appear to giggle.

For Jerome, dread is growing. Surely not nuns, surely not!

"It's beautiful isn't it?"

"Quite something. I can almost get into it."

"What?"

"The idea of monastic life. You know, up at three, a quick pray, then straight out to work?"

"No breakfast?"

"No good. No coffee!"

"You and your coffee, mister!"

One of the men is approaching the giggling sisters. He turns to Gaston and winks.

"Two for the price of one, eh Gaston?"

Gaston grimaces and ushers Jerome toward the great door. Inside they can see more nuns, a few excitedly chatting, others going about their business. From somewhere ahead wafts the blessed smell of bread, mingled not unnaturally with the smell of incense. There is a thud behind and the hall is now lit only by light from the high windows and a few candles guttering in the breeze from the slammed door.

"Would you like to eat? Sisters! We have guests!"

The other men push roughly past Jerome and Gaston making for the delicious smells, the Prioress at their head. To right and left nuns stare openly at the ragged group some of whom stare back only to be met by averted eyes, frowns or the occasional shy giggle. The giggles only increase the sickness in Jerome's gut. He tugs at Gaston's sleeve.

"They wouldn't would they, not here?"

"Like taking down from a duck, Jerome. Down from a duck."

"Shall we go in?"

"I don't think there's much to see, babe."

He is wrong. The oak doors are closed but a small wooden arrow, black lettering on a white background, indicates the route to a side door. Following the arrow they are soon standing at another door, this one set into the stone with a further wooden plaque showing the opening times.

"I thought it was a ruin!"

"So did I but it says it's open at ten. What time is it? Oops, stupid question. You don't have your watch do you?"

Since he'd known Chlöe, he'd abandoned wearing a watch at weekends, days off and for that matter days on after seven in the evening. As he had learned how time stood still when with her he'd happily dropped a life time's habit of checking his watch. Then he'd dropped the watch. She is rustling in her bag.

"What are you looking for?"

"I thought....No, here it is!"

Chlöe pulls a battered looking timepiece from the debris (his word) in the shoulder bag. He sees it is strapless, a *Casio* digital, the chrome worn away or perhaps just tarnished through neglect.

"Ha! Nine forty-seven. Not long to wait!"

"Does that still work?"

"Ish ... It's usually close enough."

The men are all in the refectory now. Just as in the great hall, light comes from the high windows, some with stained glass, some plain. Glowing candles protrude at 45 degree angles every ten paces along the walls, wax dripping to the flagged floor below. The base of each candle is at head height and Jerome finds himself wondering how the nuns reach up to light them.

"They light them before they set them in the holders."

"What?"

"The candles. It's the only way."

"How did you know I was...?"

"You are easy to read my friend. You were staring at the candles with that frown you get when you concentrate. Hey up! Food!"

A long oak trestle table with benches either side stands on the flag-stoned floor. A nun has appeared carrying loaves. The Prioress beams at her guests.

"If our Lord could feed five thousand I'm sure we can manage seven. Please, be seated."

The men shuffle into place at the table, their sly looks of lust replaced by grins as more bread appears. A young nun moves behind Jerome. A flagon, appears over his right shoulder.

"Mead?"

"Mead? What is it?"

"A beverage for the weary. We make it from honey."

"Well ..."

"Come on Jerome, sup up. It'll be a while before you're offered mead by willing sisters again."

He is about to knock on the oak door when it swings open. A woman – perhaps a little older than Chlöe – stands before him, smiling with surprise and welcome.

"Good morning."

"Bonjour. You are with the party?"

"Party?"

"Clearly not! Yes, we have a party of school-children due today. It's the reason I'm opening up on time. We're usually a little – er – relaxed this time of year. Oh! Hello."

Chlöe has appeared at his side. She nods to the woman who looks what? Embarrassed? Abashed? Cheated? Chlöe feels her hackles rising. She wonders if this woman had hoped for something more from her man's visit. She glances down; no engagement ring, but a wedding band.

"Are you à deux?"

"Oui. Ma femme, Chlöe."

And with that 'femme' all her jealousy evaporates.
The woman's next words leave Chlöe embarrassed,

"Sister Marie-Thérèse. Enchanté. Will you come in?"

No habit, no middle-aged plain-ness. But still
married to Jesus!

Nuns move from table to kitchen and back to table.
Wooden platters are gently pulled from under the arms
of men who sprawl sleeping soundly (if not silently)
amongst the meal's debris. One sister beckons to
another and they do their best to pull upright a snoring
lout. He grunts, slightly lifts his head, only for it to
slump again to his folded arms. An up-turned goblet of
mead has spilled its soporific balm beneath his sleeves,
now wet with unctuous liquor. His brown hair trails
into the mead, the ends turning black.

"Mademoiselle? Would you like a hand."

"Monsieur! Merci. I thought you all slept?"

"Some of us drink less or better handle what we do."

Gaston towers above the women. Grasping the
sleeping form under the arms, he heaves him into a
sitting position as the younger of the two nuns quickly
pulls the platter away and rights the goblet. She is at
most thirteen or fourteen. The man groans, grunts
again and his head falls to his chest. A rumbling snore
begins. Across the bread-crumb-strewn board Jerome
also sleeps. His fair hair tumbles around him, shoulders
move gently with each breath of slumber. Gaston
smiles, his heart quickening. All around nuns continue
to bustle; the meal, their hospitality a great success.

"There was a tragedy here, you know."

"Tragedy?"

"Oui. During the Hundred Years' War."

Chlöe steps nearer to Marie-Thérèse who stands just inside the door,

"How strange. I was just thinking how peaceful it all seems. Not remotely tragic. By-the-way, do you mind dogs?"

"Of course not! Did you see the vegetable patches?"

"On the way in?"

"D'accord. Look at these garden plans. They show what the sisters grew."

The nun is indicating a wall-chart. In the centre is clearly a nave and tower, the great-hall just below. To the right is a maze of cloisters. In neat rectangles to left and right of the front path are inscribed Latin names. Chlöe recognizes a few then startled points to a patch adjacent to the cimitière,

"Does that say cannabis?"

"*Cannabis Indica.*"

"As in...?"

"Bien sûr. Weed! Do you imagine all those visions were visitations?"

"Well. I..."

"The church would be a little dull without some weed!"

The hall is quiet. Two men still slump at the long table. The rest are gathered with Jerome and Gaston around a blazing fire. There are no nuns. The few clearing the table have stopped their work and moved silently away as the bell chimes for afternoon prayer. The men speak in hushed tones.

"What do you reckon then?"

"I...I'm not so sure. What would we do with it?"

"Sell it!"

"Ha! Sell it? Who to? You think the locals can afford a silver chalice?"

"Trade it then."

"For what? There's more food here than within twenty leagues!"

"It's hardly charitable, is it?"

The lowered voices stop. Heads turn to Jerome. He looks down as Gaston's eyes role upwards.

"Charitable! Why should we be charitable, blondie?"

"Because they've fed us!"

"Because they've ... Jerome, feeding wayfarers is their duty. We must be a blessing. Another sou in their heavenly coffers."

"You thinking fucking is their duty too? For charity?"

Jerome has raised his voice but his companion just leers. He nods toward a door through which a nun, a benefactor, has emerged. He grins. And beckons.

"Why don't we go back to the great hall, sister? More comfortable, non? Better fire!"

As if in the early throes of a nightmare Jerome follows the men back into the hall where the fire does, indeed, blaze beckoningly. Like the fires of hell.

"So, Jeanne d'Arc was off her head on pot!"

"Well, I don't know about the sacred Jeanne. She was just a peasant. She hadn't taken holy orders or anything. But, I'd guess the sisters just took it to, er, clear the mind. Voilà!"

She grins; a lovely smile. He is beginning to like this nun. He realizes how the surprise threatens his preconceptions. Marie-Thérèse is neither plain nor ugly, she is not covered head to foot in black and clearly uses make-up. And perfume. Perfume!

"What is your perfume?"

It is Chlöe; that magic again! Same wave-length, same question that he doesn't need to ask now. 'Actually,' he muses, 'It wouldn't be too clever to ask another woman what perfume she's wearing. Not within Chlöe's ear-shot. Nun or not!'

"Perfume? Ah! My guilty secret! *White Linen*."

"It's lovely."

"Merci."

"What did you mean by tragedy?"

"A fire! It destroyed the kitchens, dormitory and much else besides! They rebuilt some of the abbey in the seventeenth century but the order hadn't recovered so they didn't bother with the dormitory or the refectory."

"How did it happen?"

"They think it was the English."

Jerome shifts in his chair. He runs his hands through

his hair and looks at the approaching nun. She is unhurried, doesn't seem alarmed and doesn't see the men around Jerome shifting excitedly in anticipation.

"Monsieur? Can I help?"

She is no more than fifteen. A wisp of auburn hair escapes her coif; her face pale, open, innocent.

"We would ... Did you enjoy your prayer sister?"

"Monsieur? Merci. Oui. Prayer is a quiet time, a time for reflection. But, yes, I think I enjoyed it. I prayed for you."

"For me?"

"Well, for all of you. For strength and peace."

"I..."

He says no more. Eyes now down-cast, the would-be leader of the attack turns to the fire. Gaston speaks,

"Could we stay the night sister? We don't want to impose..."

"No, no! Of course. Bien sûr. I shall ask the Abbesse."

With that she disappears through the side door. Jerome sighs with relief. It is but short-lived. The night! Surely the nuns will see the trap?

"Why would the English burn down a convent?"

"Why do the English do anything? Blood-thirsty lot. Always have been."

"But a convent!"

"It's all shrouded in mystery. Some sort of raiding party looking for trouble. Probably guessed the sisters would shelter anyone who turned up. Enemies included."

"Did the defenders shelter in Religious houses?"

"Surely *anyone* can seek shelter in God's house! There would have been food. And no plague!"

"So, what happened?"

All is quiet. Jerome knows the nuns will be up and about again soon for prayer. For now they are asleep in their dormitory. Do they fear? Do any shuffle or squirm? Perhaps in anticipation? Have some prayed for deliverance? As the afternoon had turned to evening ribaldry had grown. Two of the men had made a great show for the youngest sister, twice suggesting she let down her hair; twice staring with undisguised lasciviousness at her small breasts held tight in her habit. She had smiled, blushed and then turned away confused, a little afraid.

Gaston had barely spoken during the meal of lamb and even less afterwards as the drinkers forged on. He had sat with a stern expression only occasionally moving his hand to cover his goblet as a sign he needed no more mead. The sisters had arranged pillows of down on various settles around the hall before retiring. On these the men, all bar Gaston, had stretched out. Were they now feigning sleep? Snores, grunts and farts suggest otherwise and herald a peaceful night; albeit a smelly one.

Jerome eyes Gaston who still sits as if set in stone by the fire glancing to left and right. On guard? Certainly wary. The man nearest to Jerome twists in his sleep and with a grunt rolls from the settle.

"Putain! What time is it?"

"Late!"

"Fucking settles! Only wide enough for boys! I need a bed!"

With that he struggles to his feet and shaking a companion awake makes for the cloister doorway. Other men stir. Some grin as they rub their eyes to wakefulness. There is much stretching and a muffled, "Shh...!"

"You coming, Jerome?"

Jerome is about to whisper, "Non!" but feels a familiar stirring. Not nuns! Not nuns!

"Would you like coffee?"

"Sister! You are a mind-reader!"

"No. Non! Marie-Thérèse si-tu-plais!"

Chlöe's eyes dart toward their hostess. She doesn't like that 'tu.' Not at all.

"Do you think it too early for Calvados?"

"Too earl...? Marie you're in the process of shattering illusions here! Coffee, perfume, no habit. Now hooch at eleven in the morning!"

"It's not so unusual surely? You have pastis, non?"

"Bien sûr. But..."

"Oh! I see what you mean! It should be *Chartreuse.* Or *Benedictine.* Or perhaps a Belgian Trappist beer at great strength. I'm sorry my friend. All the best hooch, as you put it, is made by monks. We have to make do with Calvados. From *Carrefour*!"

"You'll be telling us you swear next!"

"Only by Jesus! Or if my *Chanel* clutch-bag is stolen! A joke! It is a joke! Don't look like that. It's *Givenchy*! Ha! I do have some habits my sisters might frown upon."

Now Chlöe starts. The 'tu' may have been innocent. The way the nun's eyes sparkled at 'habits' was - is - quite, quite definitely all woman!

"Shouldn't we be going? We don't want to take you away from your other visitors!"

"Guests. We call our visitors guests. And it looks like the school party has been de-railed. Perhaps they have gone to the museum instead. Don't worry. I'll put the 'Gone to lunch' sign up."

She steps quickly to an ancient oak dresser and opens the top drawer. Holding a wooden plaque in her left hand, she shuts the drawer with her right and reaches down to open a dresser door. Chlöe sees several bottles (mostly pastis - *Ricard*) as Marie reaches inside to grasp a litre wine bottle. It is filled with clear liquid.

"Oh! I'd forgotten this. We should try it."

"What does the sign say?"

His question is answered as Marie lifts the plaque. It reads, 'Bienvenue! Fermé jusqu-à 15.00 heures' in blue lettering.

"We like long lunches here. Marc? It's home-brewed!"

"Where do you think you lot are going?"

"Come on Gaston! Some of us prefer women!"

"And some of us have a conscience!"

"Get you big man! A conscience! Now I've heard everything!"

Jerome starts. His tumescence is subsiding even as Gaston confronts the other man, the fellow who first fell from the settle. He is short, his hair lank and the beard long. He looks none-too-pleased to be checked by Gaston. But Gaston with a conscience! Jerome feels ashamed. The whispering is now supplanted by firm, stronger words. Gaston's stand is diverting to anger some of the energy in the hall.

"So, fatso! The deal is we want sex and have to go through you to get it?"

"That's about it."

"Right! ... What the fuck!"

There is a hammering at the door. Outside men's voices are raised. Jerome knows well the guttural Normande.

"Hey, you! Sisters! Open up! There are hungry men here!"

"Putain! English! Now what?"

"Cocks away boys! Cocks away!"

"It was very small at first with no more than twenty monks. Well, lonely peasants."

"Twenty?"

"Just a few souls gathered around the abbot. Then it changed."

"Size-wise?"

"Oui. In function as well. They had a special dormitory for lepers. Then, later, vagrants and the poor."

"Charity?"

"Bien sûr. By the thirteenth century the lepers had gone and money was pouring in to make it a place for the sick and dying. And even more monks. But around the beginning of the next it became a convent."

"Just like that?"

"It happened everywhere. Even mixed religious houses!"

"Mixed? Men and…"

"Women. Oui. There's a lovely example at Fontrevraud. Run by an Abbesse too. It's where the Lionheart is buried. Along with Henri et Eleanor. Beautiful. Together forever."

Marie-Thérèse suddenly breaks off. He looks at her, then glances at Chlöe who peers at their new friend.

"Why sad, mademoiselle?"

"It's…nothing. Another life. Let me show you the kitchens. Well, what used to be the kitchens!"

She steps to yet another aged door and, pressing lightly on the iron handle, swings it open. There before them lie any number of flag-stones, many with weeds growing between them. Roofless walls protect only an enormous stone sink. It is alone, exposed to the elements and unused for centuries.

"Voilà! All gone now. Taken along with the dormitories in the great fire! I like to think of it as a place where the sisters shared their cooking with whoever showed up. That reminds me. Are you hungry?"

"No, we couldn't!"

"Pourquoi non?"

"Well…"

"Come back into what we jokingly call the office. I've a micro-wave. And fresh bread. And do try the marc!"

"Now what?"

"Fucked if I know! Shhh…one of the sisters is coming!"

"Messieurs! Vîtes! There are English outside!"

"We know. How many?"

"I don't know but they're getting angry. And they're a good deal more awake than you!"

Jerome runs his hands through his hair. The nun has been speaking to Gaston but it is the others she looks at. Most have no boots and only Gaston is armed.

"Come on! Open up! It's cold tonight! And we need food. Hot food!"

"I must open the door!"

"Sister Margueritte! Arrête! The Reverend Mother says they are many. And they mean harm to our guests!"

The Abbesse strides toward the second nun and stares at her as if daring her to say more.

"That is indeed what I said. We must bar the doors! Sisters! To work!"

"But the cloisters! The dormitory! We can't shut

that!"

"We must do our best. God will take care of the sisters!"

All is bustle as three nuns and seven drowsy men hurry from door to door making fast each one. Soon all is quiet again. They wait, hardly daring to breathe. Voices are raised again beyond the main doorway,

"We know you are in there. We smell lamb! Now stop fucking us about and open up! We'll give you ten seconds!"

"Can I ask, Marie? How long have you been..."

"A nun?"

"Oui."

"I was called when I was nineteen. That's, let me see, sixteen years ago. Sixteen years!"

Marie suddenly sounds wistful. She raises her glass and sips at the marc. He does the same,

"Christ! Pardonnez-moi Marie. This is strong stuff!"

"Bien sûr. After a glass or two it tastes less like rubbing alcohol!"

Chlöe tries again, her curiosity aroused,

"And why?"

"Pourquoi? I don't know. When you are called it is suddenly the right ... the only thing to do!"

"But were you happy?"

"As a teenager? As much as teenagers can be. Boy-friends being, er, boys, boring times at home, not enough money for half-way decent booze. The usual. Oh! And I hated my body! Mais, c'est normale, non?"

"And now?"

"No boys. Or men. The order provides for everything. Even the perfume. Thank God we're not Poor Clares. And I'm never bored."

"Where do you live?"

"We have a house provided by the order. In Vernon."

"How many is 'we'?"

"It varies. We're a teaching order. Have you heard of the Ursulines? People come and go. Often they are moved to other parts of Europe if a teaching vacancy comes up. We even had a sister moved to Singapore! Voilà! But it's usually much closer. Paris has no end of need! I suppose at any one time we are fifteen. I've been here the longest. Well, with Madeleine..."

She breaks off. Again she looks sad. She raises her glass and takes more than a sip this time.

"You look sad Marie. You looked sad before. Is it Madeleine?"

He is surprised by Chlöe's question. There is something searchingly intimate about it. Or is it the marc? Looking somewhere between the two of them, Marie-Thérèse says quietly,

"I loved her!   Simple, non? To love a sister. To be happy working at her side. Wa .. wa .. waking up to her! Voilà! Now you know!"

"I'm sorry, I didn't mean..."

"Don't be sorry, cherie. It is old history now. And not an original story. Hardly front page news!"

"But you loved her!"

"Loved? I still love her, cherie! But she, she found another path."

"Meaning?"

"She met a student in Paris. He was about twenty I think."

"He?"

"Indeed! He! Jean-Paul. She has become his de Beauvoir, je crois!"

"Do you meet?"

"No, she wrote to me to say she was leaving the order. And that was it!"

"That's terrible!"

"Terrible? Don't they say, 'If you love some-one let them go'?"

"Well, Sting said that. It's quite a philosophy to live by!"

"Harder than being married to the Saviour? I don't think so, cherie! Now, some bread I think."

"We should go out to meet them."

"What! And be butchered? Stay calm. They may go away."

"It doesn't sound like they're going away!"

Voices and shouts come from outside. There is an occasional half-hearted thump on the door but the majority of the sounds come from elsewhere.

"They're trying all the outside doors!"

"Don't worry. They can't break in here. What's that?"

There is a scream from the cloister. Then another.

Glass shatters in the kitchen. Another scream and then,

"Burn them! No! Fuck 'em! Then burn the whole fucking place to the ground!"

The screams are louder now. Jerome is tugging at his hair. The Abbesse and Gaston stand impassively listening to the horror outside. From under the kitchen door comes an orange glow.

"Quick! Press the pillows to the base of the door. We don't want to suffocate! And press the settles to the walls in case they try breaking these..."

At that moment there is a crash from above. A burning log hurtles through the smashed panes. It bounces on the table sending sparks and flaming splinters all around. Gaston moves as only a man with his strength and agility can. Clasping the blazing wood he hurls it into the fire.

"Come on! Do as she says! Move the fucking table and settles to the walls!"

The men move as one. Frantically they shove and haul everything which might form a pyre against the walls. Some of the candles are now alight, their wicks caught by showering sparks. More blazing logs descend through smashed glass. The flagstones are being strewn with coloured, leaded panes. Outside the screams have lessened. Jerome thinks he can hear sobbing.

"Put the fuckers back in the dormitory!"

"They're nuns Ducrau! Nuns!"

"You didn't mind fucking them! Now burn the bitches!"

The screams begin again, this time screams of terror, cries of the lost.

"Reverend Mother! Reverend Mother! Tu es là? Save us ! Oh sweet Saviour, save us! Aaargh! Have mercy!"

The Abbesse has fallen to her knees. In a slow, mournful decline, she spreads herself on the flagstones. Jerome sees her shoulders heaving with sobs and hears the whispered,

"Forgive them Lord. They know not what they do."

"She was lovely!"

"Quite something! And a nun!"

"You got a thing for nuns, Mister?"

"Must be my English side. No! I'm joking, baby! Makes you think though!"

"What?"

"Nuns having it off with each other! And with the occasional bloke!"

"Like priests!"

"Pretty much. Though if you think about it, for priests and monks, having it off with each other *is* the occasional bloke!"

"Ha ha! She lost her though didn't she?"

"To a man!"

"It doesn't matter does it? Man or woman. It's still loss. Pantam! Not the river!"

All is quiet in the hall. Beyond the walls, the occasional crash signifies a roof beam collapsing or masonry falling. Dawn's light spreads through the devastation of the hall. Piled settles, broken glass, and twisted lead strips lie on the floor. The men huddle around Gaston. None of them look at the nuns, all now prostrate; all muttering and sobbing. Jerome's gut muscles are tight, his hair greasy with the heat of the night. A night of fire.

"Bastards wanted to roast us alive!"

"Gaston! Would you have done the same?"

"You gone pious now, Jerome? I shall if I catch up with them! Come on! We have prey to track!"

XX

"Have you read *Justine*?"

"No, what is it?"

"One of de Sade's novels. It was banned!"

"Too raunchy?"

"Too everything. The book club's suggestion."

She had joined the book club saying she needed more stimulation and added it was sure to be a good way to meet local women. He had bitten his tongue holding back the thought, 'These local women only have the time to sit and discuss books because their husbands trudge to the city every day!' Who was he to criticize, anyway?

He loved the trudging, the coming home, the domesticity of it all. He loved the fact Chlöe was already considering a local job helping out at the nursery instead of doing her own, less regular, train journeys into Paris. And for all he knew some – if not all – of the local couples had sex lives as varied and – what was the word? – formidable as his own. He tried to imagine Mme Alphand grasping her old man as he came through the door and saying, "It's coq-au-vin, but you're to have me first Pierre. Cock sur la table! Voilâ!" He grins.

"When do you go?"

"Starts next week. We have to take a list of suggestions. Any ideas?"

"How about *Daniel Martin*? You're on that now."

"No good, baby. It's great but my copy's in translation. The books need to be originally in French."

"How about Sartre, Genet, Gide?"

"You'll be suggesting Proust next!"

"Proust."

"Ha ha."

So Chlöe had gone to her first meeting. List-less but not listless. And had returned with a gleam in her eye. And six books.

She had posed the *Justine* question a month later after an entertaining evening over wine and 'a few nibbles' with her new associates. The first meeting had started slow and business-like, building to a round of "What are you reading now?" A few replied, "I just don't have the time." Then a relaxing and luxurious "little sit-me-down and pick-me-up" as their hostess put it. Chlöe found herself on, or rather in, the plushest sofa she had ever experienced. She sank into the cushions falling straightaway into a reverie about being there with her 'lovely man.'

"Un Muscat?"

Startled, she opens her eyes. She blushes crimson.

"Oui, merci."

"This is nice isn't it? Such a good idea. Where do you live?"

"Rue Claude Monet. The little cottage on the first bend past the Café de la Théâtre."

"Do you go to la Café?"

"No, we prefer Raymonde's brasserie. He's got a bit

of a thing with our dog."

"How delightful. I thought you were Americans."

"No, they let us have it. Been there just over a year now."

"Mon dieu! A year! Doesn't time fly? Shows you how much I get out. And how old I am. I'm ashamed, I had no idea the Americans had gone. Still, it could be worse. Hélène is virtually next door and I haven't seen her for ages. Hélène, do come and meet ... what is your name, my dear?"

"Chlöe."

"Chlöe!"

Chlöe's hostess sashays away in search of the Muscat. 'I'm not surprised she doesn't see the neighbours. This garden must be three hectares!' she thinks, quickly followed by, 'Still, we've only seen ours a dozen times. Unless you count the kids and their boom boxes.'

The Americans had been right. The children next door had graduated from arguing at full volume to carrying round huge music systems on their shoulders. Invariably they were listening to different music, the volume steadily increasing as they competed for dominance. It had prompted at least one rebuke during a particularly cacophonous morning.

"It's like living next door to a bloody Charles Ives symphony! Merde!"

Chlôe had promised herself that she would look up

Charles Ives. Wondering how he knew these things, she loved him a little more.

"Bonjour, je m'appelle Hélène. Enchanté."

Towering above her is a tall, positively giantesque, picture of elegance. All flowing silk and Hermès clutch bag.

"Chlöe. Do sit down."

"Merci. Encore enchanté C'est bon, non?"

"Yes, it's lovely. And such a beautiful house."

Lowering herself into the sofa, the new arrival grimaces. Chlöe wonders if her house comment has been an indiscretion. If so, it isn't one to deter Hélène. She leans forward, conspiratorially,

"Her husband's money. Still this is a 'no man' evening isn't it? They'd love to think us little women have nothing better to do than talk about them. Have you read it?"

"What?"

"*Little Women*. Lovely book. Loved it as a child."

"No, desolée."

"What are you reading now, cherie?"

"Two. John Fowles and Iain Banks."

"En Anglais?"

"No, in translation. *Daniel Martin* and *The Wasp Factory*."

"Good."

"Marvelous, but the Banks is nasty and violent."

"And in translation?"

"Oui, So that's out. What were you going to suggest?"

"*Justine.*"

"*Justine*? Who's it by?"

"De Sade. Banned in eighteendot. Thought I'd suggest it so I finally got round to reading it. It's been in the library forever."

"I didn't know there was a library in the town."

Hélène looks momentarily taken aback. Eyebrows arched and with the barest trace of a grin she says,

"Cherie, there's no *town* library. I meant ours. My husband refers to it as his 'little indulgence in the East wing,' bless him."

"You have your own library, a bibliothèque chez vous?"

"I know but one gets so bored without something to read!"

"You have *Justine*?"

"Premier edition, cherie. Very rare. It's probably on the eighteenth century shelf along with Diderot and Descartes."

Chlôe resists the temptation to point out that René Descartes was decidedly seventeenth century. She has something else on her mind.

"Why are the books stored in centuries? There must be hundreds on the later shelves. Really unbalanced."

"Thousands, cherie. Thousands. But you're right. It's actually in the middle that the collection's most modest. Not that much between the fifth and eighth centuries and none printed of course. All parchment. Even some vellum. Lovely feel."

"And before the fifth century?"

"Much better. The Romans were a prolific lot, and the Greeks of course."

"It's not all original, surely?"

"Ha! You are a hoot. Of course not. The documents are mostly original but we have goodness knows how many books on Greece and Rome and they all go onto those shelves too. Even if the book's recent."

"Ah … Je comprends. But the documents are very precious, no?"

"Some of them probably priceless but Guillaume isn't short of a sou."

"Your husband? Does he have a favourite shelf?"

"He's strictly nineteenth century. Hugo, Balzac, Zola. I just can't get on with them. *Les Miserables* must be the most apt title in history. As for *Germinal*. Talk about bleak! Makes Dickens look like soap opera."

"But that's what it is, non?"

"What? Soap opera?"

"Dickens. They originally came out as weeklies. He had to keep the readers on their toes."

"Well, he must have changed them a lot as books. *Martin Chuzzlewit* takes forever to get going."

"Your husband..."

"Guillaume."

"Oui, Guillaume. He has the full set?"

"Cherie, we have Dickens coming out of our ears. But Balzac, he takes the biscuit. We must have five first editions of *La Comedie Humaine*. Complete. From eighteen eighty odd I think. Older than me!"

Hélène pauses and smiles demurely but a reassuring compliment isn't forthcoming.

"Do you know, he not only published *Les Chouans* himself, he reviewed it in umpteen pamphlets? Using pseudonyms!"

"Modern marketing."

"But you'd need serious marketing. I liked *Les Chouans*. A proper swash-buckler. But some of the others! Opening paragraphs that go on for weeks, dreadful bourgeoisie mired in debt. Drab little *Ursule Mirouet*."

Chlôe is feeling more and more out of her depth. She likes Dickens and makes a mental note to herself to get hold of *Martin Chuzzlewit*. And *Ursule Mirouet* for good measure.

"So you're recommending *Justine*?"

"Well, I prefer *The Confessions,* but they're rather dense for the book club. And very long. Six or seven hundred pages."

"De Sade, aussi?"

"Non, sounds like it should be, doesn't it? Rousseau."

"Good?"

"Formidable. He wrote it to go one up on his critics. He confessed everything. Even the spanking!"

"Spanking?"

"Didn't you know, cherie? Dear Jean-Jacques was, erm, turned on when a governess spanked him as a child. He preferred a little walloping the rest of his life. It could have been worse."

"Worse?"

Hélène eases forward slightly. Chlöe can smell her perfume now. Not, she is surprised to discover, *Chanel* but something altogether more subtle and musky.

"Descartes had a bit of a thing for cross-eyed women. Ah, the Muscat. Merci Anna-Clair."

First Hélène, then Chlöe take the proffered glasses. Chlôe is deep in thought, 'Confessing everything! I wonder?' And so it began.

XXI

"I've had enough now."

"Enough?"

"This war, the killing..."

"Ha! Why don't you ask Mauseau if you can go home?"

"Do you ...? Non, you jest."

"My friend. You could walk away. Or creep away in the night. But, you wouldn't get far!"

"Pourquoi?"

"Wolves, hunger. Mauseau would send men after you."

"And then?"

"It wouldn't be pretty. See that man there?"

Gaston nods towards what appears to be a scarecrow stretched out on the ground. Jerome cranes his head trying to make out the prostrate form. He blinks as whatever it is moves slightly, twisting in the glare of the sun. A crow settles at arm's length from the prostrate form and hops toward it.

"What?"

"Come. I'll show you a deserter."

With that Gaston heaves himself upright. Beckoning to Jerome he moves quickly up the slope. As they get closer he suddenly claps his hands. The crow eyes him and with an insolent shuffle the lazy beats of its black wings takes him higher into the blue of the cloudless sky where he circles – waiting. Jerome already knows what they will find. "Deserter" had hit home.

"He can't get it up, you know!"

"What?"

"Guillaume. Can't get it up. Well not with me. Even when he was barely sixty he'd hump away for ages. Just couldn't come. That's one reason he used to go to his whores."

"Why?"

"Because whores will do, er, other things."

"Other things, Hélène?"

"Well, God Chlöe, I don't know. Dress up, leather, rubber … all that I suppose."

Chlöe is taken aback – for the second time in less than a minute. Hélène's declaration about her husband had come out of the blue. Now Chlöe's thought is unvoiced; it is somehow, quaint that Hélène doesn't approve of dressing up.

"I..."

"Don't worry cherie. It doesn't bother me. It means he leaves me alone."

"Don't you miss it?"

"At my age? Ha!"

She crumbles and she says, barely audibly,

"You get used to it. But, yes, I do miss the feel of a man's weight."

"I understand, Hélène."

"You do? But your man ..."

" Of course! But to be without his body on mine!"

" Unthinkable?"

"It's bad enough when he's away for a few days, but..."

Chloe had talked to him about the "weight thing", as he called it. He had been surprised,

"I don't feel that way at all. The weight of a woman. I don't think about it."

"But it turns you on when I'm riding you!"

"Of course. But that's because of the look on your face, bouncing away, pushing to get me deeper in. You don't really weigh anything at all."

So they had tried it with Chloe laying flat, not moving, just lying still as he pulls gently at her hair.

"Well?"

"Sorry babe. You just don't weigh enough!"

Hélène's next question brings her out of the reverie.

"Does he worry about you being unfaithful?"

"Oui, non! Oui – all the time."

"And are you?"

"No time Hélène!"

"No time! That's a terrible thing to say! If you wanted someone else you'd find the time. I hope you've never said that to him!"

Had she? Hélène almost barks,

"'No time' is *not* the right reply. The answer is, "I only want him." "No time" makes it sound like you squeeze him into your busy day!"

"Does it?"

This is no scarecrow. They stand above the stretched

out form of a man. A man who still lives – just. His face is covered in wounds; small holes have been torn into the flesh and dried blood surrounds each one. As Jerome stares a maggot detaches itself from a cheek and rolls, bloated, to the ground. The crows have done their work and the eye sockets offer only dark emptiness. Again the body twitches. Jerome's eyes trace a line from the terrible remains of the face down the left arm. It seems broken, snapped at the elbow and tied at the wrist to a stave.

"Where are his hands?"

"Deserters don't need hands my friend. The only fighting he is doing is for his last breath."

Jerome cannot tear his gaze away from the mutilation at his feet. The man's hands have been either chopped or sawn away. The stave is joined somehow to another beneath the body. They form an X, the legs tied at the knees to the wooden frame. Again the man twitches. His mouth opens. There is no tongue. Jerome thinks, distractedly, 'that must be agony lying on that wooden cross!' He nods towards Gaston's knife.

"Aren't you going to?"

"No, my friend. Mercy for him could mean death for us!"

The body twitches again, a groan escaping the terrible mouth.

Jerome and Gaston turn as one. Behind them all is silence. The crow circles lower. Jerome turns in time to see the carrion-lover drop and land close to the prostrate remains. With one hop it alights on the victim's shoulder.

"Still want to go home?"

"Not that way. Who knows, Mauseau might send you after me!"

"I don't doubt it. He'd guess I could work out where you'd go."

"How could you do that?"

"Come on, my friend. You don't know these parts, this countryside. You'd head straight back the way we've come."

"I might keep on going just to fool you!"

"You...? Ha! Then you would walk into the enemy's hands!"

"Why would that matter? I'd just join with them instead!"

Gaston says nothing. He is pained – and mystified at the pain – by Jerome's words.

"And if we are met in battle?"

"One or both of us might be dead before it came to that!"

The crow picks furiously at the man's face. The corpse lies still. Two more crows swerve down to join the feast. No more twitching, no groans, only the slight sounds of the tearing of flesh.

"Anyway, I'm going nowhere. If and when I die it will be by your side, not by your knife."

A lump is in Gaston's throat as he replies,

"Merci, mon ami. Merci."

XXII

The knight's charger is passive as Jerome strokes the great chestnut neck. The black tail swishes from left to right as if brushing flies. Annoyance? Pleasure? He presses his hand harder to the muscle and the tail sweeps again. Now a hoof paws the ground; once, twice. Jerome lowers his eyes.

Something protrudes from just below the right knee. He looks more intently. A dart; small, clotted blood at the point of entry. Carefully kneeling, Jerome feels around the wound. There is a hardness under the skin, like a stone. The dart has been embedded, unseen for some time, a callous forming. The charger quietens, no longer scraping the soil. Man and beast wait. Jerome feels the horse's hot breath on his neck.

"Gaston, your knife."

The big man has come to see what his friend is doing; he stands behind him admiring Jerome's gentle exploration of the injury.

"You shouldn't go messing with that. The animal don't looked pained. Best let sleeping dogs..."

"Sshh.. I can't.."

"You can. That's a steward's job. The knight's not bothered. Nor should you be."

But Gaston hands him the knife, the blade honed as ever. Stroking the charger's chest with his left hand, Jerome pushes his shoulder to the haunch and feels the pressure returned. They are now joined in tense harmony, the least movement meeting its match in the other's response. Slowly, oh so slowly, Jerome leans down. His hand finds again the base of the dart. He presses his shoulder to the chest above him and brings the blade close to the cutting point...

"Hey, you! Qu'est ce que vous faites?"

"Don't make a fuss little man. My friend is doing your job for you."

"You can't touch my master's horse! Vous ..."

The argument is cut short with a muffled grunt. Still pressed hard against the other, neither animal nor man has moved. Jerome doesn't look up but he knows Gaston's hand will be clamped over the steward's mouth. Or worse.

"Calme. Doucement, mon ami."

Whispering now, Jerome touches the blade to the bulbous growth, the dart's shaft plain to see and he hopes not too deep within. A little blood, an easing, and there it is! He clenches his fist around the peg of wood and metal. It is not barbed, only a primitive cross-bow bolt. Blood flows more freely. Still the stallion doesn't move. Jerome eases away from the pulsing muscle and stands.

Now he looks the beast in the eye. Deep brown, almost black and glistening with wariness and relief as if a bee-sting has been withdrawn. The great head bows back down to the scraped earth and nuzzles the soil for tufts of grass. He chews, apparently unconcerned. Jerome wipes the sweat from his brow and turns to Gaston who holds the steward off the ground, dangling like a puppet. Terror in his eyes but still alive, Jerome is pleased to note.

"You should take better care of your master's horse."

"They're all the same these stewards. Something for nothing."

With that, Gaston unceremoniously drops the wretch to his feet. He is a short, slim man with a stubbled and pock-marked face, jutting chin and lank hair. His thin, hooked nose trails snot. He wipes the smear away with the back of a hand burned by the sun and already as wrinkled as an old man's. His eyes dart from Jerome to Gaston. Now he stares at the stallion still passively chewing at the grass. He seems confused but, with a curse, settles on Gaston for his muttered threat,

"You won't hear the last of this, oaf!"

"Oo, I'm scared. Tell your master what you've just witnessed. We'll see who won't hear the last of it."

"You think he'll believe you or me, fat man? Voilà!"

Gaston takes a step forward and the steward turns on his heels to scurry away. Jerome runs his hands through his hair.

"Mon ami. You know your stuff. Where'd you learn to calm horses so easily?"

"It's not so easy. But it helps not to be frightened. They pick up fear and prefer a strong hand."

"Strong hand! Ha! Little thing like you. The brute could've pushed you over with one nudge!"

"I'd have nudged back."

Gaston smiles; he is learning to like Jerome. He has noticed how calm he can be but at the same time how disturbed by Gaston's own instinctive brutality. He envies Jerome's looks, his fair hair, the way he can sit lost in day-dreams. Gaston doesn't day-dream – too much fear, too much hurt, too many deaths; his own hands as bloodied as any. He knows he is breaking a rule here; he is becoming fond of his young companion. He brings a hand to an ear lobe and rubs it, deep in thought.

"Well I never."

"What?"

"I do believe you were daydreaming Gaston! What was it? Home? What you'd like to do to that steward?"

"He's not worth the effort. I was just thinking."

"And?"

"I... It... It doesn't matter. We'd better get back before that skinny runt stirs up trouble."

With a last glance at the grazing charger, Jerome joins Gaston and they walk toward one of the blue and gold banners fluttering in the growing breeze. They don't speak; again Gaston is lost in thought. And Jerome...

"Fuck, oh fuck, fuck, fuck. I love that. I can feel your belly hairs on my yoni. Oh fuck!"

Pierre and Marie move as one – now faster, now slower, the rhythm builds, and Marie's legs grasping her lover's hips as he presses into her. She feels a familiar shudder building around her belly – the muscles contracting, rippling. Her thighs are quivering and a hot flush spreads through her breasts. She is breathing harshly, her lips pouting, teeth bared.

She arches, nipples swelling, aching, swelling...

"Now who's day-dreaming? Got a rod on too by the look of you!"

Jerome's hands drop to his crotch. How long has he been this way? Surely his thoughts about Marie lasted but a few seconds?

"Do you think his master will seek us out?"

"Doubt it. There's too many of us now. It'd take him a day. He won't bother. Probably have a go at the runt, with luck. Anyway, it weren't thinking about getting caught gave you that hard on! Women again? Or should I say woman?"

"Am I so easy to fathom?"

"Love-struck's what you are sonny-boy. Obsédée! But your thoughts were a little more physical, non?"

"I ..."

"Oui?"

"I was thinking about her and him. At it! I just know they're fucking."

"Christ! You're twenty four hours from being carrion and you're jealous! For all you know, they're not even together. I bet he's joined up and she's waiting for whoever gets home first. Or she's with someone else."

"He won't fight. Too much work on the land. They try and get him into this shit and he'll hide out 'til they go. And she wouldn't..."

Jerome stops mid-sentence. Does he know Marie at all? Women had been a complete mystery to him until Coquette and even then the mystery had been barely touched. What was it Coquette had really wanted? Food! She had wanted food. Hardly a sharing of souls! Would Marie pine for him? For Pierre? For any man? Pierre had said she'd wanted to fuck not listen to words. Is it poetic vision that allows him to be so certain of what she is doing now? Or is it delusion? Fears and thoughts created by a jealousy he can't control?

Now the idea of her with another – yet another – lover takes hold. Who could it be? He searches his memory. But surely there is no-one? All the men of age will have been pressed to war by now. Only fugitives and the old will remain – his father, vieux Pierre, M Jouir. The last he realizes is probably dead anyway by now. Old age (he must be fifty), plague, fever, who knows? But if Pierre and Marie are no more, where must she be? No, they are together.

"Si tu plais, mon amour, encore."

"Again? Do you never rest?"

"Why should we. This is, is … rutting, pure and simple. And our rutting is priceless. Beyond price. Are you going off me?"

"Course not. It's just, just …"

"Now you're thinking of Jerome."

"I'm…"

"Liar!"

"If I think of him it's only because I think he was such a fool not to rut with you."

"Do you think we'd have rutted? Like you and me?"

"Who knows? You'd bring out the animal in

anyone."

"So come my love ... we have so little time."

"Little time? It's not even dark and no-one will find us here. Anyway, time is all we have. But..."

"No, you don't understand. I'm leaving."

Pierre sits upright. He feels as though punched in the gut. Marie lies beside him, stroking his thigh, her beautiful eyes still wide with lust and longing. She shifts her weight to her elbow, never dropping her gaze from Pee-pee. His eyes, too, are wide. Is this fear? Sorrow? His brow furrows as he searches for the right question.

"Pourquoi?"

"Pourquoi, non?"

"Why not! Don't you love all this? Us?"

"All what? I love your body and the way we do this. But what else is there? Dishes to prepare, plates to clean, helping with the animals, clearing out the yard?"

"Well that's my life outside of you and me summed up! Apart from the dishes. What of yours?"

"Ha ha! That is my life, lover. We are the same. The only thing I don't do is the horses and logging. Look at my hands!"

Pierre takes her left hand in his. Calloused, scarred; a new cut on the palm. It is not so different from his own. Smaller, cleaner but still the hand of a worker – a peasant.

"What's wrong with it? It's a beautiful hand!"

"My hands age faster than any other part of me. I can't stay here Pierre. I want, no I need something

more. At least for a time."

"We could have a baby! I'd look after you. Your work would be easier..."

"Easier! Are you mad? Have you seen how old and tired the mothers are here? They don't stop their daily labour. Not for an instant."

"You could. You c..."

"I'd go mad. And how many village women have only one child? We are like rabbits."

"Well we are Marie."

She smiles. Pierre senses a new calm in her and leans forward to kiss her cheek. But she gently steers his mouth to hers. He almost misses her words as she pulls away and presses her lips to his head,

"Anyway, my buck. We don't have to wait. I'm, I'm ... We are having a baby."

"What's wrong?"

They are sitting on the terrace he had laboriously made from flagstones. They had been conjured up by Chlöe from who-knows-where. It had been a labour of love with the promise of a night of love to follow. The day has been warm, post-croissants, *Le Monde* and coffee. It is quiet, a day off work for them both and the neighbours' children at school, the only sounds the hirondelles and a vague traffic hum in the distance. On such days they would talk. And how they talked! He had never known a – what was the word – *anything* like this. All the chat, talk, conversation; the love, excitement. And such frank talk of sex! He smiled as he remembered again the time at Raymonde's when she'd shouted about his cock. She has started this morning's chat in typically enigmatic fashion.

"Have you ever noticed how many great artists have surnames beginning with an 'M'?"

Followed by: "And does it matter it's the thirteenth letter of the alphabet?"

"That's two questions. You always ask two."

"Do I? Well, what's the answer?"

"There you go again. Two more. Or three I suppose because I don't know which of the first two you want me to answer."

She leans forward and pokes him hard. Twisting away, he smiles.

"I love you."

"Just answer the question Mister Clever-Dick."

"I thought you liked my clever dick."

"No, baby, I *really* like it. But question one first."

"Which was? Oh, I know, the letter 'M.' I dunno ... Monet, Manet, Matisse, Morisot."

"All French."

"Magritte."

"Belgian."

"Really? Are you sure?"

"Actually, Matisse was technically Belgian too."

"How do you know this stuff?"

"I used to love it. I read loads on them when I got out."

"Out?"

She turns away saying, quietly,

"Another time baby. Anyway, don't stop."

Distracted now, he tries to focus again, the "out" playing on his mind.

"Modigliani, Millet, Meissonnier."

"He of *La Compagne de France*?"

"Now who's a clever Dick?"

"Don't stop, baby, I love it when it when you're showing off."

He stops, momentarily distracted again ("out?"), a look of hurt crossing his face.

"C'mon, Mister, just kidding."

"I wasn't showing off!"

"You can be so sensitive! Come on."

"Malouel."

"Who's he?"

"He did a lovely little pieta in about fourteen hundred. You can see it in the Louvre. Moreau, Macke, Marc, Mondrian."

"Now you're definitely showing off! Haven't we had Mondrian?"

"Non."

He pauses. Chlöe looks at him with a new respect.

"Is that it?"

"It? That must be twenty plus. What's the point?"

"Well they all start with an 'M', the thirteenth letter and thirteen is meant to be unlucky. And I tell what, you named thirteen too"

"Oooo, spooky. I'm not sure Monet was that unlucky. And he had such a sense of peace about his work. Look at the water lilies."

"What's so peaceful about water? Anyway, I prefer Matisse. Give me the south any day."

She looks, just for a moment, sad, then thoughtful, her brow furrowing as always.

"Matisse loved the water."

"I know, but he painted it as he thought it should look, not how it is."

"How is it?"

"Deadly. Michelangelo! Ha!"

He is startled back to "out" but equally thrown, first by the "deadly" and then by "Michelangelo."

"How so, deadly?"

"Who, Michelangelo? He was you know. Thousands of people must have almost broken their necks looking up at the ceiling in the Sistine chapel. Mind you, his David will have given comfort to loads of guys with small parts."

"Stop messing. You said water is deadly."

"Well it is. People drown in it."

"Not if they can swim."

"What if you are wrecked mid-Atlantic? Or if someone holds your head under?"

"Christ! Who would do that? You'd drown. Horrible. It's meant to be the worst way to go."

Now Chloe looks startled.

"I always think it would be kind of, I dunno, OK."

"God no. I can think of much better ways."

"Do any of them feature being in bed with me by any chance?"

"All of 'em, baby."

He stands, leaning forward slightly and kisses her neck. He nuzzles into the familiar soft hair and again the "out" wriggles into consciousness. But Chlöe is already cupping her hand around his balls hanging down between his legs in the warm summer air.

"I love your balls. Do you think I could get them into my mouth?"

"Both of them?"

"Let's see, shall we?"

"Oh... Ha! Marquet, Marval."

"Are you naming your parts? "D'accord. I draw Marquet in thus ahm. Mwawal gww,gww,.."

"Christ! You can. You'll choke."

Gently releasing him, she stands.

"They're beautiful, Mister. Bit of a mouthful tho'."

"Even...."

"Don't say it. My mouth isn't that big is it? And what about the last two ems? Did you make them up?"

"Course not. They were mates of Matisse."

"I like this game. Do we know any more?"

They walk as one to the little bookshelf in the kitchen. He had put it up in a burst of domesticity; crooked but good enough. There is an idiosyncratic collection of books, mostly dog-eared paperbacks; *The Wasp Factory, The Penguin Guide to Jazz: 1972*, André Simon's *A Wine Primer* – all three in English – Robert's *La Cuisine Des Épices,* Androuet's *Guide du Fromage,* biographies of Sartre, Genet and Marie Antoinette, John Berger's *Pig Earth* and in the middle of the odd collection, *L'Aquerelle.* Chlöe reaches for

L'Aquerelle.

"We really need some better shelves, baby. You won't find many in there. All water-colourists."

"Look, there's your Macke. And Manet. And Mondrian. Marc. Ah ha! Ewald Mataré. Un autre."

They open *L'Aquerelle* at page 57. *Passage de fleuve au bord du Rhin* is mostly in subdued tones – ochres, caramels, a grey-blue hill-side with an impossible to accurately name (yellow, ochre, cream?) sky above. In the foreground possibly sixteen or seventeen hay-stacks lead the eye to the central river running across the whole. Reflected in its – still? – waters are clouds, on the far bank cypresses, wheat fields and a strangely angular white roofed building. The effect is calming. Until,

"Those hay-stacks look like breasts. Just look at the pointy mamelons on them."

"They don't look like breasts."

As he says it, he immediately sees what she means. Eyes scanning the remaining hay-stacks he finds two more.

"Ok, they're tits. That river doesn't look deadly though. Well, not to me."

Chlöe catches her breath.

"Let's go back outside. Unless you think maybe André Simon has some artists. Other than piss-artists."

"Mïro!"

"There's no prize you know. Still, not bad. How could we have forgotten Mïro?"

"I think we should stop. This will bug us all day."

Again she looks a little downcast, forlorn even,

"Well, we have all day. You're off work 'til Thursday."

"Ok, but just one more each."

They make their way back to the terrace. It is warmer now, the coffee dregs dried dull brown, tarring the cups. They lapse into a contented silence. Only the occasional furrowing of Chlöe's brow gives a clue to the intensity of her thought. He, however, looks asleep. But he too is deep in thought striving to reach beyond a new-found pre-occupation with drowning.

"Massenet."

"He was a composer!"

"Un artist, non?"

"By that reckoning we could have Mozart or Mahler. Throw in Maupassant and Molière for good measure! Sorry, baby. Shouting. Must be the lack of pastis."

"You weren't but pastis is a good idea."

Another new habit. A 'blessed ritual' as he might say. The five, sometimes four, o'clock pastis, most often the cheaper *Berger* but on happy days…

"*Ricard*?"

"Bien sûr. Merci."

"Maigret?"

"Maigret wasn't an artist. He wasn't even a real person."

"He was for me. My dad used to watch him on TV all the time."

"So, it's now artists, composers, authors, playwrights *and* fictional detectives."

A warm glow is spreading from his stomach as the

Ricard takes effect. Like her, he is smiling broadly, "out" forgotten for the time being.

"No baby, we'll stick to the rules."

"Shame. I was gonna have Mickey Mouse."

"Have me instead."

He stands and turns toward the door.

"No. Here."

"Ici? Mais nos voisins!"

"I haven't heard them come back yet, honey."

Neither has he. As Chlöe stands, turns and leans forward on to the table he feels a familiar stirring. Pulling her makeshift dressing gown – his shirt, he notices – above her buttocks he steps away for a moment.

"God, I love your arse!"

Chloe parts her legs and guides him inside her, moaning a little. And then, as he pushes harder, gasping.

"Gently baby. No, fuck me, Mister, just fuck me!"

"Allo. Vous êtes là?"

"I thought they weren't back!"

"I hadn't heard them!"

He is pulling out of her, his balls now swinging back and forth, his erection a little too strong to either tuck away or allow an immediate response to the caller who as it happens is not a neighbour, but Hélène. Chlöe' is silently thankful her friend is not quite tall enough to see over the fence.

"Cherie. Tu as oublié? It is the book club tonight. Une demie heure. I shall come to the front, non? So you can get dressed."

They hear Hélène's tinkling laughter as she walks away.

"God, how did she see us? She must be two metres tall!"

But he has already seen a thin crack between two, admittedly elderly, fence panels and an eye-sized hole where a knot has fallen out.

"Hmmm...People would normally have to pay for a show like that."

"Don't laugh, baby. It's not funny. It's embarrassing."

Chlöe is hurrying through the kitchen as her new friend raps at the door.

"Hélène. Thank you so much for coming. I *had* forgotten."

"Et le livre? How did you get on with the good Madame?"

To his horror, this month's choice had been *Madame Bovary*. He had put his head in his hands and run his fingers through his hair. Another habit she had grown to love.

"Bloody Flaubert. And five hundred pages of Flaubert at that."

"It's quite big print though. It won't take me long."

And, true to form, it hadn't. He was amazed at the speed she could read. Something she had learned "inside" she had said. "Inside" and now, "out"? She is answering Hélène:

"Oui. Je l'ai fini."

"Would you like a pastis? Vous l'aimez?"

"Cheri, I thought Chlöe was never going to ask. Merci."

And then turning to Chlöe, with a smile playing around her mouth, she leans forward to say under her breath.

"Who is he, cherie?"

"Mon homme."

"Well, yes. I could see he isn't a boy. Charming. Quite, quite charming."

Chlöe feels a sudden pang across her chest which seems to tighten. Is this jealousy? She doesn't *do* jealousy.

"You must be very happy, cherie."

That's what it is! Happiness. Pride. Pride of ownership! He is hers, all hers. He reappears with the pastis and some hastily donned jeans and offers it to Hélène.

"Merci. It looks warm outside. Shall we?"

She leads him and a subdued Chlöe to the table. Brushing – what? Ash? Dust? Sex? – from a chair, Hélène lowers herself onto it. Chlöe can't help thinking that for such a tall woman even sitting down has a certain elegance.

"This is nice. Charming. How many rooms do you have?"

"We count the courtyard as a room in the summer but it's really a two up, two down."

"Parfait. Pour un couple. Et l'amour, non? But you have no children?"

Chlöe suddenly stands and stumbles back into the

kitchen.

"Did I say something wrong, cherie?"

XXIII

In retrospect though not, he suspects, very often Jerome imagines he will blame himself for the death of "the skinny runt". Just as he and Gaston were about to settle down for the night under a loose-woven hide-away of boughs and jerkins the steward had appeared. Without a sound he had rushed at Gaston who spun around. Did this bear of a man have eyes in the back of his head? With a great sweeping blow Gaston sent his assailant flying.

Now he lies whimpering at Gaston's feet, his shoulders twisted at an impossible angle, his left arm twitching uncontrollably. Jerome had never seen another human so rat-like; long, lank hair swept back to reveal a down-covered fore-head, immensely thick eyebrows and deep brown, almost black, eyes. Not so different from the charger he had so conspicuously failed to look after to Jerome's satisfaction, though tiny by comparison.

The nose is elongated, jutting from a whisker-covered face; what little skin shows through the whiskers is a deep brown, browner than the fore-arms protruding from his sleeves. They are also covered in black hair. Jerome can't draw his eyes from the hands; long, hairy fingers tipped with vicious looking nails. They look sharpened. Yellow and curved, more like claws; talons. The man is bare-foot and the soles of his feet, the left leg now beginning to shake, are revealed. A hiss escapes Jerome's lips. The feet too are hairy, covered by pale brown fur-like hair. He feels an arm around his shoulders.

"Our steward looks like a bloody rat!"

Gaston's voice is harsh. There is no compassion for the rodent twitching on the ground beneath him.

"Now, what do we do with rats my friend?"

"Drown them?"

Jerome is barely aware of his reply. It is natural, nothing more. At home rats unfortunate enough to be cornered by himself or Pierre were unceremoniously despatched in the nearest horse trough. They were known to carry disease and were a constant threat to the chickens. It was rumoured that adult males would attack lambs or even babes-in-arms as they slept though Jerome had never heard of anyone ever discovering a rat attacking a baby.

"Drown 'em? I'm not humpin' this bastard to the moat. Anyway there's barely any water in it. It's been filled with straw. Come on you fuck! On your feet."

There is a gasp and a flash of bared teeth and then the man is across Gaston's right shoulder like a sack of corn. His eyes dart from left to right, his mouth opens and closes like a landed fish. His teeth protrude from pinched lips and he looks pleadingly at Jerome as Gaston strides away. Jerome follows as quickly as he can, stumbling in the half light. Soon a familiar smell drifts from ahead of the three-some. Horses! Gaston is ...!

Jerome suddenly understands. They are at the horse trough within a few more strides and, without faltering in his steps, Gaston heaves his burden into the water. There is the briefest of struggles, a series of bubbles rise to burst at the surface, and all is still. Gaston pulls the dripping corpse out of the trough and says, regretfully,

"We'll have to bury the runt now!"

Their makeshift shelter feels cold. Dawn is breaking. Jerome rubs his eyes and yawns; not a stretch and arch but a quiet exhalation. He doesn't want to wake Gaston who lies pressed against him. He can feel the big man's manhood against his side. It is hard. Jerome shuffles slightly but Gaston who is indeed awake shuffles with him. Jerome feels an arm – lazily? innocently? – cross his side. His friend's hand rests on his belly. For but a moment. Jerome holds his breath as Gaston's hand moves down, down.

He feels himself responding. He shifts slightly but to no avail. The dawn is cold and the sweat on his chest colder. An image of a knife, the blade lethally honed, wells up and he wants to say – what? 'Arrête!' 'Non!' But no word comes. He shakes a little as the hand snakes inside his breeches. It is surprisingly gentle but doesn't dispel the fear. He feels his shaft responding more and more to the big man's stroking. He can also feel Gaston pressing harder against his lower back.

He says nothing as Gaston's hand pulls at his right shoulder pushing him down to the earth. Tears are in his eyes as the hand goes back to its stroking and then, quickly and easily, slides the breeches over his erection and down past his thighs exposing him. To what? He doesn't have to wait long as Gaston's mouth closes over his shaft's head. Now it is hot and starting to throb with animal desire in response to the sucking, licking, probing. Gaston's head moves down further. He feels the hot tongue around his balls and then – underneath. He shudders as the tongue continues its probe then a finger pushes carefully inside him.

He is squirming now, a tense pleasure starting to course through him. He feels the leggings removed and now ... a new sensation. Something else is probing him. Something fatter than the finger, something hard and insistent. There is a sharp pain, but it is momentary as his friend's (lover's? attacker's?) own shaft eases into him. Now Gaston begins to thrust, Jerome's hips responding in kind as the great cock lifts him from the ground. It is pushing, pushing, withdrawing, pushing again.

Despite the pain, now sharp and continuous, he feels himself growing, now pressing hard to Gaston's vast stomach and then, then his own belly is wet as he comes, the sticky sap hot against his skin. Something like shame overwhelms him but seconds later, he feels Gaston pulsing inside him. A groan escapes the bigger man as he feels his own release, the pent up desires of another night with Jerome finally spent.

It is over. Jerome pushes his hands through his hair and, for the first time, looks at Gaston. He sits cross-legged an arm's length away.

"Time for breakfast my young friend?"

"Er, oui. D'accord."

"Je t'aime mon ami."

And they leave the shelter together as if nothing has

happened. As if Jerome - still wet, Gaston's seed still seeping from him - has not experienced fearful violation from a man with the power to crush him. For Gaston, now smiling, it has been an act of love to rival any.

"What a way to start the day, eh? To begin the day with the gift of love. Today would be a good day to die, ami!"

"Yes, I could die today Gaston. With any luck."

Now Jerome is silent. He pads alongside Gaston who is smiling broadly, a look that might, to a romantic, be described as 'faraway' in his eyes. Now he breaks into a whistle. Frère Jacques of all things! Jerome's confusion mounts. Gaston is happy, almost gay.

For all his brutality some kind of joy has broken through the fierce exterior. Jerome has seen this before. He goes back, back, searching. And there it is; a memory of his mother's expression moments after his sister's birth. All that pain, exertion, sweat; the stink as her bowels moved with the final push. Blood, the baby's head, tiny shoulders forced out with a rush of red and a piercing shriek from his mother. Then peace. A slap, a cry; the delicate and surely fearsomely robust bundle passed to her who's eyes are wide, shining, the beads of sweat, the shit all irrelevant now. Such a look of joy! Love. Love at first sight!

Jerome stops in his tracks. What had Gaston said? Something about a gift? A gift of love! The big man whistles on, oblivious to his conquered friend still standing thunderstruck. Jerome is absorbed exploring each feeling as it comes to him. There's a sickness in his gut. Fear? Anger? The sickness settles to a dull ache. Is this love? No, he knows love if that is what he feels for Marie.

This is visceral. There is a word for this feeling. Loathing! And with that understanding another waves courses through him. This time it is fear. If Gaston loves him, he will try to have him again. He will succeed. He is sore, his hips still feel the crushing weight as he was carefully then harshly penetrated. Coquette had the good sense, though hardly planned, to soil herself. If he had done the same would Gaston have stopped overwhelmed by disgust? He doubts it. Rather he would have made some foul joke and continued buggering away.

Jerome's gorge rises as the dullness becomes sharper with memory. He feels sick, nauseated beyond redemption. And still he doesn't move. He can see Gaston has also stopped and is calling to him, the words not carrying in the freshening breeze. He runs his hand through his hair, the effort bringing on another stomach cramp. Tentatively, he steps forward, amazed to find he is not falling to the ground. Gaston is waving and raising a hand to his mouth. He has found something to eat.

XXIV

After that first visit Hélène made it a regular habit to call on book club night. Initially, mid-afternoon when it fell on a week-end and, by the third visit, at noon. Noon was no good. No good at all.

"Can you have a word with her?"

"Who?"

"Hélène. She's seriously interfering with us. No *Le Monde*, no post-coital coffee."

"Get you! Post-coital coffee!"

"Well I happen to love all that."

"I know, baby. Me too but she *is* lonely. And I think a bit sad."

"Well invite her on different days. Make it a proper invitation. Give her times."

And she had. Hélène comes as bid on the week-end, sometimes for dinner, pre-dinner pastis or lunch. She is invariably punctual, never outstays her welcome and, to Chlöe's mind, grateful. She has said as much.

"This is very special for me, cherie. I like spending time with you. I get so, so,… "

She looks down and quickly turns away.

"Sad?"

"Non, normalement, non. Pour moi la tristesse est interdit."

"Interdit! Forbidden? Pourquoi?"

Hélène cautiously looks around as if suspecting a

hidden camera.

"Don't worry, Hélène. There's no CCTV here."

"I know. But you'd be surprised what one can see – and hear – through that little hole in the fence!"

She smiles. Chlöe blushes.

"Don't worry, cherie. I haven't told a soul. But it was, er, quite something!"

The younger woman is by now crimson. She gasps a little and blurts out,

"Forbidden. What did you mean by 'Forbidden'?"

"It is a short story, made long by my resentment and my tendency to mull."

"Mull? You dwell on things?"

"I have a lot of time on my hands, cherie. It is too easy to get distracted by the past."

"Go on ... Please."

"My parents said I was light-headed, too young, too bright-eyed and bushy tailed, too ... I don't know, too everything to get married when I did. Mais, l'amour. Tu sais?"

"Oh yes, I know."

"I thought Guillaume wonderful. Good at sport, a career ahead of him. I saw it all. The big house, the garden, children, dinner parties, even the library!"

"But?"

"He had his first affair, well dalliance anyway, the day we married."

"On your wedding day!"

"He and some drunken friends stayed out until some unearthly hour the night before and ended up in a club.

In Paris. Of all places. Can you imagine. We lived in Evreux and he had his stag night and his little whore in Paris. Near the Moulin Rouge I wouldn't be surprised."

"Evreux? When did you live there?"

"Born there, cherie. Why do you ask?"

"Oh nothing. I lived there once."

"Did you indeed? It's fate; neighbours then, neighbours now. Well, almost neighbours. Did you hear that awful story about the abduction. What was the little girl's name?"

"Burle. Louise Burle."

"What a memory! Where was I?"

"Guillaume's stag night."

"Ah, oui. I didn't know of course. Not at the time. I was told by one of his drinking buddies after we'd been together for three years."

"Why on earth did he tell you? After three years! That's cruel. Unnecessary."

"Men are like that, cherie. Little cruelties, harsh words, thoughtlessness. I don't think they can help it. All part of that ridiculous hunter-gatherer instinct. They just say it straight. Brutish, but honest. He probably thought that by telling me of my husband's infidelity, he could have me himself!"

"Guillaume wasn't honest was he? He didn't come to you on your wedding day and confess,"

"Agreed. C'est vrai, malheureusement! But I'm not sure he even remembered. He'd been terribly drunk. He looked shocking waiting in the nave!"

Chlöe is about to reply but checks herself. She

doesn't believe a man could forget a night with a Parisienne whore, however drunk he might have been.

"So why did his friend tell you after so long? Had you asked?"

"That's two questions, cherie. Do you often do that? No, sorry, I don't mean to offend. Oh, is that the time? Pastis. Where is that lovely man of yours?"

As if on cue he appears at the kitchen door, complete with the freshly walked dog.

"Down Pantam. Get down!"

Hélène is rising, the steaming animal nuzzling her coat. He is panting and, just as a gob of saliva drips toward a very elegant boot...

"Pantam. What a charming name. And don't dribble on me you messy thing!"

"Pantam! Down! In the house! On your bed! Chlöe wanted to call him Bertrand."

"Why?"

"She's got a bit of a thing about a nineteenth century criminal called Bertrand."

"He wasn't really a criminal. I think he was mad. A bit touched."

"Really? What did he do?"

"Not now baby. Anyway I prefer Pantam."

With plaintive eyes the dog casts his head down and lopes into the house.

"I'm so sorry, Hélène. It'll rub off."

"Pastis? A little *Ricard*."

He has somehow taken the dog in hand, fetched a pastis (with ice!) *and* changed from muddied boots to trainers.

"Merci. What a marvel he is, cherie."

And Chlöe feels a familiar tightening in her chest. Perhaps, he *is* a marvel. Does she deserve marvels?

"I was just telling your lovely wife what bastards men can be."

"But, we're not mar..."

"Well, you know what I mean."

"You'll join us for an apéritif?"

"Bien sûr but am I interrupting?"

And she loves him again. Polite, attentive. A bastard? She looks at him carefully, brow furrowing.

"What's up, baby?"

"Oh! 'Baby.' How lovely. Do you always call each other 'baby'? I shouldn't ask. None of my business."

"Do we need any eggs or milk?"

"Both. Et legumes."

"The veg man is coming today."

"Oh yeah. Forgot. We could do with some cashews to go with the pastis too. Oh, pastis!"

"Desolée. I've finished your lovely *Ricard*."

"Don't worry Hélène. It's why God created water. I won't be long."

And he kisses Chlöe on the forehead. Hélène begins to rise but he leans forward and kisses her first on the left and then the right cheek. Reaching into his pocket to check for notes he walks away. They hear the front door close.

"What was all that about?"

"What?"

"You know. You must have been gassing for an hour. A three pastis hour at that!"

"It – she – was fascinating."

"Tell me about it while I make dinner."

She follows him into the kitchen, loathe to leave the little table in their courtyard, but she already knows him as a creature of habit; a man who seems calm but needs to be on the go all the time unless exhausted by their love-making. She leans back against the dresser watching him work; sharpening the fish knife. 'How can he bear to do it that way round with the blade drawn fast and efficiently toward his left hand holding the steel?'

He lays the knife down and begins to de-scale the fish; a saupe. As he delights in telling her, it is half the price of grey mullet, itself half the price of red. The fish is meaty too, a steely grey. But it first needs de-scaling with a clever studded implement bought for the task. Then the gutting, de-finning and the rest. She thinks of poor Marie Antoinette as he severs the head and can't resist leaning over to look around his shoulder as the guts spill from the underbelly cut.

What is this macabre interest? Marie A? Bertrand? Images rise. She has hoped to see an undigested shrimp or even a tiny fish but he scoops the detritus away before she can examine it further. She knows the de-scaling sometimes irritates him as finger nail sized jewels fly over the chopping board. She knows too that they can be a real pain to clean off as they adhere to the wood just as they had seamlessly stuck to the fish itself before being scraped away. He drops the head and fins into a pan and turns to the main task. Filleting saupe isn't as straightforward as the fishmonger makes it look. For the red-faced man behind the iced slab at the shop a fast downward slash away from the head on each side and voilà! Two sizeable fillets.

She has noticed that he prefers a more careful approach inserting the blade into the flesh by the dorsal bone. "Dorsal!" he had said. "That's good!" "Well even I know it's not called a backbone, Mister!" Then he slices away from the bone, gently negotiating the blade's path across the ribs to the underbelly now lying flayed on the board. The process repeated, both fillets are placed on a plate while the remaining bones are added to the pan. Leek, carrots, fennel and whatever herbs he has foraged join the mix along with a litre of water and voilà! Ten minutes of hard boiling later the stock is allowed to steep until deemed ready.

"It's fish tonight, then."

"No! Yeah. Bien sûr. Fancy Thai rice with it? I'll do it in the stock."

"Lovely."

"Go on then."

"What?"

"What did Hélène have to say?"

Sipping her pastis and eyeing his gently swaying hips (a habit since a chiropractor – a fellow commuter he had struck up a Sudoku conversation with - had said it was good for the posture), Chlöe quietly begins,

"I don't think she's very happy."

"And?"

"Guillaume's such a prick!"

"Rich prick though, baby."

"Don't be clever! Rich pricks are still pricks! He's on a dating web-site. *Inter-chat!*"

"Putain! But he must be seventy!"

"And married."

"And married."

"He's not the first, honey. For all we know, half of Giverny visits *Inter-chat*. Cuts her up though."

"How long?"

"What?"

"How long's he been doing it?"

"Years. Well not years on the web obviously but now in between affairs. Or during affairs for all I know. Does it matter?"

"I just wondered why she stays. Why he does it."

"It started on his wedding day!"

"But that's long before the web. What was it? Forty years ago?"

"Not the dating. He fucked another woman. On his wedding day. Well, during the stag do. In Paris!"

"Christ! Did they marry there?"

"No, Evreux. But he went there for his stag night the night before. Says he can't remember anything about it. He was so drunk."

"Does that make it better?"

Chlöe pauses. Does it make it better? What if she

couldn't remember something terrible? But she can … and drags herself back to the present.

"Hélène says once she found out the best day of her life turned to the worst. Just like that!"

"Quel surprise! Had it been the best?"

"How do you mean?"

"Well weddings are always meant to be the best day of your life aren't they? But think of all the pfaff and preparation. Getting your hair just so, making sure the bridesmaids don't get too drunk. All that. I bet half the people who get married are regretting it before they walk up the aisle! Probably too late to back out. And if he was that pissed she'd have smelled the booze on him. It's hot in here. Let's go outside."

"Ok, baby. Where were we? Oh yeah, you would think she'd have smelled the booze, wouldn't you? She was probably too wrapped up with getting the day right in other ways, like you say. It's hard to imagine her backing out. Anyway, she didn't really talk about that. It was mostly about all his years of screwing around and now the *Inter-chat* stuff."

He doesn't reply. He too has visited *Inter-chat.* A message arrived as spam and, like a flame-drawn moth he had clicked on. Not just the once either. But enough times to know that calling it a dating site was, at best, imaginative.

"Apparently most of the guys on these sites are twice the age of the women. Hélène says the women look like they've had their photos taken by a professional photographer."

"I know...They do."

"How do yo...? Comment..?"

"Look at that!"

"I've seen them, baby."

"What?"

"The swallows and the martins – les hirondelles. Fantastic! And the swifts, always so high. Anyway, Mister. The dating site!"

"Better class of fly up there. More bugs on an evening like this. Isn't it lovely the way we do this?"

"What?"

"Point things out to each other. Kind of, I don't know..."

"Shares the moment?"

"Exactement."

"There's a sadness though."

"Here we go, you and your balancing ideas..."

"What do you mean?"

"It's like it's hard for you to stay with something positive."

"That's not fair. Is it?"

"Often. C'mon, what sadness can here be in us enjoying swallows and talking about the moment?"

"I...I don't..."

"Baby!"

"Ok, it's just that sometime in the future ... if we're not together... One of us will look at swallows..."

"Or stars."

"Trees, pictures by Monet, dogs like Pantam..."

"Dogs like Pantam?"

"Whatever. We'll see these things and feel sad. Like there's a hole deep inside."

"Hmmm. One solution then."

"Which is?"

"We never split up and we die together!"

"You can't know when you're going to die, Mister. Or, maybe you can ... "

XXV

"It's not all brutality my friend."

"Life?"

"War."

"It feels fairly brutal to me. Or unfairly."

"Unfair?" Pourquoi?"

"Most of these men haven't asked to be here. They don't want to be running scared every day. Death around every corner!"

"Hardly every corner. Until last night, we hadn't seen hide nor hair of any opposition for weeks. It's getting boring."

"But that's worse Gaston. Bored, happy to find some food and the.."

"Then?"

"Some fool charge at men we take to be the enemy who are minding their own business out hunting or setting camp."

"Take to be...?"

But Gaston knows that Jerome speaks the truth. The evening before they had surprised a group of eight men settling down to a meagre supper of rabbit and what looked suspiciously like roasted dog. A cry of, "Charge," had gone up and he had found himself automatically running at a bare-chested fellow clutching some meat. He just had time to appreciate the man's muscularity when a cross-bow bolt had zipped past his ear and torn a gaping hole in the man's throat. He had dropped to his knees, a look of surprise on his face and, still holding fast to his supper, pitched forward. The other men had struggled to their feet but it was over in seconds.

Two more had died before drawing blades and lay sprawled across each other. A fourth, fair-haired, no more than fifteen years of age, had managed to stand boldly in front of his fate before taking a swinging axe full in his chest. As the blood gushed from the terrible wound a bolt had struck his temple and, as surprised as his fallen comrades, he had dropped silently to the ground. The others were surrounded and gave up all resistance. They had been dragged off into the trees, their screams for mercy soon cut short.

Jerome had been silent over a breakfast that was quite definitely dog. Gaston had sought to reassure him with his words about brutality.

"What do you mean? 'Take to be' the enemy?"

"What?"

"You said we take them to be the enemy."

"Well, we just do what we're told don't we? Those men last night could have been anyone!"

"Anyone with swords?"

"But we couldn't see their blades could we? Not until they stood up!"

"What would you rather? That we march up and say, 'Friend or foe?'?"

"It would be a start!"

"And if they were foe?"

"They'd have stood more of a chance."

"A chance! Merde! It's not a game my friend!"

"Well, what if they had turned out to be friends?"

"Then only one dead. The first would have got his."

"And him because you were charging at him like a bull!"

"It wasn't me that killed him. It was a crossbowman!"

"I know. I know. I'm just tired of all this killing. I wish..."

"What?"

"I wish I hadn't joined. I could be..."

But where could he be? Jerome had willingly gone to war. He hadn't been seized like so many and forced to join the butchery. Perhaps Auguste had been right, his son's escapade a pointless sacrifice. Thoughtfully, he chews on the meat; a curious taste, not gamey, yet not like the mutton so familiar to him.

"How's the dog?"

"Strange. It's like..."

"Dog?"

That was it! Jerome retches. The meat has little taste but there is something horribly canine about the smell. He can almost imagine... He retches again.

"Here! Don't waste it! Pass that leg over!"

Jerome hands the rapidly cooling haunch to Gaston who tears at the meat with his teeth, wiping his mouth with the back of a sleeve as he swallows.

Jerome's reverie returns. What if he hadn't volunteered? Could he have stayed knowing that Pierre and Marie were... Marie! Always Marie!

She stands swaying, her small breasts pushed against the cloth of Pierre's shirt, a shirt she has borrowed as protection from today's burning sun. It is too big for her, far too big, but it protects her shoulders from the rays and allows freedom of movement in the wheat. She scythes slowly and thoughtfully, a right to left sweep that cuts evenly. Not far behind another bundles the precious crop into sheaves. She knows they will rest soon and old Pascal will draw his cart alongside so yet another labourer can load it with the harvest.

She no longer enjoys the work, sometimes wondering if she ever did. It had seemed so exciting a few years back. Being allowed to use her father's scythe for the first time had been a kind of initiation. Sharpening it a real pleasure. But this was what women did, what their lives were for. Labour and babies. It had never seemed romantic to her. To bear children, labour in the fields or in the byre, taking time to prepare supper for a man's home-coming. Sharpening the scythe had been a slight adventure, her father patiently demonstrating how to draw the stone along the blade to give a fine edge.

But the adventure had palled. It is more like drudgery now, sun-kissed drudgery admittedly but a seasonal labour without end. She still thinks of mother-hood. Thanks to Pierre she knows that some things adults do are, almost, liberating; at least for a moment. She strokes the shirt, still thoughtful, a little sadder now. A face drifts into view, fair-haired, a handsome face. A man who habitually runs his hands through his hair. A man who ... She wipes away a tear.

Jerome runs his hands through his hair. They are greasy with dog meat. He can't help but notice how his hair suddenly smells, smells of dog!

"Come on then. Let's be havin' yer! Time to move."

He doesn't recognise the voice, a voice of authority. "Another fool to lead us," as Gaston might say. Thoughts of Marie recede as he stands to get a better view of the speaker. The man is tall, almost as tall as Gaston. He has a fine leather jerkin studded with metal, a belt round his waist complete with a scabbard from which juts the sword hilt, leather bound again and topped with a double pommel. This man looks like he knows what he is about; at least in the world of killing other men.

"Manseau!"

The man turns at his name being called and strides towards his commander. As he does, he sweeps his hand through his hair. It is long, jet-black and clean! Jerome finds himself admiring him despite himself. This man has found the time to wash his hair.

"He's pretty."

"Gaston! Where have you been?"

"Went for a piss and I get back and you're all dewy-eyed over Monsieur Leather-Britches!"

"Dewy... I'm not! I was just wondering how he'd found time to wash his hair."

"Found time ... Give you are hard-on did he?"

"No! Just seems odd."

"Nothing odd about it. Some of these regulars get up to all sorts of things while the rest of us are grubbing around for something to eat. Especially the ones in charge. You should see the fucking knights. Servants, men to strap their armour on, buff their shields, sharpen their blades. They wear silk gambesons under the cuirass. Silk! Grooms for the horses. Christ! The horses are better treated than us!"

Pierre is deep in thought. He draws the brush along the flank of Auguste's cart-horse with slow, patient strokes. Despite the heat, the beast is barely sweating. Despite the heat and a morning hauling great tranches of felled saplings from the copse. They stand together, man and horse, in Auguste's byre. A byre where ... even as he smiles with the memory, a familiar voice comes from the door-way,

"Pierre. Pee-pee. Tu veux manger?"

She stands in his shirt, bread and cheese held out for him. The shirt reaches to just above her knees, the calves strong, tanned.

"Oui. Merci, Marie. Merci."

She walks toward him, a swaying walk that stirs him; despite, or perhaps because of, the heat. Her heat.

"You look lovely."

"Merci."

"I love you wearing my shirt!"

"I like it too. It smells of you, lover. Come on, have some bread."

They sit in the open door-way, a slight breeze

stirring the air in the byre. As she moves to reach for the bread, he catches a glimpse, just a glimpse … the stirring is more insistent.

"I love your cunt. Ta chatte!"

"I know lover. But we don't have time. See me later!"

"What do you mean? 'Get up to things'?"

"Who? What?"

"Leather-Britches and the others. You said they get up to things while we're grubbing around."

"Ah! That. Haven't you noticed they never kip down with us? They're always on higher ground. Some of the buggers even have tents!"

"So?"

"So, what do you think goes on when they're safely under cover?"

"Planning the next day's advance?"

"Pla... Ha! Does this feel like it's planned? We just walk north or west all the time, sometimes north-west. It doesn't take much planning to walk! No, my friend, they're eating, bathing, playing cards. Probably getting a bit too!"

"Getting a bit?"

"Fucking, Jerome. Fucking!"

"Fucking! Who are they going to find to fuck out here?"

Gaston looks at his friend and smiles,

"Do I have to spell it out? Again?"

"No. Oh!"

"Serfs will do anything for some extra food or the promise of a better job."

"Better job?"

"Haven't you noticed? There's a pecking order. Personal servants, sword-sharpeners, dressers."

"Dressers?"

"Well, not for the likes of Manseau. But for the knights. Bien sûr. They can't put that lot on without help. And moving up the pecking order means more chance of eating better food, getting a good night's sleep. It's the simple things."

"And the hair? Do you think Manseau has a serf to wash his hair?"

"Wash my hair lover."

"Now?"

"Si tu plais."

"But..."

"Oh come on. I'm all sweaty now. And the floor's all dusty. I've got straw in my hair. I must look a mess!"

"You look beautiful."

The 'later' hadn't been much later at all. Bread and cheese forgotten, Marie had only feigned resistance as Pierre had tugged his shirt over her head and fastened his lips around an exposed nipple to probe and suck. Their love-making had been fierce, Pierre grasping her hips and pulling hard to press deeper. Auguste's cart-horse had been indifferent (or was he feigning?), chewing systematically on the hay from a sack which lay, mysteriously opened, not three paces from the writing couple.

"Merci. But I can't go back to the field like this. I look like ...!"

"Hmmm... Don't go away."

"I won't. Where...?"

Pierre has twisted to his feet and is heading for the back of the byre. Moments later he returns holding a leather bucket by its strap as water spills to the dusty floor.

"That's the horse's water!"

"So? It's not cold."

As she bends her head to the cooling water he starts to gently splash it around her fore-head, drawing handfuls of hair through the make-shift basin.

"Better?"

"Lovely."

Many, many leagues away a fair-haired man is learning about life for those in charge.

"My mum and dad definitely did. Still does in his case!"

"Work themselves into the ground?"

"Absolutely. It's like they always have to move on to bigger, better, more modern."

"More modern what?"

"Houses, cars. More toilets, bedrooms, more gadgets. It's a bourgeois thing. They're slaves to houses and cars. Or maybe slaves to the idea that bigger means better. I don't know."

"What it's all about?"

"They're not unique. They've just bought into the

whole thing of living in the biggest house they can afford when they die."

"They'll probably die in hospital, anyway. But they could make it easier."

"How?"

"They book into a fabulous hotel for two nights. Chandeliers, leather chairs, whatever."

"Then?"

"They kill themselves surrounded by the trappings of success! Voilà!"

They are walking towards the brasserie, Pantam, loping along on the newly bought extensible leash ("He'll throttle himself!" from Chlöe. He hadn't – so far). The conversation about workaholism had started the moment he had plonked himself down at the kitchen table after the evening commute. About to suggest a bath complete with pastis, she had, prompted by Pantam, urged him to go instead to Raymonde's. He had needed little encouragement and their talk had continued for a few minutes before her suicide idea brought him to a halt, half smiling, half grimacing, lost in admiration at her logic. His musing comes to a sudden end, the mood gone in an instant.

"What's going on?"

"Where?"

"Behind you!"

He turns, stares, any hopes of a quiet chat shattered as quickly as his contemplation of Chlöe. A police van

169

and two cars, Peugeots, are blocking one of the routes into the square. One has stopped so close to the corner doorway to the bar any exit is impossible. People he doesn't recognise are standing outside the Tabac next door. Not the Tabac he uses he is vaguely pleased to note. Two, tall and – inevitably – elegant women watch the developing drama as a gendarme somehow squeezes from the bar doorway. He hauls a half dressed man behind him. The man swears as his head hits first the door frame and then a car wing mirror. His body, bare to the waist, is covered in tattoos. He is muscley, a hard torso that can only be the result of too little food and too much exercise. He glances at Chlöe who is also staring at the victim with a mixture of pity and ... is that admiration?

"Nice body."

"Shame about the tattoos. And the fact he's being arrested!"

Before he can continue, he sees the man pitched head-long to the ground. Chlöe shudders, flinching in sympathy. The man seems about to shout but thinks better of it as the gendarme hauls him to his feet and thumps on the side of the police van. The rear doors swing open and a second gendarme springs out.

The first gendarme is of average build, sweating profusely at the effort involved in keeping tight hold on his live cargo. But the man who emerges from the van resembles a hippo. A huge head, hands like hams and he seems to have no neck. Absurdly, he sports a Chaplinesque moustache. Or perhaps Hitleresque?

Manoeuvring out of the van his cap slips off to reveal a bald head, the baldness of age not fashion. He looks well past retirement age. Pulling his new charge to his feet, he unceremoniously pushes him inside the van. Another clash of door and head; another curse. A gendarme's cap comes flying out as the two doors are slammed shut. Almost immediately a drumming is heard from within, a slow rhythm, fast building to a rat-a-tat-tat of blows and a fusillade of battering which stops as quickly as it had begun. Only to start again after a moment's respite. Slow at first, faster. Is this desperation?

"Maybe the poor guy needs a pee."

"Eh?"

"Maybe they clobbered him before he had a chance to take a piss!"

"You reckon? Maybe he's just pissed off they're busting him."

"How do you know?"

"Well I would be, wouldn't you? It's turning into a circus!"

A crowd is gathering at the Tabac. The doors to the bar are again closed with no sign of further life from within. The saloon lights illuminate nothing, revealing no movement. He wonders where the other gendarmes are. The lack of anything much to watch hasn't deterred the growing crowd of on-lookers. Occasionally one points at the van, a silent rebuke against the angry tattoo that still comes; less passionately now. Chlöe thinks she can see Hélène in the throng. Her height gives her the best view of the unfolding scene. Now two gendarmes emerge from the bar. They are laughing, the taller man banging his fist on the police car roof as he squeezes past. Chlöe can just hear his cry of:

"Move this fucking vehicle. Merde!"

"Charming! He sounds mighty pissed off."

"What do you think's been happening?"

"I dun … Oh Lord, Hélène's seen us!"

Sure enough the vision in the hat is striding towards them.

"Cou-cou. Cheries! Cheries! C'est moi."

"Hello Hélène. What have you been up to?"

"What have I…?"

"All these police!"

"All these…? Oh, you silly boy. I see. They're nothing to do with me. Some sort of raid I think."

"Drugs?"

"Unreturned library books!"

He smiles at Hélène's witticism. The spectacle of something actually happening in the square seems to have put her in a good mood.

"I didn't know Giverny had any drug dealers."

"Come on, it's a modern town. It's got its fair share. A bit obvious though isn't it?"

"What?"

"The old bar on the square. Like some scene from a 'sixties film."

"Handy for the Tabac though."

Again Hélène's remark makes him grin. Across the square what had looked to be a major theatrical production seems to have settled into a one-Act play. The van, complete with the drumming captive has pulled away from the kerb allowing one of the two police cars to reverse from the bar door-way. As he watches, yet another gendarme steps out of the bar and, smiling a greeting at the crowd, strides toward the throng at the Tabac. He can just hear,

"Bonsoir, mes amis. Fun's over. No more show today. Move on please, move on."

XXVI

"Look at them! Anyone would think those boy-soldiers were at home after a day in the fields!"

Gaston is smiling benignly. Anyone under fifteen is now a "boy-soldier" for Gaston. They rush back and forth along the river bank. The Epte is in full flood, swollen by melting snow, the ground to either side hard with winter frost. The game, such as it is, is a team contest though the players are all dressed the same making the two teams indistinguishable. A roughly spherical globe of leather makes its way from hand to hand, foot to foot, first moving to left and then, from the two observers' vantage point, to right.

Jerome struggles to fathom the purpose of the game. As he watches, the leather globe disappears under a mound of heaving bodies and then spins out. It is ignored completely as a full-scale fight develops. Cries of encouragement and pain mix in equal measure and a high-pitched yell of "No gouging!" rents the air. The mêlée disperses and a fleet-footed lad with legs bare beneath his tunic spins away and picks up the ball. He is away! Not for long. Felled by a clod of mud hurled from the throng he drops to his knees, the ball spinning from his hands and bobbling to a stop perilously close to the fast flowing Epte.

"Is that fair?"

"Is that f...? Jerome, Jerome. Is anything?"

"Why is it men do this? Pourquoi?"

"Do what?"

"Watch a bunch of kids kicking a ball around."

"I don... Hey, ref! Foul!"

They had meant to walk the dog. Despite the rain, the appeal of a morning in bed with *Le Monde* and each other. Despite the promise of ... But today is the last day before her four days in Rouen. Worse, as far as he is concerned, four days in a log cabin with her boss. Her boss! His reaction at the news had been from Chlöe's point of view, all too predictable.

"Christ! A log cabin at *Centre Parcs*. Couldn't you have just booked separate hotel rooms?"

"No baby, you know what Marcel's like. Mean! The cabin's cheaper. Anyway the art fair is at *Centre Parcs*. I quite like it. There's no cars, lots of places to jog. There's a big pool at this one. Heated!"

"And a boss! I bet he'll be on heat too!"

"We'll have separate rooms!"

"Sep...! I wonder how long that'll last!"

"Come on, mister. I'm not going to shag him!"

"Not going to...? But you'll eat together, chat over breakfast. You'll have to shower!"

"But not together, lovely. What do you want me to do? Say, 'No, sorry, my boyfriend gets jealous.'?"

"Yes!. No. Non! Of course not but I fucking hate it when you go away. Especially with Monsieur Tightarse!"

A truce had been called, two weeks had gone by and now the trip loomed before them. Hence the walk with Pantam; their last chance to walk him à deux for five days. The rain has neither deterred them nor the youngsters playing football on the school fields. The drizzle is insistent, often gusted to sheets by the wind. He stands transfixed as the lads shunt the ball upfield. He is remembering, remembering...

XXVII

They have been walking since dawn. A long, straggling line of men four, sometimes five, more-or-less abreast. There is little talk, no cheer and no shade from the beating sun. They have passed only one village, the huts long since deserted, a barn with a collapsed thatch and no sign of life; not even the occasional crow to pick at carrion. There is no carrion. Every now and then a halt is called and the men gratefully slump to the ground or relieve themselves in the nearest ditch before sitting alongside the others.

All the ditches have been dry, the one small river they have passed, barely a stream now. The water had been still, covered in an uninviting green weed that had provoked Jerome to warn Gaston against filling his flask. Somewhere behind trail the regular men, behind them the crossbow-men and behind them, the knights and their entourage. Jerome now knows the knights are stipendiaries, each paid a regular wage for their service.

Each rest stop has lasted longer, getting back on his feet has, for Jerome, been more and more of a trial. Now, finally, Manseau has called a longer break.

"Get something to eat men."

"Something to eat! The man's a fucking jester! I'll be chewing on my belt next!"

Manseau has walked quickly away as the hungry men sit or sprawl on the parched ground.

"How's that hand of yours my friend?"

"Throbs a fair bit but I'm used to it. My guts are rumbling fit to bust though!"

"Perhaps we should follow Leather-Britches. I bet he's got a little something stashed away."

"I'm sure he has but it'll only lead to trouble."

"Not with friends in high places."

"Ha! Since when do you have friends in high places?"

"Since I did a certain dresser a favour."

"Dresser?"

"A serf of one of the knights."

"Which knight?"

"Which kni...! How the fuck do I know? I was with his dresser, didn't even see the bloody knight. Too dark."

"Too dar... What were you up to?"

"I was ... introducing his dresser to man-hood."

"Yours?"

"And his. Lovely body. Thin, soft ha..."

"Je comprends Gaston. I don't need the details!"

"It was his first time. Lovely."

"How old? No, don't tell me."

"I don't know. Thirteen, fourteen. Old enough. More to the point he said we can go back for some food when we get the chance."

"Back! It would take us an hour and we'll be on the move again by then."

Despite himself, Jerome stands. Soon he is padding alongside a grinning Gaston. The pair pass dozens of prostrate forms. Few are eating, most are sleeping in the late morning heat. They pass a group of crossbow carriers. Two argue, their voices echoing behind Gaston and Jerome as they press forward. Soon Jerome sees a series of tents, high-sided, banners drooping dully in the wind-less air. They are pitched in a field to the left, sounds of merriment coming from the two closest. Gaston turns and, without altering his pace, strides toward the nearest awning. Jerome stares. There, on a spit the length of Gaston, is a young boar roasting in the heat from a blazing fire.

"I told you the knights don't go hungry!"

"I know. But where...?"

"What they don't bring by cart they kill. Probably borrow a few crossbow-men for the morning!"

"While we're half starved and slogging along in the sun!"

Gaston stops. He looks at Jerome as a bear might observe a wounded cub.

"You have a lot to learn my friend. Come on. Let's find my even younger friend."

They reluctantly walk past the haunting smells of cooking meat and on to a smaller tent where, outside the entrance, two chargers are pawing at the ground. Almost immediately a smiling boy emerges. He looks excitedly at Gaston, fear and something almost welcoming in his eyes. Without hesitating, Gaston strides up to him and lifts him off the ground before crushing him in his great arms.

"Gaston! Non! Someone will see."

"Come on boy. Give me a kiss!"

Gaston drops the squirming lad to his feet. Jerome

can see he is blushing now, all trace of fear gone.

"Can I get you something to eat?"

"Can you...? Music to our ears eh, Jerome? Oh, manners! May I introduce my companion Jerome."

"Bonjour Monsieur. Ça va? What's wrong with your hand?"

"Oui, ça va. It's a woun... it's nothing."

"Looks like more than nothing to me. Anyway, this way."

"Marcel!"

The roar startles all three of them as they are about to enter the tent. The dresser suddenly looks pale. Fear returns.

"It's my master. He'll be wanting me to dress him."

"Now? But no-one's going anywhere yet. You haven't eaten. *We* haven't eaten and I'm sure Jerome's going to faint unless he gets some of that sanglier inside of him."

Jerome looks around but there is no sign of the knight. The cry comes again, louder this time,

"Marcel! Get your lazy arse in here!"

There is a side entrance to the larger tent Jerome hadn't seen. The flap of is open. Again, the voice comes from inside.

"Desolée. I must go or he'll use Phillipe and that'll be the end of me!"

"Not so fast Marcel. Is your name Marcel? You didn't say. Jerome and me can wait another few minutes. We'll come and watch. Come on Jerome, this should be an education!"

"You can't come inside! He'll kill me!"

"Let him try! Don't worry, we'll stand outside. Just leave the flap open."

Marcel disappears into the tent. By cautious manoeuvring Jerome and Gaston are able, unseen, to peer inside. Jerome hasn't expected a running commentary from Gaston but as the two men watch the dressing ritual the throbbing from his hand subsides. Even the hunger pangs abate a little.

For all his shouting and bluster, the knight is no taller than Jerome and not much taller than Marcel who busies himself just out of view. The knight's body, at least what can be seen through various undergarments, is pallid. Only his face and hands are tanned. The hands are elegant; they look barely strong enough to grip reins, let alone control a horse *and* grasp a sword or axe. The face is unmarked, not particularly handsome, but the face of a man who expects to be obeyed. A man of, perhaps, twenty-five. Old enough to command, old enough to die. Young and wealthy enough to think the remorseless fighting an adventure.

Just as Gaston had suggested, he wears a silken gambeson and stands, a picture of hauteur and vulnerability, awaiting Marcel's ministrations. Gaston begins his whispered commentary as Marcel's arm appears, a jacket grasped in his outstretched hand. The knight grunts and takes the jacket swinging it smoothly round his shoulders before plunging one arm down through a sleeve.

"His pourpoint. Goes under the armour. Look, here comes the breast plate. Fucking heavy; iron. Rather him than me!"

Marcel steps into their line of vision momentarily blocking the spectacle though he is clearly wrestling with the breastplate. By the time he steps away both he and the knight are sweating. The knight glowers at him.

"Re-tie the neck strap. No! Don't bother, I'll do it. Get the back plates."

Marcel steps out of view only to immediately return holding three iron plates, each connected to the other by short leather straps.

"This is going to be complicated. I hope our new friend can tie knots!"

This time Marcel works faster. Soon the knight, still with no britches, stands in full view, the body armour all in place, poitrine and back plates held by a series of leather ties.

"Looks like a trussed fucking chicken! Not so keen on the legs though. Not much meat on them. Like the dog! It's a wonder he can stand on those thin pins! Oh, here we go!"

A swirl of black from the right, a hand, faster than Gaston can quite register is thrust into the air, and a pair of leather breeches are grasped.

"Christ! He may be a little squirt but he can move! Not at his most elegant now though, eh?"

The knight, weighed down by the plate armour is struggling to don the breeches. He curses as his pale legs disappear into the dark leather. One more haul past genitals that Gaston spies and ignores, a grin of triumph on his face, and the breeches are in place.

"He might be strong but his balls are like walnuts, mon ami!"

"Marcel. Mes cuisses!"

The thigh protectors appear on command and the knight straps them on. Moments later greaves, of cuir bouilli, are handed to him and he bends to buckle them on as well. Now he stands, barefoot.

"Is this going to take much longer? I can smell the wild boar. I bet the bastards are tucking in!"

"Are you not entertained? Look. Our peacock is almost there!"

Marcel reappears and hands the knight, now beginning to look like a knight, two round plates, each burnished, each with leather straps attached. Gaston whispers that these are called poleyns. The knight, moving faster now, buckles the plates to the cuisses. Again Marcel steps out of view to the side. Again he returns, this time with two more-or-less identical metal sleeves which he straps around the knight's proffered fore-arms. A whisper from Gaston,

"The vambraces. Some of the archers use them. Handy. Stops their arms getting shredded every time they let fly. Hello, there's more yet."

This time Marcel is carrying sleeves broader than the vambraces. They are of plate. The knight stands patiently as his serf attaches these rerebraces to the vambraces on the forearms. The knight says something to Marcel who makes a show of tightening various buckles and straps before standing clear. Jerome can just hear,

"Not bad boy. You're getting better. Now, get me the gorget. I can do without an arrow in the throat!"

Marcel takes longer now; sounds of metal on metal

come from within as he searches for the neck-plate. A triumphant cry and his arm can be seen holding out two curved pieces of metal about as wide as his hand and again joined by leather. The knight takes the gorget and, closing the plates around his neck, knots the straps. Now he is almost entirely covered; body, thighs, calves, knees, fore-arms, upper-arms and throat are all encased in either leather or metal.

"How much longer? I'm beyond hungry now."

"Shhh..my friend. Only the sabatons and helmet to go. Oh, and the gauntlets of course. I doubt if he'll put the helmet or gauntlets on in this heat."

"What are sabatons?"

"Look."

Marcel is kneeling at the knight's feet wrestling with a complicated series of riveted plates which he eventually managers to secure to the knight's raised left foot. Slamming the sabaton to the ground, the knight raises the other leg, almost kneeing Marcel with a burnished poleyn. Marcel clumsily straps the second sabaton to the knight's right foot, stands and, head lowered, backs away, out of view, The knight walks, awkwardly at first, then with a more confident if ungainly gait through the tent flap into the glare of the sun.

Behind him appears another servant carrying metal-studded gloves and a helmet, burnished like a mirror, complete with riveted visor. The two walk away from Gaston and Jerome without noticing either.

"Poor sod's going to get heat-stroke in that little lot today."

"Don't 'poor sod' him! Save your sympathy. Have you any idea what all that bloody armour is worth! He'll keep clear of any fighting unless we lay siege somewhere. No, my friend, don't you worry about Monsieur Shiny Helmet. He looks more suited to tournaments than actually fighting. Time to eat?"

"I... Oh God, the boar's been taken off the spit! How long have we been watching?"

The sun is at its zenith as Jerome and Gaston look, forlornly, at the fire's embers. The meat has indeed gone; only a faint smell remains as spilt fat spits and crackles.

"That group on the slope. Why do they wear blue and white?"

Jerome points at some fifty-plus men standing as if awaiting battle orders. They are, to a man, wearing blue jerkins and each has a white bandana around his forehead. Most stand easy, a few gaze toward the chateau. All are armed. Swords mostly, the leather scabbards streaked with white diagonals. Gaston doesn't look up. He adjusts his crotch.

"Crème de la crème, my boy. Crème de la crème."

"Meaning?"

"Meaning, they're in blue so we won't kill our own when it gets rough. You can recognize them easily, see. Being blue and white."

"But how are we to make out the rest of us. We all look the same."

"Same as them on the other side too."

"That's what I mean! Up close we won't know them from us!"

"I don't think that much matters to our captains boy. As long as the enemy's dead out-number ours by sun-down that's good enough. No doubt that lot in the fortresse will have an elite corps too to even things up. Hey up! Gate's opening. What did I tell you?"

Jerome faces the fortress. He hears his own "Uhh" of surprise. Perhaps a hundred men stride out from the gate to fan out and stand line abreast. There are a dozen with cross-bows and many more with vicious looking short axes. He knows the fearsome damage these can do when hurled. The men are in red. From head to foot. Like a red tongue slinking from a dragon's maw they spread out before him.

She moves slowly now, hips gently away. There is promise here; the promise to fulfil, to love, to offer herself spread-eagled under her man. Her tongue snakes from barely parted lips and she raises her arm above her head, the elbow crooked. The hand first strokes then tugs at her hair dragging her head to one side. This then is the promise of abandon. Her hair is dark, but not as dark as that revealed by her raised arm. Further down, the raven curls that only one man here shall see are covered by the frayed ends of a man's tunic. She strokes her right arm down her side, across her stomach and down, down....

"Do you sing?"

"What, when...?"

"Do you sing? You know, 'La la la,' in the shower, wherever?"

"Have you heard me sing?"

"Never. That's why I wondered. You have that kind of tuneless whistle though, sometimes."

"Thanks! Did once."

"Really? In public?"

"Don't look so shocked, Mister. I was pulled up on stage at some club at three in the morning. Not that far from where we met, actually."

"Were you drunk?"

"Are you kidding? Three in the morning in a club in Montmartre. *Everyone* was drunk. I'm sure the band thought I was someone else! They were all out of it too. I only knew one song all the way through."

"Which was?"

"Etta James. *I'd rather Go Blind.*"

"How did it go?"

"The song?"

"No, I know the song. The performance."

"We took a while to find the right key. The pianist started in E flat. Way too low for me. There was a huddle among the band. Then the drummer of all people said something about A and B minor. Off we went. I don't remember much about it but I love the song. I sang it pretty much motionless."

Chlöe stands and pads towards him. She sways her hips and raises a hand to her hair which she tugs, pulling her head to one side. He feels himself getting excited now. In the gentlest possible way. She gazes at him as if he is the only man in the room. He is. She almost whispers,

"Something told me ... it was over ..."

Jerome lies still – very still. No leaves this time but there is a smell, sweet and sickly. The weight above him shifts; a groan, then nothing. He squints upwards and sees clouds, some grey, mostly white, scudding across a blue background. 'Sky,' he thinks, pleased that he is alive enough to at least recognize the heavens.

The blue is framed by straggling fronds. Wool? How can it be wool? Some of the fronds merge like, like... hair! It is hair! He shifts again, opens his mouth to better breathe ... it is immediately filled with a sticky gush of, of ... That taste! Blood! His? Suddenly the blue and white canopy is revealed in a blinding flash of light. Instinctively he closes his eyes against the glare.

"Come on, my lad. Let's be havin' you. On your feet Jerome. I thought you was done for!"

Jerome feels himself hauled upright. Standing unsteadily and opening his eyes, first carefully and then wide with relief he sees a familiar bulk. A bulk that guffaws and clasps him so that he feels the air forced from his aching lungs again. This smell he knows. He tenses as he feels a swelling against his stomach. Pulling away, Jerome takes in the scene. Gaston stands grinning, already idly stroking the tumescence pushing at his breeches.

Beyond Gaston, the fortress is outlined, implacable against the sky. Men are moving amongst the fallen who are mostly in russet and green but a good number in the blue and white of his elite comrades. 'Not so elite when you're dead,' he thinks. His guts tense as he spots several horses in their death agonies. This is too much: as he leans forward to retch the 'weight' is revealed. At his feet lies a man – Phillipe? Antoine? – who he vaguely recognizes. From his left eye protrudes an arrow. Blood still flows through the matted hair from another wound, the skull almost clove in two from a terrible blow. The dead man is contorted as if thrown aside like some rag doll. Gaston's work.

"You could have suffocated under him! What would you do without me, my friend?"

Concern makes Gaston choke a little on his words. Something approaching affection is here. Jerome retches again. Crushed by a fallen comrade only to be saved by a rapist! The world no longer makes sense.

"How did we do?"

"Ha! See for yourself. Lost more than two hundred, barely threatened the gate. Not our finest hour. Let's go and eat!"

As they trudge back toward the hill camp Jerome strains for memory. There is little to be found; cries, screams, "Allez," a confused babble fills him like mist. He yearns for sleep.

He is dreaming, the curse of battle for a blessed hour forgotten. It is a dream which feels familiar. The kind you can almost know to be a dream though the knowledge brings neither control nor awakening.

He and Pierre are stacking wood. This must surely have happened many times. Sawn six months before, the logs are almost dry, soon to be ready for use. The stacks are two logs deep and perhaps fifty along, as neat as might be imagined. The labour isn't hard but necessary and for that reason alone never boring. Jerome has rarely known boredom at home.

Each day brings chores and tasks. These must change with the weather. All are central to survival. If the day turns to mist or rain, some indoor work awaits; in the byre, the home, wherever necessity demands. The seasons bring only a broad predictability. Planting, of course, in early spring but if the winter has been harsh and the ground too hard, then planting will be replaced by logging, seeing to the horses ... Milking. Goats ... there is always milking. It is an unending labour which only allows for satisfaction with tasks completed, survival maintained. Planning is haphazard, the changeability of weather matched by the adaptability of the workers.

As ever, they talk of what little local news they can. As ever, they soon run out of much to say.

"Do you ever worry someone will steal our firewood?"

Pierre's sudden question brings the work to a temporary halt.

"What? Who? How?"

"Perhaps a stranger passing through."

"A stranger? Here? Passing? When was the last time

we saw a stranger?"

Jerome cradles the log he has been lifting from the cart. He grins, splutters, then laughs aloud.

"Come on. When was the last time? And your stranger would need a cart. How many people with carts from outside the village have you seen?"

"That family with the dog. The big black one. Tied to the running board."

"That must have been over two months ago. We didn't even have any logs stacked then!"

"Well the soldiers then. I've seen a dozen or more in the last week. Voilà!"

It was true. Yeomen were beginning to appear regularly, usually trudging north.

"What would soldiers do with our wood?"

"Burn it. For warmth or to cook their food. Voilà!"

Jerome restricts himself to a smile and what he hopes is an expression of sympathy. He didn't believe strangers, fighting men or not, would steal their wood. Most would be from similar villages well aware that winter fuel is almost sacred. Those he has noticed have all seemed friendly enough, intent on their purpose rather than seeking trouble. And to steal wood could presage serious trouble. To be without fuel for the winter hearth was unthinkable. The work is an annual ritual. Boughs are cut to the length of a man's arm, at first stacked in piles on the outskirts to be carted closer to the homes when drier. To steal wood would be a crime against a tradition counted in numberless generations.

"I don't think so, Pierre...I..."

The dream blurs, fades to grey, then nothing. He can feel himself being shaken. It is an unfamiliar hand and early, perhaps four o'clock; for Jerome yet another cold dawn. Vaguely, he hears some birdsong; sparrows, a distant cuckoo. They are now many, many leagues from anywhere remotely familiar. The sky is mostly grey cloud, an occasional streak of pale blue or orange appearing as brush-strokes above the horizon. He has slept fitfully after Gaston's warning that today will be a day of death.

He tries a more calming image and pictures the sloping hillsides nearer home, the wood-stacking. But, as ever, the reverie is interrupted by thoughts of Marie. And Pierre. He grimaces, sighs and tries to focus. Today is not the day for idle fantasy. Today is a day for survival. And victory. But what would such mean? As a boy he already understood that the only victory *is* survival. He runs his hands through his hair.

Around him men stir. There is a smell of fear rising from them. Except for Gaston whose lumbering snores shake his great cheeks like bellows. He scans the horizon, the cloud breaking now and he sees the outlines of their goal. The fortress again, vast, implacable. Grey stone, battlements, spires, turrets. It lies perhaps five leagues across the plain. This is Falaise. A fortified township that fell all too easily to the English and now must be re-taken. Their leaders have been here before during three or four unsuccessful assaults. Beyond, still some distance, is the sea. It is a day's ride to La Manche.

He had been stirred when told of the channel that

separated the mainland from an English king who claimed the right to France. But it hadn't been the thought of England so very near. It had been the idea of swimming. Was it *possible* to swim in salt water? Salt! As precious as gold. He had never tasted it but to swim in it! Was the water white? Could fish live in it? For Jerome, the goal has little to with taking the fortress and everything to do with swimming.

Banners can just be made out hanging listlessly in a faltering breeze. They are a distraction and he drops his gaze to take in the wider scene before him. Not far from the base of the fort there are serried ranks of English bowmen. Not, he knows, crossbow-men, but the famed longbow-men of England. It is a sedate yet fearsome spectacle and one which strikes some terror into his companions.

These men are known to bring death. Death that rains from the skies like piercing hail. There is little protection and, like most of his compatriots, he wears only a leather cap. Only the knights wear heavy helmets, far too cumbersome for foot-soldiers. In any case, he knows the knights have their own vulnerabilities. Their suits are unwieldy and though he can't imagine what it must be like to face a charging, armoured, mace-wielding assassin on horseback, he knows the target for crossbow bolts is invariably the horse. And once down, a knight cannot regain his feet or move quickly enough to avoid a well-aimed axe blow.

From left to right across the plain he can see possibly three hundred archers. Beyond and behind them there will be infantrymen and cavalry. He runs his hands through his hair. His hands are sweating. The sun is behind them and is rising fast. It is not yet truly day, barely two hours since he lay down to rest. It is warm already, but still. The quiet before the storm?

He stretches and turns to see his own force. The attackers. His company had been picked up by the main army three weeks before, the mutilated crossbow-men no longer so proud as they were told to use knives and swords instead. He has yet to fathom who are, ultimately, attackers and defenders, invaders and invaded. The kindly Pascal Manseau had tried to explain some of the background to all this madness. No king of France, but many claimants, a king of England and much of France, who wanted more. Whole regions taken, restored and taken again. Madness.

A shadow, weak but énorme is cast on the ground at his feet and he feels a different hand on his shoulder, knows it is Gaston.

"Perhaps they're finishing their breakfasts, lucky bastards!"

"Who?"

"The footmen and horsemen. They'll be in that chateau waiting for the archers to do their work."

"Are we going to attack again, then?"

"Looks that way."

Jerome cranes his neck to get a better view of the men on the slopes to his left. There are many hundreds, perhaps a thousand. Those immediately to his left are dressed like him. Leather jerkins, short hose, the occasional mail shirt, probably stolen from a horseman's corpse, and blades, mostly short and of little use except at close quarters. He knows the names of a few of these men but is mindful of another of Gaston's warnings: "Don't get too friendly, friendships are as short-lived as we must be."

Further along he can see men moving into battle formation. They are better equipped, better drilled, most fully armed, many with the studded leather boots and caps he secretly envies. Mingled amongst them are crossbow-men,; a hundred or more each with a crossbow carrier at his side. There is a flurry from a standard flashing gold and crimson at their rear. He sees it held aloft, slowly making progress through the ranks before settling at the head of the force to be waved aloft. In encouragement or mockery at the defenders he knows not.

The men on foot are forming lines, thirty men across, five or six deep. He can just hear the neighing of chargers, the occasional whinny from horses he can't quite see. The horses will be pawing the muddied ground or nuzzling their grooms as their riders await the call. They are on the Eastern slope of the second rise to his left, out of sight of the observers in the castle though they must know the cavalry is here. If a siege is what awaits it will follow a familiar routine; a slow march across the plain, a charge on foot through the storm of arrow-shafts, a wheeling away as their own cavalry ride through to face whatever force emerges from the fortress gates.

His part will depend on the success of the knights as they face the onslaught from within. The knights will be backed by the crossbow-men, their bolts bringing crippling injury to the English horses, the occasional dart piercing the thin mail at the armour joints of the enemy knights. They will probably wheel again, allowing yeomen through for sometimes vicious hand-to-hand combat and, finally, he and Gaston and the others around him now will surge toward the fort's moat and drawbridge. There may be days of such attacks.

There is a final card to play. Siege towers in place of trebuchets. Great structures of newly felled pine held fast by leather, rope and mighty iron spikes driven in by men wielding hammers the like of which he has never before seen. They are topped by wooden platforms. At a smaller fortress not far to the south he has already seen them used. He watched amazed as crossbow-men and swordsman in full view of the defenders on the battlements stood fast on the platform as the towers lumbered forward.

"Excited?"

"Excited? No, I don't think that's the word."

"Scared then?"

"Not as bad as if I was at the front."

"Ah. Well I can assure you that won't happen."

"How do you know, I might get thrown in with the real fighters!"

"Only if you live long enough! But with those boots and fingers? Ha! I don't think so. In any case, my friend, Monsieur Manseau has other plans for some of us."

"Not the towers!"

"No, not the towers. If, comme d'habitude, we get

nowhere today, he wants a few of us to get into Falaise."

"Into ... ! Why?"

"Because he doesn't know what's inside. Supplies, arms, men? For all we know it's empty."

"It doesn't look empty. Those longbow-men must have been fed and watered by someone. And Manseau said that last time there were over two hundred cavalry."

"Perhaps they left."

"Why would they leave? I thought they wanted the whole territory."

Jerome has been confused by Manseau's account of the reasons for the fighting but has settled on an analogy with the fields at home. Some are owned by neighbours, their claim going back generations. His own family is one such. Others are tithed from an unseen landlord who lives, it is rumoured, in the central fort on the Ile de la Cité, adjacent to the fabled Notre-Dame. This man, a Count, has never set foot on the fields around Jerome's home. He will know something of the local seasons but virtually nothing of the people, his tithed peasants. This isn't so different from the king across the sea who regards Caen and Falaise more rightfully his but knows nothing of local custom. Nor, Jerome has realised, does he want to know.

A cry goes up, echoed by many more. The men on foot, now spearheaded by the lone standard-bearer trudge forward. To their doom.

Jerome runs his hands through his hair. He sits quietly

with Gaston and two others. Pierre ('un autre Pierre!') and Louis. Both are thirteen. Both look terrified. Gaston has no words of comfort for them and thinks tonight they will be caught. The assault had lasted most of the morning but as the midday heat had set in it had become increasingly onerous for men and horses.

There had only been one cavalry assault quickly turning to retreat as the enemy yeomen had rushed from the gates, screaming to make their charge more fearsome. It had answered one of Manseau's questions. There were many more men within the fortress. No horses had been seen but there had been no need for a cavalry charge; the attackers had broken up in disarray at the onslaught of the defenders. Many of the attackers' horses had lain quivering and whinnying, some struggling to stand, haunches and legs pierced by arrows. True horror for Jerome. It was unbearable to think what his father, the horse-loving Auguste, would have said.

An evening truce had allowed both defenders and attackers to move amongst the fallen, taking arms, occasionally finding a wounded fellow and carrying him away from the field before piling the dead onto carts to be moved to burial or pyre. The horses were despatched, their eyes pleading with anyone bringing blade to throat, the carcass quickly butchered to give meat to both sides. Manseau is speaking:

"You know how to get in?"

"Across the moat at the second bridge and through the archway to the side of the main gate."

"Won't it be guarded?"

"I doubt it. They won't be expecting anything like this so soon. And if it is ... well, you have your knives."

"And when we're in, we just saunter around finding out what we can?"

"Sauntering's probably not the best way to stay hid. But there won't be many up until just before dawn so, who knows ... sauntering might be best. Anyone who sees you will think you belong there. You need to head for the stables."

"Where are they?"

"Not that far from the main gates. We put them there when the place was ours. You can't miss them. The stink's bad and there's shit on all the approaches. Don't slip."

Jerome turns his head in Gaston's direction. He can see Manseau wasn't joking. Gaston looks at him with no trace of a smile. Then he turns to the two younger men. Men? Even Jerome sees them as boys.

"Come on you two. Let's be havin' yer. Your knives? Sharp?"

"Oui, monsieur. Do you think we'll need them?"

"Let's hope not. We'll be back before light."

With that, Gaston hastily shifts his bulk and, nodding to Manseau, beckons to Jerome and the others to follow.

"Have you read *Justine*?"

"No. Why? Who's it by?"

"De Sade."

"Closest I've come to him is that Pasolini film."

"*Hundred Nights of Sodom*?"

"*Days*. That's the one."

"How about *The Confessions*?"

"What's this? Obscure books we should all know?"

"No, baby – keep your hair on. Hélène mentioned it at book club. Rousseau."

"Oh! Don't any of your book club lot read the moderns? You were half way through *The Wasp Factory* when you joined. What happened to that?"

"Not originally in French. They read all sorts of stuff. One suggestion was *The Second Sex*."

"*The Sec*…de Beauvoir? Hardly a rom-com is it?"

"I know. A bit heavy. But they're a lovely lot and we're not so pretentious we can't thrown in some pulp."

"Like?"

"The new Bardot biog."

"Hmmm…Not exactly *Asterix*!"

"Baby…! It's good. She's quite something. Anyway have you read Rousseau? Hélène calls him 'Dear Jean-Jacques.'"

"They're probably related. I dipped into it once at a book-store. It was a bit.."

"Honest?"

"I was going to say intense. Is it on the reading list?"

"No, but it gave me an idea."

"Give us a clue."

"He was into spanking and…"

"Yeeesss…"

"No, no. Well, maybe …The point is he wrote everything down for publication. Fears, lusts, things people would have thought weak or bad."

"Or mad?"

"Probably all three."

"Like the spanking?"

"Spanking's not mad. I'm sure lots of people are into it."

"How would we know?"

"Exactement! The spanking's just an example. He confessed everything. He was ruthlessly honest. His way of saying to his critics, 'Fuck you, you want to judge me, let's hear your dirty secrets first!'"

"You're assuming he did like spanking. Maybe he was saying it to grab the readers' attention. What's wrong?"

Chlöe sits back. Her brow is furrowed and she looks hurt.

"You're not taking me seriously."

"I am missus. I am. But authors need to come up with a gimmick to sell. Marketing, it's all about marketing."

"Like your precious Roland Kirk?"

Now it is his turn to look hurt. He runs his hands through his hair. She moves closer and strokes his arm.

"Let's not argue."

He is all too happy to agree to a truce. He's long before discovered that hurting Chlöe is worse than being hurt himself. More gently now,

"Sorry, lovely. What was your idea?"

"I don't know if you'll like it."

"Don't go all girlie on me. If I don't like it, I'll say. Try me."

"Ok, I thought we could do the same thing."

"Spanking?"

"No! Well, maybe…"

"Just kidding. You mean writing it all down don't you? About us?"

"Not just about us. About whatever we are feeling, thinking, feeling ashamed of, excited by."

"Every day?"

"Well as often as we can. You could write on the train. Give you a *Sudoku* break. You must have things you don't tell me. Jealousies, hates, loves…"

"I think you know my loves…"

"Some of them. But we could do more; fears about the future, stuff from the past…"

"What for? Pourquoi?"

"So we'd know as much as possible about each other!"

"What if we get it wrong?"

"How do you mean?"

"Well, if we remember things wrong. Or if we're in a bad mood and fill it with negative stuff coz that's the mood we happen to be in? It's pretty grim on the train. If I don't do *Sudoku* I'll just be left with feeling hacked off with sitting or standing for two hours surrounded by jerks in suits. And how could we know more about each other than we knew last night?"

'It's true!' she thought. Last night had been exhilarating, precious. They had seemed to meld –

'become one' – as he had said this morning. A moment of intensity lasting fifteen, twenty minutes. Her first orgasm had gone on and on. Way past the juddering, breath-taking climaxes as he had licked and sucked, his tongue caressing her, his lips closing around her. Way beyond the moment he had slid into her the second time, her legs splayed to take him all, the belly hairs she loved so much brushing her sex; arousing her more and more. And even past the point when he collapsed making the "funny animal noises" she found so child-like yet sensual.

He had started kissing her, on the mouth this time, and there she was again; coming, coming. Chlöe rouses herself from the reverie, wet and wanting.

"I know, it, *we* can be so lovely. But that's all animal isn't it?"

"Isn't that enough?"

"Of course. When you're here with me, like now. But when we're at work I can't see you, speak to you, touch you…"

He presses his hand to her heart.

"I'm here."

"Toujours. But I want to tell you more about me and hear … read … more about you."

"For the book-club?"

"Mon Dieu, no! For us!"

"My fears and fantasies?"

"All of them. As much as you can manage to write. I sometimes think you write me."

"You? How?"

"Like that Carol Duffy poem, 'Some nights, I dreamed he'd written me, the bed a page beneath his writer's hands.'"

He stares. This woman, this lover, *his* lover has surprised, touched and persuaded him again. He wonders if there is no end to Chlöe's ability to move him.

"You might regret it!"

"Non, je ne regrets riens!"

But they will.

XXVIII

The approach has been easy; no watchmen, no fires to show their silhouettes as they bob and weave across the last league before their goal. The basin of the moat is dry and easy to cross. They now stand pressed against the fortress wall, the stones cold and hard at their backs. Jerome can hear Gaston's breath, slow and steady at his left; to his right a mixture of grunts and intakes of breath as the younger men fight their fear. For his ears only, Gaston mutters:

"Best tell those boys to button it. I wouldn't put it past one of them to crap himself once we're inside. Still, if Manseau's right about the horse-shit, a bit more won't make any odds."

He hears Gaston chuckling to himself and looks up at the ramparts. No sign of any watchers. Easing sideways the quartet, still pressed hard to the stone, make for the doorway Manseau has told them about. It is well out of sight of the smaller of the two main gates. Surely it is guarded? Jerome hears an exclamation from Gaston. Surprise? Frustration?

"Merde! The door's open. What are they up to? Quiet now!"

Jerome follows Gaston as the big man steps away from the wall. Glancing to left and right he turns and disappears from view. Jerome signals to his companions and then himself passes through the doorway. The gate is about Gaston's height and one and a half times his width; oak, studded and hinged with iron. As Gaston has said, it stands open. No light comes from the courtyard within. No light, no sound, no armed ambushers ... The four start to move across the cobbled yard scarcely able to believe their luck.

"Think our luck'll hold?"

"Shhh...!"

And then: "Think it'll be a long 'un?"

"What?"

"Siege."

"Christ, can you move your arse. I want a piss. This is no time to chat! And, yes, I do think it'll be long. Last one was bloody months. They only gave up because they ran out of horse meat!"

"Hey you! Close that fucking gate!"

Two men have emerged from a doorway, an entrance onto the courtyard unnoticed by the four interlopers. Now the two stand silhouetted against a yellow glow of fire or candle flame from within. The light has illuminated Gaston who stands transfixed in its glare. The taller of the two men has just addressed him. With a muttered, "Yes, sir," and a wink towards Jerome he strides back to the oak door and slams it shut.

"That's better fat man. The idea's to keep the fuckers out not invite them in!"

With that, the two men turn back to the light and with barely a glance at Gaston step inside. The door clicks shut, the light suddenly extinguished.

"Putain!"

"Fuck, that was close!"

"Well, I like to do what I'm told. We wouldn't want to let the enemy in would we? Ha!"

"You didn't lock it, did you?"

"The gate?"

"Oui, d'accord."

"Of course not. There's a limit. Being shut in with these juveniles is bad enough without locking us all in."

Gaston nods towards the two younger men as he speaks. No longer concerned they should hear him, he barely drops his voice.

"They're dead meat."

Jerome looks at Pierre and Louis, still terrified, now shuffling from foot to foot. He can remember his first terrors in the dark under those accursed leaves as so many were butchered. He speaks quietly,

"You two. Don't mind him. We'll make it. It's my destiny. I..."

A "Shhh..." from Gaston cuts him short. The door has re-opened. A man sways out and curses as he clutches at his belt.

"Fucking breeches! Oh, Holy Christ!"

"Pissing your pants again Guillaume? At least you made it out the door this time!"

The second speaker is big, bigger than Gaston who eyes him appreciatively as the man hauls at his own breeches and, in an arched stream, steamily urinates onto the cobbles.

"Well, my friends, there's a sight for sore eyes."

Before Gaston can speak again, he is interrupted.

"Hey you! Got nothing better to do than watch a man take a piss?"

Folding himself away after shaking the last drops to the cobbles the speaker takes a step towards Gaston. He stops at a sudden shout from inside and turns back to the open doorway.

"That'll be Leclaire doing her party trick. C'mon Monsieur Pisshead, let's get you up. Christ! You stink. What've you been drinking?"

The sounds from within are raucous; an occasional cheer, a good deal of laughter, the hubbub rising to a crescendo every few minutes. Jerome stands as if pole-axed. Leclaire! Marie? Here! It's not possible. Marie is ... where? At home in Pierre's arms of course. Where else? He forces her image from him. Surely she can't be...

"What's got into you, Jerome?"

"Nothing. Rien. I'm just being stupid. It's just that the big fella..."

"He was certainly that!"

"Bien sûr. But he said Leclaire is tonight's entertainment."

"What of it?"

"That's...she's...it's..."

"Your woman's name? And you think she's had her fill of village life and made her way to Normandy to entertain the troops?"

"No. Yes. I..."

"You really are quite mad."

"I know. It's just..."

"You miss her and hope..."

"Something like that."

"You hope to walk through that door, march up the

stairs and save her. Perhaps we could help."

"Well ... I. You're making fun of me!"

"No my friend. You are making a fool, a besotted fool, of yourself. Ob-se-dée! We've a job to do and I have no intention of being killed trying to rescue a phantom. Let's find these fucking stables before we hit more trouble."

Marie is hot. She has been dancing for an hour. She moves with abandon, no sense anyone is watching, a freedom making her twists and turns more sensual and alluring – magnetically alluring – for her rapt audience. Her elbows are crooked, hands above her head as her hips match the rhythm. The men are in raptures, the few women rapidly becoming invisible.

Marie swings and turns, her hips provocatively tempting to any that dare to touch. She has drunk little. She needs nothing but the rhythm of the hand drums to make her move thus. And the promise of course. The promise of the man who says he shall lick the sweat from her. For now she spins, swings, smiles...

"Now what are we supposed to do?"

"Check the stables. They can't be far. If there's horse we know we have a serious problem."

"And if not?"

"Life will be easy. A two month siege at most. We'll starve 'em out. C'mon."

Two months! Two months of eating less and less. As

ever the lands surrounding the fortress have been razed; no cover for any attackers nor potential food. Two months of hand to hand combat. Two months of being brutalised by Gaston. Even now Jerome can see the big man stroking himself as he looks wistfully at the door. Closed now; they can barely make out the shouts and laughter from within.

"C'mon. Don't dawdle. That lot'll be happy for a few hours yet."

Confidence is in his steps as Gaston strides away. The other three follow and with one last glance back at the guard-house Jerome turns the corner.

He seems to be in an almost identical square; cobbled, an alley leading off from the far corner and two doors facing each other in the angle of the opposite sides. There is quiet here, no sounds of revelry. A familiar smell rises from the cobbles. Jerome is taken back again. Not to images of Marie but to Pierre as together they rubbed down the horses. How long ago that seemed. How many lives lived, loved, lost.

"Merde!"

"You said it."

"Putain! They have horses. There's shit everywhere. Look where you stand. Do your best not to fall on your arses you two!"

Gaston raises an arm to point at a vast oak door. It is in shadow almost opposite them but so big it merges with the wall. They move more cautiously now, the three younger men following their leader as he steps carefully amongst the dung. As they near the stable, the horse muck is harder to avoid. A stinking pile, taller than Jerome, stands against the wall. Two pitch-forks haphazardly protrude. To the right loom the doors. Jerome can see this is no ordinary stable. The doors are three times a man's height and twice as wide. They are studded with iron, each panel broader than the length of Jerome's fore-arm. He can only guess the strength needed to push one open. A great plank of oak holds them shut.

Just above there is a light. Jerome keens. There is a small aperture in the door, a spy-hole not much bigger than his own head. Three vertical bars form a grill and a grip. Stepping forward and grasping the bars with both hands, Jerome barks a command to Gaston.

"C'mon Gaston, give us a leg up. I want to see what's inside. Christ! Not so fast. The door almost took my knee-caps off!"

Hauling himself up to the grill, his feet clasped securely in Gaston's great palms, Jerome peers into the stable.

Marie settles into a slower rhythm; sensuous, sublime. She feels sweat slowly trickling down the inside of her thighs. She smiles, gently thrusting her hips out, back and forth. There is a gratifying heaviness in her sex. She is throbbing slightly and flushes. As the redness rises from her neck she softly caresses her breasts, the nipples now hardening – erect. A man rises and walks as if in a trance towards her.

"Ne me touchez pas!"

The man stops. He stares at this terrible siren who

can command him so easily.

"Sit down Phillipe. We can't see her dance."

"Ha! Is this dance? The woman's bewitching you all!"

"Well, sit down anyway you lump. You look bewitched yourself!"

Marie has stopped. She stares at the wretch defying him to move again. This then is power. True power.

XXIX

"I'm sorry baby, I don't want to talk about Spain anymore. Let's talk about your day."

"My day? An hour and a bit on the mêtro with people who don't say a word, then eight hours with people who only talk about plastic. Except for lunch."

"What do they talk about over lunch?"

"No idea, I have my coffee on the left bank or go to our place and think about us. They're probably still talking about plastic!"

"Over an expense account bash!"

"Not sure. They only take 40 minutes. Why can't we talk about Spain?"

"You only want to grill me about Marcel!"

"I don..."

"You do. You're bloody obsessed. Obsédée! You'd think I was going to Barcelona to shag Gaudi, not photograph the place!"

"Are you? You brought shagging up. Not Gaudi. Mar..."

"Christ! Marcel! Non, non. Non!"

"That's a 'no' then?"

"Marcel's fifteen years older than me. And he's still too upset to shag anyone coz of his wife!"

"How do you know?"

"He told me. How do you think?"

"When?"

"This is like the third degree. At lunch last week."

"Lunch?"

"Oh stop it! You eat lunch, don't you? Ah, no you don't. Just coffee. Anyway he took me to lunch to discuss the trip."

"And talked about his lack of sex?"

"Well that and what he and his wife preferred."

"Preferred?"

"He used to get her to dress up."

"Go on."

"In tight leather gear. Or rubber. Turned him on."

"But you said she wasn't exactly svelte!"

"So? He didn't mind. Loved it in fact!"

"Let's get this straight. This boss of yours tells you he's into women who wear leather..."

"And rubber."

"And rubber. And he says he's not getting any. Don't you think that's a bit of a come-on?"

"What do you want me to do? Tell him to fuck off?"

"Er..."

"Baby, I need this job. We can't afford to live here without..."

She knows they can. There is no rent, they don't own the car and he earns enough for the two of them. But she enjoys her job; the company, the occasional business trip, the chats over coffee as they check the proofs. It's not art, but it's close enough and who does he think he is threatening her hard-won independence? She can't let his jealousy mess that up.

"I shall, if you want me to. We can manage."

He knows they can. There is no rent, they have no children and he earns enough. But he enjoys her independence, loves talking to her about the hours she pores over proofs as a deadline approaches. It's not art, but perhaps it is. How he hates Marcel; assured, distinguished-looking with salt and pepper hair, shorter than him but looking good for his fifty plus years. Worse, Marcel is funny, considerate, charming with women and has the huge advantage of having been widowed just over a year ago. He can almost feel the sympathy that pours his way from his entranced female staff. And he's never even met him.

"No, that's crazy. Don't give your job up. Go to Barcelona. I'll be fine."

"No you won't. You'll want to speak every day and check what I've been up to!"

"No, baby. I just love your voice."

"You're fucking impossible! I don't want to go now! Let's talk about something else? Have you thought any more about my suggestion?"

"Our confessions?"

"Yeah. Do you want to try it?"

"Well, I'd have to write my jealousies down."

"Might help you get rid of them!"

"I used to write. Not great. A bit obsessive as you might say. Not much of a style either. Kind of Enid Blyton meets Proust!"

"Five in search of times past?"

"Pretty much. I think the style would have, er, matured by now. Closer to Proust though my memory's nowhere near as good as his was."

Peace descends. Her hand reaches out for his. A frown, another smile.

"I'm throbbing, Mister!"

"Table?"

As they are making love, her legs splayed in the familiar position, moving slow and deep inside her, she forgets Barcelona, Marcel, the job ... It is after her shuddering climax that the argument hits her with a belly-tightening grip of remorse. At that moment she knows her job can be put on hold. It's close enough to art, but this is better.

XXX

Jerome cannot know this but he is about to make a mistake, a mistake that will haunt him and kill his companions. A mistake that will turn him from a fool to a murderer, victim to killer. He knows he hasn't yet killed. Luck? Judgement? Gaston has appeared each time he's been in a fix so far. Either that or found him wherever he has fallen, rarely wounded though winded beneath the weight of another's body.

He peers through the bars and involuntarily gasps. The inside of the stable is cavernous. He can't make out the rear wall at all. It is lost in shadow. The light from candle-flame not far distant from his vantage point only illuminates the scene directly in front of him. He sees three men squatting on the straw-strewn floor and a fourth, silhouetted with his back to him, standing and stretching.

The three are playing some kind of dice game. Absorbed, they don't realize they are observed. They gaze intently at the cast die, paying no attention to the high wooden stalls to left and right, harnesses and saddles hung like trophies amongst them. Jerome can see half a dozen chargers in the nearest stalls and senses many more in the shadows. He smells the familiar reek of dung, the beeswax polish of the leather and a faint smell of...what? Roast meat? Chicken? Definitely not horse flesh. Now it is his turn to be absorbed. He scans the floor around the dice players.

No plates, no evidence of a répas. But the smell is distinct and makes him hungry. Only four men! Supper lies within! Perhaps...But this is his mistake. A face (a fifth man!) appears as if by magic in front of his own.

"Merde! Qu'est ce que vous faites!"

The guard spits out the words. Jerome starts. Where has the man come from? What is he doing climbing up the inside of the great door? Words, questions, answers, fear, race through him.

"I,...I..."

"Hey, who are you? You are not Henri!"

The guard disappears from view and Jerome looks down at Gaston, The big man is smiling, sweat on his brow from the exertion of holding Jerome but apparently unconcerned.

"Gaston, let me down. They've seen..."

On cue, a small door to the left, until that moment hidden in shadow, swings open. Five men stand before the invading quartet. Before Gaston can stop him Louis starts to draw his blade. Jerome sees recognition in the eyes of one of the dice players.

"Merde! Get them before..."

But the man doesn't end his appeal. A huge hand has grasped him by the neck. With a twist and a squeeze the head jerks back. The eyes stare wildly. There is a sickening sound of bone snapping and the eyes roll up, the body falling like rags in a heap at Gaston's feet. Now Louis moves. He has seen that none of their attackers are armed. He throws himself at the nearest and they fall in a scuffling tangle of arms and legs.

"Gaston! Gaston!"

Pierre hasn't drawn blade. He stands staring at the two men struggling at his feet, moisture is seeping from his breeches. Gaston turns to him,

"My old mother wouldn't piss herself over this lot. They're not even armed."

And with that Gaston's right arm shoots out and deals one of the guard's such a blow to the head that it seems to lift from the shoulders for a brief instant. Like his companion, the man falls life-less to the ground. Pierre snaps awake, spins and runs back across the courtyard. Louis now eases himself to his feet; struggle over, his victim doesn't move. Louis seems about to speak when his eyes grow wide with surprise, a grimace of pain spreading across his young face. His hand goes down to his chest and he fingers the vicious metal points that have appeared from within his tunic. His hand is suddenly red, red with the fresh blood which now flows from the two wounds. Louis tries to speak again but sinks to his knees to reveal his assailant, pitch-fork in hand standing behind him.

"Well, fat man. Want some of this?"

"I'll deal with this clown. Get the fuck out, Jerome. Find Pierre!"

And so Jerome runs. He is vaguely aware that a fifth enemy is somewhere close. He flies across the cobbles, slipping on dung as he goes but too frightened to much care. As he turns the corner into the first court-yard he sees the door to his left wide open. No sounds of ribaldry now. Instead, a huge guard, out-lined by the light from within, is dangling a sack from his outstretched arm. No, not a sack ... Jerome skids to a halt.

"Un autre. Want some of this, boy?"

With that, the man drops his bundle and Pierre is splayed on the cobbles, his head, or what remains of his head, makes a sickening crack as the skull splits. The corpse lolls to one side and reveals a face half torn off, the left eye prised, obscenely, from its socket. Two more men appear hastily pulling up their breeches and, barely glancing at Pierre, stumble towards Jerome.

"He's mine boys! Leave the runt to me!"

Jerome instinctively steps back, tripping and beginning to fall before he can even draw his knife. But the crash to the cobbles doesn't come. Instead he is grasped by the shoulders and heaved upright. Gaston!

"Non, ami. Ils sont pour moi. Mien!"

And with that Gaston strides toward the three enemy. The smaller men make way for their bigger comrade who grins wickedly at this new fight. As he walks toward Gaston he aims a last vicious kick at Pierre's head. Torn from the neck it spins horribly across the bloodied courtyard. Jerome doesn't stop to think. With renewed energy he sprints toward the oak gate. To his left another door opens.

He just has time to see men coming out and turning toward the uproar Gaston has created. Then he is through. Now he sees Gaston running, behind him three bodies be-deck the cobbles like slaughtered sheep. The defenders from the second door-way are attempting to cut off Gaston's path but with two mighty blows he is past and heading straight for Jerome and freedom. But more men are after him now. And gaining.

"Jerome! Jerome! Aide-moi! Aide-moi!"

Will he ever be able to explain what he does next? Will he live long enough? Barely aware of his actions, Jerome slams the great oak door in Gaston's face. He hears a fearsome cry of rage from within. And then an equally fearsome scream of despair,

"Jerome.....!"

XXXI

Another Sunday. Midmorning. 'Post-rutting' as Chlöe would have it. He never ceases to be amazed how early they make love. Some mornings he will wake as the sun is rising, for the first ten minutes looking at her still sleeping. Then he will press himself to her curved back. She will mumble something inaudible and languorously slide up the bed a little. Reaching behind and pressing herself closer to him she will grasp him to guide him inside.

Sometimes this needs an added two handed action as she eases her lips apart. The first time he enters her can be slightly awkward, occasionally a little sore but she moistens and pushes harder onto him. He will grasp her hips as she bends forward more, the back of her head now half a metre away.

When spent, he will drift off to sleep only to find, an hour later, that her head is beneath the covers, her mouth closed around him. This can easily lead to their "Arc de Triomphe" finale, Chlöe sitting astride him and riding him as if her life depended on it. These minutes are close to frightening, the looks on her face fierce, his own need to push inside as deep as he can all consuming. Again, they will be spent. Again, they will hold each other.

Now he would feel both sated and energized, an energy to be spent in leaving her side in order to take

Pantam to the Tabac. He watches her stretch and close her eyes, sighing again. Tugging on jeans and, if the day is warm enough, no more than a sweat-shirt he makes his way down-stairs to where Pantam sits with thumping tail.

They step outside, the first 'bonjour' of the day within moments. Faces are increasingly familiar, names irrelevant. Today people hurry through a soft drizzle. He has forgotten his hat, a floppy leather number bought at a brocante. The drizzle clouds his vision making him grateful Pantam is so familiar with the route. As he walks Pantam pulls this way and that, stopping to inspect a series of shrubs and kerb-side stones.

He imagines Chlöe turning, stretching and twisting before pulling herself up-right. She will be sitting on the edge of the bed with arms raised above her head, crooked at the elbows. Again she will stretch, perhaps now a yawn. Now he imagines her gently swaying hips as she walks to the bath-room. Soon she will move downstairs to put the kettle on the hob. Does she whistle? He's not heard her much though he has occasionally surprised her in the middle of a vaguely tuneful rendition of something familiar. Though not tuneful enough for him to recognize the song. He can almost smell the coffee, the croissants…

"Monsieur!"

He jerks awake. Has he been asleep? No, he has arrived at the Tabac in a deep reverie.

"*Le Monde*? Comme d'habitude."

"Oui. D'accord ..."

Suddenly this is a habit. Not just a habit but one recognized by the tobacconist.

"Merci. À bientôt, Maurice."

"Merci. Bonne journée."

Twenty minutes later, the perfect part of Sunday begins, the two of them in bed, *Le Monde* open at Sudoku (*Expert* on Sundays) and the smell of coffee and croissants irresistible. His damp clothes have been discarded along with the boots, Pantam already curled up on his bed in the kitchen. "Not the kitchen!" Chlöe had exclaimed, "We can't put his bed in the kitchen." "Pourquoi?" "It's..." And in a rare victory the dog-bed had been squeezed under the table. She has toweled his hair, a vague memory rises up of imagining exactly such a scene before they had even found the cottage. Dishevelled but dry, his locks stand in spikes.

"Do you think I should get a hair-cut?"

"No."

"That's a 'No' then?"

He smiles. He loves her direct-ness. Chlöe hasn't even bothered to look up. He bends to the Sudoku. The way he suddenly spots the right number baffles him. He can look at the squares for twenty minutes, put the paper to one side, pick it up again and, Voilà! There it is; obvious all along.

"What do you think Wittgenstein would have made of Sudoku?"

"What?"

"You know, the way you suddenly see which

number fits and, Voilà!"

"I doubt if he'd have had the time to play it. He never strikes me as particularly relaxed. He'd have preferred Mots croisés."

"Same problem, baby. How is it you can stare at a clue for an hour and then it seems so obvious?"

"Too deep for a Sunday, Mister. I'll get the croissants."

"Honey."

"Yeah."

"We need to talk."

"We are, baby. We've been talking in bed all morning. In between croissants and shagging."

"I know. Just lovely. But we need to talk seriously."

"We're always serious. It's great. Oh, you've got something in mind. Let's go outside. I'll do some more coffee."

"Fab. Go down and I'll see you in a bit."

"Not coming like that then?"

"Non! Not after last time. I can do without Hélène inspecting my bits. I'll get dressed."

"But I haven't invited her for today. You said to give her a day and I'm sure it's not 'til later in the week."

"Hmmm..."

Another Sunday, another morning of chat, love, breakfast in bed. But this morning has been a little different. He has been distracted. Pretty much since the previous evening when, happily weeding the courgettes, he had noticed something new. Newly planted, newly watered and in glowing health.

Chlöe slides out of bed and, balancing two empty cups, two plates and the cafetière walks to the door.

"Shouldn't you put something on too?"

"I thought you liked this vest."

"Toujours. But... never mind. You could try the new skirt. I like that. I'll catch you up."

He looks around. The bedroom is low-ceilinged, black-painted beams crossing from side to side. Their bed is the one the Americans left behind. It's modern, but very big. On the grey ("Grey, whoever paints walls grey?" from Chlöe) walls a full length dressing mirror. It is plain, no frame ("Look what I rescued from the tip today!") but he doesn't care. It is what Chlöe shows him in the mirror (and sees herself; "My very own porn movie!") that counts. He flushes. Then, trying to push the thought of yet more sex from his mind, he picks up the jeans he had kicked off the previous night. He drags a t-shirt over his head and, shoeless, pads downstairs. Chlöe is already outside. The kettle starts its sibilant hissing as he walks past and he takes it off the heat.

"Hmm..well at least you didn't put your shoes on. Not exactly naked though are you. And me just in this vest."

"Chlöe."

"Chlöe! You never call me Chlöe. What about 'baby,' 'honey,' 'fuck-fest?'

"I don't call you fuck-fest!"

"Did once."

"Did I?"

"At the café. You were trying to stop me shouting."

"Ok. But this time it's Chlöe."

"I'll just do the coffee."

He is about to object but what is this? A disciplinary meeting? '*There's* an idea,' he thinks just as a familiar voice calls over the fence.

"Chlöe. Cou cou. Tue es là?"

"It's me Héléne. Chlöe's inside. Did you want coffee? We're out of pastis."

"No, cheri. I just wanted to see if Chlöe ... Oh, alright then. I'll go round. You are decent aren't you?"

"Utterly."

As he sits he thinks he can just make out a muttered, "Pity." He runs his hands through his hair. 'Oh, well. It will wait.'

"Cheri, cheri. How lovely to see you again so soon. And what a lovely day!"

The cloud has lifted, the rain all but stopped and the sun already strong. The courtyard is brightening up. His eyes drift to the new plantings. They seem to have grown taller. Hélène follows his gaze.

"Oh what a good idea. Are you growing tomatoes? We have so many in the greenhouses but I prefer the ones grown outside."

As Hélène stoops to look closer at the plants, Chlöe appears in the kitchen doorway.

"Coffee everybody. A croissant, Hélène?"

Hélène is now looking more intently at the greenery she has pulled from one of the stems. She rubs it between her long fingers and breathes in the scent.

"These don't smell like tomatoes. Sweet though. What are they dear? A new hybrid?"

"They're cannabis. Be careful Hélène, you don't want the sniffer dogs after you!"

"Cannabis? How delightful. What are you going to do with it?"

And Chlöe has trumped him again. The serious talk was to have been about the mysterious plants' arrival amongst *his* courgettes. He had known what they were but wanted to see what Chlöe might say. Confronted by the charmingly naïve Hélène, she hasn't batted an eyelid.

"Yes, Chlöe. What are we going to do with it? Make hemp underwear?"

"No baby. We're going to smoke it. If it's any good."

"Have you seen *The Tin Drum*? Günther Grass?"

"I haven't seen it. But I read it in translation. Why? I thought we were talking about cannabis"

"Worst bit and best bit? Worst first."

"About dope?"

"No, about the film. What more is there to say about this stuff? We'll pick it, dry it and smoke it. Agreed Hélène?"

"Oh oui. Bien sûr. Delightful. I've never tried it you know."

"Don't worry. You'll be fine. Now, *The Tin Drum*."

Again he marvels at her conversation. Where does it

come from? The instantaneous switches. Sitting in bed earlier they had been talking about, what? Not films, certainly not war films. Is it strictly a war film? No. Then what?

"Where does that come from?"

"What?"

"The question."

"I don't know. You've made me think now. Anyway, worst and best. You too, Hélène"

It's another of her games. Whatever they do together, wherever they go, she wants to know the worst and best. Always the worst first. Except, he realizes, love-making. He had once said, "You don't play this game after we've been to bed."

"What game?"

"Worst and best."

"That's coz it's all best, baby."

"All?"

"One way or another."

"C'mon, what's your answer, Mister?"

"I don't know if the film's the same at the book but ... Worst is the rape by the Russians."

"Awful."

"Best, I don't know. It's all so fucking grim."

Hélène grimaces.

"Language! I can't watch it at one sitting. Thirty minute chunks are enough. The scene in the Post Office, the moments when Alfred almost chokes on his Nazi badge!"

"I don't think that was in the book."

"Ok, how about when Oscar's dwarf lover is killed?"

"Do you two do this all the time? Incroyable! Sorry I'm interrupting."

They are oblivious now to Hélène.

"Funny thing is the bits I remember best are in Normandy."

"Paris. They don't go to Normandy in the film."

"Oh. Some of the sex is pretty good."

"You have a one track mind. Best bit?"

"Now you're asking. The part where he nuzzles her in the beach hut's amazing."

"You should have seen his uncle screwing his mum the first time!"

"Good?"

"Incredible. The actress has a lovely body. But my favourite is that scene of his mothers' conception."

"Under his grandmother's skirts?"

"Exactly. And that's what reminded me."

"What?"

"Of the film. Skirts. You said earlier how much you liked my new skirt. Charity shop."

This is why he loves her. If you can love for a reason it's this way of turning the conversation from one topic to another. All worth attending to. All her.

"Well, au revoir. Thanks for the coffee. See you at book club cherie. You two are priceless. Priceless! I look forward to the first harvest. À bientôt."

XXXII

If he lives, will he live to regret what he has done? Does he *know* what he has done? He has waited long enough outside the gate to know that Gaston is surrounded, his roars of rage turning to curses as he faces his attackers. He imagines the big man swinging out with his fists, darting left and right to avoid blows and blades.

Gaston would not let himself be taken, any terror of dying being outweighed by fear of torture or enslavement. Was the brute dead, his last words reserved for cursing Jerome?

The sound of approaching steps wakes Jerome from the reverie binding him to the door. He steps swiftly away and, not glancing upwards at the ramparts at all, plunges down the side of the moat. Compacted straw rustles, broken stems scratch at his legs as he crosses to the far side and scurries up the bank. The next league will be treacherous; there is no cover. A sharp whisper leaves the slightest trail of wind by his ear. A shaft! But the only one.

Now he runs. Still there is no outcry, no further arrows. No-one is giving chase. Perhaps his treachery has deemed him an unworthy foe. Perhaps Gaston is the bigger prize.

"Read to me."

"Now?"

"L'instant. I feel a bit tense. Please, baby."

"What?"

"Anything. No, *Lord of the Rings*."

"*Lord of the Rings*! All of it?"

"No, baby. Start at the beginning."

"It's a very good place to start."

"Hee hee. Who's been listening to *The Sound of Music* then? My mum used to read it to me. Then I read it on my own."

"*The Soun...*"

"No, *Lord of the Rings,* silly."

"How old?"

"Can't really remember. From about eight. Then I got into it. Read it, maybe six times."

"Six! By when?"

"By the time I was thirteen, no, fifteen. Actually, it was nine times."

"And you want it again?"

"I like it."

"Hmmm... Do we have a copy?"

"It's next to Talleyrand."

"The sociology of Middle Earth?"

"No, Mister! Tolkien follows alphabetically. Voilâ."

He stands and stretches, running his fingers through his hair. Avoiding the sleeping dog, he walks through the old oak doorway that leads to the front room. He frowns. The bookshelves weren't his finest moment. He recalls the clumsy push on the drill with hammer action full on. It has left a large hole in the plaster where no rawl plug will ever sit snugly. Instead of doing what was, to Chlöe at least, the obvious thing and filling the offending hole he had instead mounted four rescued planks onto a series of bricks.

Precarious at first, these had looked increasingly sturdy as they had piled the books on top. Until the very top shelf. This had a life of its own. Anything heavier than a couple of paperbacks had consistently produced an alarming tilt. He eventually persuaded Chlöe that the essential problem lay in the sloping floor rather than his literary scaffolding. Her response had been to fill a blue crystal glass with water and wisteria cut from the back fence. This now perches in the centre of the topmost plank challenging him to risk removing a tome.

He scans the second shelf. His lover's conception of 'alphabetical order' is, to his mind, pure, pure Chlöe. The first book to the left is *Americana* by one James Dunkerley. To its right, *De Niro: A biography*, Alan Dean Foster's *Alien*, Anita Brookner's *Fraud* and Antonia Fraser's *Marie Antoinette.* They are all in English bought, he remembers, at a small bookshop the previous spring. Bought by weight! Then, in French, Aldous Huxley's *Point Counter Point* and *À La Recherche du Temps Perdu*. The system, if system it is, seems to define any use of a first letter a – in title, author or imagination – as deserving a place at the beginning. "A very good place to start," he hums – and smiles. His eyes move down. Sure enough Tolkien sits next to Talleyrand both in his own tongue. But between the two? *The Erotic Imagination: French histories of perversity*, this time in English by an author rejoicing in the name Vernon A. Rosario. 'Ha!' he thinks, 'She missed that A.'

He is looking at page sixty-one, the beginning of a chapter on erotomaniacs, when he feels a hand on his shoulder. He smiles and looks up.

"Hélène! I didn't...It's..."

"You two are quite a couple. Voilà"

Hélène is grinning. He hastily puts the book back in its place and then runs his hands through his hair.

"I was, er..."

"Looking for inspiration?"

"No, Tolkien. You're back. So soon. It's not book club is it?"

"Non, cheri. I wanted to have a quick word with Chlöe. Chlöe!"

On cue, she has appeared in the doorway. One of his shirts flaps loosely open showing a flat belly, the gentle curve of one of her small breasts and a glimpse of brown nipple. His eyes follow her form that he knows so, so well, down. Her thighs are what she might call 'honed', the muscles showing against the skin he loves. Her ankles, feet, all of her, quite perfect. But between her thighs, where he loves to be, her womanhood is there for all to see. The hair is dark chestnut, the curls darkest around her mound. And the curls are plentiful. He knows they track down, down, underneath...

"Oh. Hélène. Pardon. Je ne sais. I didn't realise..."

She is adjusting the shirt making a clumsy effort to cross her legs. This only has the effect of pushing her bottom out at an angle he finds all too familiar. He feels himself swelling and drags his eyes from her to their visitor. Hélène is more than happy to witness their embarrassment. She is beaming. He knows what's coming.

"Oh, you two! You two love birds. Do you *ever* stop? Tolkien, indeed."

"But, I was running a bath. I didn't think it was book club tonight."

"It isn't. I'd forgotten something I meant to ask earlier. And don't be embarrassed, cherie. I think all this is just lovely. Your gorgeous man even had a book on perversity in his hand when I arrived. You couldn't make it up!"

"Where did you find that?"

"Next to Tolkien. Your system seems to have it there because of the opening 'T' in the title."

"Well, where else would it be?"

He is stumped. Where else *would* it be? But Hélène is looking very thoughtful. She pushes her hair – recently highlighted to show streaks of blonde and silver – above and away from her forehead and with little more than a shrug manages to ease her jacket from her shoulders. In one movement she has left him with the jacket. It is silk, *Chanel*, naturally. She perches on the edge of the sofa crossing her legs as she sits. She still looks thoughtful.

"Chloe, you'll catch your death. Do put something a little warmer on. But come back soon, I have something to ask you."

Chlöe reverses a little awkwardly to the door and,

with a giggle, spins on her heel and walks back into the kitchen. There is a muttered, "Pantam! Bougez!" followed by a shuffling and snuffling as the dog manoeuvres out of her way. He waits with Hélène, grateful the disturbance has distracted her from his subsiding tumescence.

"Do you have any pastis, my dear? C'est l'heure?"

"*Ricard* o'clock? Bien sûr. Un moment."

In the kitchen he finds a less dishevelled Chlöe struggling to pull her jeans on while simultaneously brushing her hair. She smiles and he can sense a chortle on its way but she checks herself. He nods at the bottle of *Ricard*. Levis in place Chlöe takes the bottle from the table. As she passes she brushes her hand across his crotch.

"See me later, baby. A little early for pastis, non?"

"Skip the Tolkien?"

"We'll see. Ah, Hélène, what beautiful shoes. They're lovely. They're..."

"*St Laurent*. One does one's best. Now, sit with me cherie."

He returns to sit on the wicker chair near the door so as to be present but not too conspicuous. Besides, it affords him a better view of Chlöe, her brown hair now tumbling around her face.

"You wanted to ask?"

"Oh, yes. A little more water first. Merci. Seeing your man by the books trying to understand your index system was more or less exactly what I came back to ask you. Would you like to index the library? Guillaume would pay."

"But I'm not a librarian. And what would the nursery say?"

"You wouldn't need to give that up, cherie. You could do it as often as you think necessary. Probably a few days a week at first and then less when you're satisfied things are in order."

"That's very kind. It's not a school holiday next week though. I'll be very busy with the children. I really can't Hélène?"

"Of course, whatever suits you. I think you'd like it."

"Like it! I would love it! But thank you for thinking of me Hélène, thank you for asking."

There is a knocking at the door. Then a more insistent battering. They look at each other and Chlöe moves to welcome their latest visitor.

"Who can that...?"

"You two talk all the time don't you? Marvellous. Did you spend much time talking to your mother, cheri?"

"When?"

"As a child. You seem, er, very good at talking to women. Or, at least, listening. A rare talent."

"Hmm..."

"Guillaume spent two years saying the same thing to Jean."

"Jean? Two years? Who is it, baby? Chloe?"

"It can be a blessing not having children, cheri. Oh, encore un pastis. How lovely. Where was I?"

"Two years saying the..."

"Same thing. Exactement. Do you want to know

what is it was?"

"Er, 'Wash behind your ears'?"

"Ha! Delightful. Wrong generation, darling. Getting Jean *out* of the shower would have been an achievement. Still, when he was a bit younger his room smelt like a hamster cage. And full of half-eaten suppers, dirty cups and, for some reason, tea-spoons."

"Was it, 'How many times have I told you not to do that!'?"

"Oo, Are you alright?.."

He hesitates. He knows all too clearly the expression. It isn't Guillaume who has said it. It's his own dad. His favourite question. Not a question at all. It meant, "Stop it at once!" Though once he had answered, "Thirteen today, papa. So far." His cheek had been rewarded with no supper, something of a relief considering his mother's cooking.

"Desolée, Hélène. It was something…"

"Your father used to say? D'accord. No, the constant refrain during Jean's teenage years was, 'I haven't any money.'"

"But…"

"Of course, we had a lot of money. Still do. But all Jean would ever say to his father was, "Can I have some money, papa?"'And like a shot, Guillaume would answer, "Non." Like clockwork back would come, "Pourquoi?" and he would reply, "I have no money.""

"Did it work?"

"In terms of putting Jean off? Of course not. But it drove me to distraction!"

Chlöe has opened the door and is peering out, then opens it wide. Raymonde stands before her looking flustered and more than a little miserable. Hélène, also now flustered he notices, stands as if in a trance.

"Pardon Chlöe. Desolée. Tu as des frîtes? Dans le frigo? Ton congélateur?"

"Mais, oui. Pourquoi? I think we have some in the freezer. What's up?"

"Some customers have just ordered some for lunch and I went to the freezer and…rien. Since Claudette left….I, I, forget to order stocks. I. Merde!"

Raymonde has noticed Hélène standing behind Chlöe. Both Raymonde and Hélène are reddening.

"You know each other don't you. Raymonde…"

"Yes, of course I know Hélène. I haven't seen her at the brasserie since…"

Chlöe turns. Her friend is now flushed.

"I'll just get the frîtes."

As she squeezes past Hélène she thinks she hears a vaguely familiar tune. The sound grows as she enters the kitchen. Now, she can make the song out. A cell-phone ring-tone. Curiously, it seems to be coming from her friend's hand-bag. More curiously, it is – quite distinctly now – *I Will Always Love You*. The ringing stops and she hears a muttered, "Cherie? D'accord. Chez Chlöe. Raymonde est là! À plus tard. Bisous, bisous." Hélène has materialized beside her.

"Can I speak with you, cherie? Un moment."

"Fuck you!"

"There you go again."

"What do you mean?"

"Fuck you! If I dare, I'd say you were pre-menstrual."

"Well, that's going to work isn't it? You're going to have to do better than that!"

"Why are we arguing?"

"I don't fucking know. I'm just, just…"

"Wound up?"

"Worried. I don't have enough money to last the month."

"Well use the joint account. There's enough in there."

"That's not the point. Most of it's yours."

"Ours."

"Whatever. I can't use it…"

Chlöe suddenly crumples; a picture of misery. He knows not to approach her. He had once asked her the best thing to do when she folded into herself and she had suggested a calm cuddle. He had tried it just once. The reaction?

"Leave me alone. You just want sex!"

"I…I thought…"

"Well don't think. Ne me touché pas!"

After Hélène's departure – she had waited to ensure Raymonde was no longer there – Chlöe had stormed off. In one of their many calmer moments she had once admitted that she hated building up to her period. She felt so unpredictable or, worse, predictably uptight,

240

adding,

"It's probably not the best time to remind me. It might be I'm just a bit more vulnerable but it's not like I'm reacting to nothing. You must do something to get to me!"

She had brought these moods up several times. It was usually the week after an outburst. He was always careful to agree that he must be provoking her in some way but neither of them understood what the specific provocation might be. There seemed nothing obvious. As in that first time at Montmartre it had appeared, so it seemed, from nowhere. A sudden coolness, her eyes no longer engaging his. A quiet. Then a storm, sometimes over before it had begun. At others she would stay angry and distant for an hour or more.

In Montmartre he had seen real panic in her eyes. Was it a terror he might leave? But he knew he wouldn't do that. He was already bound, head and heart. There was invariably something just beneath the surface that she was worrying about. It could be anything from things about her body (ageing was a recent recurring motif) to, in this case, money. She would allow the worry to build and then 'hormones raging' – as he had less than tactfully put it – would let fly. Her ultimate insult seemed to be, "Fuck you!" He was grateful for that; more an expression of anger and outrage than a particular accusation. He feared he wouldn't survive more specific insults. Chlöe is adept at voicing strong opinions privately between them and she rarely has a negative word about him. Her habit of sitting on such feelings leaves him with a small but persistent fear that one day she will let him have it with both barrels.

"You'll be paid for the work in Guillaume's library?"

"Lovely, it wouldn't be that much. It's not that. The nursery's great to work for. But the pay…"

"Ask Guillaume for a raise. He can afford it."

"A raise? I don't know how much he's offering yet! Anyway, I don't want to be greedy." She pauses: "Okay, I'll take it. I can't start 'til the week after next and it's not like I'll be doing much. *And* it'll be a fantastic place to work. The people at the nursery are nice too. I don't want to push my luck."

"Well take some money out of the join…"

"Don't you listen! It's not my money."

"Come on, baby…"

"Just drop it. I'll be alright."

Comme d'habitude, he knows she will be. Maybe by this very afternoon. She will be a little contrite but still wary and he will be careful not to challenge her for twenty-four hours. And then, Voilà! She will be back; all cheeriness and bonhomie. He takes longer to get over it but soon a blessed peace will reign. He will lose track of the passing days until another month is almost up. Now, how did all this start? A light dawns. She had told him that his reading could calm her. The Tolkien! He follows her to the kitchen where they both stand, abashed.

"I wouldn't put it past you to write all this stuff down."

"For what?"

"For a novel. Novelists put ordinary conversations in too you know. People get tired of nothing but lovey dovey scenes. You're not going to win many feminists over though if you say my moods are hormonal. Let's you off the hook, don't you think?"

"I'm not writ … It's not easy, you know. Keeping track of our conversations."

"Mon dieu! You're goin to tell me you *do* write them all down!"

"Only because they're fabulous."

"And you said you weren't a flatterer, Mister. I bet lots of couples have chats like ours."

"Name one!"

"That's not fair. Most of the couples we know are in the middle of splitting up. Except Hélène and Guillaume and I hate to think what they talk about. I reckon holding each other back is more typical of people."

"What do you mean?"

"Look at the couples we know that are still going. They've done the two kids and careers thing and they are so bored with each other. No spark."

"Was there ever a spark?"

"Maybe. For one of them."

"Like who?"

"Hélène."

"Well at least until her wedding day!"

"I know. She's been held back ever since."

"Not from money!"

"No, but from joy, the feeling that life is for living."

"From love?"

"More complicated, baby. Love just closes your eyes. It doesn't open them."

"Wow! How do you mean?"

"You fall in love and your eyes are closed to the person's faults, dangers…"

"Dangers?"

"Betrayal. Sharp tongue … Whatever."

"Betrayal's a bit heavy. Don't you see stars and trees and all that in a different way?"

"I do. But it's not stars or trees that will let you down, fuck off when you need them! It's the one you love who'll do that!"

"Always?"

Chlöe softens. Has she been harsh? How could he know of her betrayals?

"Maybe not always. But when one of you dies, that's a kind of betrayal."

He quietens. She goes on:

"Anyway, she seems to have discovered joy now."

"Hélène?"

"Oui. With Raymonde's missus."

"Christ! When did you discover that? Is that what you two were talking about behind closed doors? No wonder Raymonde's devastated. Do you really think some brief moments of joy can compensate for all the hurt? Do you think a few months or years of having your eyes closed is better than raising a family, having dinner parties?"

"Interminable chats over petites-fours to the same dull…no, not dull…locked-in people?"

"Locked in?"

"To their lives, their interests, each other, fears about getting the children into the` right school...all of that."

"Well, she still has Guillaume's library!"

"There's no answer to that. Would we get dull?"

"Maybe after the third child!"

He smiles, suddenly feeling overwhelmed with longing for her. Chlöe doesn't even look up as she says,

"That's not going to happen, baby."

He is startled by how firm she sounds. And confused when she picks up the conversation from earlier.

"I meant people in love. They always find each other fascinating. I knew a few people like that in Paris. Françoise and Jean-Claude par example. She'd even pretend she was interested in Paris-St-German. He'd talk about them every weekend."

"There's dedication. You don't even know who I support!"

"I ..."

"Well, lover?"

"Rugby or football?"

"Ha! I support Nîmes!"

"Are they football or rugby?"

"Both. I prefer football."

"Why on earth them? Nîmes is hardly your local team is it?"

"Don't know really. My dad took me to see them play

Paris Saint German when I was about ten and I couldn't cheer for the same team as him."

"And?"

"Nîmes lost four one and I've followed them ever since. Anyway, I haven't written about your hormones."

"Liar. I bet you have. You've said it to me."

"Well, maybe..."

"Don't push your luck, Mister. It's bad enough having my love life noted down without dissecting perfectly understandable moods."

"But..."

"But nothing. I'm worried about money and you make a glib comment about it being your treat at Raymonde's tonight. Raymonde's! Of all the places to suggest!"

"But I didn't... *That's* what I said. I'd forgotten. We'd better not ask for frîtes! Now I know what that little scene was about. Hélène almost ran out. And as for that ring-tone..."

"Don't change the subject, Mister!"

"Sorry. But you hadn't said money was tight then. Well not that tight."

"I'm sorry too, baby. I'll get over it. You'll see."

And she will. Money won't be mentioned for a while, the occasional treat like a pricier wine will appear and, at least twice in the week following the confrontation, so will a new pair of boots or a lamp looking suspiciously non-brocante. He thinks the way she acts might well drive him mad. He doesn't care.

XXXIII

"Grêlons!"

"Quoi?"

"Grêlons! God throws rocks at us!"

They had watched the sky darken, a change starting slowly enough an hour before is now complete. It had seemed to presage rain or perhaps a storm. Jerome had been about to say as much when a thud at his side was followed by one of the most curious scenes he was ever to witness. Within seconds men were screaming and running randomly about the slope trying to avoid innumerable what looked like rocks the size of his fist raining down from the glowering sky. Manseau had shouted his warning but there was nothing to be done. The men had all been out in the open, the nearest cover a league away. Already a dozen or more sprawl on the ground, their slight head-gear no protection from the hail.

There is something not quite right about the vehicles parked to his left; the long, familiar line of Peugeots, Citröens and occasional Mercedes or BMW. Pantam is his usual, snuffling self. He takes the opportunity provided by his master's thoughtful hesitation to sniff and cock his leg several times by a Renault's rear wheel.

Glancing at Pantam, his eye is caught. Voilà! Why didn't he notice before? A scan of the cars nearest to him reveals a similar story. Each and every one has upward of a dozen dents in roof, bonnet or both. There are at least two with great cracks across the windscreens. On closer inspection he can see a wing mirror hanging, forlornly, from the nearest Peugeot.

"Quite a storm, eh?"

It is Raymonde's voice. As if from nowhere he has appeared at his side.

Beside him, Chlöe hadn't stirred as he had listened to the pounding rain in the early hours. For perhaps three minutes there had been an intense clattering on the cottage roof. Too drowsy to investigate the source of the racket he had sunk back to sleep and woken, as usual, to the alarm. But now Raymonde seems poised to explain the devastation and he has finally noticed that many house roofs are no better than those of the cars. The occasional gutter hangs limply from its supports beneath the eaves, tiles are dislodged or broken. Even the bicycles propped outside the Tabac seem to be worse for wear.

"I didn't really hear much. Rain seemed very heavy."

"Rain! It was hail-stones! Grêlons! The like I've never seen before. About the size of my fist, some of them!"

Simple. Three minutes of huge hail-stones and Giverny is the scene of a battle, a battle nature has won hands down.

"How's the brasserie?"

"Don't know yet. I'm just on my way now. I've spent half an hour on the 'phone talking with the insurance about the bloody car?"

"Bad?"

"It depends. If you like bonnets looking like Normandy sand dunes, I'd say it's perfect!"

Suddenly concerned for Chlöe and the cottage, he mutters a perfunctory, "Adieu! À plus tard," to his friend and starts to walk away. Pantam is taken by surprise. Suspecting there will be no croissants for breakfast, the dog looks back at Raymonde, still standing by the Renault. Rudely jerked upright Pantam finds himself almost dragged back along the familiar side-walk. As man and dog near the front gate of the cottage, the door opens. There stands Chlöe. She has thrown on one of his jumpers that stops just below the hips, barely covering her modesty (as his mother would have said).

"Hello, lovely. You're back early. Did you get the paper? I'll put the coffee on."

He doesn't move. Quizzically, Chlöe raises an eyebrow, her forehead furrowing in confusion.

"What's up, Mister?"

"Haven't you noticed?"

"Noticed? Noticed what?"

He realizes he is being unfair. It had taken him a good ten minutes before he'd spotted the give-away details of the dented cars. His eyes stray to the cottage roof. Chlöe follows his gaze. There is a sharp intake of breath – hers.

"What's happened to next-door's gutter?"

Their part of the cottage has an old metal gutter that seems to have survived unscathed. But at his suggestion the previous summer their neighbours had opted to change theirs to plastic. It is now punctured; every fifty centimetres or so a hole the size of a large egg. At various points the hail-stones have smashed through the plastic holders connecting the gutter to the eaves and, like those he had seen earlier, the guttering has come away altogether and now hangs loose.

"Grêlons. Last night apparently. For about three minutes according to Raymonde."

"Grê...? Hail-stones? I didn't hear them. And they did this?"

"And worse. You should see the cars on the way to the Tabac!"

"Well! This'll give us something to talk about at book club tonight. Poor Guillaume!"

"Poor Guillau ...! Pourquoi?"

"His beautiful greenhouses. They'll have been smashed to bits!"

Jerome stirs in his sleep. The grêlons storm had lasted no more than minutes. But long enough to kill or maim many, many men. He's been lucky; no injuries, not even a bruise. Manseau called for a respite before the grisly task of burying the dead. Gratefully, Jerome had simply curled up on the now sodden grass and closed his eyes. The dream started at once.

"La saison commence."

"Demain."

"D'accord, demain. Soon be eating boar."

"Make a change from mutton."

"It's the hunt I love. La chasse."

Pierre and Jerome sit cross-legged in the shade. Their shelter is a willow, the boughs heavy with leaf, the tiny white blossom interspersed throughout, like snowflakes. The day is hot and both men wipe their brows as they speak. It is Pierre who has offered his preference for the hunt rather than the resulting fare. Jerome isn't so keen on either but he knows how important the meat will be for the families. What isn't eaten over the first few weeks will be dried for the winter or smoked over wood ash to be enjoyed with confiture of apples or spiced pear. His mother will delight in using every imaginable cut from the beast; ears, tail, tripes. All will be consumed. He asks:

"Do you know where they'll be? It's very dry. I haven't seen any so far this summer."

"They'll be on higher ground. Don't worry, there'll be no shortage."

"You're going to do what?"

"Go on a sanglier shoot with Guillaume."

"Go on a...? That's disgusting!"

"Why?"

"Killing innocent animals for sport!"

"It's not just for sport. Whatever we get will end up on someone's table."

"Not ours I hope!"

"It's beautiful meat. No fat!"

"It might be, but…"

"You eat pork don't you?"

"What's that got to d…?"

"Isn't it better to eat something that's run free all its life instead of pining away in some great shed?"

"No. Non! I…"

Chlöe falls silent. She feels irritation and flummoxed. Is it better? She changes tack.

"I bet Guillaume does it for sport!"

"Well, it's hard to imagine Hélène slaving over a pâté du sanglier I have to say. But Guillaume probably gives his to the charcutier to turn into sausages."

"But why are you doing it? You don't have to go on a bloody wild boar hunt to prove you're a man!"

"I know, babe. But it's a tradition! They've done it here for hundreds of years."

"Look! A sow with young. Careful."

Jerome doesn't need to be told. There are stories going back generations of those foolish enough to disturb female sangliers with their young. There's even a terrible tale of a priest who had thanked divine providence at surprising a litter of three young males only to become *their* breakfast after he, in turn, was surprised by the aggrieved sow.

The season always starts at the end of the summer to make sure enough adults born the winter before survive their vulnerable early months. Not that a stranger would understand how old the younger animals might be. After only six or seven months they are bigger, heavier and stronger than a man.

The two friends have made their way to a copse on higher ground and been immediately successful. There are five sanglier in total, the adult male nowhere to be seen. The sow and her litter, two already grown to almost the size of Pierre, are a stone throw distant within range of a well aimed arrow. But Jerome and Pierre know better than to let loose before the others arrive. A charging boar is one thing. A charging, wounded boar something altogether more dangerous.

The animals tug at the grass at their feet, chewing systematically and slowly, their eyes all the time darting to left and right for signs of danger. The sow is slightly away from the group. She is scrabbling at the base of a hazelnut, the bracken cast aside as she searches the undergrowth.

"What's the mother doing?"

"No idea. She's looking for something though. Ha! Phillipe, bienvenu."

The third man settles quietly beside Pierre and Jerome. All three are silent as from below them on the slope comes the sound of advancing hunters. To Jerome's annoyance the new arrivals are talking loudly, Auguste's occasional familiar guffaw rising above the chatter. There are three men, all with bows, alongside his father who spots Jerome and is about to raise a shout when he puts his finger to his lips instead. Jerome looks back to where the boar had been eating. The earth is scored and brown. No grass. And no sangliers.

"Where did they go?"

"The sow led the others off through that gap in the trees as soon as she heard your father and the others!"

"Will she have gone far?"

"Who knows! This lot were making enough noise to scare them off I should think."

Auguste has arrived. All four men look sheepishly at Pierre and Jerome. He is annoyed yet, in part, relieved. The animals had looked so peaceful.

"Come on, you two. Let's go up into that copse. They won't have gone far!"

Jerome and Pierre are soon standing where the family had been. Under the hazelnut are signs of the sow's investigations. He leans down to look; earth, roots, some stones and, and...in the centre of the hole is a blackened, partly chewed ... what? A cap? An old loaf? Before he can reach down Auguste has moved forward and plucked the curious mass from its hiding place. He is beaming!

"Les truffes! Les truffes! Tonight we eat well, mes amis. Let's find those boar!"

"Come on sleepy head. Time to get to work. Dreaming again?"

The voice is Laurent's, a man who seems to have barged into Jerome's life with the subtlety of a battering ram. Also fair-haired, but taller and with long tapering fingers that make Jerome think of Marie's hands. He had introduced himself the previous evening with a cheery, "Bonjour. Enchanté! Need a friend?" And that was that. Now he squats on the grass beside Jerome.

"I was dreaming about truffles."

"Truffles! Ha! Now he dreams of truffles! Merde!"

And Jerome is pulled to his feet, the memories of the past banished along with the hope he might again one day eat well.

XXXIV

"If you could write, what would you say?"

"What I say to myself, everyday."

"Qu'est ce que ce?"

"I love you. What are you doing?"

"How about, 'Do you have another?'"

"Non! Oui ..! But I don't want to know."

"Really?"

"There is another! Pierre. They will be together. She is too, too ... full of life to be alone for long"

"Even now? Anything may have happened."

"I know. But he won't leave. And why should she.....?"

"Another man. Boredom. New horizons?"

"New horiz ... ? Non. She's a village girl. Perhaps ... I think I'd send her a verse."

"A verse! You are a true romantic ... a true romantic."

"He once said that of me."

"Your friend?"

"My... Her lover. Pee-pee."

"Well, he was right. What would your verse be?"

"I don't know. Something about the life she has lived."

"Go on."

Jerome hesitates. To speak a verse! To Laurent, a man he has known for barely a day. Of all the madness, is this the worst? Or best? And he doesn't have a rhyme for Marie. Certainly not one he can conjure up in an instant.

"Come on Monsieur Troubadour. Cat got your tongue?"

"I ... It's not that easy."

"Just start. Try something with her age."

"Her age?"

"You know, at eight, I met you at the gate. At nine......."

"I knew you'd be mine."

"Ha ha! You've got it! Did you?"

"I'm not sure I even knew her family then! We met at ten. I think...."

"Then, start there."

"I...."

"Be quick Jerome, Manseau is on the prowl!"

"What's that?"

"A poem."

"Let me see."

"No, it's not finis..."

Before he can react, Chlöe has snatched the notebook from the table and reads,

"I didn't know you at ten. Then again, maybe we had already wed, you in my bed, my wife – in another life. How gorgeous you must have been at eighteen. At twenty, you must have had plenty. By twenty three, was there a hint of me.? At twenty four – sure, you wanted more. By twenty five, you were coming alive. By thirty, you were getting dirty! At thirty four...you knocked down the door!"

"I wouldn't have put it quite like that! Anyway …Thirty four! Makes me feel old."

"I know baby. But that's what happened!"

"How about thirty five?"

"Now … I'm really alive"

"At ten, you knew not men."

"Ten! I should think not! Boys only! Go on." "Were you so bold as an eleven-year old?"

"Ah ha! Very good. I wouldn't be surprised …"

"I'd rather no …"

"Pardon, mon ami. Go on."

"At sixteen. I was already thinking of what might have been."

"You or her?"

"What?"

"Sixteen?"

"Oh! Her."

"Had she had Pierre by then?"

"I think so. Don't rub it in! By twenty, you will have had plenty."

"If she lives that long! This isn't a love verse. This is a song of jealousy."

"This is how I feel."

"Come on, you lot! We need to move on."

Laurent stands and with a groan, stretches. Jerome pushes himself to his feet and runs his hands through his hair. There is a soft rain. All around others stir and haul themselves upright. The rest has been brief: 'Time for a piss, no more,' Mauseau had said before striding away to join a huddle discussing the days business. He had been away an hour, long enough for the men to settle, talk, and sleep. Now it was time to go on.

"Have you written any more?"

"Poems?"

"D'accord."

"I'm not sure that counts as a poem, baby."

"Well, I liked it. Well?"

"No. Poetry's not my thing."

They are back at the table. As ever, the love making had been suffused with passion. And, as ever, different. The first kiss had been gentle, his lips playing around hers, her pulling away slightly and then gently pecking at his neck. The kissing had continued almost flirtatiously until, now under the covers, she had taken him into her mouth, and moments later was riding him, all gentility gone.

"I liked that."

"What?"

"The gently kissing. It's kind of tentative, dead sexy,"

"Oh so you don't like it when I ....."

"No, babe. I didn't say that. It's a good contrast though. We should do that combination more often."

"No good."

"Why not?"

"Feels like a plan. Plans in bed don't work for us."

"We should try ... You know."

"I love licking your bottom. But ... it might hurt."

"Best way is me on my back. But you'd have to be as gentle as you can. We could get some gel."

"Some ge...?"

"What about the dressing up, then?"

"But that's not a plan as such. I don't know what's going to happen just because I've got my basque on. Or whatever ..."

"Do you think Mauseau can write?"

"Doubt it, why?"

"I thought perhaps you could ask him to write you a letter to Marie, or a verse!"

"I'm not cut out to be ... The shame would be too much anyway."

"Shame?"

"Him writing love letters for me. Or verse. What a curse."

"Voilà! You're a natural!"

They have been trudging for several hours. Grateful for the breeze, Mauseau has ordered them to make good time. A long line of men, four abreast, in places five, stretches before Laurent and Jerome as far as either can see. Behind, an equally long line. Most walk in silence, some seem to doze as they shuffle. There is no sign of an enemy, no villages on this route, just fields and the occasional copse. In the woods the men are at first more wary but soon settle into a rhythm, no longer looking to left and right.

"Tell me about the commuters"

"Tell you what?"

"I don't know. What they wear, what you talk about. If you fancy any of them."

"In what order?"

"Ha ha! No, seriously. It must get boring."

"I don't spend much time talking to them. A lot of them just read their papers. They look pretty much the same too. You know, brogues, pin-stripes."

"Do they look miserable?"

"Not really miserable. A bit resigned I guess."

"Going and coming back?

"Coming back they look knackered."

"And the women?"

There aren't many women. It had taken him any number of mornings to realise what was missing in the carriage; women, children. No-one who just looked relaxed either. It was the time of day of course. The families or anyone going to Paris for the shops would all start their day's travelling after breakfast and still be at the *Galaries Lafayette* by mid-morning. By which time he would be on a fourth coffee and up to his eyeballs in the latest graphic for packaging plastic products.

Yesterday's had been the best yet. A small see-through casing shaped as 007 with 'For your eyes only' embossed around the surface in tiny font. Contact lens cases! The argument in marketing no doubt had revolved around how many purchasers even knew about James Bond let alone understood the in-joke based on the film title. Over coffee some wag had suggested packaging contraceptives in a sachet marked 'Dr. No!' From there it had been a short step to a 'Diamonds are Forever' jewellery case, a 'Casino Royale' playing card holder and a 'Thunderball' jock strap. The conversation had soon slipped into ribaldry. He had liked the plastic coffin idea with lid embossed, 'You only live twice.' Suggestions for an 'Octopussy' container veered from cruel to crude.

Over sandwiches an argument developed about the best screen Bond and why France had no equivalent to Ian Fleming. His half-hearted "Simenon?" had been met with blank looks.

"Where have you gone off to Mister?"

"What?"

"In that lovely head of yours?"

"I was thin...."

How had Simenon appeared? He runs his hands through his hair.

"Never mind baby. We were only talking about commuting. And how you spend every morning with ravishing women in designer dresses."

"I don...."

"I know baby, Joke!"

"What about your morning trips to work?"

"What, all the way to the nursery or Hélène's?"

"Do you see anyone en route?"

"No-one who I'd recognise day to day. Half the time there the library's too. Hélène's out somewhere and Guillaume only appears mid-day. If he's there at all."

"Are you bored?"

"No. I love it. You should see the books! It's like being in the quietest book shop in the world."

"And the biggest."

"Don't know about that but the place is huge. And the smell!"

"Musty?"

"Not at all. It smells of leather. Some of the desks have leather inlays. It's not just the books."

"*Some* of the desks? How many are there?"

"The first one's as you go in the main doors."

"Which are what? Twelfth century oak?"

"No, They're new. Guillaume said they're cherry."

"For doors?"

"I didn't argue. They're definitely new though. When you first walk in you see lines of bookshelves running away from you down the middle of the room. They're old. At least they all look old. There are paintings on the walls left and right. No shelves."

"At the far end?"

"You can't see the far end from the door!"

"Christ! It sounds like an aircraft hanger."

"No, it's not that big but there are no windows at the far end and you have to walk half-way down the middle row to switch the lights on."

"Which is how far?"

"Maybe forty metres."

"To the far end?"

"No. To the light switch."

XXXV

Journal: It's hard writing this. I'll start with the easy stuff. I love you, our talks, our bodies, the way you smell. How I love your smell, Mister.

Chlöe stops writing and thinks for a moment, a long moment. She is playing with her almost empty coffee cup and sitting at the courtyard table; *the* table. She smiles, then frowns. He has long since gone to work. For her part, she has greeted the first bread van of the day with a cheery wave; then queued at the second. It's generally considered the best of the increasing number in Giverny and a good place to listen to local gossip.

She had overheard Mme Picard make some remark about a cremation the following week. After several minutes featuring details of the various ailments suffered by the deceased (aged ninety seven!) she instead lets her attention drift to Guy. He is notoriously hard-working but, according to Hélène, not the brightest of sparks in the embers. She had referred to him as "the dunce" though she had also suggested that a man with the hardened muscle of a labourer would have no difficulty in finding local lovers whether they be old, young, poor or draped in *Armani*. Hélène had grinned while airing her suspicions.

Guy stands now directly behind Chlöe in the queue. She can vaguely smell him. It's not unpleasant.

Perhaps, earth with a little diesel oil thrown in. She doesn't turn but knows his features well. He is fair-haired, a sun-burned face, strong forearms, forever bare and wide shoulders. She knows he will be wearing his stained blue overalls and black work boots. His hands will be grimy, nails bitten to the quick.

She has heard Guy's story before. Most mornings she can hear him declaiming, as if by rôte, that day's events. In the summer Guy is up by four-thirty and at work for the Picards by six. After the bread van he will toil until noon when he takes thirty minutes over lunch before cycling to Vernon where he will work for the Laguoiles until dark. Somewhere in that long stint of labour, as the afternoon turns to evening, he will find another thirty minutes to eat his sandwiches. He buys them ready-made from *Lidl*. Thanks to the unrelenting public announcements about his day she even knows he prefers "Gruyère et jambon avec mayo."

In the winter months, his day is shorter. Not so very different she thinks from peasant life as it has been lived forever. Up at dawn, work, bread van, work, lunch, work, sandwiches, work, home. Twice a week Guy helps out with the rubbish collection. He delights in telling any trapped in the bread queue the number of wine bottles discarded by M Laconte or the "astonishing" number of two litre ("Two litre!") *Berger* pastis bottles Mme Azzam manages to cram into her weekly ("Weekly!") recycling crate. Invariably this will prompt Guy to add that he'd always assumed "they" weren't allowed alcohol. Chlöe doesn't think Guy stupid. Many people talk about their days at work. What makes Guy's banter unusual is the sheer repetitiveness of his public talk.

This doesn't reflect some lack of acumen. He can tell you anything at all about the horses he tends at weekends. Pedigree, history, the names of the winners, jockeys and owners of numberless *Arc de Triomphes* won by those of similar stock, their Arab fore-bears, the odds for their victories, even tales from a century ago about other equestrian heroes. The repeated recitals of his days mirror more the numbing dullness of the work his few qualifications allow him. She feels a little sorry for Guy even while suspecting one more repetition of his time-table will send her screaming from the queue.

She has left the bread van complete with ficelles and croissants and returned to the cottage determined to begin her diary. The *Confessions*. Already she has decided 'diary' too weak a title, opting instead for 'journal.' The first coffee is quickly followed by a second. As she searches for inspiration it is the almost finished third at which she now gazes.

That's hardly a confession is it? You know how much our time together means to me – the loving, the talks. I'll try something harder. When I was thirteen I hated the way I looked – small tits, bottom too big, really embarrassed about my cunt.

She pauses again. "Cunt" looks too blunt in black and white. She remembers envying boys who held their penises everyday if only to urinate. They could see and examine themselves at leisure. Her own sex was a mystery to her until a friend (another Chlöe) suggested she use a mirror held between her legs. Such a disappointment. How could anyone be remotely interested in the pale slit revealed, the labia not yet developed, her pubic hair embarrassingly sparse? She barely knew her clitoris though she enjoyed the sensations as she squeezed her thighs together on her favourite chair. It was the one comfortable sofa in the apartment at Evreux.

I've told you about my embarrassment over my clit already haven't I? Do you ever think we talk too much? This is getting more difficult by the minute. Coffee break! What are you doing, Mister? How was your train ride in today? No! This is about me! Trouble is you even know my fantasies. No! Let's get off sex for a bit.

I really fancied the boulanger at Evreux. Putain! You're going to think I'm a nympho! You once said there were worse things to be. I loved you when you said that. Forget the boulanger. Start again.

I used to collect dolls. I had dozens. When I met Etienne he said he liked that about me. It made me seem younger than I was. I think I was twenty, no nineteen and a bit. He was in his twenties and liked being seen with younger women, girls really. Once I came home (I had a job at Les Mousquetierres) and my parents were away (we'd stopped speaking by then).

Found him with some of my old Barbies. He'd undressed them and pulled the legs off. Really weird. I didn't tell him, but this had happened before! I kind of liked it. It turned me on. It was like he'd ritually ended my child-hood. We had a bit of a row. I went into the kitchen to throw them into the poubelle.

When I got back into the sitting room he was just standing there with a pleading look on his face. We just kind of snogged – no hesitation – and I felt him through his jeans. I was scared, turned on, angry about the doll murders, all over the place. But I unzipped him and touched it. Then I stroked him for a few seconds and he got all breathless and really hard. It was amazing. A few dead dolls and a couple of strokes and I could see what I'd been missing. I'm sure you can guess the rest. I was so wet I thought it would turn him off.

It didn't of course. We fucked for an hour. He came almost straightaway but then played with me until his erection came back. It didn't take long. The first time he'd been inside had hurt a bit but the second time was just lovely. No, baby, not as lovely as you! But we didn't do any of the more interesting things until he came round the next week. By then all the dolls were in the poubelle and all I could think about was screwing. Bum! Sex again!

I'd started collecting dolls when I was about five, living with my gran. She'd given me this lovely little girl doll. Big head, those funny blue eyes that turned up when you moved her, little blue dress and gorgeous white shoes. Like a baby's first pair. I loved her. I used to bathe her and pretend...

This isn't very good is it? Are you bored? Asleep by now I shouldn't be surprised. But you've said you're never – ever – bored with me. Bet you didn't know Mlle Nympho collected dolls tho' did you? Start again.

Sometimes when I'm on my own at the cottage I imagine cutting myself.

Chlöe sighs and rubs her forehead. She is surprised at the candour, wonders if he will be too. Shifting her weight in the chair she puts her pen to paper again – more gingerly now.

I think of taking out one of your beautifully sharp kitchen knives. The ceramic one if only I knew where you kept it; "too sharp," you said. Then I'd open a vein. I used to cut myself. There! In black and white!

She pauses again and stares at the notebook on the table as if the words have written themselves. She fingers the top corner of the page and pulls slightly. There is the merest sound of tearing; she stops. A tear forms and begins a gentle roll down her cheek. She lets go of the page, noticing how strongly her heart now beats.

I almost ripped that last part out. Deal is we write everything, right? Almost put "right everything". How about that! Unconscious word games! How can you love me after you read this?

She stands and walks towards the kitchen door. The note-book still lies on the table, its pages ruffled by a growing breeze. As she passes his newly planted artichokes her resolve seems to return. Clenching her fist she turns and, taking two deep breaths, sits again at the table. She smoothes out the page.

From now on baby it all goes down. And do you know? There's only one thing you need to know.

Journal. Wondered about calling this a diary but 'journal' has more of a literary ring to it, non? There I go again. More pretension. You say you like the way I use language. Even if it's you who wins the language games! But I'm stuck in some sort of need to impress (1st confession. Ha!).

Knowing literary stuff impresses all sorts of people (probably only the ones who are impressed by such things – do I really want to impress them?). First fear is that you find it pretentious too though you seem to be happy enough when I'm chatting to Hélène about Sartre or whoever. Number Two: I care too much what you think of me. Do I smell OK, wear the right clothes, shave often enough? You're probably laughing at this – you say you love my face - stubbly or not – never say anything about my clothes (though YOU seem to wear them a lot), love my smell (so you say – seems to me we more often as not smell of each other) but I'm allowed some amour propre, non? There you go again

– more pretension but this is all down to Rousseau so knowing about A-P must be OK.

Where to start? I love you. Not exactly original but true. True as the wind, our breath, the third side of Tales of Topographical Oceans *by Yes (a joke – are we allowed jokes? I haven't a clue what the third side of* TOTO *is about). Could try a poem (do you get a hint of desperation here?).*

If it's sunny
I'll take my honey
And love her till we're breathless.
When it's snowy
My love for Chlöe
Like stars, is clearly, forever deathless.

Baudelaire eat your heart out!

He raises his head from the key-board and looks around the office. It is open-plan. And big, possibly 250 square metres. He knows there are fifty seven desks, all but one with dark wooden work surfaces supported by legs of grey steel. Each work space is exactly four square metres, the desks in rows of eight. Between rows two/three, four/five and six/seven there are narrow passages down which fellow workers pace for inspiration, on their way to lunch or just for a break from hours poring over the niceties of plastic production, sales and export. At the end of row seven (his row) is a large cubicle encased in glass and steel. Inside is the fifty-seventh desk. Or first, depending on your point of view. This one is all wood, though not oak. Oak is reserved for the director on the next floor up.

A leather and steel swivel chair is tucked under the desk. It's usual occupant, Paul, is on an extended sabbatical; "stress" he'd been told. It was hard to imagine being more stressed than Cyrille who sits at the junction of rows four and five, more or less in the centre of the office. Cyrille had spent his first three months barely daring to move – the distance to the main doors or even the director's office had seemed just too much for him. Nonetheless it was M Paul Autier - Directeur Étage Six - who was off sick.

He looks hard at the monitor. Lunch is twenty minutes old and he's alone in the office awaiting inspiration. So far he's written – he does a quick word count – 290 words. His eyes are drawn again to Autier's office. There are no paintings inside, no personal effects at all really; nothing to interrupt his views. From the cubicle in the corner, M Autier, when he's there, can see the entire office floor by simply looking ahead scanning right to left. Something he had taken to doing more often of late has been swivelling his chair 180 degrees so he can take in the Seine, Notre-Dame, the left-bank. And M Autier is stressed!

He places a finger on the key-board and waits. He runs his hands through his hair. With a sigh of frustration he -

Fuck this. I've been at it for 25 minutes and I've already got writer's block. What was I saying about writing a novel? Forget it, baby, I can't even keep a journal going.

Here's something. I know you know this but I don't think you realize how deep it goes. I love thinking of you when I'm on my way to work – what you're doing, what you're wearing. Coming home is formidable – I just can't wait. I love it when you're home before me; dog walked, dinner thought about if not cooked, your lovely body. Wearing my shirt. But if I'm there first it's just as good. I get all twitchy about getting the dinner ready (and the washing up done) before you get home.

I try to create the impression I've prepared the food, cleaned the ash out of the grate and walked the dog without any fuss at all. And I just happen to have squeezed in a shower for good measure. Mad or what? You're much more realistic about these things. You tell me you need space to clean the place and walking the dog is a hassle. I have no idea why I want to pretend any of my domestic labour is effortless. Trying to be a perfect bloke? Maybe.

But the hours at work can be tough if I get some bee in my bonnet about you with someone else. I get so jealous. It's usually about your ex-boss. Not always, sometimes it's strangers but that's kind of OK – less threatening. Do you have lovers? I can't quite believe someone who likes shagging as much as you doesn't have a queue.

Again, he runs his hands through his hair. The desks around him are filling up now as colleagues return from lunch. The air-conditioning hums away but as the room fills the temperature rises. Soon he is uncomfortably warm. He knows he should open the desk-top file "PlaDeau," a summary of the programme for the annual Deauville Plastics convention. Glancing around he instead returns to the file still open in front of him.

What about your ex-boss? He'd have to be blind not to have fancied you. Where was he in the queue? I was seriously jealous when you were away with him. Did he have you on his desk with his Armanis round his ankles? Did you sit over coffee while he poured his heart out? 'Crazy' you might say but someone once said the jealous person knows everything – so I guess you and someone are at it right now. You're going to think I'm pathetic after reading this. There I go again – armour propre shining thru. Actually, baby, I think I am pathetic. This love is all-consuming, maddening.

I sometimes think of you dead (honest enough?) but only to spare me the jealousy. If you're dead, you're not with someone else (unless you count people like old S-M Bertrand). This is getting like one of those Virginia Woolf stream of consciousness things. And you can't have her on the book club list; fluent in French but only wrote en Anglais. I even get jealous of the women at the book club. You can drink, talk (do you ever talk about me? I know, I know – typical male thing about being the centre of attention, even in absentia). I just think of you sitting there, glass of wine at the ready, surrounded by women thinking how beautiful you are (I bet they do).

"Not exactly a plan of things to do in Deauville is it? Water? It's getting hot in here."

Cyrille is leaning over his shoulder reading the words on screen. On the desk he has placed a plastic beaker of water. Two small ice-cubes bob on the surface.

"It's a kind of diary. I'm doing it for…"

"None of my business. It's better than *Battleships*. Enjoy the water."

XXXVI

A new van! He is grateful for the day off – courtesy of the extra working days in "the North" as Chlöe had insisted on describing Deauville. She is back at the cottage. Said she'd give it a "thorough clean." As she was reading a life of Firenczi at the time this had seemed extremely unlikely.

Quite why she was reading about an obscure Hungarian psycho-analyst he couldn't fathom. But Chlöe's reading matter had long since stopped surprising him. Whenever films were shown at the local cinema club she would insist on buying the book. As non-members they rarely went to the club. To his chagrin any visit depended on guest entry courtesy of Guillaume.

The films and subsequent book purchase could be anything from *Manon des Sources* to *The Tin Drum* (in German. German! Chlöe didn't speak a word of German.) Perhaps the life of the Hungarian analyst wasn't so different from the other biographies she had started picking up; Cohen-Salal's *Sartre*, Edmund White's *Genet.* How she found the time to read these as well as the monthly book club suggestion (this month's had been *Marie qui louche* – Simenon!) was beyond him. Perhaps it was the distinct *lack* of cleaning house!

But the new van; big, white, a vast tonnelle to shade

the customers. A rasping blare as it arrives at the spot usually considered the melon man's own, then the painfully slow opening of the awning and a gathering of the curious. Mostly retired he suspects. There are fruits et legumes, some of the latter looking none too healthy. He could swear the courgettes are curling in front of his eyes. But there is a huge bag of almonds and some enormous frisée lettuce. It isn't the produce that arrests him. Rather it is the constant chatter of the propriétaire. She seems far more interested in the local gossip than selling anything. And she is wide; her great breasts parting to reveal a décolletage into which any hormonal teenage boy would be happy to disappear.

She shuffles about breezily behind the counter, her bulk something to which she has become accustomed. Despite himself, he is drawn again and again to those breasts. They are hardly the size or shape that he idealizes. The ideal is Chlöe, pure and simple. But there remains something intriguing. How far *down* do they go? Are the nipples in proportion – dark, brown spreading? Or are they flat, pink, nondescript? And what of this woman's sex life? Wild, outrageous or dominated by fearsome self-consciousness?

"Monsieur?"

He tears himself from her breasts.

"Oui. Madame?"

"Voulez-vous quelques choses?"

What does he want? He wants answers to his un-voiced questions.

"I, I...C'est possible?"

To what? See her upper half? He notices she is sweating, a bead of moisture sliding down her neck. Also, her skin is mottled. Le mot juste; 'mottled.' Snail-sized circles of light grey and brown appear at regular intervals along her arms. The fingers too are covered in brown patches; moles and freckles. The spell is broken.

"Avez vous des pommes de..."

"Bien sûr. But they are not so fresh. Try the sweet potatoes. I have figs. Or the melons. Canteloupes"

He wonders if he has fallen into a comedy routine; an unscripted, unspoken dance of suggestiveness and sexuality. Her next question carries the day,

"Do you prefer melons firm or ripe?"

"Fir...rip...it depends."

"I have both! Most customers prefer somewhere between the two!"

He had left in a daze. Had she been flirting? Had he? Could he confess to Chlöe? Bien sûr!

"Good day so far?"

"What, you mean the twenty minutes since you left?" "OK. You OK, Mister? You look a bit dazed."

"Do you ever have fantasies about the people in the vans?"

"What? Where did that come from?"

"Well?"

"Whoa! What's happened?"

So he tells her. She laughs, looks serious, at one point looking down-cast when he talks about the

279

teenage ideal and then brightens when he speaks of his own – her.

"Sometimes."

"You do?"

"Why not? I don't fancy any of them! Besides most are women and look exhausted. There is a boulan..."

"Who?"

"Just kidding, baby. Just kidding!"

Oeufs

  Lait

  Poulet

  Liq vaisselle

  Armagnac

  Ricard

  Noix

  Crème fraiche

"Wotcha doin, lovely?"

"A shopping list."

"I can see that. I thought you were on the novel this morning."

"I am."

"With a shopping list?"

"Yep. I thought it might add realism!"

"Hmmm...Takes up a few words too I suppose?"

"Not that many. Maybe I should do the *Carrefour* list. That would use a hundred or so."

"You getting desperate, babe?"

"No. But a bit stuck."

"Try a different list."

"Like?"

"Favourite films, the women you've slept with, kinds of dogs we see in Giverny...You could even score them. 1 to 10."

"For what?"

"The films could be direction, acting, script, memorability. Dogs could be size, slobberiness, number of feet..."

"Ha ha. And the women?"

"You tell me?"

"How I'd score them?"

"Yep."

"Oh I dunno. Eyes, skin, how much they made me laugh, noisiest orgasms, pubic hair ..."

"Charming! You'd score pubic hair?"

"Absolutely. Yours would win every time."

"I should think so! Your list's a bit, er, male isn't it?"

"The laughter?"

"No, I bet you only threw that in because you're talking with me now. I don't imagine women would have the same list at all."

"Eyes?"

"Maybe. But after humour; being good to talk to, ability to listen, kindness..."

"Now who's being stereotypic?"

"How so?"

"Listening, kindness. Sounds like something out of a women's magazine. You'll be saying 'good with children' next!"

"I won't. But I'd add 'can cook.'"

"Really? Are you having me on?"

"Hmmm..."

Chlöe folds her arms. She is wearing, yet again, one of his shirts. This time blue with thin grey and red stripes. Collarless. It's *Boss* and picked up in a charity shop. He loves her in or out of his shirts. She looks fondly at the sleeve.

"Come on. Are you serious? How about having a man who wears the kind of shirts you can't resist walking round the house in?"

"You're the only man I've ever done this with. It's not about the shirt, baby. It's the smell, imagining you wearing it, the feel. Loose, comfortable ..."

"So one criterion would be 'Big enough bloke who wears comfy shirts and smells good'?"

"Ok. And, er, dick. You got me!"

"Size, width, length, feel?"

"Fit. It just has to fit right. You do. But I really don't think it's the kind of thing women in general think about much. Or at least talk about."

"Women in general? How many do you know? How about Etta and Hélène?"

"I wouldn't say they're typical."

"Who is?"

"Catherine."

"Deneuve?"

"No, course not. Catherine at the nursery."

"What do you know about Catherine?"

"Apart from the fact she's got a great body?"

"Great body! She's like a stick insect with breasts! Your body knocks hers out of sight!"

"You're biased. I've hardly got any breasts…"

"They're beautiful. Lovely, lovely nipples. As for your legs!"

"My legs are losing tone, baby. I'm thinking of running."

"Fab. I'll lick you dry when you get home!"

"You're impossible. Great body or not, she told me a bit about her love life."

"When?"

"Last week while you were away."

He had hated being away from her for the meeting. Four days in Deauville. Forty-plus men in suits discussing plastic cutlery; colour, packaging (a whole morning on packaging!), durability, disinfection, pliability, potential health hazards and (of course) marketing.

He had spent a third of the time dozing or imagining what Chloe was doing – wearing, worrying about, thinking about, how she was sleeping, *who* she might be sleeping with. He had dismissed all the local candidates but Giverny was in full-on tourist mode and packed with guys he was convinced were better built than him. Younger, flatter stomachs. Worse still, better defined abs, more good-looking, cleverer, funnier. All of them probably rich, well richer than him. American, English, no ties. The list went on. But he didn't have ties. Only his tie to Chloe, and the life she gave him and whether or not she would want him when he returned. He had resisted the temptation – more a need – to call everyday and had restricted himself to a couple of calls. Fairly short by their standards. He'd considered trying some telephone sex but she had sounded distracted. Maybe there had been a fully-abbed rich Yank waiting for her to finish the call so they could get on with some furious rutting?

He trusted her when she said she loved him and his body but what did he really know about her? Her rages (and "Fuck you!"s) gave him pause for thought. He knew that jealousy was basically the idea that someone is having a better time than you. And what better time could there be than making love with someone? Actually, it couldn't be just anyone but there always came a moment when it didn't matter who it was. He'd read that somewhere. An off-the-wall 'sixties Sartrean analyst called David Cooper. He had no idea if Dr Cooper was still alive but knew he'd been friends with Ronnie Laing, and he was certainly dead. Heart attack playing tennis somewhere in the south. Cannes probably.

The simple truth that overwhelmed him was that Chlöe was beautiful, whatever she thought about her breasts and tone, and fun. Irresistible. Surely not only to him? He'd spent most of the time avoiding the lectures. He gave 'pliability' *and* 'durability' a miss. Instead he had walked along the prom, visited a couple of small galleries (that reminded him! He had a bracelet for Chlöe!), and sat in one particular café for what seemed like years although it was no more than three hours over the four days.

The evenings had been an education. His group had opted for evening meals rather than soporific lunches. All other than himself and Cyrille were on generous expenses. So generous that the two of them had simply been included on the tabs for whoever happened to be buying that evening. The food, mostly shell-fish or steak, had been remarkable. One dinner involved a sublime Teryaki concoction as the starter and a steak/frîtes combination that took him an hour to eat.

The wines were conspicuously fine and even more conspicuously credited to company *American Express* platinum cards. His first, probably only ever *Gevrey Chambertin*, several *Grands Crus* including something extraordinary from *Chateau Durfort* and another first; a *d'Yquem*! It had been like living inside a Maigret novel. He had wondered if he might treat Chlöe to a *Durfort*. Who knows, perhaps *Carrefour* carried it? But the post-prandial events had none of the 'fifties' bonhomie of Simenon about them. The group would divide: a few "sad fuckers," as his Director called them returning to their gleaming five-star hotel rooms, the remnants going separate ways; "looking for skirt," "clubbing," "more drinking time yet, boys!"

It had been mostly the married men 'skirt-hunting' probably destined to end up in some late-night bar with nothing but remorse. He had gone along the first night but his head-ache on Day Two had been so terrible he'd promised himself to stick to water. He hadn't but he'd been happy to join the 'sad crowd' until the last night. That Friday he had found himself at 'his' café just before midnight striking up a conversation with a woman dressed head to toe in something fearsomely expensive. She had regaled him with stories of her ex-husband's numerous infidelities. He understood that discussing sex with a stranger is a code for, "I fancy you." But he didn't and hadn't pursued the conversation. Instead she had staggered off in search of her hotel and he'd retreated to his.

"I knew you got up to stuff while I'm away!"

"I don't think a drink with Catherine constitutes 'getting up to stuff'!"

"A drink?"

"Well, a bottle. Maybe a bottle and a half. She was a bit down because the kids were being infuriating and she'd had a row with Jesu. So I invited her round for a glass. Or was it five?"

"Jesu? Is she born-again or something?"

"No. Jesu's her Brazilian bloke. Gorgeous."

"Good abs?"

"Good ab...how would I know?"

"Just wondered....Didn't Catherine bring 'em up?"

"No, I told you. That's not what women talk about!"

"But you said..."

"No, no. Non! I said we don't talk about specifics. Size and all that. But she was a bit pissed by the time we had the cassoulet and she was telling me about her and Jesu."

"Not the Saviour then?"

"No, Mister. Not the Saviour. But he might be hers."

"How?"

"She said it's just lovely with him."

"Except the rows."

"Except the rows. Lover, *we* have rows. They don't make you think I don't love you do they? They don't stop you trusting me?"

He is hurled back to the jealousies of his days in Deauville. She *can't* be this good at pretending! Can she?

"What did she say then?"

"She said that before Jesu she hadn't the first idea what love was all about. And how beautifully he fits! She said their sex life is amazing! She was all conspiratorial. She whispered. Whispered! Remember we were on our own. That there was "nothing like really great sex!" Then she said it was obvious I was getting it! I felt, I felt...like someone had read me. Like I was see-through!"

"And?"

"You called. It was awful. There's Catherine in the background whimpering about how she might have blown it with Jesu and there you are in Deauville! I just wanted to tell you about my evening. But you felt so, so...distant!"

XXXVIII

Recipe II
Poulet Pascal

Ingredients: Poulet (jointed), oignons (quartered; skin on), carrottes (halved and sliced lengthways), pommes de terre (quartered; skin on), fenouil (quartered), 1 garlic head, salt, pepper, any herbs you fancy, olive oil

Method: Heat oven to mark six. Coat everything with olive oil. Scatter all ingredients into a metal roasting dish and cook for one hour.

Martini: Mix a Parisian Martini (5 parts gin and nod towards La Tour Eiffel). Drink several as dinner cooks.

To serve: Squeeze garlic onto a sliced baguette, throw the rest into a serving dish. Et voilà!

"What's that?"

"I thought I'd have a go at a cook-book."

"You don't think the world has enough cook-books?"

"Not one like this."

"Which is?"

"Recipes for busy mums!"

"Ha! What do you know about busy mums?"

"Not a lot. But I know they don't have much time."

"Much time! Busy mums are so busy, I doubt if they bother with recipe books! Probably buy everything in one mad supermarket rush. Pizza, oven ready frîtes, stuff for the freezer. You'd be better off writing something for not-so-busy-dads to help out. Now what are you doing?"

"Adding a bit."

For exceptionally busy mums. The best way to prepare this dish is to get your bloke to mix the Martini and do all the food preparation too. If you want, you might like to entertain each other in the kitchen a little. This will depend on what you are wearing but a basque is to be recommended.

"For him or her?"

"It might be two hers."

"You're impossible! How many busy mums have the inclination to put a basque on while their partner is messing around in the kitchen? Martinis too! It should be called *Recipes for Rich Busy Mums!*"

"I just thought…"

"I know baby, but you'd better stick to a novel if you don't want the harpies on you. Still, I like the basque idea. Who's Pascal?"

"An old friend. He lives in the Eighteenth Arrondissement. Or he did. Cooked me the chicken dish once. Haven't seen him for a long time."

He realises it is, indeed, a long time. He and Pascal would occasionally eat together, often drink together and talk, talk, talk. Since Chlöe his male friends have almost disappeared. He doesn't count the men he bumps into in Giverny, though he has grown close to Raymonde. He meets Nicolas from time to time when he and Chlöe fancy some honey. Nico runs the Apiculteurie, an aged "Vente en Miel" notice dominating what once had been a significant house. Even the honey now has a rather different meaning courtesy of Chlöe's insistence it had aphrodisiac properties. He had said:

"Aphrodisiac? You can't believe that. Everything's an aphrodisiac nowadays. Chocolate, oysters."

"I know baby, but you don't eat it. You put a little here. And here! Now you can lick it. If you want!"

And the honey game had joined a growing list of games. Games that turned him on just thinking about what she might have in store after his daily return from Paris.

"It would have been much worse fifty or more years ago."

"What?"

"The lives women led. Kids, cooking, washing. Go back a bit further and they'd have been in the armaments factories or in the fields. Not much time then for Poulet Pascal."

"Are you sure? The women in the office work just as hard as the men. *And* most of them are expected to go home and cook, pick the kids up from the child-minder's..."

"I don't think they're typical. You might be right

though. The less you earn, the harder you work. Their secretaries probably stay late and still go home to all the chores. We're...lucky. No, we're incredibly lucky. Look at me, I can laugh at your Poulet Pascal, sit and talk with you, nip down to Raymonde's most days. I'm sure it's why I've the energy for all this sex. It's like being en vacances compared to some of the women I know."

"You don't find the time and energy for sex because I'm irresistible then?"

"Mix me a Martini and we'll see. Shall I get the chicken?"

"No, just the basque. Do we have any honey?"

Not a game, then. Just pure sensuality. But they still play games; sex games for the head.

"Let's use a die."

"And do what?"

"You write down six things that you want to do. In bed or wherever. (She grins) Number them one to six. I'll do the same. You throw and I'll do whatever comes up."

"Like *The Dice Man*?"

"Kind of. Or woman."

"What if I write for number five we have to go for a walk?"

"S'fine. You roll a five and we'll go for a walk. As long as we have a tumble in the grass!"

"A tumble in the grass! You're lovely."

And another time.

"Next time we're in bed, you wrap a scarf round my

head so I can't see. I'll keep as still as I can and you do what you want."

"What if I want to go and make some coffee while you're trussed up?"

"Trussed up! It's only a scarf. Anyway, I'd wait."

They had played the dice game. Her number four had been for him to read to her by the fire; not a tumble to be seen. So he'd read a page or two of *The Confessions*. Then she took the book out of his hand.

"I love it when you read, baby. I love you. Voilà!"

They rarely make it beyond a throw each. And the scarf routine is always too exciting just talking about it.

It is a Saturday. A brocante is planned all morning for the square. They listen to the radio as they change, he into black jeans, she into loose grey jogging bottoms.

"Turn it off, baby! Please."

"Pourquoi? I thought you liked *France Musique?* Your homage to Sartre and all that."

"I bet Sartre didn't have to listen to *The Great Gates of Kiev* three times a week! Solo piano, orchestral versions from Makarrass to André Previn. I'm sure they've had a modern version for sax! I used to like Mussorsgsky!"

"Manguin."

"What?"

"Manguin. And Munch."

"What are you talking about?"

"More artists beginning with 'M'"

"You've been cheating! Looking them up I bet!"

"There wasn't a rule to say I couldn't…"

"But.."

"Means you might lose?"

"I didn't say that."

"But that's what you meant. You're so competitive baby…I still love you."

"I should think so. Being competitive is the key to our sex life!"

"I thought it was love!"

"That too. But I do try to keep the competition at bay by making it interesting."

"You don't have to do that. Anyway - your technique isn't up to much is it? Saying you want to have me whenever you can, in whatever position and then fucking me fast. And hard."

"I thought you liked that?"

"I love it. Real man stuff. You can be so gentle the second time though."

"I like the gentle times. The under-the-duvet times."

"So do I. Don't get me wrong. I love all that too but when you just have me…"

"Too urgent?"

"Fantastic! And you're the only man I've *ever* been able to say, 'Just give me one, Mister' to!"

"Makes you sound like a builder. Dirty?"

"Animal. Seriously animal."

"Oh, listen. The boulanger. What do you fancy. Pain au chocolat? Tarte abricot?"

"I'll go. You finish getting dressed and put some coffee on."

As Chlöe steps outside the last blast of the bread van's horn is dying away. There are half a dozen people standing talking as the "bread-lady" – as he calls the greying, pasty-faced propriétaire – adjusts the side-awning. Croissants, breads, patisserie are revealed; at the front of the counter a pile of sweets to tempt any waiting children. And provoke any parents.

"Bonjour."

"Bonjour. Ça va?"

"Oui Chlöe. Et toi ? Ça va?"

"Oui. Je crois trois croissants. Et deux ficelles. Merci."

"Deux euros, quatre-vingt. Merci. Bonne journée!"

Nodding to two other customers as she passes, Chlöe makes her way back to the cottage. He is sitting at the kitchen table poring over some sheaves of paper.

"What did you get? Croissants? Do you know it's tempting to have a go at an historical novel. A romance, even a thriller."

"Too many. Here you go. You can have the extra one."

"Too many what?"

"Historical romances. And thrillers. Umberto Eco started it. You know, *The Name of the Rose.*"

"Yeah. Then *Foucault's Pendulum.* These are good. Better than the pain-au-chocolats."

"Don't remind me. Impenetrable. Too many sub-plots, all that existential guff where suddenly the hero is making up the plot as he goes along."

"It's magical realism, lover."

"Not for me baby. Too much magic and not enough realism. I couldn't finish it."

"That's not like you. I thought you ploughed on no matter what!"

"Non! That's you! I even gave up on *Martin Chuzzlewit.*"

"In translation?"

"Bien sûr. Must be the most boring first fifty pages ever."

"Coffee? So you got to page fifty?"

"No, I skipped loads, then thought, life is too short. Thanks."

"You should be more patient."

"If I finished half the novels I'd started and given up on I'd need to *be* a patient!"

"Name another one."

"Most of Flaubert, a few Zolas…"

"*Nana*?"

"No, I loved *Nana*. And *Pot Bouille.*"

"What's that?"

"Typical Zola. Exposing the hypocrisy of the bourgeoisie. All that."

"No, what does it mean? The title?"

"A kind of pun. Apparently a pot bouille was the cooking pot used by the poor. The book's set in a Paris house where there's a kind of cooking pot of emotion, lies, hypocrisy. Good enough answer? What haven't you finished, smartass?"

"Hmmm. Pynchon's *V*, Flaubert."

"None of it?"

"Not one. Dickens has beaten me a couple of times. I gave up on *A Tale of Two Cities.*"

"You didn't!"

"First time round. 'Fraid so. I was about seventeen and Maigret was much better. Went back to it a few years back. I liked it."

"Dickens would be pleased."

"Anyway. I'm no Dickens. Even Eco – he was already some kind of expert on linguistics."

"Philology."

"Whatever. He must have known publishers. A first time novelist would never get away with it. I just fancied trying my hand at some historical fiction. Might set it during the Hundred Years' War. There's a problem though..."

"And?"

"I don't know anything about the Hundred Years' War."

"Well, it didn't last a hundred years for a start. Pour us another."

"How do you know that?"

"We did it in history. It was three, maybe four wars lasting maybe a hundred and twenty odd years."

"Putain! Maybe you should write it."

"Well, I'm in Guillaume's library three days a week. I'm sure he's loads of relevant books. Why don't you come and have a nose?"

"You think it's a good idea, then? An historical romance with added blood and guts?"

"Why not, baby? Pourquoi non?"

He can think of no reason. Other than how writing will distract him from Chlöe. How he will spend every day cursed by the need to write. How he will resent walking Pantam because it will rob him of precious time when he could be crouched over a computer keyboard. Then again, he would get to work alongside Chlöe in the library. They might even...

"We're *not* doing that!"

"What?"

"Making love in the library!"

"How..."

"The look on your face. You'd make too much noise!"

"Come on, baby. It's not a public library."

"'S'not going to be a public library either, Mister! Shagging surrounded by books isn't going to help get it written."

"Oh, I don't know ... It's not goin to happen, anyway. What's the point of writing if I can't get published? Bottom line is, I don't have any contacts in publishing and it's who you know that counts."

"That's not like you, Mister. Don't be so pessimistic."

"Look at all the dross that gets published just because the author happens to be married to a publisher or related to a writer. Or journalist."

"Maybe it gets published because those people have been brought up surrounded by words and they know how to write."

"Par example?"

"Martin Amis!"

"Un autre?"

"Dumas."

"Which one?"

"Dumas fils!"

"Very funny. Not much of a list though is it? Authors who know the system must outnumber sons and daughters of novelists ten to one."

"Like?"

"Balzac – publisher."

"And?"

"Burgess – journalist."

"Keep going."

"Virtually any twentieth century poet – Auden, Isherwood, all part of a gay underworld. Sartre, Gide, Malraux – all involved in promoting their own work via so called left wing pamphlets."

"You sound jealous."

"I, I ... You're right."

He looks so downcast that Chlöe stops, quietened by remorse. She reaches out and ruffles his hair. He immediately runs his hands through it as if in mimicry and says, miserably,

"There must be hundreds of romantic bodice-rippers published every month. And historical murder mysteries. And historical, romantic bodice ripping murder mysteries."

"Set during the Hundred Years' War?"

"Probably half a dozen a year. The era's only a sleight of hand anyway. Whatever I write's going to be about us. Conversations, sex, what we eat. I'll just write it down and set it six hundred years ago."

"All of it?"

"Ok, not all of it."

"Coffee?"

"They didn't.."

"Brasseries? Lovely cottages with electricity?"

"Ok, ok, the details would be different, but not the substance."

"Which is?"

"You, baby. You. The love, the body, the talk, the sex..."

Intrigued, Chlöe stands and leans over his shoulder to get a better look at the papers he has been shuffling.

There is no spirit in rock. The stones men will hew into building blocks or carve to their will making statues that have no spirit, no soul. The self-glorifying replicas of false men will last long past the passing of those memorialised. Churches, houses, even Roman viaducts, all will fall in time. Time measured in thousands of years, not the few decades it takes for flesh to rot. And what is flesh without spirit?

"You're hand-writing's terrible. You should've been a médecin!"

"Thanks. It's just easier to write long-hand. I can copy and edit it straight onto the computer. What do you think? Apart from the hand-writing?"

"It's not about the Hundred Years' War is it?"

"Nope. Les Cathares."

"Hmm…"

"Well?"

"Bit old hat aren't they?"

"I know, but the whole thing's fascinating. The way of life, beliefs, battles with the church. Then there's the betrayals. The Autiers, Clergues, Montsegur, Beziers. All that."

"Yeah, yeah, but…"

"But?"

"Have you read *The Perfect Heresy*?"

"Bien sûr. Fabulous."

"And it reads like a novel anyway. They all do. *The Yellow Cross, Montaillou*. All of them. You're going to be hard-pressed to beat them."

"I'm not trying to. I just think it's a good era to set a love story in. And a few betrayals."

"But it's been done, baby. The Clergues, that poor woman at Montaillou."

"Beatrice?"

"Whatever her name was. The whole history is about love and betrayal."

He stops shuffling. He knows she is right. How can he beat *The Perfect Heresy*? How can anyone? But is that the point? He doesn't write in order to surpass the books he loves. He writes because he can't stop himself. And to keep a record…

"You're only doing this so we go down in history aren't you?"

"Mind-reader. Too weird. I was just thinking … and then you come out with it. Voilà!"

"Isn't that worth recording somewhere? The way we think of things at the same moment?"

"I dunno. I bet loads of people have the same experience."

"Well that's better isn't it? More people to relate to the book!"

"What, while they're on a beach?"

"With their lovers."

"Hmmm, do you think we'd find time to read on a beach?"

"We could try it. Not the south again though. Too far. Maybe Trouville."

"Not, not Trouville!"

"Pourquoi?"

"The mussels incident!"

"Les moules ... ?

"Haven't been back since."

"You were attacked by a mussel?"

"Not funny! I went with my parents and my dad insisted we had oysters. But I felt so sorry for them I asked for mussels. Moules frîtes."

"But you like moules frîtes ... "

"I know. But the mussels weren't cooked. They were raw like the oysters. I almost ... !

So, they had taken a train. First to Paris. Then south. Via Lyons and Narbonne to Perpignan. They booked into a pension at Argelès-sur-Mer but the beach at Argelès had proved to be searingly hot, the wind gusting stinging sand into their faces. Grateful for the public showers positioned at regular intervals on the promenade, they had washed the clinging grains from their bodies and then retreated to a brasserie.

"Pizza! Pizza et frîtes! Frîtes! Moules. Moules et frîtes. It's not Cordon Bleu is it?"

"You can be such a snob. It's cheap and cheerful. And just look at the size of the portions!"

Despite her protestations, they had taken another train. This time to Collioure. In a brasserie they sat drinking coffee watching a handsome man bent to his paper. He had short-trimmed grey hair and wore tortoiseshell photochromic glasses. He had soon been joined by two others; both with cropped grey hair.

"Looks like an older persons' skin-head convention!"

"They look like they're arguing. That guy on the left is wearing a Paris Saint German shirt!"

The skinhead convention is getting animated. Random words drift their way.

"Perpignan. Narbonne. Beziers. Ha!"

"Beziers. Perpignan. Narbonne! Voilà!"

They moved on to the Fauviste museum, gazed at the balcony where Matisse could overlook the bay while he worked. They ate sea-food galore (no oysters) and then took a bus to Céret.

In la musée, absorbed in a book, she barely looks up as he says:

"Aren't we here to look at the Soutine exhibition?"

"Je préfére Jean Gris. But you can go. They're pretty much everywhere. Did you know Picasso had one of his mistresses here?"

"One?"

"So it says in the guide-book."

"That's not a guidebook."

"No, it's about medieval warfare."

"Where ...?"

"Outside. There were a pile of them. Cheap. There's all sorts about the Hundred Years' War. I thought ... "

They travelled on to Leucate and find themselves in a small apartment overlooking the central square. Below them a carousel, children yelling happily and a host of English and American tourists dominating the ice cream parlours and outdoor eateries. They had tried first at a hotel on the edge of town but it was full. As they were leaving the receptionist said she could offer an emergency bolt-hole, an apartment not a hundred and fifty metres distant. They had agreed and, barely able to believe their luck, had been given a balconied apartment overlooking the scenes of holiday indulgence outside.

"How lucky was that?"

"Par for the course, baby!"

"Par...?"

"You know what I mean. Love brings luck. Meeting for the first time, Place du Tertre, finding the cottage. Even finding that amazing Calvados! We just make memories as we go along."

He hadn't wanted to believe her. Then, or now. Such luck couldn't last.

He crumples the paper in front of him.

"What are you doing?"

"Wrong theme, wrong era. Hundred Years' War, here we come!"

"We could get into the spirit a bit to help you picture life six hundred years past."

"Throw away the radio?"

"No, I thought maybe you could wear a leather jerkin. Then we could roll around in the mud a bit."

"Roll aroun ..."

"Well, not roll. But at least not shower as often."

"We'd have to have blackened teeth."

"Not true. I bet they had healthy diets. No sugar. Mostly meat. No reason for their teeth to rot."

"Well we'd have to let ourselves stink a bit. They didn't have showers. When was the last time you let yourself stink?"

"I.."

Chlöe is suddenly quiet. She turns from him and he hears a sharp intake of breath. She is still facing away as she mutters,

"Do you really want to know?"

XXXIX

He is learning. Writing a novel is a lot more than plot. He's not even sure what his plot is to be: *Man goes off to fight in Hundred Years' War, has a few adventures, witnesses any number (four so far) of terrible acts of violence and, and...spends a lot of time thinking about what the woman he loves is getting up to.* Not a comedy, then. But equally, not much of a story line and, so far, he is terribly short of some basics; dialogue, description, motive. But he is learning. The train journeys to the office have become much more productive.

His first problem had been names. *Le Monde* supplied a few, then he wracked his brain for more. Could he have a "Chlöe?" He thought not; a problem with names is that many didn't exist in the fourteenth century and many that did have long since gone to dust. A walk around the cemetery at Giverny had been instructive, if not helpful.

Monet's plaque is clear, beautifully clean like the others for famille Monet and obviously preserved by the *Claude Monet Trust* or a local body. But Monet's death was in the twentieth century. There are others inscribed on the headstones, equally well preserved from the nineteenth and eighteenth centuries but, despite the best efforts of those who tend the graves, these are showing signs of such age that the inscriptions are barely legible. A search for those going back further had proven fruitless, most being so worn that only heraldic marks are now visible. In any case, he had reasoned, the graves in a beautifully preserved church were hardly the place to find inspiration for the names of fourteenth century peasants.

For much the same reason he discounted using the names of those he had come to know locally; Hélène was out. Despite Hélène of Troy and the Goddess Hélèna he couldn't quite imagine an Hélène so far back. Eleanor! Now, Eleanor had some mileage but was it too obvious? He doubted if the peasantry would have had the modern-day propensity to name their children after the rich, royal and famous. Assuming they knew of their existence. With Hélène there was the added problem that she was so very much herself! Wherever would he find space for a scene involving an exquisitely dressed Amazon with her very own library?

Raymonde seemed a safer bet. There would have been any number of Raymondes. Plus a few Richards and Roberts! The three Rs! But he wanted something meatier. Which is where his fellow travellers began to come into their own. Sitting stuck, pen in hand, one morning he had simply asked the man at his right what is name was.

His fellow commuter had look startled. Something like amazement crossed the man's face. Clearly a taboo had been broken. Smiling he had quietly answered, "Guillaume." Guillaume! Perfect! And it killed two birds with one stone. He could use the name and take Hélène's notorious philandering husband as some kind of model. The dour fellow opposite had been less of a success. Alphonse! Why would there be an Alphonse shuffling about on his precious pages? The man next to Alphonse looked Algerian or similar. Insulted that he hadn't been asked, he had leaned forward to whisper,

"Je m'appelle, Sadi. Bonjour."

"Enhanté. P…"

"Why you not ask my name? You not like blacks?"

"Non, desolée. I'm writing a book and I need some names for characters. I don't have any, er, people like you in the book!"

"People like me! How do you know what I'm like?"

"I, I don't. That is…"

"No blacks allowed?"

"It's set in the fourteenth century."

"Didn't they have us back then? Is it about the Arctic? We were everywhere else. We practically invented literature you know!"

"Yes, I…"

"Architecture!"

"Erm…"

"Art of all kinds, even irrigation systems. Have you been to Cordoba?"

"You win. What shall I call him? Sadi?"

"Non, Gaston."

"Gaston, that's not an Arabic name! It's a good one though."

"Most names are Arabic, my friend. But your Gaston

would need to look more like … more like him!"

They are at a station. On the platform is a huge man. He is puffing as he hauls a gigantic suitcase towards the train. So Gaston is born. But what on earth is Gaston to do? The train moves away from 'Gaston' who stands, abandoned to frustration, on the platform. They gather speed as they enter a tunnel.

Sitting opposite him now - Sadi having mysteriously disappeared - is a dark-haired woman. Beautiful in an aubergine coloured dress, black tights and slippers. Slippers! They are a pale leopard-skin design. He tears his eyes from them and looks again at her face. Her eyes are brown. They exit the tunnel; the eyes are green. Perfect lips; temptingly kissable. Her hair is drawn tightly back, a perfect forehead. A little too much make-up. He wonders about her skin. Him and skin! Her forearms are pale. The skin looks fine.

"Pardon. Comment s'appellez-vous?"

"What."

"What is your name?"

"I understood that! Why are you asking?"

"I'm writing a novel and looking for names."

"Well, that's a new one!"

"New one?"

"Pick up line."

"It's n …"

"They never are."

"What do you mean?"

"Men on trains, park benches, planes. They're brilliant at sounding genuine!"

"But ... park benches?"

"Long story. You look genuine enough. Marie."

"Enchanté. Do you want to be in a novel?"

"Oh, stop it!"

"No, really."

"You'd need my surname?"

"Well, only if..."

"Deneuve."

"As in?"

"The very same. You can't have that in your novel can you?"

"I suppose not, but Marie's good."

She looks at him harder now, weighing him up. He can't possibly know this but Marie Deneuve has a problem, a problem not connected to her famous surname. Not connected at all. Marie Deneuve is torn. Does she fall in with men where she feels an instant, possibly dangerous connection, not so different from lust? Or does she get to know a man first in the hope that love and desire will grow? So far she has tried both types; one started stalking her within weeks of them splitting up. The other turned out to be embarrassingly, horribly impotent just as she had decided the time had come to burden their friendship with sex. He can't know this.

"Are you serious?"

"Serious?"

"About writing a novel?"

"Yes, he's serious. He's been asking complete strangers their names. I've never seen so much conversation on le mêtro."

As Guillaume is speaking, they hurtle into another tunnel.

"Your eyes."

"Oui."

"They change colour in the light."

"Dix points pour l'observation. What else do you need to know? Birth-sign. Life story. Why I'm wearing slippers?"

"Are they connected?"

"I... Hmmm... I'm Capricorn, I don't really believe in it though. Hard working? Maybe. I wouldn't be sitting here before breakfast otherwise, would I? Perfectionistic? I don't think so. Would a perfectionist come out in her slippers. Year of the tiger though."

"Year ...?"

"I was born in the year of the tiger. And they are leopard-skin. Close enough for jazz. Ha! My life story's no more interesting than anyone else's. Except for the slippers."

She leans forward conspiratorially. He notices that Guillaume pretends immersion in *Le Monde* but he too has leaned forward.

"I've just left a tryst!"

"Tryst?"

"With my man. Jerome. I had to leave in something of a hurry."

He loves the "something of a hurry." The kind of thing Hélène might say. Formal. Not quite...

"In a bit of a rush."

"Je comprends. Tryst interrupted?"

"At the worst possible moment!"

The audience is growing. Marie is no longer whispering. Half a dozen fellow commuters are distracted from their *Sudokus* and *Mots croisés* or gazing avidly at the floor. They listen. One stares at the leopard-skin slippers.

"Christ! It was a nightmare! She came back!"

"She?"

"Madame Leclaire! She was meant to be out for the night and not back 'til later."

"By which time you've normally gone?"

"D'accord. You, presumably don't hang around 'til your lover's husband is back?"

Suddenly, what seems like the whole carriage's attention is turned to him. Guillaume no longer makes any pretence at reading his newspaper.

"I don ..."

"Oh, come on. A man like you isn't faithful? And I can tell you're not gay!"

"How?"

"Just look at you. Confident. Not remotely efféte!"

"Not all gays are efféte."

"So you are?"

"No. But I am faithful."

Is he? How are you meant to resist women with so much joie de vivre? He changes the subject.

"What are you listening to?"

"You."

"No, I mean on your portable player."

"The CD?"

"Oui. Who is it."

"Etta James."

"Excellent!"

From nowhere, Jerome, Gaston and Marie Leclaire have come to life.

"It's my stop ..."

"Desolée, Au revoir."

"À bien tôt. Hordahafis."

"What? "

"Goodbye. In Persian. Don't ask. Another long story. Next time, handsome."

XL

From early spring – each and every spring - some sounds, a few smells had been familiar. The crickets, hirondelles, cries from the wheeling martins, the swifts always higher and last to return to their nests after an evening of catching insects. In summer he smells the heat of growing crops, occasionally the precious stink of dung. He has watched lizards playing on sun-baked walls or darting into crevasses, just as he did as a child. He knows such as well as he knows his right hand. Jerome looks down and tears come. He no longer knows his right hand. He had been lucky; the wound had healed well, no gangrene, no poisonous death coursing through his veins.

He has learned that a mutilated hand excuses him from nothing. He is here to fight. And no doubt die. The memories are merging, hunger and exhaustion taking him. Jacques, *Frère Jacques*, Coquette, the plague village, Manseau, Louis, Pierre, Gaston. How Gaston roared through the closed door, the mud, sunsets, early morning mists, the screams, the anticipation of death, the dead ...

Few villages are welcoming now. Those that the enemy has not razed or plundered, those with a little food. In any number he has seen burnt out hovels, scarred landscapes where even the byres have been put to the torch, any pigs or cows long gone. In some a smell of charred wood or burned bodies lingers amidst the dung. At least the dung is familiar. He brings it close to his face to recall better times, times when the threat of battle and imminent death were unknown. Times when...

Then another memory will struggle to the surface. Pee-pee boasting about Marie. Had he been boasting? It hadn't seemed so. Her face in all its beauty swims before him offering momentary solace before the unseen and barely imagined face of abandonment takes over the image. Now she is fierce, wild, groaning, hoarse with desire, reddened, rage-full, absorbed in pleasure ... in Pierre ...

He throws the cow-pat to the ground and, mournfully now, slumps away to rejoin his companions in their search for welcome. And welcome occasionally comes once the villagers have understood these men are too worn down to steal, to brutalize them further.

"Bienvenu mes amis! We have little. We can share some cheese, some comfort."

"Merci, merci. Come on Jerome. Fill your belly!"

But a belly cannot be filled with such small offerings, however gladly given. There is often so little on the table he knows the family can have saved nothing for themselves. Children with hungry eyes watch as he gulps down day-old bread moistened with rot-gut cider.

At one table there are figs and fresh-caught fish. It is all he can do to stop himself wresting the silver offerings from the frightened child at his side and eating them raw. Instead he waits as the fire is lit and the trout are gutted before being speared and twisted over the smoking wood. As the smell pervades the room he grasps the bloodied guts and stuffs them into his mouth. He retches, then swallows and retches again.

Now, they have come across a lone farm. It is by a wood, the roebuck can be seen among the trees. Such plenty! And the people are kind, pleased to see men not intent on taking, taking. Soon they are inside the farm-house. It is bigger than it looked from the outside. Four or five rooms, all warmed from a blazing hearth. Venison turns on the spit. Venison! It is his first meat in weeks. The taller of his two hosts, a ruddy faced man with strong, farmer's hands and immense forearms steps quietly forward.

"Doucement, mon ami. Doucement. There is no rush, no enemy here."

But, for Jerome, the warning is too late. He has gulped down scalding meat and potatoes from the pot-bouille and is spewing it back out across the table. It traces an arc of steaming, half-chewed food and bile before splashing to the wooden surface. He feels ashamed.

"Margueritte, help our friend."

A girl, perhaps nine or ten, offers him a rag to wipe himself. She scoops his shame into a wooden bowl.

"Ce n'est pas grave. A treat for the pigs."

"You have pigs, aussi?"

"Bien sûr. Well, one. We are fattening her for winter. Margueritte, give that to Coquette. My friend. What is wrong?"

"Your pig is called Coquette?"

"D'accord. All our sows are called Coquette. After my sister."

"Ta soeur?"

"Oui. She disappeared about three years ago. Went off following some men like yourselves. Up to no good I shouldn't be surprised. She's a survivor though, Coquette. Probably found herself a bed or two for the night! Children, I hope you're not listening in!"

Jerome feels tears welling up. Can this be the same Coquette? That he should ... to the sister of...

"Tu, t'appelle?"

"Jean-Louis. Doucement. Doucement. Get yourself a little air."

Jerome stands unsteadily and walks to the open door. His companions' laughter and chatter well-up behind him. It is quiet outside, early evening, only the late cries of hirondelles can be heard as they swoop and bank gobbling up midges. The western sky is dulling red and he can see l'étoile de bergers. Some things don't change! He smiles.

Was it his father or Pee-pee who had told him it isn't a star at all? It moves, overtaking the moon and always coming from the left tracing a path just below the moon's own. Apart from the moon it is the brightest thing in the night heavens. It's called the shepherds' star because the herders can tell from its placement the direction they must take to find their way back. Even on misty nights it is visible, only disappearing when cloud cover is complete. As a child he had wondered if it was still there behind the cloud. How could he know? How can anyone? There was no means by which even the wise could see behind clouds. But still, it was curious that night after night it appeared in the same position.

It seemed reasonable...

And what is reason? He lives now in a world where men march for countless leagues in order to butcher or be butchered by other men. At other times they fall under a hail of arrows loosed by archers so far distant it is impossible to know your executioner...

"Jerome! Stop day-dreaming. Vue là. Hommes! Come back inside! Viens ici!"

He snaps back to awareness. Sure enough, he can see men approaching from the trees. He is pulled roughly into the house and the door slammed shut. Tension is palpable. All laughter and chatter has ceased.

"The children! Take them into the back-room!"

Jerome now sees there are five children, all girls. Five! The youngest is barely two years old. Too startled to protest, she is scooped into her sister's arms and carried quickly away. The other children look frightened and pale, all colour drained, all good humour vanished. Around him, his companions are grasping swords and other blades. One is dragging on the string of his cross-bow, straining to prime a hastily mounted bolt. He hurries to the window.

"Douse the light! The light! Douse the..."

Too late! The door flies open. A burly, bearded yeoman stands in front of them. He looks grim and stern. A man of war. Then he softens...

"Mes amis! Put down your arms. Voilà! It is time to go home..."

XLI

Guillaume is lonely. Alone in his study. He stares at the screen with its familiar images. There is no sound. He's had enough of the ludicrous dialogue and the faked cries of delight. The couple are moving in ways he can barely imagine but there is an emptiness to the systematic way in which first the woman, then the man lick and probe each other. His eyes stray to the shelf to his right. Balzac. Arching his back and leaning toward the book nearest to hand, he strokes the spine of *Seraphita*. Along with about thirty others, he hasn't read it.

Guillaume is tall; his height was an important part of his relationship with Hélène. It still is. His arms are thinner now, pale where they were once bronzed, with less muscle than in the days of his courting. He smiles. What does he expect? That a seventy-year-old man will still have the body of his younger self? Or a seventy-year old would miss the body of his younger self? He looks sad. He feels ... tired. He hadn't even attempted repairing the greenhouse. One glance had told him how exhausting the work would be. He knows too that he drinks too much, something else that was easier when young. Only twenty years before he would have drunk wine and cognac for much of the weekend and happily gone to work on Monday none the worse for wear. Now it takes him a day to recover from a bottle of wine. How did that happen? Age just crept up on him. He wishes he could advise younger people to go easy on their bodies. Chlöe, for instance. But younger people don't take advice. He didn't.

He rests his hand on his stomach; a little flabby. He presses. Very flabby. Guillaume sighs. Can this be why Hélène...? No, he knows why his wife no longer touches him. The visits to Paris, the weekends with prostitutes, the drunkenness at home. Sadness again. For her as well as himself. He reaches again for Balzac.

Placing the book beneath the screen, he opens it at the dedication; above the page the couple continue to gyrate.

To Madame Eveline de Hanska, née Countess Rzewuska. Madam, Here is the work you desired of me. Then some two hundred or so words acknowledging de Hanska as his muse before, *I remain, Madam, with respect, your faithful servant, De Balzac. Paris, August 23, 1835.*

Guillaume sighs again. 1835! The publication date of the volume before him is 1897 but he knows he has an earlier one. The couple seem to be taking a well-earned breather. He turns to Chapter One.

On seeing the Norwegian coast as outlined on the map, what imagination can fail to be amazed at its fantastic contour – long tongues of granite, round which the surges of the North Sea are forever moaning?

He sighs again. Only Balzac would start a novel with a thirty six word question. And a rhetorical question at that.

The couple have taken to writhing a good deal. Guillaume shuts the book. *Seraphita* can wait. His days seem long now; the occasional round of golf, the infrequent dinner parties. Hélène no longer shows off her Cordon Bleu skills. Sometimes he returns home to an empty house, a terse note left in his study to the effect that his supper is waiting in the refrigerator to be re-heated. He had confronted Hélène about this. But only once.

"Do you know, I don't expect to have some re-heated crap after a day in town. I want..."

"What do you want, cheri? A little wifey to cook for you, perhaps warm your slippers?"

"I don't wea ... My 'wifey' doesn't even warm my bed!"

A chasm had long ago opened between them. Sex was no longer something to be contemplated. To mention it was to risk...

"Well, Guillaume, we all know why that is don't we? You gave up any rights to me sharing your bed when you confessed to your little Parisienne dalliances. Don't get me wrong. You can have who you want but to spend our money on whores...!"

He hated it when she used his name. It made her

sound like the annoyed teacher and left him feeling like a chastised child.

"Come on, Hélène. You can't still hold that against..."

"Don't you, 'Come on, Hélène,' me! Once might have been forgivable but you must have spent nigh on thirty years of our marriage whoring around. I don't know which sport had the more holes. Whoring or golf!"

He had not dared to mention sex since. Hélène could be formidable in a rage. It was always a controlled rage, the venom reserved exclusively for him. And when she drew herself up to her full height! He eyes the screen again. His hand strays to the volume control...

"You swing."

"What?"

"Swing. From miserable to 'It'll be alright.'"

"Are you going to talk about my periods again? Don't go there baby!"

"No. I mean you swing from, 'It's hopeless' to 'It'll be fine' in the space of minutes."

"I don...Give mean an example."

"Like...I don't know. Money."

"Go on."

"You can be on your knees with worry about money and then you say, 'Let's go to the brasserie!' Three minutes later!"

"Give me another."

"Children."

All goes still – a deathly calm has come over Chlöe, the colour drained from her face.

"Go on."

"Well, you were so chirpy about Danielle's announcement she was pregnant."

"Donc? Normale, non?"

He runs his hands through his hair. This won't be easy.

"But only yesterday morning you were saying how stupid people were to have kids and the world was already top heavy with the human race!"

"But that doesn't mean I can't be happy for Danielle! You really don't think like a woman at all, do you, Mister?"

"Maybe I feel how a woman feels though!"

"Which means?"

"When you're sad I pick it up, right away. And when you're really down it makes me feel terrible."

"So?"

"So I'm not thinking straight when I respond. I say the wrong thing, make it worse, whatever."

"Well, there's your clue."

"Eh?"

"Don't say anything, Mister. I'm not looking for words."

"Fine. But what am I meant to do with my feelings?"

Chlöe quietens again. What *is* he meant to do with his feelings?

"Coffee, missus?"

"Balzac was a coffee freak."

"Where do you get that from?"

"Guillaume. He was in the library today. We were just chatting."

"Does he often see you in there?"

"Yes. No! It's his house!"

"And I bet he loves the fact a gorgeous woman is prowling around the library."

"I'm not."

"Gorgeous?"

"Prowling. Anyway he only pops in for coffee. You and your jealousy. He's old enough to be my dad."

"So... Johnny Halliday's old enough to be your grandfather but you fancy him."

"Christ! You get more chance to meet people than me nowadays. You must meet hundreds of people on the commute!"

"I....Let's not do this. Tell me about Balzac."

The argument about her moods seems to have evaporated.

"Hmmm...He used three different beans – Martinique, Mocha and...I can't remember the other one."

"And...?"

"He bought one in the rue de Vieilles, one in the Faubourg St Germain and whatever the other one was, in the rue de Montblanc."

"But they're half way across Paris!"

"Used to take him half a day pre métro. Voilà!"

"He more than liked the stuff. What does Guillaume

drink?"

"You wouldn't believe it! It's some Vietnamese concoction that comes out of civets' bottoms!"

"Eh?"

"The civets eat the beans. Then after they have a poo some poor sod cleans it off and roasts the beans."

"What does that cost?"

"Guillaume gets it at some boutique coffee house near the Champs-Elysées at sixty euros for a quarter kilo."

"Sixty euros! Fuck me! Have you tried it?"

"Once."

"And?"

"It tasted like coffee. It's not how I like my coffee anyway."

"Why not?"

"You weren't there, baby. You weren't there."

And with that all the jealousy, all the anger evaporates.

Guillaume pats his belly again. Three minutes of faked ecstasy has been more than enough. The screen is dark now. He is thinking about Chlöe. Her style can be quite breath-taking. He comes to the library as often as he can nowadays in the hope... He smiles; he is too old for his young assistant librarian.

Anyway, she has a boy-friend. Perhaps a live in lover? It's a vernacular wholly unfamiliar to Guillaume who can't quite find *le mot juste*. Images of the writhing couple invade his contemplation and he makes an effort to replace the gyrating actress's features with those of Chlöe. To no avail. Both the pornographic acrobats had been fair-haired, the man positively Teutonic while Chlöe is dark, her body slighter than the woman starring in *'Je dîs,Oui!'* He grins. Where do they get these titles from? Is there a committee? It must be hilarious seeing who can come up with the silliest. He has a vague memory of *'Je dîs, Non!'* from the same director. Same plot too, if you can call it plot. A woman who happens to be half-dressed surprised by the visit of a plumber, builder, electrician, whatever. Some nondescript dialogue before she puts a hand on his knee. Or crotch. She undoes his belt buckle. Then seduction, various sexual positions, denouement all pretty much identical.

But Chlöe's body, the way she sashays through the door, her bright smile, invariably cheery greeting... He can feel himself getting hard. With an effort he controls the image. Now Chlöe is reaching over the desk, showing delicious cheeks, a thong, legs parted slightly. Guillaume presses at his erection. A response! Barely aware of anything other than a growing urgency he fumbles with his fly buttons. The image is still there as he grasps himself. It's a slow fantasy: Chlöe pushing her thong to one side, a glimpse of dark, curling hair, lips parting, pressing himself to the beckoning yoni...

"Guillaume! Guillaume, arrêtez-vous. What are you doing? No. Don't tell me. I can see *exactly* what you're doing!"

Hélène stands in the doorway. She has a cup of tea in her right hand, a hand that trembles as she sets the saucer down on a polished walnut side-table. Guillaume is trying to press his erection back inside the yawning fly. Despite the hideous embarrassment of Hélène's sudden arrival, he grins. His tumescence shows no sign of dying away, itself a kind of triumph.

"Well! It's the middle of the day!"

"The middle ... Hélène my gilded sunflower, is there a right time to masturbate?"

"I...Is there...? Well, well *you* should know!"

"Desolée. I'm sorry. I thought you were out. Anyway, you never come to the study."

"Well, I don't think I'll make the same mistake again. I brought you some tea. You can go back to your porn star now. Don't let the tea go cold!"

As she leaves, Guillaume is smiling again. Porn star! If only she knew.

"You can't just do that!"

"What?"

"Fly into a "Fuck You!" mood."

"I don't."

"Well, that's how it feels. It feels like you're a different person. Bitter, angry."

"Go on Mister."

"Incredibly self-centred. It's like I don't exist."

"Far be it from me to go off the subject."

"What subject?"

"You!"

"What are you talking about?"

"It's the man thing isn't it? If the world doesn't revolve around you, you get all hurt."

"That's not fair. You try being on the receiving end of "fuck you!""

"You try being pissed off at a bloke's me, me, me-ness!"

"I......"

He pauses. Is he so self-centred? The explosions don't seem to relate to him. He runs his hand through his hair. He has a theory about Chlöe's mood swings. They have been worse of late and nowhere near as predictably cyclic as before.

"The last time wasn't about me."

"What was it about then?"

"Work."

"It..."

Now she pauses. The last time had been Friday morning. Just as he was leaving the front door a red-faced Chlöe has leaned out of the window,

"Go on, just fuck off! Ignore me, why don't you!"

Moments before, while he had been hunting yet another wayward sock, she had suddenly announced that she didn't want to go to the library.

"Guillaume will be there with his leer and his expensive coffee."

"From civets' bottoms though baby."

"Don't you dare laugh at me, I'm serious!"

"I wasn't. I...."

"Well it feels like it when you come out with some clever remark."

"I...."

"You do it all the time."

"I don't think..."

"Exactly!"

"No. I meant, I don't think it's every time."

"Don't be pedantic. It's every time as far as I'm concerned. You try being leered at and paid peanuts. It's not like it's a safe job!"

"Like mine?"

"Just fuck off!"

The sock found and no further words from Chlöe, a picture of dejection he had left the house.

"I think it's because you don't feel appreciated."

"It's n..."

"Go on."

"I think you only want me for sex!"

"Come on. You know that's not true. Anyway, you've said that even if we only wanted each other for sex, that would still be pretty good."

"There you go again. Not taking me seriously."

"I do baby. I'm just repeating...."

"Well don't! I only say that when we're fucking! Anyway, you try working for Guillaume. *He* only wants me for sex! I'm crap at the library stuff."

He runs his hand through his hair, unsure whether the door-step is the best place for a heart-to-heart,

"Not crap. Probably a bit ... eccentric?"

"Then why did Hélène ask me to do it?"

He bites his tongue. 'Charity' has uncharitably come to mind. He doesn't know why. Chlöe's classification system is some way from *Dewey*. Even their own collection in it's wildly off-kilter sequencing, bemuses him. He can't imagine what she is doing with thousands of books.

"What system are you using?"

"Alphabetical."

He inwardly groans. Before he can say anything she goes on,

"I've pretty much done the 'A's. Althuser, Aquinas, Aristotle..."

He breathes a sigh of relief.

"And?"

"Those too."

"What do you mean?"

"The 'ands'. *Pride and Prejudice, Fear and Loathing in Las Vegas, Androcles and the Lion*"

"I......"

"What's the matter?"

He grins. What *is* the matter? If Guillaume is happy to pay Chlöe to create alphabetical mayhem with his books, who is he to argue?

"Guillaume says he thinks the system is interesting."

"But how does he find the books?"

"He doesn't. I do. I can remember where they are. The only thing he insisted on was that all the Balzacs are together."

"And are they?"

"He keeps them all by his computer in the study."

"To read?"

"I think just to look at the spines. I can't imagine Guillaume reading Balzac."

"Why not?"

"I don't think he'd relate to tales of nineteenth century money-lending. He's got too much money to worry about it."

"Come down and kiss me good-bye, lovely"

XLII

"Do you realize how much time you spend writing nowadays?"

"A lot?"

"More than a lot, baby."

"Not as much as Sartre I bet."

"Who cares about bloody Sartre! What gets to me is how much of our talks you record."

"All of em!"

"All of them? Liar!"

"Ok, not all. But it's only because I can't remember them all or I get distracted. Like on the train."

"The train? Are you changing the subject?"

"No. I was stuck for names so I started asking people."

"For what?"

"Their names. For the novel."

"There wouldn't have been many with fourteenth century names. For all we know, people didn't have names."

"What?"

"Life was pretty short. Why bother?"

"Well, what if they wanted to refer to someone?"

"Maybe, they just said where the family lived. By a field they'd have been Les Champs."

"What if two families lived by a field?"

"Well, they'd have had fore-names. Ha!"

"What if two families lived by a field and had kids with the same fore-names?"

"Oh, I don't know. Maybe there was a rule against it."

Would there be a rule against it? The French do so love rules. He knows the only records of names are for the rich, privileged and the accused or witnesses. Even in the fourteenth century records had been thorough. In Latin, but thorough. In the Sorbonne he had found records of Cathar trials. Hundreds of pages in Latin and early Occitaine.

"Well, anyway, someone suggested Gaston. Thought I'd use that. Guillaume as well."

"No Chlöe?"

"Sorry babe, too modern."

"But there was a goddess Chlöe!"

"I know but I doubt if any of my peasants would have named their kids after goddesses even if they'd known about her."

"Probably didn't name many of them at all until they were sure they'd survive."

"Hmmm... I checked in the graveyard."

"Any luck?"

"No, the stones are too faded but ..."

"Peasants wouldn't have been buried there anyway."

"Mindreader!"

"Moi? Non! But it's obvious isn't it?"

"It wasn't to me until I thought about it."

"Well, I'd never thought about it 'til now. It's our talks. We discover things we knew all along. Don't write that down!"

"Why not?"

"It's too, too…"

"Sentimental?"

"That, oui. And naff."

"Naff?"

"Makes us sound the perfect bloody couple. Like we're still love-sick kids inspiring each other all the time."

"So, how old do you feel when we talk like this?"

"I don't know. Thir…No, older. Eighteen maybe sometimes my age. Sometimes about ninety."

"Ninety!"

"Yeah, it's like I've known you for a long time. Like Hélène says."

"What does Hélène say?"

"She's involved with some kind of telephone guru."

"Telephone guru! Are you serious? Putain!"

"Honest. She has long conversations with him most days. She says he's an existential counsellor in touch with auras and previous lives. Voilà!"

"Nuts then?"

"Baby! Hélène thinks he's great."

"But prev…"

"He says love passes through the centuries until you meet your soul-mate again."

"So we've known each other before. We could have

been Napoleon and Josephine. Louis and Marie-Antoinette…"

"Better still Fersen and Marie-A."

"Who?"

"Love of her life. After the Dauphin."

"Abelard and Heloise! Antony and Chlöepatra!"

"Ha ha. He's serious. Not cheap either! He's got Hélène convinced she was born on Sappho thousands of years ago!"

"So Guillaume's a woman?"

"No, Mister. Guillaume's hardly a soul-mate is he?"

"How would you know?"

"What, after the story about their wedding. And the Internet dating? Maybe some men just need it more, honey."

"I…"

What is he meant to answer to that? He's sure different couples are unbalanced in different ways, their sexual appetites just being one example. But there's more than a hint of … what is it? Ah yes. Blundering stereotype. He decides to take her on. He regrets it almost before the words have left his lips.

"I don't think you can generali…"

"Why not?"

"Well, for all we know most couples have the opposite problem and it's the woman who doesn't get enough."

"Now who's stereotyping?"

"What? How?"

"Couples. You're assuming couples are men and

women."

"I... Maybe you're right and she secretly loves all the infidelities and puts it down to his libido being out of synch with hers."

"No. She hates it. She stays for the money, the grand-children..."

"The library?"

"Who wouldn't? But soul-mates they are not."

"Are we?"

"You have to ask! We've been together since..."

"The Hundred Years' War?"

"Easily. Though I'm not sure."

"Because?"

"They wouldn't have had pedicures then would they?"

"Ped ... What?"

"You wouldn't love me without my pedicure mister."

He sits back, grinning. He loves her feet, especially her toes, the one silver toe ring nestling on the middle toe of the right foot. But he hadn't thought about their care before. He is intrigued,

"How often do you have a pedicure?"

"Not often. They're not cheap. Twice a year probably. When the lady comes round in the van."

"Van? We have a pedicure van?"

"You must have seen her. *Pieds du Pierre*."

"*Pieds du...*Who's Pierre?"

"The owner. She often calls him Pee-pee."

"Pee-pee? Pee-pee ... I wonder?"

"What?"

"It's a good nick-name that. And Pierre..."

"You're doing it aren't you? Thinking about writing it down!"

"No. I can remember Pee-pee."

"What day does the van come?"

"Keeps changing. Why?"

"I'd quite like to see him. Get a better picture."

"Well you can't. He sends his missus to do the pedicures. She drives the van too."

"And her name?"

"You're pushing your luck! Clarice. Clarice Dupont."

"I knew a Clarice Dupont."

"Knew?"

"Not like that. She was about eleven. Lived down the road. I'd have been fourteen or so. Pretty. Club-foot. The kids at school took the piss all the time."

"What happened to her?"

What *did* happen to Clarice Dupont? He searches for memories. He can vaguely recall her after school sitting with, with...Alain! Another name. He wonders how many he needs. Is it possible to dredge them all up from school-days? Daniel, Phillipe, Paul? Some potential there. Stephane. He sees him now; a shock of red hair, pale skin, misty blue eyes, thin lips.

"Hello. Hello. Where have you drifted off to?"

"School-days. I'm trying to remember the boys I knew. Well, their names at least."

"What about the teachers?"

"We weren't told their first names. Except the head."

"Who was?"

"Auguste. Auguste Manseau."

"That's a good name!"

"Now all I need is a character to fit the name."

"Or two. An Auguste and a Manseau."

He remembers Auguste well. Rumoured to be gay he was probably in his, what, thirties? This wasn't so easy. The headmaster had seemed impossibly old to him. Thirty was an unattainable age, forty beyond comprehension though to him his parents had always seemed forty. Even when in their sixties. His father had seemed to age suddenly. He'd been living away from home for a year before his first return. His father had looked older; within an hour the familiar features were all back in place.

Then he'd moved much further away; this time the gap between visits was a full five years. And this time his father was definitely older, noticeably greying, in some places white. His beard had not a trace of black. He was still tall though a little stooped, the broad shoulders now bowed. Before he had time to comment his father had said, "Stop staring. Anyone would think you hadn't set eyes on me before!" Perhaps he hadn't. He noticed now the grey eyes, the lines around them deeper than he expected. The bronzed forearms were still brown from a life-time habit of rolling up his shirt sleeves whatever the weather.

But the arms were thinner, less hairy, the wrist bones more obvious and the wrinkles on the backs of his hands ... They looked like aerial photographs of wind-whipped sand. Just below the sand, mighty rivers of blue stood out. The nails were still beautiful, almost manicured. The pedicure comes back to mind and he grins.

"What you thinking about now Mister?"

"Your feet."

"No, before that?"

"My dad. The way he seemed to age so fast."

"I bet you had long gaps between seeing him."

"Longer and longer."

"That's how it works baby. If we went for a month without seeing each other, you'd think I looked a lot older."

"Don't be daft. You always look the sa... No, that's not true. You always look different to me. You change all the time. Impeccable."

"But if we had a real gap, you'd notice wrinkles, my skin getting baggy..."

"Baggy! I don't think so. If anything you could do with a bit more...er..."

"Meat?"

"Fat."

"Am I too thin?"

"No, I didn't mean..."

"Hmmm..."

He smiles. He's back in that terrible place where he thinks he's hurt her feelings. Unbearable. As a distraction he searches again for images of his father. But it is Auguste who comes to mind. Ah yes, the chain of thought had started with Auguste. His hands? His face? No, his age. How old *had* his headmaster been?

The face lined, the hands like hams. Strong, if pale, calves. He and Phillipe had almost choked as Auguste had appeared in shorts to take a rugby session. The usual master ... now what was *he* called? Ah! Michel! Michel had most definitely been gay. Michel had been ill. The contrast between Auguste's thick-set body and his thin legs had provoked much hilarity.

"You're smiling again."

"School-days."

"Lots of nice memories?"

"A few. You?"

"Let's not ... please. Not now. How do you imagine yourself? A Proust, a Gide, a Simenon?"

He notices the sudden switch and wonders whether to pursue the school memories option. Not today,

"More like a Robinson Crusoe."

"What?"

"You know, Daniel Defoe."

"I know who wrote it. I meant, how is it you're Crusoe? You're hardly on an island are you?"

"Aren't we all?"

"Oh stop it! C'mon, seriously."

"I don't know, I just record ordinary events around me. I've become a voyeur of ordinary life."

"Such as?"

"The train through the banlieus. When I'm not listening in to other people's conversations, I'm writing down the scenery."

"Hardly inspiring."

"It's odd. Do you have any idea how many

apartments have trampolines outside? They're in the car-parks, next to the rail track, wherever."

"A lot?"

"Nearly all of them on one stretch. I gave up counting."

"Not very fourteenth century is it?"

"I know, I just can't help myself...thought it might come in useful."

"Like when your hero invents a new siege tower based on trampolines?"

"No...how did you know about the siege towers?"

"I read what you've done sometimes baby."

He is quiet. He hadn't expected this. Somehow he had imagined presenting Chlöe with a leather-bound volume after a low key book launch.

"And?"

"And what?"

"What did you think?"

"I like it. It's odd seeing us all over the place. Even five hundred odd years ago."

He suddenly feels happy. Very happy.

"There's another way I'm Crusoe."

"I'm Man Friday?"

"No, lover, you're Woman Everyday. But that's not it. It's the way writing forces you to think of the most important things there are. Like Crusoe's diary. It's full of longing for home, the need for food, fear of savages; the crucial stuff."

"Hmmm....not sure about longing for home being crucial."

"Well, a home. *Our* home."

"Do you ever talk to other people about what you're trying to do?"

"No, well occasionally on the mêtro when people spot me scribbling. And once to Raymonde."

"I bet he said the same as Hélène when I told her."

"Which was?"

"Oh darling! I've been thinking about writing a novel for ages."

"Not quite. He said, "Everyone thinks they've got a novel inside them. But it's always shite. Novels need to be outside, not inside.""

"Wow! That's almost profound."

"Turns out he started one about twenty years ago and just gave up."

"Why?"

"No real story other than loads of pseudo-autobiographical stuff. He said the love scenes made his own toes curl."

"You didn't show him yours?"

"Are you kidding? I doubt if Raymonde wants to see you and me in black and white."

"I'm not so sure. Anyway, the scenes could just be from your imagination. He wouldn't know…"

He is grinning. She smiles, then starts to quiver. A snort, another. And she's off. In between choking laughter she manages,

"Ok, he'd know. He'd know! You can't put all the sex stuff in!"

"Why not?"

"Too…too…intimate."

"But people won't know it's true."

"Baby, anyone who reads this stuff will know it has to be true."

"Well, you'd suddenly have a fan club!"

"Not me, mister. I think it's you who'll have the fan club."

"Why?"

"For a start most people who read novels are women aren't they?"

"I…"

He has read all his life. He must have read *The Little Prince* six or seven times before his teens. Then Baudelaire, Zola, Genet, Camus. All set school texts. As for Balzac! His master at school hadn't much approved of Balzac. He'd said he was, "too bloody enamoured of the petit-bourgeoisie." But despite the disapproval, or more likely spurred on by it, he had read all but two volumes of *La Comedie Humaine.* Completion had been delayed from a sense that the world might come to a juddering halt if he managed to finish the task. Now it was put off indefinitely. The unread volumes also had titles which, even now, seemed silly; *Seraphita* and *The Magic Skin.* He sits quietly. A gulf is opening between him and various friends. Raymonde. Pascal. Do either of them read novels?

"How about Guillaume?"

"Collecting first editions of the classics isn't the same as reading them. No. Novels are written for the woman's market. And you're going to wreck a few lives when this hits the bookshops!"

"How?"

"How do you think? Anyone with a tenth of the sex life you're recording is going to feel cheated!"

"But it's a love story!"

"That happens to have some sensational sex every three pages!"

"It's not every three…"

"No, but it feels like that. Anyway, even as a love story, people are going to envy the lovers. Or get sick of them. Us!"

"Isn't that the point of stories? Some people will hate them, others will love them. Or envy the characters."

Chlöe stops mid-rebuttal. He's right (damn him!). That *is* the point of stories. Especially love stories. Marketing types would call it "selling aspiration." More gently, she goes on,

"I still think it's going to cause trouble, baby. If the women who read it are remotely unhappy with their partners, they'll go looking for wonderful sex."

"Don't you think they do that already?"

"Not all of them!"

"What's wrong with some rutting?"

"Nothing, Mister. But they might come looking for you!"

"I thought half the point of reading was to escape into a fantasy world. Not go looking for it."

"You're going to say next that books keep relationships going!"

"Hadn't thought of it before, but they probably do. One way or another. You can avoid the kids, the nagging wife…"

"Or partner, or husband!"

"Both… Just by burying your head in a book. If you read adventure stories you don't even have the trouble of going on adventures. If you want some time alone and you're into techie stuff, you can pick up a manual for an hour. And you don't need to get your hands dirty. If you love music, you can spend a quiet hour with an Edith Piaf biography and skip the singing lessons."

"And the fags!"

"And the fags."

"And romance?"

"The same. Pareil. Romantic novels aren't meant to be self-help books."

"I bet self-help books work the same way."

"Eh…?"

"You buy a self-help book and you can escape into some fantasy about what it would be like to actually take the advice. Assuming you have the time to read it."

"That's a bit harsh."

"Is it? If these things worked there wouldn't be a new diet book every six weeks."

"Minutes, more like."

She grins. A momentary frostiness has melted to the warmth she loves when they talk like this. He had said he'd not thought of things that way before and there, before their very eyes – as it were – they had both come up with new ideas. But she still wasn't so sure about having her sex life held up for all to see.

"You even put the mirror in!"

"Of course. It's great."

"And you describe my, my…"

"Bush?"

"No, Mister. I was going to say pubes. You haven't put my cunt in there have you?"

"Not as such."

"Not as…what have you said?"

"Nothing yet."

"Yet!"

"Just a few notes."

"A few n…! Let's see."

She leans over his shoulder as he moves the cursor over the screen searching for a desk-top icon.

"Here we go."

He clicks on a yellow folder icon marked "Paris" and then scrolls down an enormous number of files before selecting "Beautiful." Before them, a Word document unfolds on screen. He notices that it's not unlike a flower opening though the petals are actually a large white rectangle dotted with words. Not a flower then.

"You're calling it 'Paris'?"

"It's a working title. I can't think of anything else so it'll do for now."

"Let's see then. Budge over."

Chlöe reads through quickly. There are barely seventy words:

"Beautiful. Your cunt is beautiful. I love your labia and

as for your clit…"

He gently slides his finger against her. Like a walnut. Can feel it throb. Labia dark and kind of wrinkled. Inner labia really soft. Pubes really thick. Curlier at vulva. Pink inside. Dark red deeper in. Looks like a well when he eases out.

"Like a walnut! My clit is not like a walnut!"

"I just meant size-wise. After we've been shagging for a bit anyway."

"You can't use that!"

"I haven't yet. Like I said."

"It's not wrinkly for a start! Apparently my labia are though!"

"I didn't know how else to phrase it."

"Makes me sound all dried up. I don't like it. What's this about me looking like a well?"

"Only when I've been in you for a while and then I come out. A well was the closest I could get. 'Hole' sounds crude. 'Red hole' sounds worse!"

"I'm surprised you didn't take a copy of *Tropic of Cancer* to give you inspiration!"

"I thought about it. I was trying to be original."

"I don't think 'well' quite captures it, baby. Does it really look red and deep when you pull out?"

"More wet, red and deep and, er, oozing."

"And the knot of thick pubes?"

"All there. Perfect. Dark brown."

Journal. Embarrassment – I prefer the old toilettes. We still have a couple in Giverny but right alongside the modern versions. Do you remem…. No, never mind. This is about why I prefer the holes in the ceramic. So much cleaner for a start and a much better angle for squatting. No, you guessed it – they're not the reason. When I was about 25. Actually I know exactly how old I was – too, too embarrassing. No, putain, the whole truth. This was last year – chez Hélène. Book club gathering. I went to the toilet by the front door and saw some poo floating. Flushing didn't help so I went anyway. Sod's law – when I flushed it away my little lot disappeared (do you think it ends up in the Epte?) but the original lump was still floating around – a little worse for wear but mostly intact. At that moment I heard Margot asking if anyone was inside. What to do? Not very polite is it to leave evidence of a poo, even if it isn't yours? Can you believe this? I picked it up in some loo paper and threw it out of the window! Someone probably stepped in it later or found it and assumed a drunken reveller had been caught short next to the rose bed!

Chlöe pauses. She feels a flush spreading up her neck and feels again the embarrassment of that night. She grins at the memory of spending most of the evening trying to guess who had left the offending stool in the first place. Had it been Margot? Possibly she'd been sneaking back to check it was still there. Chlöe giggles. She can't imagine that the culprit was Hélène. On reflection she can't imagine Hélène *needing* bowel movements. She smiles again, then a grimace crosses her features and she very deliberately picks up the note-book. As if searching for a witness she casts left and right before carefully pulling the recent entry from the diary.

Crumpling the paper, she places it on the corner of the table and, with a look of resignation, picks up her pen again. This time she hesitates. The pen is first twirled, then gently − pensively − sucked, then twirled again. Finally, she writes,

I spent some time at Bicêtre. You didn't know that did you? I was young, if you call fifteen young. I wasn't eating. There were so many theories about girls who don't eat. As if not eating matters. Was I getting revenge on my parents for pushing me academically? They hadn't − maybe I was punishing them for not pushing hard enough! Was I denying my sexuality, a cry for help for the family, maybe even a political protest aimed at joining with the starving African millions? My memory of it was I didn't feel hungry but that's just not complicated enough is it? One of the psychiatrists asked me some incredible questions about my dad. What she called 'abuse.' Basically, being raped by him!

If I'd had anything in my gut I'd have thrown up on the spot. I couldn't stand the idea of my dad touching me. He'd always been a grumpy sod and not much to look at. But to be "interfered with" by him as the lady

doctor put it – Yuk! The shrink said I was in denial and it had probably all happened when I was too young to remember. This made me feel even more sick. Stupid woman had me all ways. Either it happened but I was too young to remember or it had happened and I was deliberately hiding the memory from myself.

She seemed in no doubt and, when I burst into tears, that was the clincher! She said, "Let it go, dear, let it go," all sympathy and light. I wanted to murder the cow!

My dad didn't touch me. I don't remember him touching any of us – mum included – very much. But I'd have known how to stop him, even as a teenager.

Chlöe pauses again. She knows the writing so far is a form of procrastination. What needs to be said follows – loosely – from the background she has so far sketched out. But, 'It's hardly essential!' she muses. She stares at the notebook, a page now filled with her neat hand-writing. She leans back, stretching her arms wide and upward. She passes her hand across her fore-head and begins to stand. But, overcome by a new determination she resumes her seat and picks up the pen,

He'd been a lodger. Ha! Classic or what? Deflowered by the lodger! My dad could be an idle sod and used to have long periods off work when he'd spend most days down the bar. So, mum decided to take in a lodger to bring in" some extra sous" as she put it. I didn't see

much of him at first. He worked in the centre of Evreux and we were on the outskirts so by the time he got back from work I'd have eaten and was upstairs in my room. I remember that room so well. I had loads of stuffed animals and dolls – so many dolls. It was the dolls that started that thing with Etienne later.

It was one weekend, mum and dad had gone to Carrefour or somewhere and I was getting ready to go out. I came out of the bathroom and into my room and there he was – Jean. Standing in my room with one of the dolls in his hand – a Cindy I think. But – but – he'd pulled one of the legs off! He was in the middle of twisting the head really hard when I found him. He looked up and do you know what? He didn't look at all embarrassed or ashamed. He just said, "Nice doll" and handed it to me. I was really confused. I'd forgotten I just had a bath-towel wrapped round me and my hair was still dripping wet. I remember him looking at the towel for a while and then – very slowly – scanning the rest of me. A real top-to-toe job. Then, as if it was the most natural thing in the world to have been caught in someone's room wrecking a doll, he brushed past me and into the hall. As he started down the stairs I heard, "Nice legs" from under his breath! I've already written about Etienne haven't I? But Jean was the first. I'm losing it, honey. Sex and more sex.

Chlöe sits back again and shuffles back in the chair so better to see her thighs. She is wearing one of his shirts and as it parts slightly she catches sight of brown curls between her legs. "No, not bad," she sighs and bends again to the note-book. But she hesitates.

I don't know if I can write this baby. It's too hard. Worse than the "shit" incident which I'm going to throw in the bin anyway. It's not what happens next either. I've written THAT down already. Etienne and Jean weren't so different. Hope you enjoyed it. You said you have fantasies about me as a fifteen year-old didn't you? No, it's what has to follow.

This time she puts the pen down very deliberately; even straightens it in line with the note-book. Then she takes the screwed up sheet and, standing quickly, walks to the kitchen. Crumpled paper safely deposited in the poubelle, she steps to the stove and surveys the remains of the previous day's not altogether successful attempt at a curry,

"Go on, let's have a go at curry. What do you fancy, duck?"

"Duck! No-one makes curried duck!"

"I dunno. Thought it might be a Cordon-Bleu Gujerati fusion."

"Hélène would be horrified. She's Cordon-Bleu you know."

"She must have told us four times. Hmmm…OK, how about chicken? Do we have any?"

"No baby. Only cheese!"

"Fromage! I can't do a curry with cheese!"

"Defeatist!"

"Right!"

And he had done his level best. Mustard seeds (black), garlic (green), onions, chilli (red), turmeric, crushed cumin seeds were all quickly fried in oil before the addition of some huge seedless tomatoes from the melon man. Rice prepared in a fish stock, he had added camembert at the last minute and then briefly put the "curry" under the grill.

"This is shite!"

"Hmmm…"

"C'mon, baby. This is terrible. Let's go to Raymonde's. He'll still be serving."

The curry sat where they had left it on top of the stove looking worse than she might have imagined. At Raymonde's he had said, dolefully, "If only I'd had some fresh coriander," and they had both burst out laughing,

"No, baby. Coriander wouldn't help a cheese curry. Some things aren't meant to be. Now, take me home to bed. We'll wash up tomorrow."

And now she stands, the detritus before her. The coffee pot is white, complete with a glass top which is supposed to make it easier to check when the coffee is bubbling through. It looks curiously inviting. Ignoring the plates, still piled with cheese curry, she reaches out to ignite the gas. Placing the coffee pot atop the flame she languorously stretches. The shirt parts and her hand moves down, down. She feels a familiar wetness and begins to stroke, carefully at first and then more quickly.

The pot is bubbling and rattles its lid in urgent appeal. Grimacing, Chlöe stands upright. Moving the pot from the heat with her left hand she thoughtfully places her right index finger to her lips, "Later. I'll wait for my man," she says aloud to no-one as she pours a suspiciously dark stream of coffee into an unwashed mug. "Ok, here we go." Chlöe backs to the table and closing the shirt, sits. She picks up the pen. Now she presses the nib to paper with new-found urgency,

I couldn't wait for the next weekend. Mum and dad were on a trip – showing sis the sights of Honfleur as I remember – and were going to be away early Saturday to late Sunday. At the last minute, Jean asked if he could stay as he had some kind of job to finish. He said he'd be gone early Monday as it was half-term. He was a History teacher. I remember staying awake most of the Friday night. What did I expect? Was he going to creep into my room while mum and dad were still there?

He didn't. My folks left early on the Saturday and he wasn't around when I got up so I went into town with some mates. I'd pretty much forgotten about him by the time I got back but there he was! He'd been out too and had just got back in time to see some crap game show on the TV. He smiled when I walked in and – I hate to say this – I blushed; can still remember it like it was ten minutes ago.

"Don't be embarrassed Chlöe – may I call you Chlöe?"

"Sorry, I…"

"Don't apologize. I surprised you, non?"

"I, oui, non, I…merde!"

This could have gone on for hours but he suddenly stood up and asked if I'd like a coffee. No-one, well not an adult – a man – had ever asked that before.

"Oui. Merci bien."

"What have you bought?"

"Oh. Nothing. Just a dress. I'm not sure if it fits right but I can take it back. It was so lovely I couldn't.."

"Let me see."

Well you can guess the rest can't you? It's like the worst scripted soft porn flick. I went into the kitchen and put the dress on. I was just coming through the doorway and was about to ask what he thought but there he stood – his cock hanging out of his jeans like some kind of fat salami. He'd taken his shirt off too – he had nice abs but no hair on his chest. I guess he must have only been about twenty-four or five but he had the body of a teenager. Except for his dick. That was definitely man size.

"Did I startle you, Chlöe?"

"Oui, non. I..."

"Have you seen a man before?"

"Non. Not like this, I..."

"Come closer."

It was like being in a trance. I walked across and he took my hand and put it round him. It was riveting – the way it grew so fast, from fat and a bit floppy to hard. He pulled his fore-skin down and asked if I wanted to see closer. So I went down on my knees – no I didn't go down on him; I didn't know what to do. But he asked me to lick the end and I did that for a bit before he started breathing really hard. So I stopped. I was so wet. It seemed the most natural thing in the world when he put his finger in me. Then he pushed me – he was very gentle about this – onto the sofa and pulled my knickers off. Then,

"You are very beautiful, Chlöe."

"Merci. I..."

"Don't talk. Let me see you closer."

Next thing I know his head is between my legs and he's licking me like crazy. God I wanted him. I kind of pulled him upright and more or less forced him into me. It hurt a bit but I just opened my legs wider and hung onto his neck like grim death. He came really fast but I wanted more.

"You'll have to wait my love. Let's go to your room."

We ended up spending hours at it. Now I know he wasn't that good but a girl's got to start somewhere.

She puts the pen down again and sighs. The History student – he wasn't a qualified teacher at all – had left on the Monday and never returned. She picks up the mug and takes a sip of the tar-like coffee. She seems to steady herself and then picks up the pen again.

This is it then. Wetted your appetite have I, Mister? You're not going to like this next part much. No sex I'm afraid. Eating-wise I suppose things had gone down-hill after my initiation by Jean. Strictly speaking I should have been happy. Ok-ish folks, nice-enough sister, warm house, LOTS of dolls (I finally stopped even thinking about dolls after Etienne buggered off), school not too boring but it just wasn't enough. In the end, the médecin recommended a "rest" at some local bin but they were full (you'd be amazed how many people in Evreux are off their heads – half the working population is on anti-depressants) and I was sent to a clinic near the Bicêtre. Not very nice. Very famous and all that but the food! It would be enough to make anyone anorexic. And the amount of drugs they used to pump into us! I'd been told I was voluntary but they watched me like hawks to make sure I was eating. I wasn't. The food was (she glances up) *worse than your cheese curry.*
They told me I wasn't allowed week-end leave and a new shrink called me in to arrange some therapy

sessions for the next week. But I told her to "fuck off" and she said I'd "lose my privileges" whatever they were. I was told to gain half a kilo a week – not so hard when you're not doing anything. My therapist turned out to be a follower of some obscure analyst – Ferenczi. A mate of Freud's no less. She wasn't the "lie on the couch and say whatever" school. She used to push me quite hard and had a few suggestions about "re-entering the world" as if that was in MY control in a loony bin.

She wasn't bad. We chatted for an hour or more each day. I could say whatever I wanted. She didn't seem at all upset about my adventures with Jean. I'd pretty much always said whatever I wanted to most people (except dad) but with her I didn't censor anything. She looked more interested in the dolls. But only by an occasional raised eyebrow. Her lack of reaction otherwise was weird. Felt so bloody false.

Here I was, telling her about illicit under-age sex and she just wrote it all down like a shopping list. Four times a week too. Have you ever tried talking about yourself for up to six hours a week without anyone answering back! Makes you a bit mad. I told her about my worries that my breasts were too small and she said that was normal. Even told me she'd had the same worries. She pushed her chest out when she said that. A bit odd..

After a month, they sent me home. As far as anyone could tell, nothing had changed but I had a pile of pills to take every day and kept falling asleep in my lessons. Deep breath. I had ...

She stands again, stretches. Chlöe feels the shirt flop open but there is no stirring this time. Instead, she pads upstairs and, barely glancing at herself in the mirror, pulls the shirt off and looks around the room. More "evidence" – the unmade bed, the pillows askew; two on the floor. The top draw hangs at an angle where he had dragged it open this morning in a hasty search for socks. She can almost here his muttered, "Putain!" and smiles.

So many weekday mornings like this. Awake so early, aware of his whispered, "I love you," turning to him. Then somehow almost an hour later his need to rush in order to catch the train. She would bask a little once he'd gone and then, reluctantly, would herself get up dragging on his shirt, complete with his smell, before going downstairs. Today had been different; she'd known, even as they held each other, what she intended to do. Was that why the passion had been so urgent? Pulling on a sleeveless vest and wriggling into a pair of jogging bottoms, she sits again on the edge of the bed, head in hands. On auto-pilot she moves to the door and, with a last glance at the dishevelled bed linen, heads for the stairs. Seconds later she is sitting at the table and picks up the pen. No twirling, no sucking, she writes,

I had met a woman in the hospital. Very kind, a bit mad I think. She kept looking at my waist and calling me Marie Antoinette. Told me a terrible story about one of the queen's lovers. Fersen. Other days she'd call me

Empress Josephine and would ask if I'd ever been to Elba. We got on fine. She wasn't allowed out on leave so when I got out I used to visit her. I'm pretty sure I was her only contact with the outside world.

She said she was related to Simone de Beauvoir and lived in a big house near Le Havre. Said she kept prize-winning cats and a huge art collection including two Monets, a Picasso and a Matisse. I didn't believe any of this but who knows? Maybe she really was a mad millionairess! She definitely wasn't 99 years old. She looked about forty. But she told me that she was about to celebrate her 100th birthday but didn't want a big fuss.

Mind you, if she had been a hundred it would have made one of her stories a bit more plausible, though not much. She said she'd been raped by Proust in his Paris apartment and his asthma had been induced by guilt!

Then she told me she had killed a baby. I believed that.

XLIII

It's been a long day. Le mêtro had been stifling, the train almost as bad. He had sat for hours in the, thankfully, air-conditioned office as various colleagues had passed by on their way to the coffee machine, only to walk back with barely a glance. He had been pre-occupied with a novel where the plot eluded him and with the thought of Chlöe waiting at home. Though she probably wasn't. Was it book night? Perhaps she was walking Pantam?

The train had been unusually quiet, the sense of needing to get home almost palpable. Passengers had jostled, shoved their way into the throng and then forced their way back to the doors with not a word. The usual apologies for the occasional crushed toe were either muted or absent.

Now he is walking toward the front door. It is open – not a good sign. His jacket is already off. And then on the path as Pantam rushes to greet him.

"Merde! I love you too boy but it's hot. Chlöe."

"Oui. Entrée."

"Bit formal isn…oh!"

"Hello. I was just leaving."

"Not on my account, Hélène."

"I just popped in for a coffee. Chlöe's upstairs. I think she's had a tough day."

"She's....?"

Thinking about it, he realizes the, "Entrée" had come from the bedroom. He is at once concerned and irritated. Chlöe's had a tough day! Chlöe hasn't been sitting on stifling trains surrounded by stifled passengers. Chlöe hasn't been sitting in an air-conditioned prison unable to think of a plot line. Chlöe...

"Hello, Mister."

And it's gone! All the heat of the day, all the frustration replaced by a calm that stops him in his tracks. She steps past the now subdued Pantam and puts her arms around his neck.

"Hello, beautiful!"

But it's not him that's beautiful; at least he doesn't feel it. It's way too hot. But Chlöe! She is wearing a short green dress he hasn't seen before. The cut is low. Her breasts...

"Like it?"

"Love it, but how...?"

"I bought a prop-up bra. It's all in the wiring!"

He puts his hands gently – then more firmly – in the small of her back. Then down...

"Don't mind me, you two!"

"Oh, Hélène. I'm so sor...You must think us so rude!"

"Not rude, Chlöe. In love and lust. It's quite lovely to behold!"

"Pastis?"

"If you're sure. Merci. I'll stay for just one. If that's all right with your good woman!"

Moments later, the trio are sitting in the warmth of the last of the sun's rays. His shirt is unbuttoned, Chlöe has tossed her sandals somewhere and even their visitor is relaxing. Until Pantam puts a large head into her lap.

"Pan...!"

"It's alright cherie. He means no harm. Though his mouth is a little, er, wet!"

"Come on Pantam. Lie down!"

"What were you talking about?"

"Before you got home? This and that but just before you arrived...It's odd. Hél...You tell him Hélène. It's your story."

"Well, if you're sure I'm not intruding, cherie. I'll just make myself a little more comfortable. I was telling Chlöe about the widows."

"Widows? Les veuves?"

"Oui. Our little town, well what used to be little, has some sad tales. Have you ever noticed how few men of my, um, years there are?"

"In Giverny?"

"Well not in all of Giverny. But around here."

"No, I..."

In truth, he isn't that interested in men or women of Hélène's age. Or any age. Other than those that might be turned into passing characters in his book. He thinks, 'has he noticed?' There were a number of men of his age or slightly older but men in their sixties? Was Hélène in her sixties?

"How old are you?"

"Old enough to consider that a very rude question! Take my word for it; Guillaume is a rarity. Don't smile! I don't mean like that! He's still alive!"

"Who are these widows?"

"Marie-Ange, Felicité, Lisette, Angela, Cybille, Vivienne. And half the book club. No! More than half!"

"What happened to the men?"

"Most of them just died. A combination of too much hard work and hard liquor! Marie-Ange's husband went off with a younger woman. Came back with his tail between his legs after a year and died in his own bed. Cybille, I don't know. She arrived already widowed and has stayed single. But Lisette...!"

"What happened to her old man?"

"I'll get another pastis. Do you want some cashews, lovely?"

He is distracted. He hasn't quite forgotten Chlöe. How could he – her smell is everywhere! But he had been absorbed.

"Oui. Merci."

"Hélène?"

"Need you ask? Do the stars come out at night?"

As Chlöe stands, a slight gust of breeze lifts the hem of her green dress. Hélène blushes as Chlöe quickly pulls the hem down and picks up the glasses. With what he thinks is a positive swirl she moves toward the kitchen door. He can make out the beginnings of a snorting laugh as she closes it behind her.

"Where were we?"

"Admiring Chlöe's bottom!"

"Exactement. No, I was telling you about Lisette. Her poor husband drowned!"

"Drowned?"

"Well they think so. It was horrible. A few years back we had flash floods. We'd had weeks of rain and every once in a while the river would burst its banks. The water came from nowhere. Most people stayed in of course but Lisette's husband had to go into town for the baby."

"Baby?"

"Lisette's grandson. They were looking after him while the mum and dad were in Paris for the weekend. They'd gone to see a show by Malcolm Maclaren. Some time after his Sex Pistols years so I understand."

"Do you know the Sex Pistols?"

"No, cherie. But I know of them. We do have television you know!"

"Thanks baby. Wow, that's strong!"

"Sorry, I had a bit of a laugh ... coughing fit. Spilt some. Too strong?"

"No, it's fine. The cashews will soak it up."

"Merde! I forgot the cash..."

Chlöe stands again. Holding her dress in place she returns to the kitchen.

"How did he drown?"

"Malcolm Macl... Oh, Lisette's husband! They found the car at the top of a land-slide. The theory is that he got out to walk because the road was being washed away and he slipped."

"Into the river?"

"No, not the river. The road wasn't by the river. He slipped into a vineyard."

"A vineyard! But we don't have vineyards in Giverny!"

"Not any more. We had one. But after the accident it was torn up."

"But how does someone drown in a vineyard? Couldn't he have grabbed a vine?"

"There was a channel flowing down one of the rows and a pool had collected at the bottom. They think he slipped and slid into the pool. He couldn't swim."

"Did they find the body? It must have been there somewhere!"

"Not at first. The mud had sucked him under. But they found his boot near the pool and his car keys at the top of the slope. Voilà! C'est tout."

His mind is racing. Could he have a mud-slide scene? Why not? But there would have to be something different about it. No car for a start. Barely looking at Hélène he stands; with a muttered, "Desolée," he scoops up a leather hold-all from the kitchen floor and heads for the front door.

"Mister! Where are you....?"

"Sorry lovely – burst of inspiration. I'll see you at the café. Je t'aime. Au revoir!"

"That must be the world's biggest lap-top!"

"We all got one. Cheap bulk offer."

"Well, don't use it here."

"Why not? I thought I might throw some atmosphere into the novel."

"At Raymonde's!"

"Hmmm..Something might happen worth writing down."

"Like the wind blowing that woman's dress up over her head? Made you look!"

The café is crowded. They sit surrounded by tourists basking in the warm evening air, not a regular to be seen. Pantam lies panting at Chlöe's feet while he types. Pantam's surprise had been almost as complete as Chlöe and Hélène's but he would never hesitate at the possibility of a walk. Who knows? There could be a croissant or similar awaiting.

Chlöe had apologised to her friend, reminded her where to find the pastis and hurried out closely followed by Pantam. She'd settled at his table and waited patiently for an acknowledgment. Without looking up from the screen he had simply stroked her arm. Surely he didn't intend to sit in silence? Hence the lap-top comment.

The wind comes in gusts, though there are no skirts being blown about. The computer has been a mixed blessing. As Chlöe has more than once pointed out it is bulky, bought by the company as part of a job lot. His colleagues don't seem to use theirs much other than to check profit margins on intricate graphs or play one of several games that came ready loaded. For himself, the need to carry pens and paper hasn't disappeared as the battery life and the sheer weight (some six kilos) makes it both unreliable and unwieldy. Twice he has lost an hour's work. After re-typing what he could remember he remains haunted by the suspicion he has forgotten a crucial scene or descriptive passage. This is the first time he has brought it to Raymonde's and, as ever, finds himself lost in the intricacies of plot and the need to observe other café-goers. Rather than attend to Chlöe.

"What?"

"I didn't say anything."

"I thought..."

"Well I didn't, baby. There's no point while you're staring at the screen. I bet this was how it was for couples where one was a TV addict."

"Still is, probably."

A woman in black, a large gold crucifix round her neck, sits behind Chlöe. She is having a desultory conversation with a woman, this one in blue, whose back is turned to them. She chews thoughtfully at a baguette only half listening to her companion's chatter. She's not having much luck with the baguette as a sliver of what could be ham or pastrami slithers to the table-top. Toying with the stray meat, it is half way to her mouth when she sees Pantam.

"Hey! Chien!"

Pantam raises his head. Half rising to his feet, he thinks better of it and rests his head on his mistress's knee.

"I think that woman behind you wants to give

Pantam some of her lunch."

"How on earth...? You're not writing this down are you?"

"Typing."

"How have you described her?"

"Just turn around and you'll see her."

"No, I want to see what you've typed first. See if you capture her."

"I've just said she's in black with a gold crucifix."

Chlöe turns. The woman has given up on Pantam and is talking with her friend slugging at a bottle of Coca Cola.

"She's tanned. Nice watch. Wedding ring ... and engagement ring. Crosses her legs under the table. She really is in black, isn't she? Head to toe."

"You should write it, not me."

"Well, I thought 'black with crucifix' was a bit sparse. And you don't say anything about her hair. It's dyed blonde, grey and black roots."

"It might not be relevant."

"To what? She's not going to be a major character is she?"

"Did fourteenth century peasants dye their hair?"

"Henna."

"Oh. Really? I thought that was the rich. But if you say so."

"And what about the bikers?"

"Bikers?"

"You must have see ... well, heard them at least!"

"I was concentrating."

"Concentrating? You missed the bikers? About a dozen, I'd say. Quite a racket too."

"They definitely didn't have bikers in the fourteenth century."

"Or Coca Cola!"

"I didn't mention that. You did!"

"So that's why it's just the crucifix and the fact she's in black?

"I can't say anything about her tanned legs. Didn't notice actually."

"Liar! She has nice legs. Why can't you say anything about them?"

"For a start she must be fifty if she's a day. You wouldn't know it from her face. No lines."

"And?"

"I don't have any fifty year old women in the book. Mine are either younger or used up. Or both. Sun-burned arms is about the most you get. I don't expect there was much call for shaving legs and sun-bathing during the Hundred Years' War."

"Well you could up-date it."

"How so?"

"Have a contemporary love story too."

"Too much like *The French Lieutenant's Woman.*"

"So? That sold in spades. It's no problem using a scenario that's been used before. There are probably hundreds of books that do the same thing. Splitting love stories across the years."

"Centuries?"

"Hmm....Don't know about that but the idea is sound

enough. Just look at Fowles. It made his fortune! You could set one half in Ancient Rome. It would still work."

"I don't think so! Researching the bloody fourteenth century is bad enough without starting over with Julius Caesar!"

They lapse into an uneasy silence. Chlöe distractedly scratches Pantam's head. Playing with her coffee cup, she glances shyly at the man opposite her. Does she know him at all? He moves so quickly nowadays from a contented calm to being agitated and combative. He is typing again. She sighs,

"I think that book's your other woman, Mister."

"Eh?"

"I th ... Never mind. Come on Pantam. Let's leave Victor Hugo to connect with his alter-ego."

"Marie Antoinette, Matisse, de Maupassant, de Gaulle, Monet, Balzac, Charlemagne. What do they all have in common?"

"Er, they're all dead?"

"Exactement ! So what did *they* know?"

"What...? Ha ha. You could say that about anyone who's dead!"

"I do."

"Maybe they enjoyed their lives."

"Maybe. But that's worse isn't it?"

"Worse? How?"

"Because there they were having a good time and bang! Mortality strikes!"

"More like immortality."

"Only on paper, lovely. *They* don't know they're in every history book you can think of. They're dead! Voilà!"

"I... What's your point?"

"It's my version of existentialism."

"Your...? How?"

"We should all learn from their deaths."

"Don't become famous?"

"Non! Live life while you can because death's round the corner. We could have been struck dead by grêlons! And then that's it! We're history and the best you can hope for is to be in a book!"

"Are you building up to a plan?"

"Don't go to work today. Stay home."

"I kinda like time at work."

As he says it, he knows it is barely true. He's alive at work. Just. How else would he discern the increasingly dreadful flavour of the coffee as the morning grinds on? How else would he know and feel just how boring plastics can be? But it's not living as Chlöe means it.

"Go on. I'll skip the library. You phone in sick."

"Then?"

Chlöe pauses. She knows she has stirred him. May have even captured him for the day. But she barely hears her next words. They are as unexpected to her as they are to him.

"Let's go to Evreux."

She had regretted her suggestion the moment it was uttered but, to her surprise, he had proven keen; Pantam even more so. For her, the first hour following his call to the office had been a mixture of luxuriating under the duvet from which Pantam had been rapidly banished down-stairs and a distracting, creeping dread.

Her usual sense of being lost to the moment had been sporadic. Sensing a distance he had pulled her to him until she felt crushed. Struggling a little for breath, she whispers:

"Shall we stay here?"

"No, no. I like the idea of Evreux. Let's do it."

Pantam had been loaded into the *Clio,* now on permanent loan from Raymonde. They had decided against a picnic opting only for a bottle of *Evian*. After checking the tank was at least half full, they negotiate the smaller streets of Giverny before finding the Route Nationale. The speed increases. He dozes as Chlöe drives. Her sense of foreboding and regret grow in equal measure but within an hour and a half they are parked anyway. To her consternation, he makes straight for a church of dull red stone. There is a Norman tower with restored mullions around the windows.

"Eleven o one!"

"What is?"

"Look at the plaque. 'This church was dedicated by Bernard, loyal churchman to William of Normandy and consecrated by Friar Benet in AD 1101.' You don't suppose that was *the* William of Normandy."

"No baby. I'm sure you need me as an historical researcher! We were on Henri Premier by then. William was long dead."

"Like Marie Antoinette, Balzac etc, etc."

"Ha ha. Don't start."

"Just joking. Great though isn't it? This plaque says the main part was re-built in thirteen fifty. During the Hundred Years' War!"

"You are funny!"

"Why?"

"You just get excited over the oddest things."

"You don't like it?"

"No, it's not that. It just takes me by surprise."

He moves forward but she steps back and reaches for his hand.

"Come on, lover. Let's have a look at some of the other sights."

"The shops?"

"No! Well, maybe a quick look before we eat. There are some funny little boutiquey places nearer the centre."

They check Pantam has a rear window lowered just enough to allow in what little breeze there is, then walk hand in hand towards the centre of Evreux. Some feels unfamiliar to Chlöe. A new road, buildings where there were none and a new car park where buildings once stood, several dead-end streets. Not quite a new town but she begins to breathe easier.

XLIV

The cover is pink. Pink! Why, oh, why? Pourquoi? Why do designers insist on it? For what? For the pleasure it gives to a tanned woman with stylish hopes as she rides le mêtro? He looks, looks again. There is no doubt, she is absorbed. Gone! She wears a green V-neck sweater. No socks, so thin ankles are revealed between white shoes and the pale blue denim of her jeans. These are not designer jeans! No rips, no conspicuous label, Just cheap, thin denim. From *Carrefour,* he thinks. Unkindly.

Her head barely moves as she scrupulously scans each page. The evening sun streams into the carriage. She wears small glasses with brown frames, the lenses thick and shaped like lozenges. The overall effect is to increase the look of concentration on her gaunt face. There is nothing much to signify this stranger; all is perfectly ordinary. Except the look. Her eyes bore into the page.

He sits back, full of foreboding. Is this what it is like to write a popular book? A book with a pink cover! But readers who sit transfixed by the words on the page ... No doubt the plot is full of tricks like leaving each chapter a cliff hanger. Then it will lure the reader down a few blind allies before ...

He starts. She has changed her glasses. And she still reads. But they are beyond the banlieu now. Maybe she is not what she seems. Perhaps the nondescript air is a disguise. The glasses are not nondescript. Not at all. These look serious. The frames are studded with glass beads. They are a different brown, almost translucent. Now he sees her hair. Not lank as it looked in the tunnels but auburn, a clean, vibrant auburn.

He starts again. Almost his stop. Only thirty minutes to go before Chlöe. Will she wear the green dress?

Their first trip out in the car had been a revelation.

"God I'm wet!"

"I know baby."

"No, I mean my dress .....! I've gushed!"

"Great!"

"Not great! Look at this seat!"

She had uneasily fussed for a while and then settled before pressing the accelerator slowly. As they leave the car she smiles:

"I know why you love me."

"Why?"

"Coz I'm so, so fucking skanky"

"Bulls-eye! Voila!

From the carriage he can see row upon row of vegetables. Artichokes, tomatoes, beans, even peppers run parallel to the track. They thrive beyond wire fencing in one of Giverny's many allotments. The borders, what he can make out of them as the train slows, seem immaculate. There is no-one to be seen at work. There never is this time of day, but still the rows are so tidy, so free of weeds. They resemble some exhibition at a horticultural show where an army of gardeners toils from morn to dusk. But the allotment is empty for now.

All summer by seven o'clock the retired men-folk will have torn themselves from their televisions and occupied the vegetable patches. By half past eight they will be joined by commuters, tired, well-fed and ready for the whole point of their drudgery in Paris. To be able to plant vegetables on the edge of Monet's town pretending they too will one day re-create his garden. They won't have a Japanese foot-bridge and probably no giant studios.

'How does this happen?', he thinks. Families devote themselves to a lifetime of labour, the parents seeing little of each other and less of the children in order to live in a country house with astronomic rent and leave the place altogether for two weeks of the year to lie on a hot beach somewhere. He knows he is lucky. After all, it's Chlöe he goes home to everyday. But he also feels trapped in the grind of the commute and the figures. Today the calculations concerned an order for two hundred thousand plastic cups for a garden centre near Aix-en-Provence. The lunchtime coffee, more figures, the return home. And all the while thinking of Chlöe and looking forward to the weekend.

Does this make him a modern man? Or a drudge? Again he drifts to a time before such enslavement. Well, he tries.

And try though he might, the slavery of humankind seems endless. Infinite. He skips to the earliest days of the industrial revolution. But it's still there. Enslavement to the factory or to the land. The mill-owner or landlord. Before Louis and Marie-Antoinette then. No good. If you weren't in the military risking life and limb for a pittance, then it was a shop-keeper up to your ears in debt. Beyond Paris it's straight back to the hovel. Even the courtiers were in train to the whims of the aristocracy and their excesses. This is no good, no good at all. What about the Franks? More slavery. Of their own, and the conquered.

"Our stop."

"Pardon?"

"Our stop, Monsieur. You were day-dreaming."

With a nod of thanks he joins the 'evening shuffle' as Chlöe calls it. At what seems like dawn there is a dash out of the door, a run half way down the road. A double fast walk along the old railway track to the station at Vernon where the morning shuffle begins. Now for the evening shuffle, through the great wooden and glass doors at the entrance into the V.I.P. car park. "V.I.P? It just means they pay some extortionate annual fee so they don't have to walk from home!" Chlöe again.

A man that he has seen dozens of times in the last year strides towards a gleaming Audi. He feels he should know his name. He doesn't. With a click and a flash of the side-lights the door is unlocked from at least twenty metres away. The man visibly sighs as he opens the driver's door. It is starting to rain. Thin, only drizzle, but the wind is getting up and his face moistens quickly as the droplets run down his cheeks.

Now, where might she be? He loses track of the days so easily. There are 'Chlöe' days. Almost every day she is waiting at the cottage. Then there are weekends. He understands these, looks forward to them as a shipwrecked man scans the horizon for a sail. Of course, book club evenings where he might have to face thirty minutes (two *Ricards*!) worth of Hélène before she and Chlöe move off to "literary gossip for rich folk." Not Chlöe this time but his own rather churlish phrase. A phrase she had immediately corrected with a sharp, "Less of the literary, Mister! You think we have time to discuss books?"

What is it to be tonight? He has automatically turned for Raymonde's. It will be getting busy. If the drizzle eases, the summer's heat will dry the outside tables faster than Raymonde can say, "Voila!" Monet's church is to his right. Already? He is walking faster, the rain barely noticeable. There is something about the church. Something? A peel of the bells splits the evening quiet. Now he notices the two limousines. Antique Mercedes parked by the lych-gate. Normally there is no parking allowed. *Parking interdit 24 heures* notices are discretely positioned every twenty metres. Normally... A man appears at the church door and as it swings open on its great iron hinges he hears ... Mendelssohn! Mendelssohn! Of course! The black coated stranger walks quickly to a spot to the left of the flag-stone path and opens the leather shoulder bag he carries.

As he raises the camera to his eye the bells peel again and the beaming couple step from the doorway. Her wedding dress is cream. She is bare at the shoulders with a cream hair-band holding back almost black hair. The dress is nipped at the waist, the whole neat, understated and by the look of the yellow diamond on her ring finger, expensive. The groom wears a grey morning suit, no hat, but a cream button-hole matching his new wife's dress. They stand, her arm linked in his as the photographer barks commands.

"Un peu à gauche. Oui, parfait. Now forward a little. Madame, look at your husband. Parfait. Baissez. Oui. Et encore."

So it goes on; the couple kissing on command, laughing, smiling, now a shot of the bride alone with her bouquet. Where did *that* come from? It needs two hands to hold it. Now one of the groom on one knee.

"Voila! Et, les autres!"

Guests emerge from the doorway. A silver-haired, impeccably dressed older man leans down to kiss the bride. His daughter? Daughter-in-law? He is accompanied by a red haired woman half his age in - 'Oh no!' – cream. More women emerge, some the same age as the couple – his age – others probably brides-maids. More guests emerge. This is getting peculiar – he knows how small the church is inside. The new arrivals are mixed ages. A frail looking woman stands leaning on a young man's arm. Her hair looks mauve. Recently permed, the only word is bouffant. Others stand close to the bride's left. Friends or relatives; all are in cream. He grins. It is like watching a well dressed dairy convention.

The photographer is grouping the guests for snaps of the couple, children, the main guests; now the men, now the women. More are coming out now, the tidal wave of cream finally being broken by pastel shades, some darker hues, even a purple! And then ... a short green dress, familiar tanned legs, the flash of a silver bracelet. Those eyes! Chlöe is all smiles. The last to leave the church she hastens past the throng and, beaming, walks past the photographer with hardly a glance ... and abruptly stops.

"Chlöe?"

"Oh! Mon Dieu...!"

"You didn't say......."

"I......Oh Christ! This is embarrassing!"

"Who....?"

"Come on, let's go.

She links her arm through his and they step under the lych-gate and into the road. He can feel her trembling beside him as they turn to the right. Towards Raymonde's. A small sob escapes what he guesses to be gritted teeth.

"I'm sorry, baby. Desolée."

"No need. I just thought you would have told me that you were invited to a wedding.

Now barely a whisper,

"But I wasn't."

"You weren't'! But, how...?"

"This is shite! You're going to think I am so stupid."

"No I'm not. Tell me."

"I finished at the library, nipped home, put the dress on for you and, and....."

"Go on."

"I was on my way to the brasserie and saw the bride arrive. She looked so lovely, And, I......I followed her in!"

"You.....?"

"Well her and the bridesmaids and her dad."

"The man with the silver hair?"

"Him. Lovely isn't he? You're going to look like him one day mister."

"Then?"

"I just stood at the back. No-one noticed. The ushers had already sat down. It was fab."

"I'm sure. But why?"

They are arriving at the brasserie gate. The flagstones steam in the early evening heat, a haze rising from the ground. No customers are at the outside tables yet but a few wait hesitantly at the cafe door, a smog of cigarette smoke visible behind the glass.

"Do you think they'll ever ban it?"

"What, marriage?"

"No. Smoking."

"Why would anyone ban smoking?"

"Oh, I don't know. Health reasons, the cancer police, the way it makes your clothes smell even if you don't smoke."

"I can't see the government banning it because it makes your clothes smell. And cancer keeps countless people in work."

"Who?"

"Doctors, nurses, specialists in oncology centres, hospice workers."

"Don't forget the tobacco industry!"

"And the advertisers. Anyway, stop changing the subject. Look there's two chairs under the tonnelle, They're dry."

They are maneuvering into position when the brasserie door swings open. Raymonde emerges from a fog of tobacco smoke. Behind him, four or five customers hover at the doorway, all clutching coffee cups and cigarettes.

"Bonjour mes amis, Ça va?"

"Oui, ça va Raymonde. Deux cafés si tu plais."

"Bien ... Et Pantam? Il n'est pas là?"

"Non. Chez nous."

"You look thoughtful cherie."

"I...."

"She's been to a wedding."

"She's ...? At the church? When?"

"It just finished. The guests are probably at the reception as we speak."

"Big affair?"

"Pretty big. Rich folk too."

"Friends?"

"She didn't know anyone there."

"She? Do I feel a story coming on? Attendez. I'll get the coffee!"

They talk with Raymonde, interrupted only by his occupational need to wipe dry a chair, fetch coffee or greet new customers. They continue to talk walking home toward the setting sun, a great orange orb spreading red and gold across the roof-tops. Despite Pantam's best efforts they talk through the doorway and into the kitchen. Still no wiser, he feels her hands slip around his waist as he slices onions at the marble surface adjoining the stove. She nuzzles her head into his back.

"Forgive me, Mister?"

"What's to forgive? You went to a stranger's wedding on a whim. As long as you don't make a habit of it...."

There is an intake of breath.

"That wasn't the first time, was it? You didn't mention *that* to Raymonde. Or me!"

"Non! Not the first time. But it's not a habit."

"Then, why....?"

He turns. Her lovely face is a picture of misery.

"I imagine...."

"Go on."

"I imagine. No, this is so stupid."

"Don't stop now."

"I imagine it's us!"

He hasn't expected this. Now it is he who feels stupid. Of course!

"I didn't think ..."

"Oh I know. I don't want to get married either but there's something lovely about the ceremony, the people in their Sunday best. The hope, the commitment in the words ..."

"They're only words"

"I know ... But sometimes the couples look so in love that you can almost believe ..."

"Do we need a ceremony?"

"No. I......I don't know."

"Will you marry me?"

"That's not...not....not"

"What I'm meant to say? Well, I said it. What's your answer, lovely one?"

XLV

"Are the love-birds in?"

"What time is it?"

"About seven."

"Seven! Christ! What can Hélène want at seven in the morning?"

"Coo-eee. Are you there, cheries?"

"Oh Lord, did you leave the door off the latch? I think she's downstairs. I'll go…"

"No, baby, she's my friend, I'll go down."

Chlöe slides from the bed and shakes her hair. With a glance at the mirror she is gone. Only to return seconds later.

"Oops. Better put some clothes on."

He buries his head under the duvet and closes his eyes. He knows sleep won't come; too intrigued by what Chlöe might be discovering it is his turn to slide from the bed. Walking cautiously to the door he prises it open a fraction to better hear the voices below.

"But you must come. C'est tradition!"

"But, Hélène, we go every weekend and often in the evening for coffee. I'm sure Raymonde thinks we should have shares in the place. What's so special about today?"

He hears a sharp intake of breath, a pause in the conversation. A pause that grows until he wonders if their visitor has left. Or possibly died. What *is* so special about today? His alarm had gone off as usual. As usual he had pressed le bouton before the increasing volume woke the sleeping form at his side. He had leaned over and whispered, "I love you." As usual she had stirred, turned to him and...they had been rudely brought back to the social world by the voice from downstairs. He looks at the clock. 'Christ! Seven-fifteen!' He'll miss the train. Almost running back towards the bed he pulls on the trousers unceremoniously thrown to the floor the previous night. His shirt is downstairs; along with a reviving coffee. Who knows where his socks might be? Without a backwards glance he hops to the door buckling his belt as he goes and is in mid head-long flight down the none-too-steady stairs when he his brought to a sudden halt.

Chlöe and Hélène are standing at the base, the former nonchalantly toying with her hair. Hélène stands, an amused expression on her face. She first raises her eyes to his, and then one eyebrow arches in a fashion that manages to be simultaneously quizzical and condescending.

"You can slow down, baby. We're going to the café for breakfast. Hélène has kindly invited us. It's tradition."

"Trad...? Isn't work a tradition?"

"Oh my dear. He's as bad as you."

He looks at the two women and for a moment sees himself as another might. Trousered only, frozen on the stairs, the day's stubble yet to be razored off. Wild eyed. Definitely wild eyed.

"It's July the fourteenth, baby."

"What?"

"July…"

Like a deflated inner tube his body relaxes, then almost slumps against the banister. Juillet quatorze! No reason to go to work. No work. Most of France will still be in bed thanking their ancestors for the storming of the Bastille.

"And every year there's a little breakfast gathering at Raymonde's. Isn't that lovely? And so sweet of Hélène to think of us. You look great by the way, but I think Raymonde would prefer us both fully dressed."

So far there are eleven around the joined tables. He recognizes a few; Cecille, Mathieu, Boris. These last two from brief conversations on the platform before all three bury their heads in Le Monde. Cecille he can't quite place; Ah! the Tabac, she serves at the Tabac. Laurent is here too. And Mme Bordette, as ever dressed simply and, he doesn't doubt, expensively.

"Ah! Pascal. Bienvenu. Come, sit with me, cheri."

Hélène is beckoning the new arrival. Despite the gathering heat of the morning Pascal wears a heavy coat and black beret. He moves towards the group dragging one leg slightly; the left, its calf encased in a metal cage suspending some kind of heavy black boot. The club foot makes his gait similar to a three-legged dog that always sways slightly at the rump perhaps because of the physical effort required to walk in a straight line. With a sigh he accepts the proffered chair and slumps back in it, exhausted by his entrance.

"Chlöe, Pascal."

"Enchanté."

"No, my dear. It is I who feels enchanted."

And with that, the club foot, the awkwardness, the breathless exertion all vanish. Pascal smiles and inclines his head toward Chlöe who blushes.

"Oh, Pascal you are such a charmer. Be careful, her man's watching you! Don't make him jealous."

He is startled. Is Hélène a mind-reader? Can he be jealous of a man so unkempt, so clumsy, so... inelegant? That's the word, 'inelegant.' Immediately he is ashamed; not of the jealousy – he knows this will be a constant in his love for Chlöe – but of his judgementalism. Who is he to sneer at clumsiness? And as for charm; Chlöe has already told him how he can charm and how jealous that can make her. He leans toward Pascal.

"Enchanté. Je m'appel P..."

"Oui, je le sais. Pascal. How do you find our little town?"

"It's, er, interesting."

"Interesting! Oh what a dead word. Do you hate it that much?"

"I..."

"Now, now Pascal, let's not start yet. The others are arriving."

Start? Start what? He had assumed this was just a

gathering of locals who liked to indulge in convivial chat. Hélène's admonition seems to imply something more serious, or at least more considered. He sees Chlöe looking at the new arrivals. There are two women he doesn't recognize at all and a small, rather mousey looking man following in their wake. He, at least, is dressed for the weather; sandals, shorts showing thin white legs, a loose white shirt and a jacket slung over his shoulder. The shirt reveals a bird-like chest and, the sleeves rolled up, terribly thin arms even paler than the legs. From his left wrist dangles a large watch continuously threatening to slide over his clenched hand. With his other hand he adjusts, rotates, fingers the watch strap mindful of its imminent descent to the flagstones.

"Marie, Felicité, Jean-Louis, welcome. Ah, croissants. Merci, Raymonde."

Croissants, coffee, pain et confiture have appeared as if by magic while he has been watching the mismatched trio; the women almost haughty in their figure-hugging summer dresses, Jean Louis positively servile in his more comfortable outfit. The hubbub around the table grows. These people seem to know each other well. He guesses a few of the women are in the book club. Perhaps the men bump into each other at the Tabac or Raymonde's. But why would they make this an annual occasion? Is there a secret society in Giverny? A society of mostly rich people dedicated to preserving that symbol of the freedom of the people, the release of the murderers and others from the

Bastille? It hardly seems likely. He thinks back; in his own child-hood little was made of the fourteenth other than a day off school, his mother and father suddenly thrown together all day on a week-day with no work to go to and nothing to do but argue.

Fireworks! Ah, yes, there were definitely fireworks in the evening, and not just the sparks produced by his parents' bickering. He would spend the day out with his various friends playing hide-and-seek, or having knowing (and not so knowing) conversations about girls held in secret in Claude's kitchen. Claude! He had forgotten; the neighbours' son, an only and much loved child who delighted in beating him at every game imaginable; table-tennis, darts, bezique, boules. He remembers Claude as hugely successful with girls. If "success" meant the number of girls prepared to give kisses.

Then another memory. This one is vague (how old was he?). He was dimly aware of events in Paris spewing out from the radio. Renewed fears of rioting to make the events of that May seem a mere rehearsal for a summer of unrest. 1968! How long ago it now seemed...

"Cheri, you are lost in thought. Do tell!"

"I..."

"Don't be shy, we are all friends here. At least for today."

He is aware the tables have gone quiet and several quizzical looks are aimed at him. Not aggressive, merely inquisitive. The breakfast has largely been cleared away. His remains the only untouched croissant.

"Nineteen sixty eight. I was thinking of nineteen sixty eight."

"Bravo. Parfait. How very appropriate."

"Appropriate?"

"Our little club, cherie. Our annual celebration of ..."

"Student riots?"

"No, my dear. *Not* the riots though I'm sure Pascal would have something to say about those dark days."

At this Pascal bridles but, warily eyeing Hélène, bites his tongue.

"We meet to celebrate our freedom; to say what we will, live as well as we can, our right to discuss without fear of retribution or rebuff, to strike. Above all, cheri, to be taken seriously. As citizens. Voilà!"

There are some murmurings of assent. Hélène looks a little overwhelmed by her own eloquence.

"So, this is a debating society?"

"Voilà!"

"For one day a year."

"Your man can be a little obtuse, Chlöe. Do explain."

Chlöe is looking at him. She is slightly wild, obviously caught by her friend's rhetoric and torn in her sudden role of go-between. She opens her mouth but it is Pascal who speaks.

"Mon ami, we are not a debating society. We meet to celebrate our freedom to debate, challenge and to strike. Our constitution preserves the right. In my less modest moments I see us as a less abstruse group to the one that met during the war at Café Flore. Voilà!"

"The Café F...! Who am I? Sartre?"

"What a good beginning? Can we start now, Hélène?"

"Bien sûr, Pascal. Commence!"

"I think we are all Sartre in our own way."

"Eh? I'd rather be Cocteau, or Gîde!"

"Excellent. Throw in Genet if you like."

"De Beauvoir!" Hélène excitedly adds.

"Always speaking up for the little woman," from Jean-Louis. Jean-Louis!

Marie interjects, her gorge rising, "Little woman! I hardly think she was a little woman, Jean-Louis!"

"D'accord. But I think Pascal's point was ... what was your point Pascal?"

"That we are all Sartre, Genet, even de Beauvoir."

"How?"

At this point Raymonde speaks up.

"Yes, how? I'm not Sartre. Or that queer Genet! And who was de Beauvoir?"

"Come along Raymonde. You know very well who Simone de Beauvoir was!"

"Oui, bien sûr. A joke! But I still don't see how we can all be straights, gays, men and women. And dead intellectuals to boot!"

"Because, my wonderful friend, we carry them in all that we think and do. Voilà! It's why we're here."

"On the planet? In Giverny?"

"No. Non! It's why we gather together every year."

Suddenly, he understands. It's all here. The right to

talk and debate. A tradition carried through Marat (though he was murdered!), Rousseau (imprisoned!), Verlaine, the writings of Balzac. He searches in desperation for a relevant Balzac novel but can only come up with *Les Chouans*. Hardly a philosophical work. Then, Malraux and the sacred circle spending hours at the Café Flore. And all because of Mme Guillotine and the storming of the Bastille. He sits back. It is gloriously sunny. Tobacco smoke wafts around the table. He is very, very happy.

"Well I don't get it! I'm not a queer or a woman. And if I was, I wouldn't be Genet or de Beauvoir. Fucking criminal and aristocrat! And it wasn't 'til I set up in business that I even had juillet quatorze off. It has always been le premier mai for the workers. Voilà!"

"Raymonde. Raymonde. Don't get excited. Shall we have more coffee? Encore du café?"

"Oh, that's right. Suddenly I'm the waiter again. Get your own fucking coffee. Putain!"

With this, Raymonde stands. He looks, for a moment, as if he will say more but thinking better of it trudges to the edge of the terrace where he sits disconsolately against the wall.

"Still find Giverny 'interesting' mon ami?"

He jerks back to Pascal who, infuriatingly, seems amused.

"It's, it's... crazy, frightening, maddening, er, extraordinary. And you do this every year?"

He turns again to look at Raymonde who has been joined by Chlöe. She seems to be comforting him. His shoulders are shaking. Anger? Rage? Sadness? Another stands. This time it's Jean-Louis who moves to sit by Raymonde.

"Well, Pascal. At the very least you must do as Raymonde suggested and get some more coffee. Perhaps it's time for a little break. what *lovely* weather we've had so far this summer, don't you agree?"

It is late afternoon. The group has long since dispersed. Things had become more heated after a round of pastis at 11.30 and far too much wine over a lunch that had mysteriously appeared from hampers provided by Mme Bordette.

The wine had been in litre bottles, all without labels, all tasting somehow of the sea. Jean-Louis had declared it to be *Banyuls*, thus provoking another discourse on the pretentiousness of the bourgeoisie. Inevitably, this has led back to the ways in which Sartre and his ilk, with the exception of Genet, only played at being friends of the ordinary man. Jean-Louis had *apologized* for knowing the wine's origins and looked immensely relieved when Marie had said,

"For God's sake, Jean-Louis, don't say 'sorry' for knowing things. I bet Pascal knows where the foie-gras comes from, don't you dear?"

Pascal had reddened and poured himself another *Ricard* before saying, quietly.

"Perigord."

"Voilà!"

It had gone on in much the same vein until well after three o'clock when a drunken Marie had signalled to Jean-Louis her intention to leave. Within minutes, after several "Adieus" only five remained. He couldn't help feeling a little disappointed. Had he held his own in the discussions? He could barely remember some of the conversation. He had found himself disquieted by Raymonde's reactions. At other times he had felt entirely out of his depth. He should have another go at *Being and Nothingness* – fuck it! Life was too short! At the same time he had been utterly filled with desire for Chlöe and strangely detached. This was after all meant to be an annual *celebration*, but it seemed to have brought nothing but conflict terribly reminiscent of his parents' rows.

"Is it always like this?"

"Bien sûr. It is our way, cheri, like bull-fighting with none of the physical courage. Pascal is such a bore, don't you think? He's the reason we only do it once a year!"

Hélène speaks quietly. She too is a little drunk.

"And as for that nonsense about the wine! Pascal can tell you the origins of any wine and even the slopes the vines grow on but for one day of the year he turns it into a political debate."

"What does he do?"

"For a living? *Now* who's being bourgeois? Pardon. He owns *Pastis Bertrand*."

"He *owns Pastis Bertrand*!"

"Well, he has a major stake. I'm sure it's why he

pretends all the sympathies with the workers. Pure guilt. His family is Catholic, going back generations. Pre-revolutionary generations. Voilà! He's a sexist so-and-so too. At least he has that in common with Sartre! Did you notice how quiet the women were? Even Chlöe!"

It was true; Marie had said little, Cecille and Felicité nothing at all and Mme Bordette had limited herself to comments about the weather and the contents of her hampers. For her part, Chlöe had been too wrapped up in Raymonde's misery to contribute much.

"It didn't used to be like this. We used to meet, eat, drink coffee, talk and debate. Sometimes monthly, sometimes more. It started like a book club without the books. Then one year Pascal climbed onto his high horse and only Jean-Louis and myself would take him on. So we agreed to do it once a year."

"Why didn't you ask Pascal to leave?"

"Leave? My dear, we aren't a club! We don't have rules or membership fees. We just want to celebrate the..."

"Freedom to hurt and humiliate each other?"

Chlöe has roused herself. She has been intently following the conversation. Now she is angry.

"Poor Raymonde! I'm surprised he has you all round at all. *And* he gives you croissants!"

Hélène is startled. A pained look crosses her face and she squints lopsidedly as she replies.

"Raymonde is a generous man, cherie. But I don't think he feels humiliated. If he did, he'd close the café for the day and send us on our way."

"People can do all sorts of things when they're humiliated. All sorts."

With that Chlöe stands, almost violently, and head bowed lurches across the terrace.

"Pardon Hélène, I'd better make sure she gets home in one piece. À bientôt."

The note-book lies on the kitchen table. A pen juts from the centre. Perhaps she has been writing today. Glancing around and feeling to his surprise more than a little furtive he cautiously opens at the page where the pen lies. Again looking behind, he picks up the slim writing pad.

It was Simone de Beauvoir's pretend relative who first put the idea into my head. It had been a long time ago but something she once said had stuck, "My theory is that for every child born one must die!" I'd had no real idea what she was talking about. But half the time she didn't either.

My head had hardly been straight at the time and things had got worse. Do you know what three years' worth of psychiatric drugs can do to you? I'd been on goodness knows how many. Sometimes I couldn't sleep, sometimes it was all I could do to get up in the morning. My periods had been all over the place. And my libido! Pretty much dormant except for bursts of horniness you wouldn't believe babe. Etienne had struck ultra lucky. And my eating? After all that, no change; still wasn't hungry. It never occurred to any of the so-called professionals that maybe I was just made that way. After all, I hadn't starved to death!

Her talk about de Beauvoir used to make me think of Sartre – not that she ever mentioned him. But it spurred me to read the old goat. Do you remember that part right at the end of Roads to Freedom when Matthieu pulls the trigger and just keeps on firing at the Germans? What was that about? Meaninglessness? Responsibility? What did he SAY? "Freedom!" To kill someone else at random. Just some poor soldier doing his job. I saw 'The Vanishing' too. Same idea; random killing as the ultimate kick.

It was three months after Etienne had fucked off. Long enough to know I was pregnant. Even getting that confirmed was a pain. Not having a period for two months in a row had been par for the course. It was when my nipples started getting sore that I bought the tester. Voilà! Pregnant and considered bonkers. Lucky girl, heh? I'd given up on visiting the clinic; the shrink didn't mind. I'm sure she had lots of other people to drug up.

But Evreux! It was so boring. College was a drag – when I could be arsed to go. I was really pissed off with my so-called family too. Two parents who argued in between rows. A mum working all hours and a dad who swanned about like we were the nouveau rîche. I was convinced it was all meaningless – you cured me of that, baby! But I guess you were too late.

I found her sitting on a step. Pretty, but with eyes

that didn't quite stay in line. She was blind. Her parents hadn't even given her sun-glasses! She was late for school. I was impressed – she used to walk all the way to school, about two kilometres, all by herself. But that day she'd stubbed her toe and was sitting waiting for the pain to pass. She wasn't making any fuss, just sitting. What was she? Seven? Eight? The papers would have told me eventually but I didn't bother much with papers – before or after.

She seemed pleased to meet me and I said I was called Josephine.

"Comme la femme de Napoleon?"

"Oui, d'accord. Et vous?"

"Louise. Je m'appelle Louise. Louise Burle."

She sounded really happy to be in la Famille Burle but when I asked her to tell me more she looked sad. Said her parents were out all the time. Working. I was sympathetic. Asked her where she lived and suggested we should go home and check she hadn't hurt her toe too badly. She was happy enough to miss school. Said they wouldn't mind.

So we walked for a while and she told me how much she missed her dog that had disappeared the week before. I asked if it was a seeing-eye dog and she said she'd never had one! She must have been like a bat the way she could get about without being able to see. But she was very modest about it. It had never been different for her.

She couldn't see. Her death was a kind of blessing for us both. Blindness is a kind of living death, non? She didn't see me approach. I'd taken a knife from the kitchen draw while she'd been listening to a story tape but I didn't have the guts. So I filled the bath and asked her if she wanted to cool down. It was so bloody hot that day – a Monday. She didn't seem at all surprised by the idea of a bath mid-morning though I think she said something about la piscine being better. She came into the salle de bain, undressed (I congratulated her on how easily she did that despite not seeing) and climbed in.

The rest was – easy. She didn't struggle much. I saw a burst of bubbles and that was it really. She looked so peaceful. I took her body and wrapped it in a towel and took her to the woods. There were leaves covering a muddy part at the edge of the pond but I don't really remember any of that. Funny, I remember humming – Frère Jacques. Then I went home and waited. But no-one came."

He stands transfixed. Appalled. He has been reading for but five minutes getting more and more engrossed, desperate to look away, but drawn again and again to the note-book and its terrible denouement. His world – their world – is tumbling down around him. So many images – the log fire, Pantam, the brasserie, the bedroom mirror, their garden, the love-making. All turning to dust, dying before his eyes. He hears a foot-step and turns, almost afraid. Chlöe sees the open note-book and catches her breath.

Absurdly, he says:

"But being blind isn't like being dead! She still had her sense of hearing, her taste!"

Then more cruelly: "And she'd have felt herself being pushed under, the water filling her lungs!"

"I know, baby. I know. No need to spell it out."

"No nee...No need! What were you thinking?"

"I, I wasn't really."

"But you'd planned it!"

"I know. Once the idea was in my head..."

He feels sick. Another image, this time of a fair-haired little girl. Lying in a bath asleep. No, dead!

"What colour was her hair?"

"Fair. Why?"

"I...I don't kno...Urrghhh"

He retches, dry but how his chest heaves.

"Well, you wanted to know if I'd make things up to shock you!"

A ray of hope!

"Did you? Please say yo..."

"No, baby. Non. What did you expect? We said the whole truth, nothing hidden."

"Christ! You make it sound like it was my fault!"

"I didn't mean that. I just meant that writing it all down was sure to lead to something one of us didn't like."

"Didn't like! Didn't like! This isn't about me not liking something! This is about you...murderi...murdering a child. A fucking blind child!"

"It was a long time ago."

"A long ... putain!"

He sits down, head in hands his shoulders slump forward. He runs his hands through his hair. Curiously, he notices a spot on the wall where the plaster is cracking. 'Another job,' he thinks. And then, 'This is so mad, so mad.'

"Is it being a long time ago meant to make it better?"

"Not better. But easier. I got over it. You can too. In time..."

"What about her poor parents? Did they get over it? Putain! Putain! Please tell me you made it up!"

She is silent. She looks at him with a half smile, a smile of sympathy. But she says nothing. A peace has come over her. Chlöe has made her confession. It is still Bastille Day.

XLVI

Journal: I'm not sure about this diary business. Things I took to be the same – we are different in more ways than I might imagine. Your entries about sex are a good example – the conversation we had about cocks mattering or not. You say that, for you, there is no memory of another man (me, for instance). If you have gone to the trouble of bedding him, he becomes a man in his own right. New, different, certainly. But you're not comparing. You're studying, appreciating, smelling. I think your way is better. With time they all just merge, you said. You can remember that some were better than others but no specifics. Did you once say the shags that stand out are the awful ones?

For me, not to compare, contrast would be impossible. The breasts not yours, the skin another's, the smell! How could the smell approach you, yours, us? Pure, pure sex. And chat? Precious moments in the sun? Post-coital (pre-coital) rituals? The games? I don't believe it possible. And yet the jealousy remains. Maybe it's the man I am envious of – his explorations, his excitement; as precious to him as our times are to me. Lucky bastard! Or maybe it's that old adage about jealousy being the jealous person thinking the other person's having a better time. But I don't think it can be that; I get jealous when I'm having a perfectly good time - though not as good when we're together.

Would you take a lover long enough to find out about him? For a night/three/a week? Would you wake to him, make love, hold him as you hold me? Would you make him breakfast, sit calmly drinking coffee in one of his shirts, your legs slowly opening so he sees, sees…? Or would it be for an afternoon only? An afternoon of frantic shagging and a curt, 'au revoir.'

You see the problem? I am possessed by you. Obsédée. Is that fair? Dare I think you feel the same? Or is it my male thing about possession? Am I transferring my desires onto you? This gets complicated doesn't it? If I'm doing that, then surely I should plant my jealousies onto you as well? Let me stand back. Do the impossible – step outside of myself to look at my fears. I follow the thought through and I have a new theory. You are suffering too – you too believe I am exploring, enjoying. Are you generous enough to hope, through your hurt, that I am? I'm not that generous with you. My possessiveness is extreme, unfair. To wish you happiness with another man is too much for me.

It's no problem imagining you with Claudette, Raymonde, Héléne. You enjoying their company, entertaining them as much – more – as they yours. But Jésu! A different story. What did you call him? 'Gorgeous!' I noticed.

Do you remember our first Noël? Well, do you? Are you reading this, baby? It was, what? Three years ago? You were in blue? No, I was in green. Ha ha! Actually, I was in heaven. Snow, a log fire. The dog. Did we even have a name for the brute? I remember you wanted to call him Jerome. Whoever calls a dog Jerome? I remember, I remember,

"C'est un bon nom."
"Jerome? Pourquoi?"
 "Pourquoi non?"
"Why not? Why not!"

And of course I couldn't think of a reason. You could have called him François Mitterrand for all I cared. I was convinced you would come up with Rousseau or even Diderot. You can imagine the scene at the engraver's when I order the collar-tag:
"Quel nom?"
"Diderot."
"Excellent. J'aime Diderot. Un philosophe profonde."
Hmmm. Or, maybe.
"Diderot! What kind of name is that for a dog? Call him Bernard."
"Pourquoi Bernard?"
"Il est un bon philosophe, St Bernard. No, maybe Bertrand."
So what did we call him? Pantam. What kind of name is Pantam?
It was cold that Christmas. Snow everywhere. Too cold to go out much and the vans didn't come every day – just too icy. We played cards – euchre. We feasted on fish for Christmas Eve and then woke up to champagne on the day itself. Yet-to-be-named Pantam

wanted a walk at midday but you weren't having any of it. Too busy having me if I recall. We finally got up at about four. Ash in the grate, freezing house, dog sulking at the back door. You suggested having a look at Giverny in the cold but it was already almost dark. Then:

"I've got a game."

"Quel surprise. Un joue pour Noël. Et... ?"

"You pretend to be Santa and knock on the front door. I'll let you in and you can give me a present."

"It's fucking freezing out there!"

And you cast your eyes down, the way you did – so beautiful. So bloody irresistible. And I trudged out, waited all of five seconds and banged. Hard. The door opened –

"Christ! Where did you? What?"

And there you stood – Mme Claus incarnate. If Mme Claus usually wears a red and white mini-dress barely covering the tops of her thighs – and nothing else. I just had time to turn the stove on before you took me upstairs to get a better look. Which was how we came to have our lamb at midnight.

We even had a domestic routine going for a while around Noël, didn't we? Remember? Noël is no big deal in Giverny. A few days off work, a parade complete with Santa on an ass. Santa! I thought it was

Jesus on the donkey. The kids go down to the *salle de fête*, play some games, a few presents – all the usual stuff. The richer folk come with the grand-children; quite a sight later as they all pile into the church for midnight mass. Chanel galore. Even Dolce and Gabbana – Margot, wasn't it? They must all know Monet is buried metres from the door. Pretty pissed too. So we would do all that, then back to our cottage for a little present opening. How you loved it – you were incredible – the house looked like a Christmas card. Log-fire, tinsel over everything, you in full Mme Claus regalia by two in the morning.

And the presents! I still don't know how you did it – truffle oil (perfect), those biographies (Zola one year, Auden, Napoleon, Marie-Antoinette)! A magazine (always a magazine – angling (!), animal husbandry, wood-turning – one year you slipped up and said I'd find National Geographic boring. I didn't. It's great. Where else could you discover there are a million lakes in Alaska?), chocolate covered everything from figs to a dildo that made your eyes water.

We'd get up mid afternoon after experimenting with the dildo or me reading one of the biogs to you. Some champagne or blanquette, then you would say, "I'll cook." But we'd go back to bed and eat much later. The dog would get his walk the following afternoon. You would be hungover and promising not to drink for, what, an hour?

The second year we watched Baisse Moi on TV. How you hated it. The rape is horrible, the revenge *understandable and the moral baffling. That's when I discovered you had no fantasies around violence at all. Just the tentative stuff about me holding your wrists and a soupçon of bondage - you loved the control didn't you, honey? My guess is that the blindfold game was one-sided for just that reason. Remember?*

"Let's play."

"Play? We've been playing with M Chocodildo all afternoon."

"No, I want to blind-fold you."

"Hmmm… And?"

"Trust me, baby."

Sometimes I sit and watch the fire, Pantam at my side. He basks, if a dog can bask, in the heat and attention as I ruffle his fur at the neck. The fire spits and crackles, in the background a vague roar – like approaching trains – as the smoke rushes up the chimney. Do you remember our little "incident"? How the pompiers arrived at the front door hammering away.

"What's that banging?"

"Us."

"No, downstairs. Someone's battering on the door!"

I went down to find a room filled with smoke and the fire blazing away – all yellows, reds, oranges and blues. The hammering continued so I answered the door, hoping it wasn't Hélène who'd already seen quite

408

enough of me post-coitally.

"Oui."
"Un feu. Vous avez un feu."
"Oui, d'accord. Et?"

The pompiers marched in and went straight to the fire. One, bringing up the rear, hauled a hose with him.

"La chiminée! C'est dangereuse!"

Then I clocked it. Cinders were raining down into the street. We were, how should I say? Alight.

I grabbed a coat and stepped outside to join a small crowd admiring our neglectful handiwork. Smoke and flames billowing out. Just as I was about to rush back in to rescue you there was a "whoosh" and a kind of "whump" and a huge cloud of steam and smoke shot from the chimney and all went quiet. Inside, the man with the hose had obviously done his thing. Our curious neighbours drifted away and I came back in to find one of the pompiers playing with Pantam; another opening windows to free the choking smoke. And the other two? None too bashfully, they were staring at you as you made coffee – dressed in one of my shirts, wide open and, for anyone with eyes, showing the most beautiful bush a man could ask for.

"Cafe?"

How cool could you be? Two flustered men averting their gaze then sneaking looks, another supposedly playing with the dog while eyeing you all the time and the fourth, bright red if I remember right, leaning across the window-sill so no-one would see his stiffy.

"Merci, madam, merci."

We talked about it on and off for weeks, always laughing, invariably ending in you suggesting a four-fireman fantasy and then …

Whenever I sit watching the fire nowadays I see you, us, a group of uniformed voyeurs and a panting dog. I guess it makes life less lonely.

Well, memories and France Musique. You were right about FM. They can be so far up their own arses it's a wonder they don't suffocate. How can these clowns talk so sincerely about some 1960s' accordionist? But where else can you listen to uninterrupted Coltrane or Miles for two hours? They even had Rahsann Roland Kirk on recently. I told you my dad saw him once in some smoky club in the 18th arondissement didn't I? He said it was stunning – as was the night with my mother. And you know he told me it was the night I was conceived! Dunno if it's true but it's a nice thought. Mind you, I thought we'd conceived any number of times. Sometimes you just, kind of, know.

I've almost finished the novel – just like we'd said; a proper one. I stole lots of it from us. More importantly, from you. I checked out the Mazerkinde, got lost for a couple of days in the library at the Sorbonne and then found myself stuck deep in a tale about the Hundred Years' War. It's full of love, desertion, fear, a few battle scenes and murder. Giverny's in there too though you wouldn't recognize it – apart from the church. Long before dear Monet got himself buried there of course. I hope a vague sense of the beauty he saw comes through.

I don't think I'll stay here much longer. It's – I'm – too sad except when I write. It's foggy today so even when I look outside for a bit of inspiration all I see is mist and there's a limit to the number of times you can describe a wall.

Do you remember what you said when I told you about the advance for Paris? The novel's called Paris.

"You're a sucker for it, baby."

"For what?"

"Flattery. You're not alone. Look at the things you say to me. How can a girl resist?"

"I don't flatter you."

"You tell me I'm beautiful, sexy, smart. Then there's the skin. You go on about my skin like it's…"

"Heaven?"

"There you go again!"

"I just say it how I find it – you."

"And my slap? You think it's sexy when I'm putting my make-up on?"

"Every time."

"You'll be saying you like my poo next!"

"There's nothing wrong with your poo. Nice torpedoes. No smell."

"Putain!"

"That too."

"I know. But it's a bit weird."

"No, baby. It's love. And I reckon any man would say the same. You're gorgeous. Fact. What's not to love? Are you surprised I'm jealous?"

"Who are you jealous of? You say you like it when other men look twice at me!"

"I do. But when I'm away I can't help thinking…"

"Well don't. I'm too busy sorting Guillaume's library and doing my thing at the nursery."

"There's always Guillaume himself. Rich. On the razz twenty four seven."

"Please…!"

"What did you mean about the flattery?"

We were in the courtyard. A balmy day. Wisps of cloud way above but otherwise a blue, blue sky; Pantam panting – as ever – in the sun. We'd been talking about the mad publishing advance for the novel. 2,000 Euros. You'd looked shocked, then smiled, then looked sad. You thought it must be a trick. Who would give an advance, let alone one so high, for a first novel?

"He's buttering you up. Why would he want it?

You're not a Genet. You're not even an Iain Banks. Neither of them got much first time round."

"Genet was offered 30,000 francs in the 'forties for three books. One of them turned out to be *The Thief's Journal*!"

"So now you are Genet!"

"No. But why would he flatter me with an offer? Any offer?"

"Has he read any of it?"

"I sent him a précis and a few sample chapters. He liked it."

"Liked it! He must have loved it. Bet he liked the sex scenes. Voyeur!"

"He didn't say. But mostly he liked the idea, especially all the factual stuff about Paris. He loves Paris. Thinks it would be a…"

"Good plug for Paris?"

"Hardly. Don't think Paris needs any PR. No, he thinks it would make a good film. He's got some mates in the movie business."

"Even so. Why you? Why now? It just doesn't seem real. You only met him a couple of weeks ago."

It was true. I'd been deep in Sudoku and a pony-tailed man had asked if I minded anyone sitting next to me. A commuter speaking! Never mind being so polite. We started chatting. Edouard turned out to be a publisher. He said his biggest sellers were obscure European philosophy texts and out-of-copyright snippets from the masters – Zola and Dickens were a speciality.

Then we talked about my pathetic struggles to find a way into the system with Paris and from there to deeper conversation about plot, the need to have potentially film-friendly dialogue and the publishing zeitgeist - an obsession with murder and mystery, particularly what Edouard called "Gothic who-dunnits." Paris - or at least the opening chapters - had been a long way from a "whodunit," Gothic or otherwise, at that point. It was just meant to be a modern love story coupled with an historical Romance with some blood and guts thrown in to keep the tension up. Edouard asked to see a sample and – within a week – he'd suggested another meeting where he made the mad offer; an advance allowing me to finish the novel at leisure. Plus two provisos. First, it had to be a bloody Gothic murder mystery. Second, I shouldn't approach any other publisher via an agent. I didn't and Paris changed at a rate of knots. I'm not stupid, you know. I suspected Edouard of acting nefariously but couldn't for the life of me think what the secret agenda could be.

"He might be just mad, you know."

"Who?"

"This Edouard. He might spend his time flattering up-and-coming novelists to make his morning commute more entertaining."

"But why meet me? Why buy me lunch?"

"Maybe he fancies you! Or really wants to meet me. See what your heroine's like in the flesh."

"He could just ask."

"I hope you wouldn't say, 'Yes.'"

"Why not?"

"Too embarrassing. He's virtually seen me shagging you anyway!"

I'd been twitchy, probably run my hands through my hair. You were only voicing my own doubts. And yet, yet... What if Edouard was - is - the real thing? Get behind me, temptation! Too much hope. Too much disappointment lying in wait. I didn't doubt the sense in Edouard's suggestion for the novel's new direction. Until a bit back I'd even enjoyed writing it with a new theme. At least I felt like I knew where it might be heading. And if Edouard turns out to be a flattering fruit-cake? So what? Paris will be finally finished and off my mind; I can get back to the business of...What? Walking the dog? Commuting? Planting my garden, cooking for myself...

"Sorry, baby."

"Why?"

"I didn't mean to bring you down. I just don't want you to be hurt. You're too trusting... Edouard might be OK."

I set myself a target of a thousand words a day. They reckon it's the best way – Lesley Thomas used to do a couple of thousand before 11 o'clock. Simenon more – he probably indulged in a Maigret style lunch afterwards. Maybe, I should get a pipe. Well, at least, a pastis. But they're not the same anymore – no ritual, no gorgeous woman to love – no chance of Hélène popping round for a viewing. Christ! Who's that?

"Bonjour."

"Hélène! I was just, er, writing about you."

"Something nice I hope."

"No, I'd only just mentioned your name."

"Spooky. Ça va?"

"Oui, non, je ne sais."

"No sign of Chlöe?"

"No."

"Poor you. Can I come in?"

"Bien sûr. Un café?"

"Pastis, si tu plais."

"How's life?"

"Slow. The book club feels empty without Chlöe."

"You try living here without her."

"Maybe you should move, cheri."

"Where would I go? Though I've been thinking about it."

"Can I sit down."

"Sorry. The fire's going. Let's sit there."

"Do you remember your chimney fire?"

"Remember it! I've just been describing it in my diary."

"You keep a journal?"

"Oui."

"How very Rousseau of you."

"Not quite. I'm not as honest as he was."

"Did you describe what you and Chlöe were up to when the chimney caught fire?"

"How do you know about that?"

"Well, one might have guessed. But I didn't need to. It was the talk of the town for days. You can't just appear in the street mid-afternoon looking like you've been at it without people talking. Quite made their day I imagine! How lovely, France Musique! I love the chat in between pieces, don't you?"

"Hmmm…"

"They do overdo the jazz though. Who can listen to so much John, John, what is the name I'm looking for, cheri?"

"Coltrane?"

"That's it. John Coltrane. My husband even insisted I listened to some awful cacophony on Monday. A man playing three instruments at once!"

"Roland Kirk."

"Exactement. Dreadful! Guillaume and I are…très different. Perhaps Chlöe told you. No, I know she told you. You didn't have secrets did you? Such a lovely way to be. But, you are young."

"What's age got to do with it? There's not much point in a couple being together if they can't talk. Honestly."

"You sound like her. Idealistic to the core. If couples could talk surely they wouldn't get divorced, argue? Have affairs. Probably wouldn't need to get married in the first place. Another pastis, darling. If I may. Do you have anything to eat? What's that?"

"An experiment."

"An … It looks a little … yellow."

"I know. I tried it last night. I added turmeric, shallots and tarragon to a pommes de terre gratin.

"And?"

"Would you like some?"

"Why not?"

"I'll heat it through."

"No my dear. Just a spoonful as it is, si tu plais. And perhaps, un autre pastis."

This was getting tricky. I could see Hélène getting drunk and confessing all. I gave her the pastis – Berger. And a spoonful of the Gratin Indienne as I called it.

"Merci, cheri. Oh my word! This is divine. Not enough salt, but otherwise … Now where was I? Can I take my coat off? The fire's very warm. Ah, yes. Affaires."

Here it comes.

"My husband didn't have affairs as such. He used to go on business trips. Funny how many of them featured trips to the red light districts. He particularly liked some little whore near Montmartre. Probably took her to the Folies Bergère as well. There, what do you think?"

"It's your life Hélène. Who am I to comment?"

"Or judge."

"I'm not that judgemental. Anyway, I'm sorry he hurt you. But there must have been signs for a while?"

"From day one, darling. But, he was a man after all."

"A man who was seeing other women. Doesn't that reflect on the women too?"

"Hardly. They were doing a job."

Hélène pauses, sipping her drink thoughtfully.

"We're all doing a job aren't we cheri? Looking after the children, organizing the house-hold. I know at least two of our neighbours who've whored themselves into wed-lock for the husband's money. Do you have a little to eat? Or smoke?"

"I didn't know you smoked."

"Few people do, dear. Chlöe does. Now you. A privileged elite Do you have any *Ricard*? I don't get on with these others. Desolée. I must sound very rude."

"Not at all. I don't like *Ricard* anymore, though."

"I see. Celebrations only, eh?"

"Chlöe and I would..."

"I'm sorry, dear. I didn't mean to pry. *Berger* it is. Less water this time, though."

"It's in the jug in front of you. You poured."

"So it is. So I did. I think I'm getting a little drunk. Time for that cigarette. Should I go outside?"

Hélène makes no attempt to move. He notices that somehow she has managed to take off her boots which now sit warming by the fire.

"It's OK, you can smoke inside. I do occasionally, especially on days like this."

"Awful isn't it? You can see the mist rising off the river. You don't see much of that in dear Claude's paintings do you? All light and beauty. Pissarro got it right, I think."

They are shockingly and stridently interrupted by a blast of Whitney Houston.

"What?"

"Pardon, cheri. C'est mon portable."

"You have *I Will Always Love You* for a ring-tone?"

"Only for one caller. Excuse-moi."

With that, she turns away and whispers into the phone: 'Bien sûr.' 'Toujours'. She mentions his name. He vaguely sees her rubbing her ankles together at that point.

"Pardon. Claudette."

"Claudette from the brasserie. Etta?"

"The very same."

"But I thought she had left with someone else."

"She did. But we met when she was visiting one afternoon and, I think she prefers an older woman... I'm happy to say!"

"And you have Whitney Houston for her....?"

Hélène pauses again. Slightly red – from the pastis, or from embarrassment, he can't tell – she looks him in the eye. Hers are a little wild.

"I'd have the Sex Pistols if she asked me! She ... keeps my lonely nights less lonely. Tu comprends?"

"Chlöe, er...Sorry, Hélène. I knew."

"No secrets then! We are lovers. A woman gets lonely. Masturbation soon loses its charms at my age."

There are confessions and confessions. Hélène's would have been up there with the best if she hadn't already told you. And you, me.

I'm really going to have to move.

XLVII

For Jerome the long retreat has passed in a haze. He neither knows nor cares why the army is being withdrawn. He had been told to march, walk, run – crawl if necessary – back towards Paris. Was this a regrouping? A retreat in defeat? Victory? What could 'victory' possibly mean? So many dead, maimed, disfigured for life. On both sides. And what did 'sides' mean? Those who fought for the king? Which one? Those who died for France? He barely understands what 'France' is. He knows only that he has survived, a victory of sorts. As they trudge on the men strike up the occasional song, or they talk or settle to silence. Something has changed; except for the odd stumble and curse, the men are cheerful and many smile. There is hope. Hope of a return to hearth, home and loved ones. To hot food, to ardour.

"I can't wait. My woman's going to get such a seeing to!"

"Mine too. I hope she remembers what to do!"

"Ha! Remember? Don't you think she's found another prick by now?"

Jerome flinches. The banter is not ill-meant. The two men are pushing each other in mock combat. Jerome, walking just behind, runs his hands through his hair and winces. What of Marie? Is it Pierre's body she still enjoys? He doesn't doubt that Pierre continues to provide passionate embraces, humour, the conversation and company a young woman must need. He no longer lives an illusion. Marie as his, children playing contentedly as she prepares his meal and chats about her day in the fields or at market. He knows not where such dreams came from and knows no-one in the village who might live such a life. All are worn down by the constant labour, the need to gather the harvest, see to the horses, chop and stack wood. There is no market. His imagination has given him a life unknown. It is too placid, gentle, calm. Altogether too complacent; the opposite of the jealousy that drives his mad speculation. Such scenes are too, too ... He grimaces. Pierre had understood Marie well. She was a woman, a woman needing work to survive, a fire in the hearth for warmth not romance.

Everyone he knew had been the same. Men and women toiled together in the fields, often with their children at their side or strapped to the mother's back. They would return to their hovels when the sun went down or would go into the byre to see to a cow. If they were lucky they would settle on dry straw pallets as soon as they had eaten, only to plunge straight into slumber before waking with the dawn. A curse escapes him.

"Un fou. Je suis un fou!"

"Come on Jerome, cheer up! It can't be far for you now."

The land is beginning to look familiar. Hills roll to left and right. He can see a few copses at their brows. The road seems to beckon him on. Not so far then. In distance. But in time! How much would have changed?

He wasn't sure how long he had been away. Certainly two years, perhaps three. He had kept in touch with time only for the first year, the seasons different – often grey – but still familiar. But as they had ventured further north and west only the summers seemed right. Seasons had merged; spring, even autumn, becoming one long grey winter. Spring flowers seemed late in blooming, autumn leaves either dashed to the ground before they were truly russet or holding tenaciously to twigs long after frosts had turned the ground to frozen mud and ice.

"You were one of the first from round here, weren't you? What's it been? Four years?"

Four years! Perhaps that was right. Jerome's spirits lift a fraction. Four years! So much may have happened! Perhaps Pierre has left the village? To war? Not Pee-pee! Perhaps he had left to seek court-ship to the east or south? More likely, but why should he? There were local girls and all the younger men taken. And Marie? Pregnant? Betrothed to a rich passer-by? A memory – Falaise! Surely that couldn't have been Marie? Gaston had called him mad. Obsédée. And Gaston? Surely dead? Surely... He pushes the thought away.

Perhaps Marie is also dead. Why not? There was more than enough death in the village. Beauty could not protect you. A lust for life might. He knows that fever carried away many young, the very old; forty years of age was very old. Those weakened by fearsome child-birth lasting sometimes days. Those killed by simple cuts turned septic or green with gangrene. He had twice seen rotting limbs sawn from uncles who had carried on labouring in fetid pools and then continued to clear rank ditches after cuts had started to suppurate. Both men had nicked themselves with scythes only a few days before. A few days could be a life-time around here.

He thinks of the comrades left behind, the ambush in the woods. So long ago now. Instinctively he raises his hand. Even this had been a kind of luck. The blade had been sharp, the cuts severing flesh, bone and muscle as a knife through butter. The wounds had bled for no more than half an hour, a mercifully clean cloth pressed to them. A dozen others had the fingers torn out, the stumps trailing nerves and veins. Their shrieks pervade his nightmares still. These men had been surprised to find they bled for a shorter time, but the damage was done, the stumps suppurating and gangrene soon appearing. Jerome feels sick. He can still smell the rotting flesh; rank, chokingly acrid. He stumbles and retches. A hand is proffered. Jerome looks up. No! Impossible! A new daemon?

Auguste Mazerme smiles down at his son. Great tears of joy, relief and love course down his cheeks. His soft grey eyes gaze at the prodigal returned.

"Welcome home, Jerome. Bienvenu, mon fils."

Jerome's feels his father's familiar strength as he is hauled to his feet. He looks into those grey eyes and – no shame now – allows Auguste to draw him close.

"Papa, oh papa!"

Burying his head into the safest of shoulders Jerome Mazerme begins to cry. Soft at first then choking sobs. Clinging now as tightly as he can, he hears from somewhere far away:

"Bienvenu, mon fils. Bienvenu!"

XLVIII

Can you understand a village? It looks so simple doesn't it? Perhaps three or four well established families, some incomers and then the rest; folk who have lived there for a couple of generations. Most will talk to each other at the local shop or say, "Hi" as they pass in the street. Villages are not like that. To the outsider they are as mysterious as the moon; some people won't pass the time of day, others ignore all and sundry and many will have petty grudges stemming from a long-forgotten incident or a dispute over land, light, noise...

Customs, traits and peculiarities will be set. There may be traditions or enmities lasting hundreds of years. Feuds, language and a hidden religion will carry on as all else drifts to death. There will be a distrust of outsiders, even – perhaps especially – those from the neighbouring hamlet or commune. Families can be so interwoven they have abandoned their original names in favour of combination or contraction.

When the Franks first raged through what was to become Paris one family plundered all and everything. The Mazerkinde took, despoiled, razed, ravished and ravaged person, beast and land alike. Rape was no crime; to the victor the spoiled. A strategy ensuring that the next generation and those following would be children, nephews, cousins of the invaders. And what closer – safer – tie can there be than family? The Mazerkinde were masters of this tactic. Only the

Hazermes came close to matching their ferocity. What could be more natural than declaring a truce via marriage – or what passed for marriage – between the two families? A solution sought by Henry and Eleanor of Aquitaine; a half baked plan that lead to the Hundred Years' War. At least the proposed union between Mary Queen of Scots and Phillip of France only resulted in the short-lived "Fortunate Armada", so fortunate that 30,000 men were blown and battered by the winds coursing around Scotland and Ireland. Only 5000 returned to Spain.

But for the Mazerkinde and Hazermes, what name could they take? Mazerkinde-Hazerme, Hazerme-Mazerkinde? Which family would assume primacy? Both names, in any case, too much of a mouthful for those raised to fight, kill, maim and breed brutally and fast. So Mazermes they became and as we approach the time of our tale – her story – we can be assured, as the Mazermes are assured, that their place in the tradition and history of the village is set. It is as sure as the stones of their homes or the land they have seized to own and till with whatever labour they can muster up from the frightened and unwilling.

They live on in the very language of the place. Their name has its own grammar to be used in under-the-breath tones, sparingly and with more than a little trepidation: *"They* live over the far hill," "I hope *they* aren't angry," "I wonder what *they* ssshh... those Mazermes are planning now."

No-one in our village can know – even through tales told at the bedsides of children –what the Mazerkinde and Hazermes had done to deserve their reputation. It was hundreds of years before our story begins – so no memories of the barbarism, the plunder. But there is an understanding as real as any written record. These are people to be reckoned with, a family that rules as if by decree. A family holding the land and compassionate only for others of the clan; there are many such.

How could Jerome have emerged from la famille Mazerme? Jerome the sensitive, the smiler, the dancer, the shy lover? Was it his strangeness to his kith that lead him to prove his muscle in the army? No-one had doubted his heart but his mettle was another thing – and no Mazerme in living memory had ever had the courage to leave the village of his birth for war or adventure.

XLIX

And now Jerome stares at the grate. With a little effort he could stir the ash and, perhaps, raise another fire. The kindling sits in its familiar spot to the left. It is his father's habit in the winter to rise well before dawn to bring the fire back to life.

A smile crosses Jerome's face. Merged memories of so many winter days as a child sitting with his mother, his father already gone to the fields, as she busies herself with the morning bread-making, a cold sun creeping over the horizon but the fire already blazing. He knew, even then, how lucky he was to have both mother and father still living. So many died in their twenties, the woman worn out by the triple work of house, child and field. It was common to find men in their early thirties who had already had two, or even three, child-bearing partners. It was the exhausting privilege of the last to raise the children. Six or seven children with one father but three mothers.

But not for Jerome. Auguste was considered remarkable, Jerome's mother more so. Both were still relatively hale and hearty. Both had raised all their own children; together.

Today is already warm. There is no need to rekindle the fire. Thoughts return to last night's home-coming.

"My poor son, your hand. What have you done to your hand?"

He had told the story. As he reached the part

concerning his sacrifice, Auguste stands.

"But you weren't a crossbow-man! Why Jerome? Porquoi?"

"Honour."

"Mon Dieu! Honour! What kind of honour is it to lose your fingers?"

"They might of killed me if they'd thought me a mere yeoman."

"And they might not. You bloody fool!"

"Leave him Auguste. He is alive. We should be grateful!"

Auguste reddens. Is he angry with his son, the war, the senseless carnage?

"It's the pointless deaths of all those beautiful horses I really object to!"

"The dead horses fed us!"

"The dea...! I'm sorry Jerome, none of this makes sense to me. But I am grateful!"

There is a familiar knock at the door. Familiar after so very long.

"Entrée Pierre!"

"Jerome est là?"

Jerome stands as his friend – rival – no, friend, steps inside. He hesitates. Pee-pee doesn't.

"Jerome. Mon ami!"

Somehow he finds himself swept up into Pierre's strong embrace. Despite his re-awakened jealousy, he hugs in return. Stronger and stronger.

"You are alive!"

"Oui. Voilà!"

"Your hand! How?"

And he re-tells the sorry tale. Out of the corner of his eye he sees his father becoming agitated at the second telling.

"You showed wisdom as well as courage, mon ami."

This stops him. His father steps forward and suddenly crumples into his fire-side chair. He looks old, older than Jerome has seen him. His stuffing, like that from the chair, is gone.

"They would have killed you, I'm sure. You were wise."

It is said, as simply as that. Pierre who has never known war and has barely stepped beyond the village boundaries is suddenly a supporter who inverts folly to wisdom.

"Merci. Et toi? Ça va?"

"Oui. Le bois, le travail. Plus ça change!"

"Pierre. Jerome. Shall we eat?"

It is as if he has never been away. They talk of the farm-work, how little news they ever received of the war, some deaths in the village, local arguments about inheritance, land, increasing tithes. Jerome does his utmost to feign interest. But only one thing pre-occupies him. "Obsédée!" He looks at Pee-pee engrossed in his mother's stew. He catches his eye a few times but Pierre seems absorbed in the lamb and the current topic of conversation. M Cerdan's sheep seem to have been spirited away, last seen ambling toward the copse at the river's edge. 'Marie, Marie, Marie.' She floats before him, between them, an unseen presence that holds Jerome in suspense.

"Marie?"

He has spoken aloud! The conversation stops. Jerome looks down, abashed.

"Marie? Marie Leclaire? What of her?"

"Ssshh... Auguste! He doesn't know. Perhaps Pierre can tell him. Pierre?"

All has gone quiet, a collective holding of breath.

"Well, what of Marie? Elle est où? Where is she? Is she well?"

"Two questions! You always ask two questions!"

Does he? Was this some unnoticed habit? There were two unvoiced questions right there! Perhaps it was, indeed, a habit. He runs his hands through his hair.

"Really, do I? How is she then?"

"Two more! Always two! Voilà!"

Jerome feels his fists clench. Pee-pee is playing games with him. He runs his fingers over the two stumps on his mutilated hand. Again he raises his hands to run them through his hair.

"Your hand, mon fils. Your poor hand. Pierre, stop tormenting him."

His father's eyes are full of concern as he repeats.

"Tell him, Pierre!"

"We don't know if Marie Leclaire is well. No-one has seen her since she ran away. Voilà! After her crime. Voilà!"

"Crime? Ran away?"

"Marie killed Madame Gigot's little girl. Jeanne."

Jerome gasps. He hadn't expected this. A child with Pierre, illness, even death. But murder. It wasn't possible. His – Pierre's – Marie!

"I don't believe you!"

"It is true, Jerome. Listen to Pierre."

His father's tone is quiet but very firm. He knows this tone. It never presages anything good.

"Mon Dieu! What happened?"

"No-one is sure. Marie had fallen with child by a yeoman passing through and...."

Pierre stops as Jerome slouches forward, his head almost touching the table.

"And she couldn't work outside. The winter was harsh. She was worried for the baby. She started to lodge with Madame Gigot and would look after little Jeanne when Madame was out in the fields. The Gigots had been in the habit of working as late as they could, often after sun-down. One night they worked very late indeed until the frost was too much for them. When they got back... when ..."

"Go on."

"There were no lights, no fire. Madame said later she knew at that moment something terrible had happened! They found little Jeanne in the stone basin, the water stone cold. And no sign of Marie."

"Mais, pourquoi?"

"No-one knows. There was some suggestion the pregnancy had turned her."

"But a child! She wouldn't kill a child!"

"Well, she hasn't been seen since that night. Probably went into the city to have the baby."

"No! This is impossible! Marie kills a harmless child, then runs off to have her own? In Paris! Impossible! The father? Has anyone any idea who he is?"

"Personne! He may be dead by now himself. She said he was a yeoman on the way to fight. Perhaps he was."

"And perhaps the father was really a little closer to home!"

"Clos... Why would she lie?"

"To protect someone close to her. I don't know. I, I..."

Jerome slumps again. This is madness. Why would Marie kill? Would she lie to protect Pierre? From what? There is no shame in being a father. A memory stirs. What had Gaston said? "Pregnancy is the worst thing," or something similar. But no-one in the village believed that. Besides, everyone of age had children. Everyone except himself and P... He runs his hands through his hair. The butchered stumps are hurting, a dull ache like the one in his heart. There is the occasional sharp stab of pain as if a needle...

"Pierre. You, you, ... knew her. Didn't you talk with her. Get the truth about the father? She must have told you!"

Pierre blushes and stammers,

"We, we didn't talk much. Well, sometimes about you and why you'd gone away."

This was easier. Jerome steadies himself,

"You know why I went away. For honour. To win Marie!"

At this Auguste returns to the table and looks sternly at his son.

"You don't win a woman by running away, mon fils. Not by running away!"

L

Unsent letters: I'm fucked. I feel like I've trailed thru the 100 years war – all hundred plus of them. What can I do, baby? You tell me murder is in your blood. A Leclaire? Am I to understand? Who the fuck are the Leclaires? I made them up! I don't care. I don't care about much at all now. That night I stayed staring at your crazy book system. You were asleep, upstairs. I crave Absinthe! Very Montmartre, non? What I would give to be sitting in one of those cafés as I write. How Jean-Paul Sartre is that? Hey, maybe I'm alive – I can make jokes. Pretty poor and intellectual jokes I know. I can still see the funny side. But only the funny side of me (no more than 80%).

Is there a funny side to you now? Have you been stripped to the core? Am I to see what you did as momentary madness– even an aberration of mind only to be understood by psychiatrists - or are you scarred deep in your family? A true throwback rather than an everyday degenerate (your Leclaire genes poking thru, maybe)? I can't write this. I must go and sit outside under the stars.

My love, how could you carry on with the usual things. Smiling and laughing at the legumes I brought home; the funny shaped carrots. Sitting happily on the sofa after dinner. Such love-making! Did you feel we were in our last days? What a way to go, hey? And here am I texting you from the garden. Or perhaps not.

'Hi, Soz bout that last mess. Bit drunk and v unhappy. Missing us – and we're still here. Fuckit!'

Baby, it's getting late. Tried to send a text but I can't remember if I pressed, "Send". It's maybe three in the morning and I'm as lost as two days ago. I can't imagine life without us. What, exactly, would be the point? "Life without you" implies I should do something. Phone the cops? Flee the country (no point, you wouldn't come with me)? But it doesn't matter, does it? You were doing a Rousseau – your confession wasn't a test of you was it? It was testing me.

Am I able to cast the first stone? Have I killed? Only, to my knowledge, at a distance by paying my taxes to bomb people faraway. I don't think I've killed deliberately – but I can't remember much about driving cars before I was twenty – too drunk. Maybe I did kill then. Does Marianne's abortion make me a murderer? Or at least a bystander? The most I can claim is to be an accomplice or a drunk-in-charge but not in charge enough to avoid running someone over. But you did it, didn't you? You set out to kill and you did. So, what the fuck am I to do?

I bathe the children now and I think of you – and then of us. Then I wonder. Children. Hey, I have two. Would you like Marie? She is patient, kind, great with the kids. I trust her. Not to write a confession, not to harm them or surprise me. Of course not being surprised means all sorts of things. Bed is … bed. Sex fine – never amazing. Meals are good – we eat with the kids. No danger of being caught at it by anyone – let alone dear Hélène. I haven't heard from her now for years. She sends a card at Nôel and that's it really. She couldn't understand you disappearing like that. Who could?

Every now and then there's an abduction reported in Figaro or on the radio. Same old stuff – it's in the headlines for a week, then back to what the economy is doing, or the weather, or a politician caught out. I can't help but curse the Press and feel for the parents. A part of me wonders – just wonders. But you only needed to do it once didn't you. Didn't you? The most recent was in Spain. You always said you preferred the south but Spain? I don't think so, baby.

I hid the journal. I wanted to tell Louise's parents but what would that have done? Brought them some peace. And then doubts – after all, there was no body and who'd have believed a confession from someone who'd been in Bicêtre? I don't even know why I believed it. Let me off the hook, maybe? I could blame you going away on some kind of madness. Not about me – or us. 'Cos we were pretty good weren't we? Even now, honey. Even now, despite Marie, two lovely girls and a – what do they call it? – a fresh start I just can't help but want…

Finally. Confession time. They won't find you will they? Or Louise? How could they? I know where you are – not so far. If I go back to Giverny, to me at least, it's obvious. The tree is strong now, covering you nicely. And Louise? Did she ever exist? Leclaires? What did that mean to me? A Picard. Pierre Picard. Au revoir cherie.

And you? Yes YOU – dear reader. Did you pick up my story in an airport book-store? Did you borrow it? Steal it? Is it your book-of-the-month in your quaint bourgeois book club? Where are you reading it? On a beach? A plane? Tucked up in bed? Alone? With your family safely sleeping in their little beds? Or perhaps your family has flown the coop now. Perhaps you had none. Are you single? Alone? Did you guess the ending? Did you cheat and check to see if it was worth the effort of reading to this last page? It doesn't matter.

Are all the doors locked? As locked as your heart? Do the staff in your hotel seem friendly? Do we really know anyone, even ourselves? Look around you. Are there fellow readers, sun-bathers, other passengers, hotel guests, a partner who knows little of your secret fears and desires? Does anyone look familiar? Look closer. Be assured, dear reader, I shall come for you.

Fin

The Real Press

If you enjoyed this book, take a look at the other books we have on our list at www.therealpress.co.uk

Including the new Armada novel with a difference, *Tearagh't*, by the maverick psychologist Craig Newnes.

Or the medieval thriller *Regicide*, by David Boyle, and introducing Peter Abelard as the great detective...

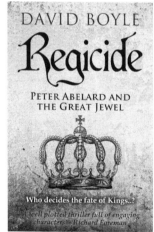